"Eva, I'm going to do everything in my power to find Brady," Austin said.

He held her gaze. "I promise you that. I know your son was in these woods. I know exactly where Justice lost the scent trail, and I feel confident that he can find it again, but not if we don't go look for it."

"Okay," Eva said. He was right. Talking only wasted energy that could be spent finding Brady.

"Great. You can wait in your car or go back to your place. As soon as we have new information—"

"No."

"What?" He stopped short, his eyes flashing with irritation, Justice tugging hard on the lead.

"I'm coming with you, Detective."

SEARCH
AND
RECOVER

New York Times Bestselling Author   **USA TODAY** Bestselling Author
SHIRLEE McCOY   MARGARET DALEY

Previously published as *Tracking Justice* and *Detection Mission*

LOVE INSPIRED
INSPIRATIONAL ROMANCE

LOVE INSPIRED®

INSPIRATIONAL ROMANCE

Recycling programs for this product may not exist in your area.

ISBN-13: 978-1-335-53485-9

Search and Recover

First published in 2018. This edition published in 2021.

Copyright © 2018 by Harlequin Books S.A.

Tracking Justice
First published in 2013. This edition published in 2021.
Copyright © 2013 by Harlequin Books S.A.

Detection Mission
First published in 2013. This edition published in 2021.
Copyright © 2013 by Harlequin Books S.A.

Special thanks and acknowledgment are given to Shirlee McCoy and Margaret Daley for their contribution to the Texas K-9 Unit miniseries.

This edition published by arrangement with Harlequin Books S.A.

For questions and comments about the quality of this book, please contact us at CustomerService@Harlequin.com.

Love Inspired
22 Adelaide St. West, 40th Floor
Toronto, Ontario M5H 4E3, Canada
www.Harlequin.com

Printed in U.S.A.

CONTENTS

TRACKING JUSTICE

Shirlee McCoy

Much thanks to extraordinary editor Emily Rodmell.
Without your guidance and expertise (and patience),
this book would not be what it is.

And to the K-9 Justice continuity authors—
Sharon Dunn, Lenora Worth, Terri Reed, Valerie Hansen
and Margaret Daley—I loved working with every one of you!
Thank you for your kindness and encouragement after my accident.
It meant the world to me.

Restore to me the joy of your salvation
and grant me a willing spirit, to sustain me.
—*Psalm* 51:12

Chapter One

Police detective Austin Black glanced at the illuminated numbers on the dashboard clock as he raced up Oak Drive. Two in the morning. Not a good time to get a call about a missing child.

Then again, there was never a good time for that; never a good time to look in the eyes of a mother or father and see terror and worry or to follow a scent trail and know that it might lead to a joyful reunion or a sorrowful goodbye.

If it led anywhere.

Sometimes trails went cold, scents were lost and the missing were never found.

Knowing that didn't make it any easier to accept.

Austin wanted to find them all. Bring them all home safe.

Hopefully, this time, he would.

He pulled into the driveway of a small, bungalow-style house, its white porch gleaming in exterior lights that glowed on either side of the door. Just four houses down from the scene of a violent crime and the theft of a trained police dog the previous afternoon. An odd coincidence.

Or maybe not.

Two calls to the same street within nine hours? Not something that happened often in a place like Sagebrush, Texas.

Justice whined, his dark nose pressed against the grate that separated him from the SUV's backseat. A three-year-old bloodhound, he was trained in search and rescue and knew when it was time to work. Knew and was ready, even after the eight-hour search they'd been on earlier.

Austin jumped out of the vehicle and started up the driveway, filing away information as he went. Lights on in the front of the house. An old station wagon parked on the curb. Windows closed. Locked?

A woman darted out the front door, pale hair flowing behind her, a loose robe flapping in the cold night air as she ran toward him. "Thank God you got here so quickly. I don't know where he could have gone."

"You called about a missing child?"

"Yes. My son."

"The dispatcher said that you don't know how long he's been gone?" Austin had heard the call go out shortly after he'd left his captain's place. Hours of searching for Slade's stolen police dog, Rio, had turned up nothing but a dead-end scent trail and mounting frustration. Austin had been exhausted and ready to go home. Now he felt wired and ready to hit the trail again.

"I thought that I heard Brady call for me, and when I walked into his room, he was gone. That was about ten minutes ago."

"Has he ever run away?"

"No."

"Ever talked about it?"

"No! Now, please, can you help me find him?" She ran back up the porch stairs, her bare feet padding on the whitewashed wood.

Austin jogged after her, stepping into a small living room. Neat as a pin except for a small pile of Legos on a light oak coffee table and a college textbook abandoned on a threadbare sofa. No sign of the woman.

"Ma'am?" he called, moving toward a narrow hallway that led toward the back of the house.

"Here." She waved from a doorway at the end of the hall. "This is my son's room."

Austin followed her into the tiny room. Blue walls. Blue bedding tangled and dripping over the side of the twin mattress. Crisp white curtains. A blanket lay on the floor near the open window, the frayed edges ruffled by the wind.

"How old is your son, Ms…?"

"Billows. Eva. He's seven."

Billows?

The name sparked a memory, but Austin couldn't quite grab hold of it. "Did you and your son have an argument about something? Maybe a missed curfew or—"

"He's *seven*. He's not even allowed to be outside by himself." Her voice broke, but her eyes were dry, her face pale and pinched with worry. A pretty face. A young one, too. Maybe twenty-three or four. Too young, it seemed, to have a seven-year-old.

"Did you argue about homework? Grades?"

"We didn't argue about anything, Officer—?"

"Detective Austin Black. I'm with Sagebrush Police Department's Special Operations K-9 Unit."

"You have a search-and-rescue dog with you?" Her face brightened, hope gleaming in her emerald eyes. "I can give you something of his. A shirt or—"

"Hold on." He grabbed her arm as she tried to move past. "I need to get a little more information first."

"Find my son. *Then* I'll give you whatever information you want."

"Unfortunately, without the information, I won't know where to begin searching for your son."

"How about you start out there?" She gestured out the window.

"Was it open when you came in the room?"

"Yes. And the curtains were just like that. One hanging outside. Like, maybe…" She pressed her lips together.

"What?"

"It looks like someone carried Brady out the window, and Brady grabbed the curtain to try to keep from being taken. But I don't know how anyone could have gotten into his room. The window was locked. *All* the doors and windows were locked."

He nodded. He could see the scenario she'd outlined playing out. The little boy woken from a sound sleep, dragged from his bed and out the window, grabbing on to whatever he could to keep from being kidnapped.

He could see it, but that didn't mean it had happened that way. Most children were abducted by family or friends, and most didn't even know they were being abducted when it happened.

"You're sure everything was locked?"

"Of course." She frowned. "I always double-check. I have ever since…"

"What?"

"Nothing that matters. I just need to find my son."

Hiding something?

Maybe. She seemed more terrified than nervous, but that

didn't mean she didn't know something about what had happened to her son.

"Everything matters when a child is missing, Eva."

Missing.

Gone.

Disappeared.

The words just kept coming. Kept filling Eva's head and her heart and her lungs until she wasn't sure she could breathe.

"Do you need to sit down?" Detective Black touched her elbow, his dark blue eyes staring straight into hers.

"I need to find my son." The words stuck in her throat, caught on the roof of her mouth, and she didn't know if they even made a sound when they escaped through her lips.

"I'm going to help you do that. I promise. But I need to know if there's some reason why you were careful to keep your doors and windows locked. Someone you were afraid of." His voice was warm and smooth as honey straight from the hive, and Eva might actually believe every word he was saying if she weren't so terrified.

"My parents were killed two years ago, but it had nothing to do with me or my son."

"The killer was caught?"

"No."

"Is it possible—"

"It's not possible!" She nearly shouted, and Detective Black frowned. "I was estranged from my father when the murders occurred. There's no connection between my life now and what happened to my parents." She tried again. Tried to sound reasonable and responsible because she was afraid if she didn't, the detective would linger in Brady's room for hours instead of going to look for him.

"Is Brady's father around?" He leaned out the window without touching it, eyeing the packed earth beneath.

Did he see anything there?

She wanted to ask, wanted to beg him to get his dog and go after her son, wanted to go after Brady herself, run into the darkness and scream his name over and over again until she found him.

"No," she answered a little too sharply, and Detective Black raised a raven-black eyebrow.

"You're not on good terms?"

"We're not on any terms."

"When was the last time you and Brady saw him?"

"Brady has never seen him," she retorted. "The last time I saw Rick was six months before my son was born."

"Have you spoken to him on th—"

"I haven't had any contact with him since the day I told him I was pregnant. He's not in my life. He's not in Brady's life. He didn't want to be. He was married, okay? He and his wife moved to Las Vegas two months before Brady's birth. That's it. The whole story." She'd been nineteen and foolish enough to believe every lie Rick had told. It didn't hurt like it used to, but admitting it to the detective still made her blush.

"Is there anyone else? A boyfriend? Fiancé?"

"No. Just me and Brady. That's all there's ever been." She swallowed hard and turned away. Holding back tears because crying wouldn't solve her problems. Wouldn't help her son.

"When did you last see Brady?"

"I checked on him at midnight. Right before I went to bed. He was sleeping."

"You went to bed after that?"

"Yes! I went to bed. I fell asleep. I thought I heard Brady call for me, and I went to his room. He was gone. Now, will you please go find him?"

"I will. A soon as—"

The doorbell rang and Eva jumped, her heart soaring with wild hope.

Brady.

Please, God, let it be him.

She shoved past Detective Black, not caring about niceties. Not caring about anything but getting to the door, opening it, seeing Brady's face.

Only it wasn't him.

Her heart sank as she looked into the eyes of a uniformed officer.

"Ms. Billows? I'm Officer Desmond Cunningham. We have a report of a missing child?"

"My son. There's already a detective here."

"He's with our K-9 Unit. He'll start searching for your son while I interview you."

Thank You, God. Thank You, thank You, thank You.

She stepped back so he could enter the house, wishing she'd had time to straighten up the living room, put the sofa cover over her threadbare couch. A twenty-dollar Goodwill find that worked fine for her and Brady but wasn't great for company.

Such a silly thing to think about.

Such a stupid thing when her son was missing.

She pressed a hand to her stomach, sick with dread and fear.

"He's been gone for twenty minutes already," she said, the horror of the words filling her mouth with the coppery taste of blood.

"It takes a little time to get a search team mobilized, ma'am, but we'll have plenty of people out here before you know it." Officer Cunningham offered a reassuring smile, his dark eyes filled with sympathy.

Seeing it there in the depth of his gaze was too difficult, made the tears she'd been holding back too tempting. She turned away, met Detective Black's steady gaze.

Deep blue. Bottomless. Unreadable.

"Were you home this afternoon, Eva?" he asked, and she shook her head because she wasn't sure she could speak without tears rolling down her cheeks.

"Was Brady?"

"He was with his babysitter. Mrs. Daphne lives two doors down," she managed to say past the lump in her throat.

"Is that close to Slade McNeal's place?" he asked.

And odd question, but she'd answer whatever he asked if it meant getting him outside searching for Brady.

"Yes."

Detective Black and Officer Cunningham exchanged a look she couldn't read. One that excluded her, made her even more terrified than she already was.

"What's going on?"

"Captain McNeal's father was attacked today. His dog, Rio, was stolen. The person responsible is still on the loose."

"What does that have to do with Brady?" she asked, but she knew, the cold icy feeling in her heart making her shake.

"It's going to be okay." Detective Black walked across the room and opened the front door. "I'm going to get Justice. Eva, if you want to get a photo of your son and an article of his clothing. Something that he wore today, preferably. I'll be back in a minute."

She ran into Brady's room, trying not to think about Slade's father, his missing K-9 partner. Trying not to think about how pale and quiet Brady had been when she'd picked him up from Mrs. Daphne's house.

He hadn't eaten much for dinner.

Maybe he'd just been sick. A stomach virus. Kids got those all the time.

She wanted to believe that accounted for his silence at the dinner table, his desire to go to bed early.

Check the window again, Momma. Did you check it?

The words seemed to echo in Brady's empty room.

She should have asked him why he was worried about the window lock. Should have pressed him about his day, asked just one more time if everything was okay.

If she had—

"Did you find something?" Detective Black walked into the room, a bloodhound padding along beside him. Orange vest and droopy ears, a wet nose and big, dark eyes. Brady would have loved to see him.

The thought burned behind Eva's eyes, and she ran to the closet, yanked out the T-shirt Brady had worn to school.

Blue today. Orange tomorrow!

"This is the shirt he wore today." She handed the detective Brady's T-shirt before she gave into temptation and pressed it to her face, inhaled her son's little-boy scent.

Please, God. Please.

"He asked me to check the window lock twice. He seemed quiet at dinner. I thought he might be getting sick, but maybe…" Her guilt spilled out, and she had to stop the words so that the tears didn't spill out, too.

"Your son's disappearance might not have anything to do with what happened at Slade's house."

"But you think that it does?"

"Do you have a recent photo?" He didn't respond to her comment, and she knew that he did.

She hadn't realized she could be any more petrified than she'd been when she'd walked into Brady's room and seen his open window.

She could be.

She *was*.

Cold air blew in, carrying a hint of rain or snow.

And, somewhere out in the darkness, Brady was scared and probably calling for her.

A tear dripped down her cheek.

"Eva, I need that photo," Detective Black said gently, and she ran from the room, ran into hers.

So close to Brady's.

She'd planned it that way when she'd decided which of the three bedrooms she'd take and which Brady would have.

So close, but she hadn't heard a sound until he'd cried for her.

She grabbed the framed school photo from her nightstand, pressed it to her chest.

"Got it?" Detective Black walked into the room with his bloodhound, and Eva didn't care that she'd left her waitressing uniform in a stack on a chair. She didn't care that a pile of college books and papers lay beside her bed. She didn't care about anything but handing him the photo and watching him walk out the door to find her son.

"This was taken a few months ago." She handed him the photo, and he studied it for a moment.

"Cute kid," he said with a small smile, and she nodded because she couldn't speak past the tears that clogged her throat.

The doorbell rang again. This time she didn't run to answer it. Didn't believe that somehow Brady would magically appear on the porch, tired and scared but with some explanation that would make sense. Maybe some story about sleepwalking or thinking that Mrs. Daphne's dog was outside whining for his attention.

She walked into the living room, her heart heavy and aching, her chest tight.

Captain Slade McNeal stood near the front door, his dark hair mussed, his face drawn and weary. "Eva, I'm sorry I couldn't be here sooner. I had to wait for my son's babysitter to arrive."

"It's okay." Her voice sounded hollow and old.

"Have you found any evidence, Cunningham?" Slade turned to the patrol officer.

"I checked the back window. It looks like someone popped the lock on it. I've already called for an evidence team."

"Good. Are you going to take Justice out to track Brady, Austin?"

"Yes. We'll start around back and work our way from there."

"I'll come with you." Eva pulled her old wool coat from the closet near the door. There was no way she could put Brady's life in someone else's hands. No way she could trust that anyone else would look as hard or as long as she would. He was her son, after all. Her responsibility.

"The best thing you can do for your son is stay here and answer the captain's questions. The more information you provide, the faster we can narrow down our search." Austin walked onto the porch, and she followed.

He might not want her to help with the search, but she had no intention of staying behind. Brady needed her, and she needed to be there for him. That was the way it had been from the moment he was born, the bond between them so strong that she'd thought that nothing would ever tear them apart.

Something had.

Some*one* had.

She clenched her fist.

Brady was okay. He had to be.

"I've called in Lee Calloway. I'll have him question the neighbors while I work with Cunningham and the evidence team." Slade stepped outside, and Eva walked down the porch stairs, letting him approach Detective Black. They could talk all they wanted. She was going to look for her son.

Please, God, just let him be okay. Please, help me find him. Please.

She could not lose her son.

Wouldn't lose him.

If that meant searching alone while the police collected evidence and speculated on the who and why and how of Brady's kidnapping, so be it.

Chapter Two

Justice whined impatiently as Austin followed Eva around the side of the house. She stood near the window, staring aimlessly into the backyard, her arms wrapped around her waist.

"You need to go back inside," he said.

"I need to find my son, Detective. He's my life."

"I know." Austin didn't have children yet, but he'd heard the same story dozens of times over his years in search and rescue. He knew the depth of fear and longing, the hope and despair that lived in a parent's heart when a child disappeared. "I'm going to help you do that, but you need to help me."

"By going inside and answering a thousand questions?" she asked, her eyes shimmering with tears. None fell. She looked young, but tough. Like someone who'd lived through trouble, and who expected to live through more.

"If that's what it takes to find Brady, then, yes."

"I can't go back inside."

"You have to, because the longer I have to stand here talking to you, the longer it's going to take me to get started on the search."

"I—"

"Go inside, Eva." He cut her off, crouched near Justice and held out Brady's shirt. "Ready, boy?"

Justice snuffled the fabric, then bent his long snout to the ground. He circled the area, bypassing Eva, who didn't seem at all interested in following orders.

"Do you think he can find Brady's scent?" she asked.

"Yes."

"Will it lead us to Brady?"

"Hopefully."

"What—"

"Justice is ready to track. I can't let him start until you're inside."

His words were like a splash of ice water in Eva's face.

Of course, he couldn't start the search while she stood there asking questions.

She blinked back hot tears, hating the weakness that made her want to beg and plead and cry. She was strong. She had to be, but she didn't feel strong. She felt weak and scared, and she wanted to hover around Austin until he promised that he'd bring Brady home to her.

She pivoted, willing to do anything to have Brady back.

"Eva," Detective Black called as she reached the corner of the house.

"Yes?" She stopped, but she didn't turn to face him. She didn't want him to see her despair.

"I'll do everything I can to bring Brady home to you."

She did turn then, wanting to thank him for the reassurance. The words died as she watched him hold Brady's little shirt out to the dog.

Justice huffed out a breath and barked.

"Seek," Detective Black commanded, and the bloodhound took off, his handler running along behind him. Across the backyard, into the neighbor's. Out onto the street beyond.

She lost sight of them there.

If she could have, she would have followed them, but she knew she had to go back. Do what she'd been told. Answer dozens of questions that might, if God were willing, bring her son home.

He certainly hadn't been willing to bring her parents' murderer to justice, but she had to believe that this time He'd answer her prayers.

Please, God. Please.

She walked around to the front of the house, skirting by several police officers who were standing on the front porch. Three police cars were parked on the curb, another one across the street. One in the driveway. Lots of people, and that had to be a good thing.

Didn't it?

She hoped so, because every minute that passed was a minute that Brady was alone with...

She cut the thought off. Didn't want to acknowledge what had been floating around in her head since Detective Black had mentioned the crime at Slade's house.

Had Brady seen something?

He shouldn't have. He wasn't allowed to play outside by himself, and Mrs. Daphne didn't like being outside in the cold. Arthritis, she always said, and who was Eva to say differently? At seventy, Mrs. Daphne deserved to stay inside if it was what she wanted. The rule was, Brady stayed inside with her. A tough one for him to want to follow. He was high energy and active, and he loved being outdoors.

Had he skirted the rule?

Snuck outside or convinced Mrs. Daphne to let him go?

Her house was close enough to Slade's for Brady to have had a clear view of it from the yard. But could he have seen enough to make him the target of a criminal?

She didn't know. Didn't even want to speculate. All she wanted was her son.

She walked back inside, tried to return the smile that Slade offered. "Do you have some questions for me? Because if you don't—"

"I do. Officer Cunningham is working with the evidence team, and I'll be conducting the interview. This should only take a few minutes."

"All right." She sat on the edge of the couch, her body trembling and cold.

"Was Brady with Mrs. Daphne today?"

"Yes."

"What time did you pick him up?"

"Six."

"Did he mention anything unusual about his day? Anything that concerned you or him?"

"Nothing. He did seem…quiet." She knew where the conversation was heading, and she took a deep breath, tried to relax.

He narrowed his eyes. "You heard what happened at my house yesterday afternoon?"

"Yes. Detective Black told me."

"Then you know that my father was attacked and Rio was stolen. Do you think it's possible that Brady saw what happened?"

"He didn't mention it, but I guess anything is possible."

Slade jotted something in a notebook, asked another question and another.

Eva answered all of them as best she could. She couldn't collapse, couldn't let herself give in to the emotions that beat like bat wings in her stomach. She wanted to, though. Almost wished she had someone to lean on. Someone who could put an arm around her shoulder and tell her everything would be all right. There was no one. She wasn't sure there ever had been.

The clock on the fireplace mantel ticked the time away. Five minutes. Ten. Fifteen.

Nearly an hour since Eva had realized Brady was gone.

An hour that he'd been missing. An hour that he'd been terrified, cold. Hungry, because he always was.

She wiped clammy hands on her pajama pants, swallowed down bile. "Are we almost done, Slade?"

"I just have a few more questions to ask."

"I've already answered dozens, and I've answered some of them more than once."

"We have to be thorough, Eva. It's the only way to get your son back."

"The only way to get my son back is to go out and look for him. That's what I'm going to do." She stood, her legs shaky. "Where's Detective Black?"

"Tracking Brady. If things go well, your son will be home before dawn."

"And if they don't?"

"I can't answer that, Eva. Sometimes kids are returned home in an hour or two. Sometimes it takes longer."

She sucked in a breath. "And sometimes it doesn't happen at all?"

"I think you know the answer to that. I also think that you know we'll do everything we can to bring Brady home to you."

She'd wanted reassurance.

She'd gotten truth, instead.

She should be thankful for it but she just felt sick, her stomach heaving, stars dancing in front of her eyes. "I need some air."

She ran outside, letting cold air bathe her hot face.

"Is everything okay, Ms. Billows?" Officer Cunningham asked, stepping away from a group of officers he'd been talking to.

"Do you know where Detective Black is?" If Slade couldn't give her an exact location, maybe he could.

"He's organizing the search team."

"Where?"

"Headquarters are at the east entrance of the Lost Woods. We have a team setting up there. I'm sure Captain McNeal explained everything to you."

Eva nodded as if he had, but she'd been told nothing. Maybe Slade hadn't known. Maybe he just hadn't told her. The second seemed more likely than the first. He'd taken several phone calls during the interview. At some point, he must have been told that Detective Black was setting up at the Lost Woods.

He had chosen not to share the information.

It didn't surprise her. She'd learned all about police silence after her parents' deaths.

She walked back inside, grabbed her purse, slipped her feet into old sneakers.

"Where are you heading?" Slade asked.

"I told you that I was going to go look for my son."

"I can't recommend that."

"Can you stop me?" Because unless he had a legal reason to keep her at the house, she didn't plan on being there. Not for a minute longer.

He hesitated, then sighed. "You're not a suspect, and you've answered all my questions. As long as I can get in touch with you if I need to, I guess I can't keep you here."

"I have my cell phone." She jotted the number on a scrap

of paper and handed it to him, trying hard not to look into his eyes. She respected Slade. He was a good man who'd always been a good neighbor, but if his son, Caleb, were the one missing, he wouldn't be sitting in his house answering questions while other people searched.

"Just be sure you don't get in the way of the search, Eva. If you do, it won't help Brady."

"I know. I just need to...be doing something." She grabbed Brady's coat from the closet, telling herself that she was bringing it to him. That she'd go to the Lost Woods and see him standing with the search team, cold but fine.

She jogged down the porch stairs and across the yard, unlocking the station wagon and sliding in behind the wheel. She slammed the door closed as several people called out to her. A few were neighbors. One was a stranger, a reporter maybe.

She didn't care.

All she cared about was Brady.

"Please, for once, just start!" she muttered as she shoved the key into the ignition. The starter clicked once, then again. Finally, the engine sputtered to life and she pulled away from the curb, glad for once for her father's advice. *Never park in the driveway or the garage, kid. If you do, it'll be too easy for the police to block in your vehicle and keep you from running.*

Yeah, Ernie had been overflowing with little tidbits of information. Especially when he'd been drinking.

A police cruiser pulled in behind her, lights on. No sirens, though. No doubt Slade had called in a tail. He'd probably call it an escort. Either way, Eva knew her rights, and she didn't stop or slow down. That was another thing Ernie had taught her.

He'd also taught her that people couldn't be trusted. Not strangers, not friends and certainly not family. A good lesson that she'd forgotten once and would never forget again.

The road leading out of the neighborhood was nearly empty, the moon hanging low above distant trees. A quarter mile, and she was outside Sagebrush city limits, sparse trees and thick scrub lining the two-lane highway. She knew the way to the Lost Woods. There weren't many people in Sagebrush who didn't. The place was legend, the deep wilderness a siren's song that had called more than one explorer to his doom.

She shivered, flicking on the heater and grimacing as cold air blew out of the vent. The car was a junker, but it ran. Until she finished school and got a better-paying job, there was no way she could afford better. It didn't matter. She and Brady had what they needed and they had each other. She'd told herself that often over the years. She'd believed it, too. As much as she cringed when she thought about the mistake she'd made, the lies she'd bought into, the things she'd given away, she couldn't regret Brady.

A tear slipped down her cheek. The second of the night, and if she wasn't careful there would be more. She tightened her grip on the steering wheel, her fingernails digging into hard plastic as she turned onto the narrow road that led to the east entrance of the woods.

If Justice *had* tracked Brady to the woods, it meant he'd found the trail and been on it for nearly half a mile. Good news, but Eva didn't want to think about Brady wandering through the wilderness. Anything could happen in the thick shelter of the Lost Woods. Anything could be lost there and never found again.

She pulled in behind a line of police cars, search-and-rescue vehicles and TV-news vans. A crowd of people stood in the glow of several oversize spotlights, huddled around a long table, staring at something spread across its top. A tall broad-shouldered man gestured to the table and then to the entrance of the woods, his sweeping motion including stately pine trees crowded close and giant oaks that seemed to bar entrance to the forest's dark interior.

Detective Austin Black.

Exactly the man Eva wanted to see.

She grabbed Brady's coat and jumped out of the station wagon, ignoring the officer who was getting out of the patrol car behind her.

"Detective Black!" she called, pushing past a couple of news photographers.

"Come on over." He didn't look surprised to see her. Had probably been warned that she was on her way. Good, because she didn't want to waste more time arguing about whether or not she should be there.

She squeezed in between him and a dark-haired officer who held the leash of a border collie.

"What's going on?" she asked.

"Justice and I tracked your son to the entrance of the woods. We were able to follow the scent trail to a stream about a half mile in. We lost it there, but I think Justice can pick it up again. We'll have four teams working quadrants from here." Detective Black jabbed at a map of the Lost Woods, the cool leather of his jacket brushing her cheek. She caught a whiff of pine needles and soap and some indefinably masculine thing. It settled into the pit of her stomach, mixing with her fear and worry, the combination shivering through her blood, lodging in the base of her skull. It pounded there. The beginning of a migraine.

She took a deep breath, trying to ignore the stabbing pain and concentrate on the map.

"Do you really think he's in the woods?"

"It's not what I think that matters. It's what Justice's nose says, and it's saying your son went into the woods. I don't know yet whether or not he's come out."

"Is it possible that he ran from his kidnapper and came here on his own?" That would be so much easier to think about than Brady with someone who had beaten a man just a few hours ago.

"His kidnapper was still with him at the stream. I found footprints on the bank. One child-size print. Three adult boot prints."

"There's more than one kidnapper?"

"I didn't say that. I just said there were multiple footprints." He turned his attention back to the team.

"We're going to split up from here. I'd like you to cover that section, Lee." He used a highlighter to mark a rectangle of forest, and the man beside him nodded. He marked two other sections, calling out names of people Eva didn't know, but who she had to trust to do everything they could to find her son.

"I'll take the last quadrant," he said, marking the spot. Acres of land. That's what he was talking about. Miles of wilderness they had to search, and Brady maybe somewhere in the middle of it.

"Any questions?" Austin asked.

No one on the search team seemed to have any.

Eva did.

She wanted to know what the temperature was, wanted to know how long it would take for a little boy dressed in nothing but flannel pajamas to succumb to hypothermia. She wanted to know what kind of person would beat an elderly man, steal a dog, kidnap a child, and she wanted to know how likely it was that Brady was still ali—

No.

She already knew the answer to the last one. He *was* alive.

She could feel it in her gut. She backed away from the table and the map and the group, because she couldn't bear to look at that expanse of wilderness and picture her son lost somewhere in the middle of it. Something bumped into the back of her legs. Or maybe she bumped into it. Whatever the case, she nearly fell over.

"Careful." A warm hand wrapped around her wrist, and she looked straight into Detective Black's midnight-blue eyes. Thick black lashes, laugh lines fanning out from the corners. Handsome, hard-edged and someone she desperately wanted to believe in.

"I'm okay." She pulled away, looked down at the thing that she'd tripped over.

The *dog*.

Justice, with his tongue lolling and his dark eyes gleaming, his droopy face matched by his droopy ears. He looked sweet and a little silly, and Eva thought again that Brady would love to meet him.

She touched his head, feeling knobby bones beneath velvety fur. "Brady would love you."

"Hopefully they'll meet soon." Austin scratched the bloodhound behind his ears, crouched and held Brady's shirt in front of him. A *piece* of Brady's shirt.

His favorite blue one, cut into pieces.

She'd buy him another one when he got home. Maybe she'd buy him four, because the little savings that she'd managed to secret away didn't matter if he wasn't around when she spent it.

She swallowed hard as Austin put the square of fabric into a plastic bag, tucked it into a backpack and shoved a hardhat fitted with a searchlight onto his head.

"How long do you think it will take to find him?" she asked.

"I don't know, and it wouldn't be fair to you if I speculated. I'll be calling updates in to Captain McNeal, though. He should be here shortly." He gazed down at her. "Why don't you wait for him in your car so you don't get hounded by the press?"

"I—"

Austin issued a command to Justice and walked away, obviously not interested in a discussion.

That was fine.

Eva wasn't interested in one, either.

She followed him across the small clearing that narrowed onto a hiking path, buttoning her coat against the cold wind as they walked deeper into the blackness of the woods.

Chapter Three

Eva didn't plan to give up. She was bound and determined to help find her son.

That much was obvious.

It was also obvious that having her wandering around in the Lost Woods could only lead to trouble. Dozens of hikers had been lost there over the years. Some had been recovered. Many hadn't.

Austin had been on plenty of search-and-rescue missions in the thousand-acre wilderness. He knew the area well, and even *he* got turned around on occasion.

"You need to go back to base camp," he barked over his shoulder, Justice tugging at the lead, anxious to be given his head.

Eva didn't reply.

Not a word.

Not even a hint that she'd heard.

He pulled Justice to a stop, aggravated, annoyed and frustrated.

"I'm searching for your son, Eva. You're slowing me down."

"I have his coat. It's cold tonight. He's going to need it." She held out a thick blue coat, her arm shaking, her voice steady.

"Thanks." He took it, tucked it into his backpack, not bothering to explain that he had plenty of blankets and knew how to warm someone with hypothermia.

"Do you think he's okay? It's freezing out here, and he's just a little guy."

"We're in the forties. That's well above freezing."

"You know what I mean, Detective."

"Austin." He urged Justice to seek again, not willing to stop for a conversation. Not wanting to spend any more time trying to assuage Eva's worry. She needed to go back and wait. It was as simple as that.

Unfortunately, forcing the issue and dragging her back would waste time they didn't have.

Forty-three degrees *was* cold. Especially for a kid who wasn't dressed for the weather.

"If he's still with his kidnapper, do you think that—"

"Eva, I don't have time for a question-and-answer game, okay? If you want to have that, then go back to the head of the trail. I'm sure Slade is there. He can answer every question you want to ask."

"I can't go back. Not when Brady is out here somewhere."

"You'll be helping him more if you go back. Do you understand that you're slowing me down?"

"Go as fast as you want. I can keep up."

"For how long?"

"As long as it takes."

"That could be hours. You know that, right?"

She didn't respond, and he glanced over his shoulder, irritated by her presence. She was a wrench in the works, a roadblock getting in the way of the smooth teamwork that he and

Justice usually achieved without effort. "This is your son's life that we're talking about, Eva."

"I know," she said simply. No dramatics. No tears.

"Then you'll understand why it's better for me and Justice to do this alone."

"Let me ask you something, Austin. Do you have any idea how it feels to wake up in the middle of the night and realize that your child is missing?

"No," he responded honestly.

"Then you can't understand why I need to be here."

"You're wrong. I *can* understand. But finding the missing is what Justice and I are trained to do. We put everything we have into it every time. You can trust us with your son's life."

"I don't trust anyone. Especially not when it comes to Brady."

"This time, you don't have a choice."

"Sure I do. I trusted the police to find my parents' murderer. That hasn't happened. I trusted Brady's father to keep his promises. Look where that got me." She laughed, the sound achingly sad. "Now, I trust God and myself. That's it."

"I'm not anyone you've dealt with before, Eva. Maybe you should keep that in mind."

"What's that supposed to mean?"

"When I'm on search and rescue, every person I'm looking for is my family. I don't leave family behind. Not ever. As long as there's a chance of recovering Brady, I'll be out here searching for him."

"Who decides when there isn't a chance?" she asked quietly.

"Time." He shoved through thick foliage, holding back branches so they didn't slap her in the face.

"How much time?" Eva persisted.

"I don't know. Every situation is different."

"I can't go home without him." Her voice quivered, and

Austin remembered the softness in her eyes when she'd held her son's photograph. The lone tear that had slid down her cheek. She was tough, but she was also a mother whose child was missing.

"Then let's both pray that you don't have to," he said, because he wouldn't promise that he'd find Brady. No matter how much he wanted to. He'd gone down that path before. It had ended in tragedy and heartache.

For a moment, Eva was silent.

Maybe she was waiting for the vows that Austin wouldn't make, hoping that he'd reassure her, tell her that finding Brady was a certainty.

"Thanks," she finally said. Nothing else. No begging or pleading for a guarantee.

"For what?"

"For not feeding me a bunch of lies about how certain you are that you'll find my son."

"You deserve the truth, and the truth is, I can't promise a good outcome, but I'm going to do everything that I can to make sure we have one. Come on. Let's pick up the pace."

He loosened his hold on the leash, allowing Justice more slack. The bloodhound leaped forward, his paws scrambling in the thick layer of fallen leaves and pine needles. They'd searched this area before, and Justice followed the scent trail easily, baying once and then taking off.

Austin ran behind him, his feet pounding on packed earth and slippery leaves. No thought of Eva and whether or not she could keep up, just focusing on the feel of the lead in his hand, the tug of Justice's muscular body, the tension that surrounded both of them.

Justice stopped at a small creek, sniffing the ground and moving back and forth across the creek bed. He stopped at a small flag, his tail wagging slightly as he acknowledged the area that they'd searched so intently, the prints that Austin had cast and photographed.

"Seek," Austin urged, and Justice bent his nose to the ground again, his ears dragging along the wet creek bank.

Nothing.

Another ten minutes. Fifteen.

He pulled Justice up with a quick command, bent to study a small footprint pressed into the earth. Five toes. A little heel.

A little boy walking with his kidnapper or running from him?

Eva crouched beside him, her pants dragging in the mud, her sneakers caked with it. "His feet must be so cold."

"Kids are pretty hardy." He tried not to think about the children who hadn't been. The lifeless bodies he'd found on riverbanks and in deep forests. Tried not to remember little Anna Lynn. Missing for four days before Austin had finally been able to bring her back to her parents. She'd been the daughter of one of his closest friends.

The search hadn't ended the way he'd wanted it to.

Never again.

That's what he'd told himself. No more emotional involvement. No more allowing himself to be so personally invested. But how could he not be when a little kid was lost, scared and alone?

He shoved the thoughts away and stood. "He headed downhill from here. We picked up the trail at a creek there. Come on."

He led the way down the steep hill, Justice panting behind him. He gave the bloodhound a minute to lap water from the cool creek, then pulled the shirt from his pack again.

"Seek!" he commanded.

Justice raised his head, sniffing the air.

"Seek!" Austin encouraged, and Justice ran to the edge of the creek, snuffled at the ground.

Nothing.

"Do you—"

"How about we just let him work?" Austin cut Eva off. He needed to focus. Needed to keep moving. Time was ticking by. Brady was still missing. As much as Austin had tried to play it cool with Eva, he knew how quickly a child could become hypothermic. Especially a wet child. Brady had walked through two creeks and there was a hint of moisture in the cold air. The clouds might open at any moment, pouring down rain or ice.

Please, Lord, help us find him before then.

He let Justice work the area around the creek for fifteen minutes, then led him from the water, Eva pressing in so close that he could hear her soft breath, feel the warmth of her body through layers of cloth. She had a presence about her, and even in silence, she was difficult to ignore.

In the distance a dog barked, and Justice cocked his head to the side, then bent it to the ground again. Still nothing.

Brady and his captor might have come this way a couple of hours ago, the scent trail diluted by time and forest life, but giving up wasn't an option. Not now. Not an hour from now. Until Brady was home, Austin would keep searching.

Slow. That's the way they were moving, circling one area after another as Justice nosed the ground. Eva didn't say another word. No questions. No idle chatter. She just followed along, stayed out of the way, and let Austin and his blood-hound do their job. She wanted to run, though. Race past them both screaming Brady's name. Hoping he would answer.

Dim light filtered through the tree canopy, the first rays of the rising sun breaking through the forest's gloom. The area felt empty, Justice's soft huffs seeming to fade into the expanse of wilderness that surrounded them. They moved up a steep ridge, crisscrossing the leaf-strewn ground as Justice searched for the trail. He paused, nose to the air, body taut. One quick bark and he strained against the leash, his powerful body plowing through thick foliage.

"Do you think he's found Brady?" Eva panted as she shoved through a tangle of tree branches. Her hair snagged on a twig, and she yanked away, her eyes tearing from pain, her pulse humming with hope and fear.

"He's found the scent again. How far we'll be able to track it is hard to say." Austin's answer was brief, his breathing unlabored. He didn't even look winded, his long legs eating up the ground as he followed Justice.

"I can't believe that Brady walked this far."

And she didn't want to picture all the ways that he might have gotten there if he *hadn't* walked. Carried? Dragged?

"I've tracked kids that have walked farther." Another brief answer. Fine. If Austin still wanted silence, she'd give it to him.

She didn't speak again as they crested the ridge and ran down the other side. Justice stopped at the bottom, and Eva's heart stopped with him. If he lost the trail, would he find it again?

Justice barked, his body seeming to vibrate with energy as he strained against the leash. They were heading into hill country, the woods deepening, the feeling of being cut off from time and place growing. They ran along the edge of a steep ravine, following a game trail that wound its way through the forest. No sign of anyone or anything, but Eva was sure they were being watched. Unseen eyes staring out of the shadowy woods and tracking their movements.

A branch snapped to their right, and Austin stopped, pulling Justice up short and issuing a sharp command for the dog to cease. His dark hair gleamed in the early-morning sunlight, his hard face shadowed with the beginnings of a beard. If Eva had been alone in the woods and seen him, she'd have walked the other way.

He gestured her over, pressing his finger to his lips as she moved in close.

Another branch snapped and Eva tensed, sure that someone would step out of the woods.

Silence fell. Thick. Heavy. Expectant.

Austin pulled back his jacket, his hand falling to the gun belt at his waist, his icy gaze scanning the forest. Justice stood beside him, hackles raised, body stiff. What did he sense? A bear? A deer? A person?

Several minutes passed and Justice relaxed, settling onto his haunches, his floppy ears whipping as he shook his sturdy body.

Gone. Whatever had been in the trees, but Eva still felt the threat, still wondered what or who had been watching.

"Let's go," Austin said, issuing a command for Justice to seek. The dog jumped up, nose to the ground, energy pouring through his body. Seconds later he barked, straining against the leash as he led them up a steep incline.

They ran up another hill, plunged down it again. Wove their way through trees and up to a cliff that overlooked the forest, following a path that seemed disjointed and erratic. A trail laid by a frantic, scared little boy?

Dear God, she hoped so.

She wanted to crest the next rise, round the next tree, see Brady standing there waiting for her.

She tripped, slid a few feet forward on her hands and knees, the earth near the cliff's edge crumbling and falling away. A thirty-foot drop, at least. Her heart jumped, and she scooted back.

"Careful." Austin appeared at her side, tugged her upright,

his hands on her waist. There. Gone. So quickly she should barely have felt them. She did, though, his touch burning deep, reminding her of things better forgotten. Her cheeks heated, but there wasn't time to think about it or to care.

Justice scrambled up a steep hill, his paws churning up leaves and dirt. Austin followed easily, grabbing tree branches and fists full of foliage as he fought his way to the top. Eva slipped and slid behind them.

Austin grabbed her hand as she neared the top, tugging her onto a ridge that overlooked the forest. A mountain of foliage shot up to the right. To the left, the ground fell away. A hundred feet below the trees huddled close, their winter-bare branches revealing glimpses of the forest floor.

Not a safe place for a seven-year-old boy, and Eva's heart jolted with panic.

"What if he fell?" she whispered, the words barely carrying past the lump in her throat.

"He didn't. Justice is still locked on to his scent. Come on." Austin let the dog pull ahead again, and they skimmed the edge of the cliff, the slippery leaves and loose dirt slowing their progress.

Eva glanced into the abyss to the left, her head swimming as she imagined Brady falling head over heels.

Please, God. Let him be okay.

A fat branch slapped her cheek, the stinging pain barely registering past the hollow thud of her fear. She felt sick with it, her stomach and chest tight, her breathing labored. Everything she loved was wrapped up in Brady.

Austin stopped short and she ran into his back, her feet slipping on thick leaves as she tried to catch her balance.

He snagged her arm, pulling her forward as he crouched near Justice. The dog whined excitedly, his deep bark breaking the morning stillness.

"Release," Austin said, and Justice backed away, dropping down beneath a thick-trunked oak and panting heavily.

"Look at this." Austin pointed to something half-hidden by leaves and dirt. At first Eva couldn't make out what it was. White and gray and brown fuzz covered by forest debris. A splash of bright blue.

"Is it an animal?" she asked, leaning closer, the truth suddenly right there in front of her face. Blue plastic eyes, a shiny black nose, white fluffy face.

"A *stuffed* animal," he responded.

"Snowflake! Brady must have brought it with him." She reached for it, and he captured her hand, gently pulling it back.

"It's evidence, Eva. We don't want it contaminated." He lifted the stuffed dog with a gloved hand, tucked it into a plastic bag he pulled from his pack.

"He was here! Brady was here!" She stood, whirling around, frantically searching for some other sign that her son was close.

"Yeah. And it looks like he was alone this time. Look." Austin pointed to a small footprint in the dusty earth. Bare. Every toe clearly defined. Another was just a few inches away. No sign of boot prints like the ones at the creek.

That was good.

Right?

"He must be terrified." She wanted to cry but couldn't let the tears come.

"I'm going to radio in and get the other search teams to the area. We'll do better consolidating our efforts. Drink this while I get people organized." He handed her an energy drink, poured water into a small dish for Justice.

Maybe Eva should have opened her energy drink, drank it up as quickly as Justice lapped up his water. But she felt too sick, her head throbbing endlessly, her stomach churning. Worry beat a rapid pulse through her blood, and she wanted to sit down and close her eyes. Open them again and find herself back in bed, Brady safe in the room beside hers.

"We're set." Austin clipped his radio into place, frowned at Eva's still-full bottle. "You're not going to do Brady any good if you're dehydrated and exhausted."

He took the bottle from her hand, opened it and handed it back to her, his fingers warm and callused. There was something comforting about that. Something nice and a little too wonderful about the way it felt to look into his face, see his concern and his determination.

She swallowed a few large gulps of the energy drink. Took two more sips for good measure, and then recapped the lid.

"Happy?" she asked, feeling vulnerable beneath his steady scrutiny.

"I'd be happier if you let me call someone to escort you out of the woods, but since I don't want to waste time arguing, I think it's best if I just say yes." He tucked Justice's empty bowl into his pack, took the energy drink and did the same. "Seek!"

They were off again, and Eva had to swallow hard to keep the drink from coming back up. Her stomach heaved, but Justice was on the trail, lunging against his collar and leash, his orange vest bright in the watery dawn light.

He ran like the best think in the world lay at the end of the scent trail he was following, ran like he couldn't wait to be united with the boy that he was seeking. Ran like it mattered, and Eva thought that if she ever gave in to Brady's begging for a puppy, she'd get him a bloodhound. Maybe Austin could give them some tips on how to train a dog. Maybe...

She shoved the thought away.

Thinking ahead, planning for Brady's return...that was one thing. Planning to include Austin in their lives after Brady was found, that was something she wouldn't allow herself to do.

Sweat trickled down her face as they raced past trees and

headed up a small hill. Sunlight speckled the ground with gold and warmed the winter chill, the world a blur of gold and green and brown, the only sound Justice's frantic barks and Eva's panting breath.

Something snapped behind her, the sound so loud and startling she turned, caught a glimpse of a dark figure deep in the woods. There. Gone. There again. Moving away from them, but somehow sinister in the forest stillness.

"You okay?" Austin asked, and she realized she'd stopped, was searching the trees.

"I saw someone." She pointed to the area where the figure had disappeared.

"Probably search and rescue."

"He wasn't wearing an orange vest like yours, and he didn't have a dog."

An explosion ripped through the morning quiet. One short sharp report and then another.

A gun!

Austin shouted something, and she was falling, colors swirling around her as she landed hard on the thick pine carpet.

Chapter Four

"Stay down," Austin whispered, his breath brushing her ear. Justice nudged her cheek but she didn't move, barely even jumped as another shot rang out.

Her heart thundered, her body braced for the bullet's impact. When it didn't come, she tried to get up and find cover, but Austin's body pressed over hers, holding her still.

"They're not shooting at us, but let's make sure we don't get caught in the crossfire."

"Brady—" She tried to move, but he was a solid wall of muscle, and she couldn't budge him.

"Dying isn't going to help your son, Eva."

"What if they're shooting at him?"

He was speaking into his radio and didn't respond.

She didn't think he would have, anyway. Whatever was happening, it was out of either of their control. Another shot rang out, and she flinched, her body screaming for her to get up, find Brady and make sure he was safe.

Something crashed in the underbrush to their right, and Eva turned her head, saw the gun in Austin's hand.

"Stay here." He left her lying on cold, hard earth, her heart pounding frantically, the thick coppery taste of fear in her mouth.

She lifted her head, watching as he moved away. Crouched low. Silent. If she hadn't been looking at him, she wouldn't have known he was there. Leaves rustled in a thicket a hundred yards away, and he froze. Eva froze, too, her muscles taut with fear.

"Police. Come out with your hands where I can see them," he commanded. More rustling. A soft sigh that might have been a moan. A woman stumbled from the thick tangle of overgrowth, blood streaming down her face. She fell to her knees. Managed to stand up again. Confused. Dazed. Not dangerous. That's what Eva thought, and Austin must have thought the same. He holstered his gun.

"Ma'am, are you okay?" Austin asked, moving toward her.

"What's going on? Where am I?" she replied, her gaze darting from Austin to Justice and then settling on Eva.

"The Lost Woods. You're hurt, and you need to lie down." Eva took her arm, tried to help her to the ground.

"What happened?" She touched her head, frowning at her blood-tinged fingers.

"I was hoping you could tell us." Austin pulled off his jacket, dropped it onto the woman's shoulders, his gaze scanning the forest. Danger still lurked there, but Justice lay docile in the shadows of a large oak, his big head resting on his paws.

"I...don't remember. I think..." Her gaze dropped to his gun holster, her eyes widening. "No!"

"Ma'am, I'm with the Sagebrush Police Department. Just relax, okay?" Austin put a hand on her shoulder, but she shrugged away, her eyes wild.

"Everything is going to be fine. I'm going to call for a rescue crew to come and transport you out of the forest."

"No!" she said again, whirling away, Austin's coat dropping to the ground as she plunged back into the thicket.

Austin started after her, heard the snap of branches and Justice's quiet bark. Not danger, but someone was coming. He turned, stepping in front of Eva just in case.

"What—"

He put his hand up, cutting off her words as he caught sight of an orange vest. Search and rescue. Hopefully, a police officer. Justice was on Brady's scent, and Austin didn't want to stop the search to chase after the injured woman or to find the person who had been firing shots at her.

"Hey! Austin! I heard gunfire and your call for backup. Is everything okay?" Detective Lee Calloway called out as he approached with his border collie, Kip. A fellow member of the Special Operations K-9 Unit, Lee had been a good friend and coworker for years. His dog, Kip, specialized in cadaver detection. Hopefully, Kip wouldn't have to put those skills to use in their search for Brady.

"We're fine, but there's an injured woman heading west. She may know who the shooter was."

"How bad are the injuries?"

"It was hard to tell. She had a head wound, and she seemed confused. Could be a concussion or a fractured skull."

"You want me to go after her or the missing boy?" Lee asked.

"Justice already has Brady's scent. Go after Jane Doe. And watch your back while you're at it. Someone is wandering around firing shots."

"Will do. You have a description of the woman for me?"

"Aside from the bleeding head wound?"

"Aside from that." Lee smiled, but his eyes were shadowed.

Yesterday had been long for the entire team. The discovery of Slade's injured father and the realization that Rio had been taken had hit the unit hard.

"Long blond hair. About five-five. Slim build."

"Got it. I'll radio in when I find her."

After Lee headed west with Kip, Austin shrugged into his coat and backpack. Eva hovered a few feet away, her skin pale, her arms hugging her waist.

He didn't ask if she was ready.

He knew she would be. Even if she wasn't, she wouldn't admit it.

"Come on, boy," he urged, and Justice lumbered to his feet. "Seek!"

Justice took off, barking wildly.

Close.

They were close.

Austin felt it in the tension on the lead, the way Justice's muscles pulled taut. The bloodhound wanted to get to the end of the trail, wanted to find the person they were seeking, wanted it more than he wanted to sleep or eat or play. That's what made him a great search-and-rescue dog, his prey drive completely refocused into a stunning display of canine determination.

They crested one more rise, plunged down into a ravine, the ground slick with mud and dead leaves. Justice bayed once and again, frantically clawing at the ground in an effort to move more quickly.

A dozen yards ahead, a rocky outcrop sheltered a small pool of stagnant water. Beyond that, Austin could make out thick foliage partially hiding what looked like the opening of a cave. Six feet high and maybe four feet wide, it was the perfect hiding place for a scared little boy. His heart lurched, and he unhooked Justice. Let him race ahead, his frantic alerts ringing through the cool dawn.

"Is that a cave? He's there, isn't he? Brady! Brady!" Eva ran toward the cave, and Austin snagged the back of her coat, pulling her up short.

"Wait here while I check things out."

"Check what out? He's there. Justice is going crazy trying to tell us that."

"I know, but I need to go in first. We heard gunfire earlier, and I don't want you in the middle of more of it," he said.

"He's in there. I know he is." She tried to twist away, but he kept hold of her coat.

"We don't know—"

"He's there." She looked into his eyes, and he saw hope in the depth of her gaze. Saw it in her face.

He wanted to believe that it was justified, but there was no telling what he'd find in the cave. As much as Austin wanted to think they were running toward a live rescue, things might not turn out that way. He didn't want Eva to find her son's lifeless body. Didn't want her to see what he'd seen too many times.

Maybe she saw that in *his* face.

She stilled, her green eyes staring into his, her long gold lashes sweeping her cheek and brow. She had eyes like her son's. He felt the weight of the picture that he'd tucked into his coat pocket. Felt the weight of her dreams and hopes piled on his shoulders.

"You think he might be dead," she rasped, and he couldn't deny it.

"Wait here," he said again, letting go of her coat and running toward the cave.

Thick muck sucked at his boots and splashed up his pant legs, the stagnant pool of water shallow and brown. Eva splashed through it behind him. Obviously unwilling to listen to his request.

He reached the cave a few steps ahead of her, ducked down and moved into dank blackness, following the sound of Justice's fading barks. A few large rocks butted against the side of the cave, and he skirted around them. From there, the opening narrowed until Austin's shoulders brushed the walls. Even crouched, his head touched the ceiling. He maneuvered sideways for several minutes, but short of shrinking down to child-size there was no way he could go farther.

"What's going on? Why are we stopping?" Eva pressed in as if she wanted to shove him out of the way and hunt for Brady herself.

"It's too narrow. Going farther wouldn't be safe."

"I'm smaller than you. Let me go."

"We'll both have to back out first. No way can you squeeze past me."

"Okay." She backed up and he followed, his headlamp flashing on dark gray rock and moist brown earth. The cave went deeper than he'd expected, curving to the left, whatever lay behind the curve hidden in darkness.

Justice's long howl echoed against the walls, bouncing through the darkness, and Austin snagged Eva's hand. "Hold on! Justice is alerting. He's found something. Try calling your son."

"Brady? It's Mom. Are you in there?" Eva called past the lump of terror and hope in her throat. What if he *was* there, but couldn't answer? What if he was injured or...

"Momma?" The word was faint, but she heard it. Wanted to climb straight through Austin to follow the sound.

"Yes. It's me. I have Snowflake, too. I found him out in the woods while I was looking for you. Come on out, and we can all go home together." She tried to keep her voice steady, but she was so relieved, so thankful, her body felt weak with it.

"I can't." He was crying. She could hear the tears in his voice, and if the walls hadn't been pressing so tight, if Austin hadn't been wedged so firmly into the opening, she would have gone to her son.

"Ask him if he's stuck, and ask him if there's a dog with him," Austin urged.

"Are you stuck, sweetie?"

"I'm lost. I got inside here, but I can't get out. It's too dark."

"Is there a dog with you, Brady?"

"Yes, but I didn't pet him."

"Those are the rules for normal times, but for today, you can pet the dog. He's special. Like Captain Slade's dog."

"Are you hurt, Brady? Can you walk?" Austin called out.

"Momma, are you still there? Who's that with you?" The fear in his voice was unmistakable, and her heart ached for everything he'd been through, her arms aching to pull him close, let him know that he was finally safe.

"A police detective. He and his dog have been helping me find you. Are you hurt?"

"No, and I can walk, too. And I petted the dog. He's soft… and he licked my face."

"His name is Justice," Austin said. "Do you feel the harness on his back?"

"Yes."

"If you hold on to that, Justice will lead you all the way out of the cave."

"Really?"

"Absolutely. Are you holding on?"

"Yes."

"Justice, come!" Austin ordered, and then nudged Eva. "Let's head out where there's more room to maneuver."

"But—"

"Justice found your son, Eva. Are you really not going to trust him to lead him out of the cave?" he asked as his radio crackled.

No. She wasn't going to trust him. Not if she had a choice. Trust was something given and then broken. She'd found that out one too many times. She backed up, anyway because the last thing she wanted was for all of them to get stuck in the cave because she'd succumbed to fear.

Austin's voice rumbled into the darkness as he called in their coordinates and asked for a rescue unit. Eva tried to let his words comfort her. If he was calling for transportation, he must believe that Brady and Justice would make their way out.

Sunlight speckled the dirt floor near her feet, and she stopped, cold, crisp air swirling around her ankles. She pressed a hand to Austin's back, stopping him before they collided. Firm muscle contracted beneath her palm, and she pulled her hand away, her heart thumping painfully.

Brady. He was all that mattered, and he hadn't appeared yet. Hadn't called out again.

"Brady?" she called, but he didn't answer. "What if—"

"He's coming." Austin pulled off his pack, rifled through it and took out a thermal blanket.

"I don't hear him or Justice."

"Justice already found what he was looking for. He's done alerting, and Brady probably couldn't hear you calling. The cave is a lot deeper than I anticipated." He sighed. "I'm glad you were with me. I don't know if your son would have come out otherwise."

His words took her by surprise. She'd thought him to be a little arrogant, a lot bossy. Not the kind of guy who would admit that he'd been wrong. Not the kind who she would have expected to give other people credit.

Then again, she'd never been the best judge of character. She certainly hadn't been when it came to Rick.

"Things always work out the way they're supposed to." Her mother used to say that to Eva. It had taken a lot of years for her to believe it.

"True, and this time, they worked out the way that we both wanted them to." He smiled, and it transformed his face, made him approachable in the easy charming way that would have appealed to her if she ever allowed any man to do that.

"Momma? Where are you?" Brady called, his voice muffled and distant.

Her heart jerked, the need to go to him so strong that she took a step deeper into the cave, peered into its shadowy depths.

"I'm right here, buddy. Are you still with Justice?"

"Yes, but it's dark, and I'm cold. I want to go home."

"Just keep walking, then. You'll be out of there before you know it," she called, hoping the words would comfort him.

"Use this. Brady might be able to see the light once he gets closer." Austin handed her his headlamp, and she shone it into the cave. The light bounced off gray walls and brown floors. She wanted it to bounce off Brady's pale blond hair and freckled face.

She watched the narrow opening, her head pounding in time with her frantic heart. Finally, something moved in the darkness, a shifting of shadows that drew closer and closer, until the shadows had color and shape and form and Brady was in her arms. Clutching him close, she felt him shivering, his skin cold to the touch.

"You're freezing." Eva took off her coat and wrapped him in it, alarmed at his paleness. Scratches and dried blood scored his cheek and arms, and his feet were so caked with mud that she could barely see his toes. His pajama bottoms were torn at both knees, the skin peeking from beneath the fabric raw and bleeding.

"That's because I was cold all night. I was shaking I was so cold."

"Let's warm you up, okay?" She wrapped her arms around him, rubbing his back and trying to will some of her warmth into his cold little body.

"How are you doing, sport?" Austin wrapped the blanket around both of them, then crouched close, Justice panting contentedly near his feet.

"Okay. Are you the police?" Brady's eyes were wide, his teeth chattering, his lips so pale they faded into his skin.

"Yes. I'm Detective Austin Black. You already met my partner, Justice."

"He's a cool dog. I always wanted a dog, but Momma says that we're too busy to have one."

"It's not fair to have a dog if you don't have time," Austin responded diplomatically as he tucked the edges of the blanket around Brady's head.

"If I had a dog, those bad men would have stayed away from me."

"What bad men?" Austin pulled a juice box from his pack, popped a straw into it and handed it to Brady.

"They're not nice. They beat mean old Mr. McNeal and they took Rio."

"You saw the man who did that?" Eva asked, taking the untouched juice box from his hand and looking into his face. His lip trembled, his eyes swimming with tears.

"Yes," he whispered, looking away, obviously ashamed of something.

"How? You can't see Captain McNeal's house from Mrs. Daphne's."

"I walked Fluffy. Mrs. Daphne said that I could, because

I was bored and I didn't want to watch stupid old TV anymore," he wailed.

Despite herself, Eva couldn't be upset. She couldn't even bring herself to remind him of the rule that he'd broken. Not yet. That would come when he was warm and clean and safe again.

"We'll talk about that later."

"How many men did you see, Brady?"

"Two. The man with the brown hair and the man with the red hair. The man with the red hair is meanest. He hit me right here, because I started crying when he brought me to the woods." Brady touched his cheek, tears spilling down his face. "He hit Mr. McNeal, too. With a brick. I even saw him do it. Then he pushed Rio right into a van and saw me."

"It's okay, buddy." Eva pressed his head to her shoulder.

"What happened next, sport?" Austin asked gently.

"The man with the red hair yelled for the other man to get me. Me and Fluffy ran really fast, though, and he didn't catch us."

"Why didn't you tell me about this, Brady? We could have called the police and made sure you were safe." Eva brushed Brady's hair from his forehead and looked into his denim-blue eyes. Rick's eyes, but so much softer and sweeter than his had been.

"Because you told me not ever to go walking by myself, and I didn't want to get into trouble." He started crying in earnest, his face scrunched up and so full of misery that Eva's heart broke.

"It's okay." She patted his back, and met Austin's eyes, anxious to get her shivering, sobbing son out of the cave and to safety. "How long until the rescue team arrives?"

"Ten or fifteen minutes. It might be best if we bring him out into the sun while we wait. He's hypothermic, and the sooner we get him warmed up, the better." He hooked Justice to his lead. "Ready to get out of here, Brady?"

"Yes." Brady didn't even lift his head. Exhausted, bruised and terrified, but he was alive. That was all that mattered.

Thank You, God.

Thank You, thank You, thank You.

Dawn peeked through the thick trees and dappled the ground with yellow-gold light as they walked out of the cave. Eva hadn't noticed the beauty of the forest while they were searching for Brady. Now she couldn't stop noticing. The tall pines stretching toward the blue sky. The red-brown earth beneath their feet. The soft sound of birds greeting the day.

Justice growled deep in his throat, the fur on his scruff standing on end, his nose pointed toward the rise above the cave.

"Go back into the cave," Austin shouted.

She didn't ask why. Didn't stop to think about who might be coming. She ran, feet slipping on slick ground, Brady in her arms, all the beauty of the morning fading into cold, stark terror.

Chapter Five

She set Brady down at the mouth of the cave, shielding him with her body as she shooed him away from the opening.

"Are they back, Momma? Are the bad men back?" Brady cried, his eyes wide in his stark white face.

"I don't—"

A shot rang out, the sound reverberating through the cave. Close.

Too close.

"Let's go farther in, buddy." She nudged Brady in front of her, urging him deeper into the cave until the walls narrowed and Eva couldn't move forward any farther. She could hear nothing but her heartbeat and the soft rasping of Brady's breath. If Brady's bad men were following, they'd have easy targets, cave walls to either side, no room for Eva to move forward. Brady could, though.

"I want you to do what you did before, Brady. Run deeper into the cave, okay? Not too far. Keep your hand on the wall and count twenty steps. As soon as you're done, turn right around this way so you know how to get out."

"No, Momma!"

"Yes. I'll have the detective send Justice in for you as soon as it's safe." She gave him a gentle shove, listening as his feet padded in the darkness. She counted his steps. Only ten, but she didn't want to call for him to keep going. She didn't want him any farther away than he needed to be.

She eased back the way she'd come, silently picking her way through the darkness, her hand sliding along the rough rock wall. She didn't know where Austin had gone, didn't know if the gunshot she'd heard had been from his gun or someone else's. The thought of him crumbling to the ground, blood flowing from a bullet wound, made her stomach ache and her pulse pound harder. He and Justice had saved Brady's life. Without them, her son would still be lost and shivering in the cave.

She shuddered at the thought, stepping out into the coolness of the cave's mouth. Thick foliage blocked her view of the shallow pool beyond it, but the morning had gone silent as death. Not a bird singing. No small animals rustling in the woods. Nothing, and that petrified her almost as much as the gunshot had. She searched the ground, grabbing a fist-size rock and creeping to the cave entrance. She peered through the overgrowth of shrubs and weeds, searching the landscape beyond.

Nothing.

No one.

Wait!

Her heart jumped as something moved in the forest. A man. Narrow build. Slim shoulders. Tall and thin, his red hair gleaming in the morning sun.

One of Brady's bad men. Where was the other?

And where were Austin and Justice?

She clutched the rock as the red-haired man made his descent. He glanced to his left and called to someone. Another man, picking his way into the ravine from the opposite slope. The only way out of the cave and into the woods was a straight path through the two of them.

The red-haired man stumbled the last few feet into the muck and dead leaves, his mud-brown eyes seeming to burn straight into Eva's.

She stumbled back and pressed close to the side wall of the cave. She didn't stand a chance against a bullet, but as long as Brady stayed deep in the cave, he'd be fine.

Please, God, let him be fine.

"Momma? Are they gone?" Brady called out, his words bouncing off the granite walls and ringing through the unnatural silence.

That was all it took.

An explosion of sound, and a bullet whizzed past Eva's head, slammed into the cave wall, bits of granite showering her hair and face. She dove to the ground, scrambling away on her hands and knees, screaming for Brady to stay where he was.

Someone shouted, but Eva didn't hear the words past the echoing sound of gunfire.

Austin shouted another warning as he stepped from behind an outcrop of rocks and fired. His first shot hit home, dropping the redheaded perp who was closest to the cave. The other man retreated, racing back up the ravine and dodging behind a thick oak. Austin fired again, his bullet slamming into the tree's trunk. No way could he chase the man through the forest while Eva and Brady were alone in the cave. He called for backup and warned the approaching rescue team of the presence of the armed man as he ran to the cave.

He'd seen Eva behind the foliage, her pale face peering

out, and he'd wanted to shout for her to take cover. He hadn't wanted to warn his targets, though. He hoped that he'd made the right choice. Hoped that she wasn't lying in a pool of blood on the other side of the winter-dry brush.

He paused at the fallen man's side, checked for a pulse, knowing that he wouldn't find one. He'd done what he had to, but there was no joy in it.

"Is he dead?" Eva peered out of from the cave entrance, her hair a tangled mess around her shoulders, her eyes dull and tired.

"Yes." He shifted to block her view. "Are you and Brady okay?"

"Yes." An engine rumbled in the distance, and she glanced up the slope. "I guess that's our ride out of here. I'll tell Brady he can come out of hiding."

"Keep him in the cave, okay? I don't think it would be good for him to see this."

She glanced at the body, nodded and slipped back into the cave.

Austin patted the deceased's pockets, searching for ID. Nothing. They'd have to ID him by fingerprints or dental records.

He walked into the cave and unleashed Justice.

"Stay," he commanded, and the bloodhound dropped onto his haunches, his tongue lolling out, what looked like a contented smile on his hang-dog face. He'd found the prize, discovered the missing, and he'd probably spend the rest of the day lying on the couch back at Austin's place.

"Can I pet your dog, Mr. Detective?" Brady asked as he walked from the deepest part of the cave, his white-blond hair dirty and spiking up around his head, the scratches on his face and arms livid. He'd lost his blanket and Eva's coat somewhere and shook violently. Austin pulled out another blanket and tucked it around his shoulders, concerned with his pallid complexion, his colorless lips, the vague look in his bright blue eyes.

"If it's okay with your mom." Austin glanced at Eva, who was clutching Brady's shoulder as if she were afraid that letting go would mean losing him again.

She nodded, and Austin called Justice to Brady's side.

"You can pet him, but only if you call me Austin and stay in the cave until I come tell you it's okay to come out. You also have to stay wrapped up real tight in this blanket, okay?"

"Okay."

Austin waited while Brady settled in beside Justice, smiling a little as the boy wrapped his arms around the dog's solid back and pulled the blanket over both of them. He'd soak in some of Justice's warmth. A good thing while they waited for rescue.

"I'll be right back." Austin stepped out of the cave and into the cold, sunny day. A few clouds edged across the horizon, the hint of moisture he'd felt earlier coalescing into a brewing storm.

The sound of approaching vehicles grew louder as he covered the perp's face with the blanket, said a silent prayer for the family of the man. The deceased might have chosen a dark path, but his family would still mourn his loss.

A four-wheeler roared into view, splashing through the small pool and stopping a few feet from the cave. A dark-haired woman jumped off. Austin knew her. Laurel Stanley worked as an emergency-room nurse and volunteered with San Antonio Search and Rescue. They'd dated a few times, but they both had busy lives and lived in cities they loved. Neither planned to move, and that, as much as anything, had kept the relationship from blooming.

"Hey, Austin! You've found the boy?"

"In the cave. Hypothermic. Shaky, but conscious."

"The sooner we get him out of here, the better, then." She hurried into the cave as a four-wheeler driven by a uniformed police officer arrived. Austin briefed him quickly, watching as he took off again, heading in the direction that the second perp had disappeared. More than likely, the guy was long gone by now, but they'd keep looking, keep hunting until he was in custody.

Two more four-wheelers roared toward Austin, the forest alive with sound and movement. The teams would need to take photos, collect evidence. Protocol always dictated, but when it came to lethal force, it was even more important that it be followed precisely.

He walked to the mouth of the cave, stepping back as Eva carried Brady out, Laurel right behind them.

"I'm transporting now, Austin. We'll bring them to Sagebrush General. I've already called ahead to let them know we're coming," she said.

"I'll make sure we have a man there." He wanted twenty-four-hour protection for Brady until they had the second perp in custody. Whatever Brady had witnessed, whoever he'd seen, it had been enough to put him in the sights of some very dangerous men.

"Thanks for everything, Austin," Eva said as she climbed onto the four-wheeler, Brady leaning against her shoulder, his eyes closed. Maybe she thought that this was the end, that they were done now that her son was safe. They were far from it, but he wouldn't tell her that. Not when she looked so relieved to be leaving the Lost Woods.

He stepped away from the four-wheeler, watching as Laurel drove away. He should be feeling relief, elation. The normal high that came from a successful mission. Instead, he felt worried, anxiety gnawing at him as he turned to the evidence team that was working the scene.

"Funny seeing her here," a short, wiry police officer said, his gaze on the retreating vehicle.

"Who?"

"Eva Billows. Last time I saw her, we were working her parents' murders. Shame that she's had so much trouble. Her father might have been a weasel, but she seems like a good kid.

"She mentioned her parents' murders."

"A bad scene. The bodies had been there for a couple of days before she found them."

The words sparked a memory—the murder of a couple in their double-wide trailer. The husband had been beaten and then shot execution-style. The wife had been shot in the chest. Their daughter had discovered the bodies when her mother hadn't shown up to babysit. The story had made local news because of the brutal nature of the crime and the horror of the young woman walking in on the scene. Austin hadn't worked the case, but he remembered the police station buzzing during the investigation.

"What were her folks' names?" He couldn't remember, but he thought there'd been some connection to a small-time drug ring. Some reason to believe that the crime had been retribution.

"Ernie and Tonya Billows," the officer said.

No wonder Eva's name had sounded familiar.

"Any leads on the case?"

"A few fingerprints that we couldn't match to anyone who didn't have an alibi. One or two sets that weren't in the system. No murder weapon. No suspects. The trail has gone cold, but that doesn't mean we're not still actively working it. Why?"

"I think what happened to Eva's son is connected to the attack on Captain McNeal's father and the theft of Rio, but if there are other avenues I need to check out, it would be good to know now."

"I don't think there is. Ernie was a small-time criminal. Not someone who would be remembered this long."

"What about his wife?" Austin queried.

"Just one of those sad women who got caught up with the wrong guy and couldn't ever quite disentangle herself from him. The way I see things, if you want to figure out who kidnapped the Billows boy, you just need to find out who this guy was working with." He gestured to the body.

"Hopefully, someone will track him down before he gets out of these woods and disappears into Sagebrush."

"You got a good look at him, right?" the officer asked.

"Not as good as I would have liked. Just what I called in over the radio. Dark hair. Medium build. Five-ten, max. Maybe a hundred and seventy pounds. No distinguishing features that I could see."

"I'll run that through the computer back at the station. We might get lucky and pull up someone you recognize. Internal affairs is going to want to interview you. From what I see, this was a clear case of self-defense and appropriate use of lethal force, but you know how these things work."

"All too well." Austin sighed.

"If you want to head back to the station, you can get the interview over with and get on with your day," the officer offered. "When I get back to the precinct, I'll email you the Billows file. You can look through it yourself. Maybe there's something we missed."

"Thanks." He called Justice, hooked the leash to his collar and scratched behind his ears.

Justice shook his big head, his ears flapping, his nose sniffing the air as if he were wondering what had happened to the prize he'd spent half the night searching for.

"You did good, boy," Austin said. "You found him. Now, all we have to do is keep him safe."

Justice cocked his head to the side, his dark brown eyes soulful. Then he barked as if he understood exactly what Austin was saying.

Chapter Six

Twenty minutes of winding, bumpy pathways, a quick ride in an ambulance, an hour of doctors prodding and poking Brady while Eva answered an endless barrage of police questions, and finally...*finally*...it was over. Brady was settled under thick blankets, his blond hair brushed back from a bruised forehead, his eyes closed. Eva touched his scraped cheek, felt his still-cool skin. A few more hours, and he would have succumbed to hypothermia.

The thought made her physically ill.

She'd been so close to losing him.

Too close.

It felt like her fault. No matter how many times she told herself that it wasn't, she couldn't shake the feeling that she should have kept him safe.

In the years since her parents' murders, she'd done everything that she could to create a predictable routine and *normal* life for Brady. A life that was nothing like the one she'd had as a kid. No police officers banging on the doors at all hours of the night. No hoodlums visiting in the wee hours of the morning threatening violence if a debt wasn't paid or a secret kept. All Eva wanted was to be a typical mother, doing typical things with her typical son. She didn't want drama. Didn't want danger. Didn't want any of the things that she'd grown up with.

A few more months of college and she'd have her teaching degree. She planned to apply to school districts far away from Sagebrush, Texas. Go somewhere north where there was snow and freezing weather in the winter. Where the days were longer in the summer and the air clear and crisp rather than humid. She planned to make a brand-new life where no one knew about her father.

But plans meant nothing if Brady wasn't part of them.

Her life.

Her heart.

Being his mother had forced her to become stronger. More self-sufficient. Much more patient and willing to wait on God's plans.

Most of the time.

Lately, she'd felt unsettled and discontent. As if the life she'd built for herself wasn't enough. As if there was something special waiting just around the corner. She'd wanted to run to whatever it was, grab it with both hands.

Instead, she just kept plodding along, doing the same things she'd been doing since Brady's birth—working as a waitress at Arianna's Café, going to school part-time, striving to provide a good life for her son.

She touched his cheek again, her chest tight. He still felt too cold. She pulled the covers up around his shoulders, wishing she could go home and get his favorite blanket. Wishing she could smooth the frown that marred his brow as he slept.

"Momma?" He opened his eyes. Looking in them was like

looking into his father's. Only Rick's gaze had always been calculating, his smiles designed to disarm and manipulate.

"You okay?" She lifted Brady's hand, careful of the scrapes and cuts in his palm.

"I need to ask you something." His voice had a raspy quality that worried her. She wanted to ring for a nurse, demand that the doctor check on Brady again, but he was already hooked up to IV fluids, already warming up beneath a layer of blankets. There wasn't much more that could be done.

"What is it, sweetie?"

"Do you think they're going to come here?"

"Who?" she asked, but she knew, and the knowledge shivered through her.

"The bad men. Will they come to the hospital?"

"Of course not." She hoped. Prayed. Wanted to believe.

"How do you know?"

"There's a police officer sitting right outside the door. He'll keep the bad guys away."

"What if he doesn't?"

"He will, okay? The bad guys will be too scared to come around him."

"I wish Austin and Justice were there instead."

"They're busy."

"Looking for someone else who needs help?"

"Looking for the man who kidnapped you. They're going to put him in jail. Then you won't ever have to worry about him again."

"There were two men, Momma. Remember?"

She couldn't forget. The body lying beneath the blanket, the gun close beside it. Thank goodness Brady had been too tired to pay attention to the scene outside the cave. "They already took care of one of them."

"So, just one more?"

"Yes."

"Maybe Austin and Justice will come here after they find the bad guy."

"Sweetheart, they already helped us, and there are so many more people they can do that for."

"But they really liked me. Justice licked my hand and Austin even called me sport."

"Of course they liked you. *Everyone* likes you. But Austin and Justice have a very important job, and they don't have time to visit people at the hospital—"

Someone knocked, and Eva jumped, angling her body so she was between Brady and the door.

"Who is it?"

"Austin."

"I knew he would come! I knew it, Momma!" The hero worship in Brady's eyes was unmistakable, and Eva wanted to tell him not to put his hopes in Austin. He'd only be disappointed.

That was her life experience.

She didn't want to taint her son with it, but she didn't want him hurt, either.

"Come on in," she called, and Austin walked in.

No more police uniform. Just faded jeans and a fitted black T-shirt, his abs taut beneath the fabric. He had his leather bomber jacket under his arm and scuffed cowboy boots on his feet, and she didn't think she'd ever seen anyone look quite so good.

Her cheeks heated, and she looked away, refusing to acknowledge the butterflies in her stomach or the little skip of her heart when he moved close.

"How are you doing, sport?" he asked.

"My head hurts and my throat hurts and my knees hurt, too. They got all beat up when that mean guy pushed me and made me fall. See?" Brady shoved all the blankets away and rolled up the little blue pajama pants that the hospital staff had dressed him in. Both of his knees were bandaged, one of them wrapped tight. A bruised kneecap, the doctor had said.

Eva hated to imagine the amount of force it would take to knock a child down so violently that his kneecap bruised.

"You need to stay warm, remember?" She slid the pant legs back down and pulled the covers back to his chin, her elbow bumping Austin's solid thigh.

She blushed again.

Called herself every kind of fool.

The man had saved her son. *Of course* she found him attractive. It didn't mean anything.

"I don't like all these blankets on me, Momma. I'm hot."

"Then why are your hands and cheeks cold?"

"Because…" He couldn't think of a good reason and fell back onto his pillow, his gaze jumping to Austin. "Where is Justice?"

"Home. He worked hard last night, and he needed a little time off."

"Momma said you were both out looking for the bad guy. She said you were going to throw him in jail so that he never came and got me again."

"Your mom is right. There are lots of police out looking for him."

"But you're here."

"I have to take a little vacation. Once I'm back at work, I'll be out looking for the bad guy every day."

"A vacation?" Eva asked even though she knew it didn't matter. As long as there were other officers working to protect Brady, she didn't need to know where Austin would be or what he'd be doing.

"Administrative leave." He dropped into a chair, not of-

fering further explanation. It took a moment for the words
to sink in.

"I'm sorry."

"It's nothing to do with you or Brady, Eva. It's just procedure. The way things are going, I should be back to work in
a couple of days."

"That fast?" She wasn't sure she believed it, but then she'd
made it a habit to *not* know how the police department worked.

"You've been interviewed by a police officer already, right?"

"Yes." She'd answered dozens of questions while the doctor examined Brady.

"He was from internal affairs. They're moving quickly on
things because the investigation is fairly cut and dry, and because I'm lead investigator in another case."

"The one involving Slade's father?"

"That's right. There are other officers that can take over if
I can't proceed, but there's no reason to think I won't be able
to. What happened was justified, and I followed protocol."
He crossed his feet at the ankles. If being put on administrative leave bothered him, it didn't show.

She narrowed her eyes. "So, if you're on leave, why are
you here?"

"To check on Brady."

"That wasn't necessary, Austin."

"Wasn't it?" he asked mildly, and she felt small and petty.

"I think it's my turn to apologize. I didn't mean that the
way it sounded. After all that you've done, you're welcome to
visit Brady anytime you want."

"And, next time, you're welcome to bring Justice," Brady
said, and Austin chuckled, the sound as warm as a summer
breeze and about ten times as nice.

"Not to the hospital, sport, but I'll bring him by your house
once you get home."

"I don't know if Momma will let him come. She doesn't like dogs. She says they're mean and they bite."

"Not *all* dogs, Brady. I've told you that. Some dogs are perfectly nice." Eva's cheeks were pink, her gaze skittering away from Austin's.

He made her uncomfortable. He could see that, but he didn't plan on leaving. He might be on administrative leave, but that didn't mean he couldn't do a little investigating.

"But you said that we couldn't have a dog because we don't have the time for it and because they can be fishes and mean."

"Fishes?" Austin asked, and Eva offered a slight smile.

"*Vicious*. He's a typical seven-year-old. Sometimes he needs his ears cleaned out."

"And sometimes I need to plug them up." Brady yawned, his eyelids drooping, a dark bruise on his forehead livid against his pale skin.

"Why don't you close your eyes for a while?" Austin suggested, but Brady shook his head.

"I think you'll be gone when I wake up."

"Maybe I will be, but I'll come back again."

"You will?" Brady implored.

"Of course." He patted the little boy's hand, ignoring Eva's scowl. "And even better, if you sleep now, you'll get strong enough to go home a lot more quickly. Then I'll be able to visit you at your house."

"With Justice!" Brady made it sound like Austin had just offered the moon, and Austin's heart melted a little more than he wanted it to. A little more than he should allow it to.

He'd been down that road before.

It hadn't ended well.

He wouldn't go down it again.

"Yes," he responded, because he couldn't say no to Brady.

He'd just have to be careful. Make sure that he didn't get pulled in any deeper than he already had been.

Brady nodded, but his eyes were already closed, his arm flung up over his head, an IV needle taped to it. A long scratch snaked from his wrist to his elbow and what looked like finger marks bruised the inside of his arm. His kidnappers hadn't been gentle with him. Of course, they probably hadn't expected that he'd be alive to complain to anyone.

"You don't have to come by to visit, Austin. I know that you were just trying to be kind, and I appreciate that, but I can tell Brady that you're busy. He'll understand," Eva whispered, and he looked into her eyes, felt the breath leave his lungs at the impact of that one glance.

He hadn't noticed how green her eyes were, how soft and misty. Hadn't noticed her flawless skin or her full, pink lips. He'd been working, and that had been his only focus. Now he was on leave, his focus on Brady and on Eva because it had nowhere else to be. Not his empty house. Not even his tired K-9 partner, who'd seemed more interested in lying on the sofa than playing a game of fetch in the backyard.

Truth be told, that's what had driven Austin to visit Brady.

He'd wanted to know that the seven-year-old was okay, but he'd also wanted to reassure himself that what he did, the things that had kept him tied to his work and away from the life he'd always wanted to build, were worthwhile.

They were. He knew it, but there were times when he wanted more. A wife. Kids. A loud and busy house to go home to.

"If you want me to leave, Eva, I will." He stood, ready to walk out of the hospital, go back to his house and wait for the phone to ring and IA to give him the all-clear to go back to work. He needed to sleep anyway, catch up on the hours he'd missed while he was searching for Rio and for Brady.

"Wait." She touched his arm as he moved past, her fingers trailing heat as they slid away. "I..."

"What?"

"You don't have to leave. Brady has been dozing fitfully, and he could wake up any minute. If he does, he'll be happy if you're here."

"What about you?"

She shrugged. "I don't mind if you stay."

"You don't owe me anything, Eva. You don't have to allow me to be here out of some kind of obligation. If I make you uncomfortable—"

"You don't!" She protested a little too loudly, and Brady shifted in his sleep, turning on his side and moaning softly.

"You don't," Eva repeated in a hushed voice as she brushed hair from Brady's forehead. She looked beautiful standing there, her expression as soft as her eyes, her lips curved into a small frown. Not as young as Austin had thought. Closer to thirty than to twenty.

"Knock, knock!" A female voice called, and the door opened. A tall, thin woman walked into the room, an over-size stuffed dog in her arms. Austin knew her. She owned Arianna's Café, a busy restaurant in the heart of downtown Sagebrush.

"Arianna! What are you doing here?" Eva's brow furrowed, her eyes shadowed and wary.

"You've been working for me since you were in high school. Did you think I wouldn't come visit your son while he was in the hospital?"

"How did you know he was here?"

"You're all over the news. I have to say, I'm a little upset that I didn't hear it straight from you, but I suppose you've been busy. How is he?" She approached the bed and dropped the dog onto the end of it.

"Hypothermic, bruised, still scared. Things could be worse, though."

"Of course they could. I hear that he was taken right out of his bedroom window. Not surprising that someone could break into your place like that. The house is nearly falling down, it's so old."

"It was built in the 1920s, Arianna, so it's not that old and it's not even close to falling down."

"It's not secure, though. You have to admit that. Maybe it would be best if the two of you came to my place for a while. I have a state-of-the-art security system, and with my work schedule, I'm not home that much. You'll have the place mostly to yourself."

"I appreciate the offer, but I'll get new windows and locks and have a security system installed at our place. We'll be fine."

"I hope you're right. If you change your mind, the offer will stay open. Perhaps this will help with the expense of having your house secured." She pulled an envelope from her purse and held it out. "I know that things are tight for you while you're in college."

"Arianna, I can't take that." Eva's gaze shot to Austin, her cheeks pink.

"Don't be silly. Of course you can. Besides, it's not just from me. When your coworkers heard that Brady was in the hospital, they took up a collection to help."

"Tell them that I really appreciate it." Eva took the envelope, but she didn't look happy about it.

"I'm sure that you'll be able to tell them yourself. You'll need a few days off, but I thought you could come in on Wednesday. That gives Brady five days to recover. I'm sure he'll be back in school by then."

"I—"

"You'll call me if there's a problem, but I'll assume that

there won't be. I need to get back to the café." She hurried out of the room.

"Your boss, huh?" Austin watched as Eva tucked the envelope into her purse. She didn't open it. He wondered if she planned to use the money or to return it.

"Yes."

"You didn't seem thrilled to see her."

"I was just surprised." More than surprised. Eva had actually been shocked, but she didn't tell Austin that. She hadn't expected him, either. Hadn't really expected anyone but law enforcement and medical staff. She had friends at church, work and school, but she hadn't called any of them.

Do it yourself, hon. Whatever it is you want to accomplish, make sure you don't ever count on anyone else to help you achieve it.

She could hear her mother's words echoing from the past, and she walked to the bed, picked up the large, plush dog that Arianna had dropped there and placed it on one of the two chairs that sat near the window. It was just like Arianna to offer something so ostentatious. She enjoyed her status as benevolent benefactress when it suited her. Not that she wasn't a good boss; she was simply a demanding one.

"Nice dog." Austin touched the stuffed dog's head. "Food would be nicer. I don't know about you, but I'm starving. How about I get us both something from the cafeteria?"

"I'm not very hungry."

"Which means you *are* a little hungry." Austin smoothed his dark hair and offered a tired smile. He had circles under his eyes and the shadow of a beard on his jaw, and she could lose herself in his smile if she let herself.

"You go ahead and eat, but I'm fine."

"I'll be back in a few minutes." He left the room, left her just the way she'd thought she wanted to be—alone.

It didn't feel as good as she wanted it to.

She lifted the big white dog, hugged it to her chest, fighting back tears that she had no business shedding. Brady was safe. The police had promised to make sure he stayed that way.

They'd also promised to find her parents' killer.

She didn't want to think about that, or about what it might mean if they didn't follow through on their newest promise.

She wouldn't allow herself to imagine that Austin might somehow make things turn out differently than they had before. He seemed like a nice guy, a caring one. A person who could be depended on.

That didn't mean that *she* would depend on him.

Brady was her responsibility—his well-being, his emotional health, all of it resting squarely on her shoulders. She couldn't risk his life or happiness on the hope that someone would help them. Just had to keep going on the way she had been, doing the best she could on her own.

Chapter Seven

Austin nodded to the police officer stationed outside Brady's door and walked down the hall. A bank of elevators stood across from the nurses' station, and he pressed the call button, waiting impatiently for the door to open.

He was hungry, tired and oddly anxious to return to Brady's room. It might have had something to do with Eva's misty green eyes and her soft smile.

"Austin!" Slade McNeal called out, and Austin pivoted, saw his boss hurrying down the hall toward him.

"I didn't realize you were here."

"It's where all the action is, so I guess it's the place to be," he said wryly.

"How is your father doing?"

"The same. Still in a coma but holding his own."

"I'm sorry, Slade. You know that I'm praying for him."

"I appreciate it." Slade smoothed his hair, which was just beginning to gray. The captain had been through a lot in the past few years, and it showed, but his passion for his job and his son hadn't changed. "Good job tracking Brady Billows. How is *he* doing?"

"He's exhausted and bruised, but there doesn't seem to be anything wrong with him that time won't heal."

"Glad to hear it. I got a call from internal affairs about a half hour ago."

"Yeah?"

"You should get cleared to return to work late tomorrow or the following day. In the meantime, Lee will work any leads we get on your cases. He'll keep you posted."

"Right now, Brady is the only lead we have. He witnessed the attack on your father and saw Rio being put into a van."

"My father said 'bay' before he lost consciousness. It's possible that he saw Brady and was trying to let us know that there was a witness."

"Knowing what we know now, I'd say it's more than possible. Was Lee able to find Jane Doe?"

"She was transported to the hospital about an hour ago. Lee tried to interview her, but she's barely lucid and says she doesn't know who she is or where she's from."

"You checked fingerprints and missing-persons reports?"

"Her fingerprints don't match anyone in the system. No one fitting her description has been reported missing. She may as well have fallen out of the sky."

"One more cog in the wheel, huh?"

"Unfortunately."

The elevator door opened and they stepped in.

"Are you heading home?" Austin asked.

"I have to. My son isn't doing well with Rio gone. He was up half the night crying, and the babysitter said that he's crying again. I don't feel right leaving him for too long."

"As soon as I'm given the clear, I'll get back on the case,

Slade. You know that I'll do everything I can to find Rio quickly."

"That's why I asked you to take the lead."

"Who's taking the lead on the Billows case?" Austin queried.

"Since Brady has been found, I'm letting Cunningham handle closing the missing person's case. Eva has already been interviewed. We'll interview Brady when he's a little stronger."

"How about our deceased perp? Do we have an ID?"

"The medical examiner is going to pull prints, and we'll try to get a match. I'll let you know if we get a hit." They stepped off the elevator and walked to the exit. The sun shone bright beyond the glass doors, but clouds loomed large on the horizon. The rain would arrive soon, washing away scent trails and evidence.

Austin watched as Slade made his way across the parking lot, wishing he could have offered his friend more than words. He'd hoped to find Rio within an hour of getting the call that he'd been stolen, but they were eighteen hours out from the crime, and all he had was a dead perp, a description of another one and a seven-year-old witness.

More than he'd had the previous day, but not enough to make an arrest or to return Rio.

He grabbed a couple of sandwiches from the cafeteria, threw a couple of bags of chips on the tray with them. He grabbed a banana and an apple and tossed two packages of cookies in with the mix. Brady might like a snack later.

The cashier smiled a little too brightly as she rang him up, her bleached-blond hair brassy and her makeup just on the wrong side of subtle.

"You're a police officer, aren't you?" she asked as she slowly punched in the code for the banana.

"That's right."

"I knew it. Guy doesn't need to wear a uniform for me to recognize when he's in law enforcement. I'm intuitive that way."

"I'm sure you are," he muttered, and her smile broadened.

"Must be an exciting job, being a cop."

"It has its moments."

"Maybe we could get together sometime? You could tell me about it? I love everything that has to do with law enforcement." She beamed at him. "I'm always watching those true-crime shows at home. You know the ones I'm talking about?"

"Yes." He handed her cash and mentally hurried her through the process of counting out his change. A few years ago, her invitation would have flattered him, and he might have been tempted to take her up on it. He'd grown up a lot since his relationship with Candace had ended. Grown up and realized that a surface relationship with a pretty woman who liked his job more than she liked him was not what he wanted.

"So, what do you say? Want to get together after my shift? I get off at—"

"I'm sorry. Things are hectic right now, and my schedule is full."

"Oh." She handed him his change, looking more confused than upset. As if she couldn't quite figure out if she'd been rejected. "Maybe another time."

He didn't respond. Just thanked her and walked away.

Since he'd broken things off with Candace two years ago, he hadn't spent much time pursuing his old dreams. Family and forever tucked away in the old Victorian he'd spent the past five years restoring. He'd bought it planning to fill the rooms with kids and happiness, but work took him away more than any family deserved, and he'd given up the thought of having what he'd missed out on when he was a boy.

He knocked on Brady's door and pushed it open with his

foot. The chair near the bed was empty, but Brady was exactly where he'd been when Austin had left, lying under thick blankets and sleeping deeply, his arm stretched above his head. He looked tiny and helpless, swallowed up by the bed and the room, and Austin felt the same softening of his heart that he'd felt earlier. He steeled himself against it the same way he had dozens of times before. Getting involved wasn't an option, but he couldn't seem to make himself put the food down and leave, either.

"You're back." Eva stepped out of the bathroom, her hair pulled into a high ponytail that showed off her slender neck and high cheekbones, her face dewy as if she'd just washed it.

Beautiful.

Very beautiful, and Austin's heart did more than soften, it burned hot in his chest.

"I told you that I would be." He dropped the food on the table, studied her pale face. The whole seemed greater than the sum of its parts. Large misty eyes, high cheekbones, a slightly-too-long nose speckled with freckles. Sharp chin, widow's peak and perfectly arched brows just a shade darker than her pale hair. She should have looked austere and unapproachable. Instead, she looked like the girl next door, everyone's best friend. The kind of person anyone would want on his side.

"People don't always do what they say. I'd think that someone in your line of work would know that." She shifted uncomfortably, fiddling with the end of her ponytail and avoiding his gaze.

"And *I'd* think that someone dealing with a person in my line of work would expect something different from him than what she'd expect from most people." He turned his attention to his sandwich, almost felt her relief, the sigh of her easing tension.

"Police are just like everyone else. We both know that." She smiled to take any sting out of the words. Nice, but guarded, that was the impression that Austin got, and he wondered what it would be like to push past the wall she'd built. See what lay on the other side of it.

"You're quite the cynic." He handed her a sandwich and settled into a chair beside the bed. He didn't have to work, so he might as well be there.

"Not really. I'm just a realist." She took the other chair, smoothed the covers on the bed, laid her palm against Brady's cheek.

"Because of what happened to your parents?"

"What about what happened to them?" She unwrapped her sandwich, a frown line marring the smooth skin of her forehead.

"Their murderer was never found. Maybe you blame the police for that. Think that we didn't work hard enough to find the killer. Maybe that's what's made you such a...realist when it comes to guys like me."

"I was a realist way before my parents' murders. Besides, you weren't part of the case at all, and the officers who were investigating did the best they could with what they had." She sighed. "Do I think they could have done more? Probably. But my father wasn't the kind of guy who endeared himself to law enforcement. I'm not sure they cared all that much about getting justice for him. I'm not sure I can blame them for that, either."

"What about getting justice for your mother?"

Her smile fell away, and she set the sandwich on the table. "What is it you want to know, Austin?"

"Nothing really." But he *was* curious about her family. About her criminal father and her mother. About the people who had made her the woman she'd become.

"Then why bring up my mother?"

"Someone mentioned her today. An officer who worked the case."

"What did he say?" She lifted the top piece of bread off her sandwich and tossed a pickle into the trash can.

"That she was a nice lady who got caught up with the wrong man and could never quite free herself from him."

"That's one way to put it."

He raised a brow. "What's your way?"

"She fell in love with a man who was abusive and cruel, and she stayed with him until he killed her." Her words were cold, her eyes icy.

"You think your father killed your mother?" If so, it wasn't a theory he'd heard mentioned before.

"I think his crime got her killed, and I think that's pretty much the same thing." She took a bite of the sandwich, then wrapped it up again.

"Finished?"

"I've lost my appetite." An easy thing for Eva to do when she thought about her parents.

Two years, and she could still see her mother lying in a pool of blood, her eyes open and blank. Could still smell death, the scent of it filling the trailer where Eva had grown up. Still see the flies swarming in thick clouds above the bodies.

She gagged, nearly lost what little of the sandwich she'd eaten.

"Hey. It's okay." Austin pressed a cool palm to the back of her neck, urged her head down between her knees.

"I'm okay," she mumbled, but she wasn't sure she was. It had been a long night, and she hadn't slept, and his cool palm felt like it was the only thing holding her to the world.

"Here. Drink this." He poured water from the pitcher and handed her the glass. She took a sip, flinching as he pressed a cold, damp towel to the back of her neck.

"That's cold."

"That's the point." He smiled, his eyes crinkling at the corners. Tired eyes and such dark blue that Eva thought they were exactly the color of the sky at midnight. They pulled her into their beauty just as easily, made her want to search for something more than the things she'd spent the past seven years striving for.

"Thanks." She nudged his hand away, holding the towel herself and crossing the room to stare out the window. She needed a little space to clear her head because he was starting to get to her. Starting to make her notice things that she hadn't noticed in a lot of years, that she hadn't ever planned to notice again.

Brady cried out, the sound breaking through Eva's thoughts, pulling her back to the room and her son.

"Brady?" She brushed soft hair from his forehead, smiling as his eyes opened. "How are you doing, buddy?"

"I had a bad dream."

"Did you?" Had he forgotten that it was all real? Did he think that everything that had happened was a nightmare? She almost hoped so. Would almost rather him believe that he'd had a nightmare than have him relive the terror.

"Yes. I dreamed the bad man came for me again. I dreamed he climbed right in the window and took me, and this time you didn't find me."

"I won't let that happen, Brady. I promise." She lifted his cold hand and smiled, but his attention was on Austin.

"I thought you left," he said.

Austin shook his head and stepped close to the bed. "Not yet."

"I'm glad. That bad guy won't come in the window while you're here."

"Even if I wasn't here, no one could get in the window. We're too high up."

"We are?"

"Sure. Want to see?"

"Okay." Brady pushed aside the covers, his little arms trembling, his movements uncoordinated. Bruises peeked out from under the cuffs of his pajama pants, the long scratch on his forearm angry and red.

"You need to stay in be—"

She didn't have a chance to finish. Austin lifted Brady from the bed and carried him to the window, rolling the IV pole beside him.

"See that? We're four stories up. The only way for the bad guy to get in this window would be for him to fly, and no one can do that."

"I guess you're right." Brady frowned, his head resting against Austin's shoulder, his eyes shadowed. He looked comfortable, his body relaxed, and Eva thought he might drift to sleep again. Right there in Austin's arms. Her palms itched to pull Brady away. Her mind screamed that she'd be making a big mistake if she didn't.

She wasn't the only one who could be hurt if she let Austin deeper into their lives. There'd been a time when she'd wanted nothing more than to know that her son would have a father and a mother raising him. She'd believed with everything in her that she and Rick were going to get married, that they'd have a beautiful house and a beautiful family.

That was before she'd learned that Rick was married.

Such a silly childish dream, and she'd outgrown it a long time ago. Still, seeing Austin and Brady together made her heart ache for all the things that might have been.

"You need to get back under the covers," she said, her voice husky and tight.

"I'm not tired, Momma." But his eyes were closed again.

Austin eased him back into bed and tucked the covers up around his shoulders, the gentleness in his face adding to the ache in Eva's heart.

"You should probably go," she said, and he looked into her face, his expression unreadable.

She thought for a minute that he would find an excuse to stay, but he just nodded, dropped his business card on the table near the pile of food he'd brought. "If you need anything, call."

He walked out the door, closing it softly behind him.

Alone again. Eva and Brady. Just the way it was supposed to be. So why didn't she feel happier about it?

"Did he go, Momma?" Brady whispered.

"Yes," Eva murmured.

"I don't feel safe when he's not here." A tear slipped down his cheek, and Eva wiped it away, tried to tell herself that he'd be just fine. That she could be enough for him. That they didn't need anyone or anything but God and each other.

Somehow, though, that didn't seem quite as true as it had been the previous day.

Chapter Eight

Jeb Rinehart.

Austin stared at the name, tried to match it to the body that had lain in the stagnant pool near the cave. Twenty-seven. Red hair. Brown eyes. Sallow complexion. Three convictions on drug charges. Time served for the third one. Released from prison a month ago.

Dead by Austin's hand.

His cell phone rang, and he answered as he studied Rinehart's mug shot. "Black here."

"Austin? It's Eva."

"Is Brady okay?" He set the photo on his desk, glanced at his watch. An hour since he'd left the hospital, and he hadn't expected Eva to call at all, much less call so soon. There had to be a problem. A big one.

"He's fine." She sounded distracted.

"Do you need me to come back to the hospital?"

"No," she said too quickly.

"You do need something, though, right?"

"Not really. It's just that Brady has been talking about the kidnapping. I thought that I should let you know what he's been saying." Her words were hushed as if she didn't want her son to hear.

"What's that?" He grabbed a pad of paper and a pen, adrenaline pouring through him. He might be on administrative leave, but that didn't mean he couldn't jot down a few notes and pass them along to Slade.

"There may be a third man."

"Brady said that?"

"Yes. The two men who kidnapped him were arguing. That's how he managed to get away from them. The guy with the red hair wanted to shoot Brady and bury his body in the woods." Her voice broke, and Austin's grip tightened on the phone. It was all he could do not to get in his SUV and drive back to the hospital.

He wouldn't. He'd left because he'd known he couldn't stay and not start caring too much for Brady and Eva. He needed to stay away for the same reason.

An image of little Anna Lynn flashed through his mind, her dark eyes and curly dark hair. Her chubby cheeks and excited laughter. She'd called him Uncle Austin, and he'd carried her picture in his wallet, flashed it around like a proud relative. In his heart, that's what he'd been. He'd been best friends with Anna's father since elementary school, and he'd known Anna from the day she was born.

When he'd found her on the banks of a stream deep in the Lost Woods, a piece of his heart had torn apart.

"What else did Brady say?" he asked, his tone sharper than he'd intended.

"The dark-haired man said that he didn't want any part of killing a child. He'd been paid to take the dog, not commit murder. The red-haired man told him that they didn't have a choice. If they didn't kill Brady, The Boss would kill them instead."

"The Boss?"

"That's what Brady said."

"Anything else?" he probed.

"Just that the guy with the red hair got to yelling so loud that he forgot to hold on to Brady's wrist. Brady took off. It was still dark, so he was able to hide pretty easily. He found the cave a while later and hid in it until you and Justice found him."

"Brady is a smart kid."

She exhaled softly. "I know. I just wish…"

"What?"

"That none of this had happened. I wish we were at home enjoying a quiet day together. I wish that I didn't have to worry that someone was going to come after my son again."

"It's going to be okay," he said gently.

"You can't know that, Austin."

"You're right, but I'll do everything I can to make sure it's true."

"You're not even working the case right now." She cleared her throat. "I probably should have called someone else. I don't know why I didn't."

He thought she *did* know.

He knew.

Austin didn't believe in soul mates, but when he'd looked into Eva's eyes at the hospital, he'd felt a moment of recognition so intense that he'd thought that they must have met years ago, been friends for a long time rather than simply acquaintances for a few hours. Something had jumped to life in the depth of her gaze. He'd seen it. Had known that she'd told him to leave because of it.

Attraction, chemistry, he could stick any name to it that

he wanted, and it would still be there. That didn't mean he had to act on it.

"We spent hours searching for your son together. That's plenty of reason for you to call me, Eva."

"I just...don't want to put you out." She sighed, and Austin imagined her fiddling with the end of her ponytail and staring out the hospital window.

"You're not, *and* you did the right thing in calling me. I'll pass the information on to Slade. He may want to stop by tomorrow to question Brady."

"He'll have to stop by our place. The doctor came in a few minutes ago. He thinks that Brady will be well enough to go home tomorrow morning."

"That must be a relief," Austin said.

"It is. I think we'll both feel better when we're back at home."

"Just make sure you get the security company out to your place quickly."

"I have an appointment set up for tomorrow afternoon," she confirmed. "The company can install the windows, locks and the security system. Hopefully, that will be enough to keep Brady safe."

"It's a good start. You might also want to consider getting a dog."

"Did Brady pay you to say that?"

"No, but I'm sure that he would have tried if he'd thought of it."

"For someone who just met him, you know my son well." She laughed softly, the sound as warm as a sun-drenched spring day.

"He's not shy about his desire to get a puppy, so I guess I can't take credit for a better-than-average ability to read people."

"Actually, I think you probably have a way better-than-average ability to do that. I'd better let you go. I'm sure you have a busy day planned." No more humor in her voice. No more laughter.

She disconnected, and he was left with the phone pressed to his ear, the pad of paper still sitting on the desk. He jotted a couple more notes, typed a quick email to Slade. He'd call him, too, but the information would be in the computer, and easy to access once the captain got his son settled down.

Austin glanced at his notes and frowned, circling the words that interested him most.

Paid to take the dog.

The Boss.

Kill them instead.

If Brady had heard right, someone who'd had money and power had been calling the shots yesterday.

"I thought you were on leave, Austin. Shouldn't you be home catching up on some sleep?" Valerie Salgado said.

The newest member of the Sagebrush Special Operations K-9 Unit, she came from a long line of police officers and seemed more than capable of following in the footsteps of her family. There was a softness about the rookie cop that surprised Austin, though. An openness that he hoped wouldn't be changed as months on the police force turned into years.

"I was heading that way. I just stopped in to see if the medical examiner had ID'd the deceased perp."

"Did he?" Valerie asked.

"Yes. The guy's name was Jeb Rinehart. He's served time. Was just released a few weeks ago."

"Probably would have been better for him if he'd stayed in jail." Valerie tucked a strand of long red hair behind her ear and lifted the mug shot, then leaned over Austin's shoulder and read the notes he'd written.

"Who's that?" She jabbed at *The Boss.*

"Brady Billows says that The Boss was calling the shots on Rio's theft and on Brady's kidnapping." He filled Valerie in on the information that Brady had given Eva, and she frowned.

"The victim is seven?"

"Right."

"It's easy for a kid that age to confuse information that he hears. Especially when he's under stress."

"True." But the story Brady had told was detailed, and Austin couldn't imagine that it was a product of confusion.

"But you don't think he's confused?"

"No," he said.

"If he's not, then we've got a big problem. The only way to solve it is to find the second kidnapper." She glanced at him. "What was Rinehart in jail for? Maybe we can search the database for guys who match the description you gave this morning and who have similar rap sheets to his."

"Drugs. Selling and possession."

"In that case, we might want to check with Parker."

"Check with me about what?" Parker Adams called from his desk.

"You've got some good ears, you know that, Parker?" Valerie responded.

"Only when my name is being mentioned. Who's the perp?" Parker joined them in Austin's cubicle, his dark hair slightly mussed. An undercover narcotics detective with the K-9 Unit, he knew most of the drug dealers in Sagebrush and had an ear to the pulse of the drug underground.

"Jeb Rinehart."

"I know the name. We put him away two years ago. The guy is—"

"Was," Austin cut in, and Parker frowned.

"He's your dead perp?"

"Yes."

"I'm surprised that he was involved in something that he was willing to take a bullet for. He was a small-time thug who was more interested in where he was going to get his next fix than in anything else."

"According to his kidnapping victim, Rinehart was afraid for his life," Austin explained, offering the information that Brady had provided.

"We need to find the guy he was working with. Pauly Keevers may be able to help us on that. Want me to put the word out on the street that you're looking for information?" Parker asked.

"If you think that he has information about Rinehart's friends, then, yes."

"Is there a criminal in Sagebrush who Pauly doesn't have information about?" Valerie asked. A good question. A street thug who liked to play both sides of the fence, Keevers was in the business of exchanging information for money.

"Probably not, but Keevers and Rinehart live in the same apartment complex. If I know Keevers, he knows everything there is to know about the people who live in his building. Friends. Family. Secrets. He'll know who Rinehart hung with, and he'll know who he might have been working for. For a price, he'll share that information." Parker sounded excited, and Austin had to admit, his adrenaline was pumping, too. They finally had a name, a face, a little bit of information that might lead them to more information.

"Sounds like a plan, Parker."

"Now that I'm thinking about it," Parker continued. "There's another guy you might want to talk to. Name is Camden West. He was arrested the same time as Rinehart. Booked on possession, distribution and possession of an illegal firearm. He's doing nine years in the state prison. He and Rinehart were high school buddies. Next-door neighbors."

"Cell mates?" Valerie asked.

"Doubtful, but if anyone knows what Rinehart was involved in, it's Camden West."

"I'll pay him a visit," Austin cut in.

"You're forgetting that you've been put on leave, Austin," Valerie reminded him.

"Not forgetting. Just choosing to believe that I'll be off it soon."

"If not, I'll make the visit for you. Speaking of which, I've got to do a follow-up interview with Susan Daphne."

"Brady's babysitter?" Austin wanted to be the one to interview her. Wanted to be deep into the investigation rather than heading home to catch up on sleep.

"Slade thought Brady might have mentioned something to her or that she might have heard something around the time she sent him out to walk her dog. He asked me to handle interviewing witnesses until you're reinstated."

"Thanks," Austin said, but he wasn't happy about letting Valerie or anyone else handle any part of the case he'd been assigned. He didn't start something and stop. He kept going until he found what he was looking for.

Rio. Brady's kidnapper. The Boss. *Answers.*

Lots of answers.

He turned off his computer, grabbed his coat from the back of his chair and walked outside.

Thick clouds covered the sun, their steel-gray color matching Austin's mood. He needed to get home, catch a few hours of sleep. Tomorrow was a new day, and it would bring its own set of problems.

The thought of going home didn't thrill him—the empty Victorian about as appealing as a steam bath on a summer day.

Justice was there, of course, but talking to a dog wasn't the same as talking to a person. Someone who asked questions, exchanged ideas, wanted more than a game of fetch, a bowl of dog chow and a belly rub.

He hopped into his SUV, tempted to drive to the hospital and check on Brady one last time. Only Brady was fine. He had an armed guard stationed outside his door, a mother who would give her life for him, a K-9 unit searching for his kidnapper. As long as he stayed in the hospital, the potential for danger was minimal.

So maybe Eva was really the person Austin wanted to see.

Her soft green eyes and softer smile. Her quiet laughter and guarded heart. Vulnerable but tough. That appealed to him more than he wanted it to. *She* appealed to him.

He'd admit it, but he wouldn't act on it.

Not now.

Probably not ever.

Because his life was about his work, his focus on his job. He couldn't be any other way, and that wasn't something that the women he'd dated had ever been able to understand.

Candace had been the last woman that he'd tried for. After her, he'd decided that casual dating was easier than long-term commitment and planning for the future.

But it was also emptier. Lonelier.

He frowned, turning up the radio and trying to drown out the thought.

He had a good life. A great one. He'd been blessed to have a mother who'd raised him by herself, but who'd known the meaning of sacrificial love. He'd learned a lot from her example, and he'd been determined to pull himself out of the poverty that he'd been born into, to make something of himself, to contribute to the community and to the world. It had taken time, hard work and dedication, but he'd done it. If his mother had lived, she would have been proud.

She'd also have told him that there was more to life than work. More to happiness than a job or financial success.

She'd have been right, but Austin's course was set, and he didn't plan to veer from it.

No matter how tempting Eva might be.

Chapter Nine

Maybe another night in the hospital would have been best, Eva thought as she chopped onions for soup stock. Brady sat silent and morose at the kitchen table, his skin so pale it was almost translucent.

"You need to eat some of your sandwich, sweetie," she said, tossing the onions into the pot.

"I'm not hungry, Momma."

"I know that you don't *feel* hungry, but the doctor said you need to eat. If you don't, you might end up back in the hospital."

He sighed and took a tiny bite of sandwich, the bruise on his forehead deep purple. The scratches on his cheek looked raw, and his battered knees peeked out from beneath faded pajama shorts. He hadn't wanted bandages, and she'd let him have his way. They were both grumpy from too little sleep, and choosing her battles had seemed like the right thing to do.

She tossed diced carrots in with the onions, threw celery in on top of that. A big pot of chicken noodle soup would last most of the week. A good thing since money would be tight for a while. The security system and new locks had cost a small fortune, and despite her coworkers' donation, Eva hadn't been able to afford new windows. She'd have to pinch pennies in order to have them installed, and that's exactly what she planned to do.

She also needed to write a thank-you note to her coworkers and bake some cookies to bring in for the café's staff on Wednesday. But all she really wanted to do was get through the day, tuck Brady into bed, lie down beside him and sleep until the sun came up.

She glanced at the clock.

Three in the afternoon.

They had a long way to go before either of them would be going to bed.

"I think that I'm finished, Momma. May I go play with my blocks?" Brady slid his plate away, the sandwich barely touched. She'd made his favorite, too. Grilled cheese with ham.

"As soon as I finish this." She placed a large stewing chicken into the pot and poured water over it.

"I can play in the living room by myself, Momma." Brady scowled.

He was right.

Logically, she knew it.

But she hadn't been logical since she'd walked into his bedroom and seen his empty bed and open window.

"I know you can, but how about you give me a hand, instead? Find the big lid that we use for the stew pot, okay?"

He moved like an old man, crossing the small kitchen and bending gingerly to look through the cupboard next to the stove.

"Never mind, buddy. I'll find it." She crouched beside him,

touching his forehead, his cheek, his scratched-up hand. "You go ahead and play with your blocks. Just make sure that you stay in the living room. No going outside or anything."

"I won't. I promise." He offered a tiny smile, nothing like the full-out ones he usually gave, and limped from the room.

She had to force herself not to follow.

He'd be okay in the living room, the curtains pulled closed over the windows, the door locked, a police cruiser parked at the curb in front of the house.

Slade had promised twenty-four-hour protection until Brady's kidnapper was caught, and so far, he'd followed through. He'd had two patrol cars escort her home, a police officer walk her inside and search the entire house.

Eva shouldn't feel as if Brady could disappear at any moment, but she did.

She peered into the living room, watching as Brady dumped a small plastic container full of blocks onto the floor. He looked so little, so vulnerable.

An image flashed through her mind. Brady at the hospital, cradled in Austin's arms. He'd looked safe there. Protected.

She shoved the image away, stalking back to the soup pot, adding salt and pepper and digging the lid out of the cupboard. She turned down the gas, left the stock to simmer. A few hours and she could remove the chicken. If Brady was up to it, he could help her peel chicken from the bones.

The doorbell rang, and she jumped.

"Don't answer it, Brady!" she yelled as she wiped her hands on a dishcloth and ran into the living room.

Brady sat wide-eyed on the floor, his eyes shadowed, his body still. She'd never wanted to see terror on her son's face, but she saw it now, and she wanted so much to turn the clock back, be in his room when the kidnappers tried to take him, protect him so that he never had to know the kind of fear she'd lived with as a child.

"Who is it, Momma?"

"I don't know." She looked out the peephole, saw dark hair and midnight-blue eyes.

Austin.

Her heart leaped for him, but she refused to admit just how pleased she was to see him.

"Hold on!" She turned off the alarm, opened the door and let him in.

She'd spent most of the night telling herself that Austin wasn't anything like she remembered him to be. Not as handsome. Not as strong. Not as compelling.

She'd been wrong.

He was even more of all of those things.

Justice padded along beside him, his nose to the wood floor, his long ears brushing through the dust that she hadn't had a chance to sweep up. He lumbered across the room, sniffing Brady's hair and his neck.

Brady giggled, patting the fur near Justice's neck.

"I think my son has found a new best friend," Eva said, closing the door and dropping onto the sofa, more relaxed than she'd been in hours. She didn't bother thinking about what that meant, just enjoyed the feeling of not being alone and not being scared.

"I think Justice has found a new best friend, too," Austin responded with a smile as Justice plopped his head onto Brady's legs and looked at him adoringly. "Want me to call him off?"

"And devastate them both? I don't think so."

"Good, because I'm beat, and I'd rather just sit here and watch them smile at each other." He dropped onto the sofa beside her despite the fact that the old rocking chair would have been a perfectly good seat.

Eva could have moved.

She didn't.

Just sat there feeling his warmth despite the fact that they weren't touching, inhaling winter air and spicy cologne. He smelled like the outdoors, only better, and that was something she should definitely not be noticing.

"It sounds like Brady and I weren't the only ones who didn't sleep well last night."

"I slept well. Then I decided that since I had some time off, I'd do some work on my house. I spent the morning refinishing the hardwood floor on the first level. The old muscles aren't used to all that work." He stretched his arms above his head and winced, his biceps bulging against soft cotton.

His muscles were anything but old.

Her cheeks heated, and she turned her attention back to Brady and Justice. "Do you really think Justice is smiling, because he looks more like he's frowning to me?"

"Don't let his hangdog expression fool you, Eva. Justice is almost always smiling. Aren't you, boy?"

Justice didn't raise his head, but his tail thumped.

"I suppose that he's so well trained that he helped you finish your floors. Maybe even handled a room all by himself."

"I wish. He spent most of the time lying in a sunny spot on the back porch." Austin laughed, the sound rumbling through the sofa cushions and settling somewhere in the vicinity of Eva's heart.

"Do you have any idea when the two of you will be back on the job?" she asked, shifting a little, trying to put more distance between them. His scent followed her, his heat still seeming to seep into her bones, warm her as nothing had in a very long time.

"I got a call from internal affairs this morning. They've

almost completed their investigation. As soon as they do, I'll be back at work."

"I'm glad. I hate to think that you're on leave because of me and Brady."

"Not because of either of you. Because of Jeb Rinehart."

"Who?"

"The red-haired thug who kidnapped Brady."

"You were able to identify him?"

"The medical examiner took his prints. We were able to match them through our data bank."

"How about his partner?" she asked.

"Nothing yet."

She bit her lip. "Too bad. I was hoping this would all be over quickly."

"It still could be. We're only twenty-four hours out."

"That's a lifetime when your child is in danger."

"I know," he said and sounded like he really did. "We're doing everything that we can to make sure Brady stays safe until we find the person responsible for his kidnapping."

"I'm just…worried. He's scared, and he's not sleeping. He woke from nightmares so many times last night, I lost track of the number." She sighed wearily. "It's not just the physical injuries that I'm worried about. It's the emotional stuff. No parent wants to see her child suffer."

"I know that, too." His gaze was on Brady, his eyes shadowed and dark, his lips pressed tight as if he knew exactly how it felt to care so deeply about someone that nothing else mattered.

"Do you have children, Austin?" she asked and regretted the question immediately. Too personal. Not her business. Something someone only asked when she cared a lot about the answer.

"I haven't had time for marriage or family. My job is pretty intense, and I spend a lot of time away from home. It just didn't seem fair to bring a wife and kids into that."

"People do it all the time." She really *did* need to stop talking.

"So maybe the real truth is that I just haven't met a woman I'd want to build a family with." He studied her face, his gaze a physical touch that lingered on her eyes, her cheeks, her chin, landed briefly on her lips and then slowly moved away.

"I'd better check on my stock." She jumped up, her cheeks fiery, but he snagged her hand, pulled her back down.

"There's no need to run, Eva."

"I'm not," she muttered, but she settled back into her seat, her long legs folded under her, a knee poking out from a hole in her jeans. She'd braided her hair, and it fell in a long rope over her shoulder. Neat as a pin, and Austin had the absurd desire to loosen it up.

"Could have fooled me." He stood, stretching the kinks from his muscles and putting a little distance between them. He hadn't stopped by to make a play for Eva. The opposite was true. He'd stopped by to convince himself that what he'd felt when he'd looked into her eyes was nothing more than imagination brought on by exhaustion.

He'd been wrong.

"I wasn't running, and I do need to check on my soup stock, but I guess you didn't just stop by to see how Brady was doing. So why don't you tell me why you *are* here." She pulled her knees to her chest, wrapped her arms around her shins. Her knuckles were red and a little raw, the skin cracked. She worked hard and it showed, and that appealed to Austin way more than he thought it should.

"Your parents' case file was emailed to me this morning. I spent a little time looking through it."

"And?" She seemed to sink into herself, her eyes suddenly distant, the misty green faded to a muted hazel.

"Jeb Rinehart was mentioned in it." That had been a surprise, and Austin hadn't been able to accept it as coincidental.

"I'm not surprised," she admitted.

"No?"

"I'm sure you've seen my father's record. He dabbled in just about anything that could make him money, and most of the things he dabbled in were illegal."

Austin *had* seen it. Ernie's rap sheet had been several pages long. Mostly petty stuff that couldn't keep him in jail for long. A few domestic-violence charges that had been dropped by his wife before they'd ever gone to trial. "Your father did seem to have an affinity for trouble."

"He also had an affinity for alcohol and temper tantrums."

"You weren't close?"

"We weren't even in the same universe." She sighed, rubbed the back of her neck. "Look, Ernie had one goal in life—to make himself happy. He did whatever he wanted, whenever he wanted, and he didn't care who he hurt in the process. The fact that he was somehow connected to a guy who'd be willing to kidnap and mu—" Her gaze cut to Brady. "It's not a surprise."

"Do you remember your father ever mentioning Rinehart?"

"No. Never. But I wasn't a part of his life after Brady was born."

"How about your mother?"

"We were close, but Ernie was always first with her. If she'd ever had to choose between him and me, I knew what her decision would be. I guess, in the end, that's what happened." She smiled, her eyes sad.

She'd grown up hard.

Just looking at her father's police record proved that.

"I'm sorry."

"For what?"

"Stirring up old memories."

"You're doing your job. You don't have to apologize for that." She stood and stretched, offering a tired smile. "I really had better go check on my soup stock before it boils over."

She walked from the room, and Austin was sure that she wished she could walk away from her past easily.

He heard her moving around, silverware clinking, water running. Domestic noises that seemed so much homier when someone else was making them.

He didn't follow.

She needed space. He'd give it to her, but he had more questions he wanted to ask. About the case. About her father. About her.

"Do you want to play blocks with me?" Brady asked, and Austin dropped down onto the floor beside him, worried by his paleness and the somberness in his eyes. Kids shouldn't be scared, and he was. That wasn't okay. Not by a long shot.

"Sure. What are you building?"

"A jail. I'm going to put all the bad guys in it."

"Good thinking. You build the jail. I'll find the bad guys and lock them inside it."

"Will you throw away the jail key?"

"Isn't that the way it's always done?" He pressed a block into place and Brady grinned, some of his anxiety seeming to slip away.

"Yes!"

"Then let's get to work. Where do you want this one?" He handed Brady a long gray block, smiling as he snapped it into place.

Maybe he couldn't be on the case yet, but he *could* provide a little distraction for a kid who obviously needed it.

And right at that moment, that seemed just as important as anything else he could be doing.

Chapter Ten

Brady's laughter drifted into the kitchen, Austin's warm chuckle following right behind it.

Eva tried to ignore both.

She couldn't.

Somehow, in the short amount of time he'd been alone with Brady, Austin had managed to do something that Eva hadn't been able to do in an entire day—distract Brady from his fear.

She frowned, staring into the stew pot, the chicken bobbing in the golden liquid. Looking at it made her stomach churn. A migraine nudged at the back of her head. She rubbed the spot, pressing her fingers into taut tense muscles.

"Headache?" Austin's words startled her, his silent entrance into the kitchen a surprise.

She met his gaze, found herself lost in midnight skies and starry vistas. She'd never seen eyes like his. Ever.

"A little." She stood on her toes, grabbed a generic pain reliever from the cupboard above the fridge, her hands shaking for reasons she refused to acknowledge. She couldn't pop the lid, and Austin took it.

"Let me help." He flipped open the cap with enough ease to make her cheeks heat.

"Thanks. It was a long night, and I'm still exhausted."

"Maybe you should take a page from Brady's book and lie down for a while." He leaned his hip against the counter, his broad frame taking up more than its fair share of room in the tiny kitchen. She scooted past, filling a glass with water and chugging it down with the pain reliever.

"He's lying down?"

"Yes. We built a block jail, and then his eyelids started drooping. I figured it was time for him to get some sleep."

"I better check on him."

"Justice is with him. He'll alert if there's anything to worry about." He snagged her wrist, pulling her back when she would have walked out of the kitchen.

"Austin—"

"Relax, Eva. I just want to ask you a few more questions." His hand dropped away. She was free to leave the kitchen or to stay.

Or maybe not.

Because her feet felt glued to the floor, her gaze stuck to his, and no matter how many times her brain said that she should go, her heart said that she should stay. "What questions?"

"Brady mentioned a third party that Rinehart and his partner were working for. I'm wondering if your father could have been working for him, too."

"Ernie always worked for someone. He lacked the drive and initiative to ever make a go of things on his own."

"Do you remember him mentioning a particular job or name?"

"We weren't on speaking terms when he died," she said flatly.

"How about your mother? Did she—"

"My mother had nothing to do with my father's crimes." Eva had said that a hundred times after the murders. Ernie might have deserved what he'd gotten, but Tonya had been an innocent bystander, killed simply because of who she had been married to.

"I know she didn't. Everyone on the force knows the same. Your mother was in the wrong place at the wrong time, and she died because of it. It's a horrible thing, Eva. Everyone agrees, but it's possible that she did know the person who killed her, and it's possible she knew why," Austin replied, the gentleness in his voice making her eyes burn and her throat ache.

No way would she cry.

Not in front of him.

Crying is for babies, kid, and you're not that. Keep those tears flowing, and I'll give you something to cry about. Ernie's voice seemed to taunt her from the past, the words ones she'd been hearing for nearly three decades.

"Mom has been dead for over two years. Whatever she knew is gone with her. Whoever she saw in those last moments, it was my father she reached for. When I found their bodies, she was holding his hand. She'd been shot in the chest, and instead of grabbing the phone and calling for help, she reached for him, held on to him." She shoved the memory away, dropping into a chair, suddenly so tired, she didn't think her legs would hold her.

"I'm sorry. Again."

"You don't need to be. You just need to know that my mother was more loyal to my father than to anything else. Even if she'd known who he was working for, she'd never have told anyone."

"All right." He straightened, staring into her eyes. She thought that he planned to sit in the chair next to hers, ask questions that had nothing to do with her parents or the case. Maybe tell her about his life, his day, his job.

She wanted that.

Wanted it so much that she knew she had to send him away.

"I'm beat. I probably should lie down for a while." She forced herself to stand.

"Then I'd better get out of your hair." Austin didn't want to, though. He wanted to stay a while longer. Sit in the warm kitchen, inhaling the savory aroma of the stock that simmered on the stove and talking to Eva.

He walked into the living room, grabbed his coat from the couch and slipped it on. He'd spent the past seven years working on the police force and volunteering as a search-and-rescue worker. He was used to being busy. Used to working cases, being around coworkers, spending weekends training.

He wasn't used to idle time. Having it obviously didn't suit him. He dreaded taking Justice back to their quiet house. Dreaded another evening spent in front of the TV. Dreaded facing the part of himself that still longed for something to fill the downtime. Some*one* to fill it.

"Are you leaving already, Austin?" Brady asked sleepily, his small frame splayed out on the couch. Justice was scrunched in next to him, his big tan head on Brady's legs. They looked so comfortable and content, Austin hated to separate them.

"I'm afraid so."

"Does Justice have to go with you?"

Austin nodded. "Yes. He needs to eat dinner and spend some time running around in our backyard."

"Are you going to run around with him?"

"I'll probably throw the ball for him a couple of times. He loves to play fetch."

"I could throw the ball for him. I love to play fetch, too!"

Austin chuckled. "Sorry, buddy, but I don't think you're up to that. Maybe another day."

"Okay. So after you and Justice play fetch, are you going to look for the bad guy?"

"Not yet. I'm still on vacation, but I have some buddies who are working really hard to find the guy who kidnapped you."

"You're the best, though." Brady's eyes were wide and blue and so filled with sincerity that Austin had to smile.

"So are you."

"Can you visit me again tomorrow?"

"He's really busy, Brady," Eva responded before Austin could.

"Not so busy that I can't stop in and see a friend. Unless you'd rather I not?" He looked into Eva's eyes, saw his own confusion in the depth of her gaze. Almost wished that she'd tell him to stay away. Mostly wished that she wouldn't.

Don't get emotionally involved. Don't give yourself a chance to lose another piece of your heart.

That's what he'd been telling himself for twenty-four hours. The problem was, he wasn't listening.

"Austin…" Eva began.

"What?"

She glanced at her son. "Nothing. I guess we'll see you tomorrow."

"See you then," he responded as he opened the front door, walked out into cold winter air. It cooled the heat that flowed through him every time he was with Eva, reminded him of his humanity.

He could fail Brady and Eva so easily.

He could do everything in his power to make sure that Brady stayed safe, to track down his kidnapper, to give him back the life he'd had before Rio was stolen. He could work endless hours and devote every waking moment to it and things could still turn out badly.

He acknowledged that, but he also acknowledged that he had no choice but to follow through. To give as much as he had to keep Brady safe. It was what he did, and he couldn't turn his back on it any more than the sun could decide not to rise in the morning.

He let Justice into the back of the SUV, then climbed into the driver's seat, turning up the volume of the radio as he backed out of the driveway. Eva's living-room curtains fluttered and then moved aside. Austin thought Brady would be standing there, thought that he'd have to call Eva and tell her to keep her son from the windows. She stood there instead, her long braid hanging over her shoulder in a silky rope of gold.

She lifted a hand, and he returned the wave. Felt his heart catch and his mind go because he wanted to see the same thing when he left his own place every morning. Wanted to head out to work knowing that someone was waiting for him to return.

Not a good direction for his mind to be heading.

He was happy with his life.

Happy with his work.

Happy, but he thought that maybe he could be happier.

A family, children, love.

Those were things that everyone craved.

He sighed, ran a hand down his jaw.

In the past few years, all Austin had done was run from one case to the next, one missing person to the next. He'd tracked and trailed and hunted, and he didn't have one regret.

He wanted more, though.

So much more than a job and a house and friends.

Unfortunately, right at that moment, those were his only options. Most of his friends were busy with their families and Saturday plans. His house still stunk from the layers of varnish he'd applied to the floor, and his coworkers would probably boot him out the door if he showed up at the office again.

That didn't mean he couldn't keep busy and help with the case. As a matter of fact, he could pay a visit to Jeb Rinehart's buddy Camden West and start things moving in the direction he planned to take them once internal affairs allowed him to return to work.

He drove a few houses up the road, parked behind Slade McNeal's SUV and got out.

"Want to visit an old friend?" he asked Justice as he opened the back of the SUV and let him out. Justice raised his head, took a long deep sniff of air and barked enthusiastically. He knew where they were. They'd been there dozens of times before.

This time, though, Rio wouldn't be around to play with.

His father, Chief, would be, though. A retired service dog, he'd been one of the best. Now he was a family pet, enjoying his golden years.

He probably missed Rio. Slade's son, Caleb, was missing him, too. At five years old, Slade's little boy had already lost his mother in a bombing that had been meant for Slade. Two years later, he was still struggling to come to terms with that loss. Losing Rio had to have set him back in his recovery.

Maybe a visit with Justice would cheer Caleb up, and while they were visiting, Austin would try to talk Slade into letting him pay a visit to the state prison. Camden West had some information that Austin was interested in, and the sooner he got it, the happier he'd be.

Sure, he wasn't officially on duty, but that didn't mean he couldn't pursue a lead.

He rang the doorbell and waited for Slade to open the door.

Chapter Eleven

Two hours later, he was on his way, darkness sliding across the horizon as he made the ninety-mile trek to the state prison, his uniform crisp and comfortable, his firearm in its holster.

Back at work.

Slade had been excited to give him the news, and Austin had been happy to hear it.

Internal affairs had deemed the case cut-and-dried. Austin had acted appropriately and according to the guidelines set up by the office. A witness had confirmed it. Bullets from the deceased's gun had been found in and around the cave where Eva and Brady had been hiding. Because the perp had refused to lay down his firearm, Austin had been given no choice but to use deadly force.

He'd known that he'd acted according to policy, but it felt good to know that others agreed.

It felt even better to be on the job again, searching for Brady's kidnapper and for Rio.

Slade's house had felt emptier without the German shepherd

in it, and the weight of Austin's responsibility to his friend, his boss, his team weighed heavily on his shoulders. Forty-eight hours without a good lead, and the case was going cold fast.

Maybe his visit with Camden West would be the key to heating it back up again. If West and Rinehart had been as close as Parker seemed to think, there had to be some interesting information to glean from it. One name. That's all Austin needed. If he got it, he could run with it and hopefully run straight into The Boss.

His cell phone rang as he pulled up to the prison gates and handed the guard his ID. He ignored it as he was waved into the parking area.

Moments later, it rang again.

He answered quickly, anxious to get into the building and start his meeting. "Austin Black."

"I hear you're looking for some information." The voice was vaguely familiar. Austin's pulse jumped, adrenaline pulsing through him. The fish had finally taken the bait. All he had to do was reel in the line.

"Pauly Keevers, right?"

"You guessed it, Detective. So, *are* you looking for information or not?" A small-time criminal with his fingers in more pies than Austin cared to count, Pauly would do just about anything for a buck, including selling out friends and family. Bad news for Pauly's associates, but good news for the Sagebrush Police Department.

"That depends on what information you have to offer. Do you know Jeb Rinehart?"

"Knew him. I heard you blew out his brains, though, so I guess we'd better keep things past tense. Me? I'm in no mood to meet up with him in the afterlife, so I think I'll try to stay on your good side, Detective."

"Were you and Rinehart close friends or not?"

"I wouldn't say we were friends. We lived in the same apartment building."

"Did you talk to him much?"

"Nah. He kept to himself. Had a temper, the way I hear it. That's not the kind of person I want to associate with. Too dangerous."

And betraying friends for money wasn't?

Austin kept the thought to himself, leaning back in his seat and staring out at the purple-black night.

"I'm sure that didn't keep you from collecting information about the guy."

"I'm in the business of information, Detective. You know that."

"So you know who Rinehart hung out with?" Austin pressed.

"I do."

"Do you also know that Rinehart kidnapped a young boy? That he's a suspect in an attack against Captain McNeal's father, and that—"

"He's suspected of stealing the captain's police dog? Yeah, I know. I know lots of things."

"Like?"

"Come on, Detective, you know me better than that." Keevers's mocking laughter drifted across the line.

"How much is it going to take to get you to talk?"

"That depends on what you want me to talk about."

Austin clenched his jaw. "I told you that I'm not in the mood for games, Pauly."

"No game. I have information about Rinehart, but I have other information, too. The first you can get pretty cheap. Five hundred bucks, and I'll give you a list of Rinehart's friends and the people he was hanging with this past month. Ten thousand, and I'll give you the rest of what I know."

Ten thousand dollars?

That was an astronomical amount. Not something a Sagebrush snitch would ever think to ask for. Unless he had something bigger than big to share. The thought made the hair on the back of Austin's neck stand on end.

"Five hundred is steep. I'll give you three, and the list better be complete." He kept his tone even as he responded. No sense in letting Keevers know that he was interested.

"What about the rest?"

"There isn't much I can think of that would be worth ten thousand dollars, Pauly."

"This will be. I guarantee it."

"I'll have to check with my captain."

"You go ahead and do that, Detective, but the longer you wait, the higher the price goes."

"And the more annoyed you make me, the lower your payday for the list of Rinehart's friends will be. We're at three hundred now. In another ten seconds, we'll be down to two-fifty."

"Now, wait a minute—"

"I can get the names myself. We both know it. Maybe it will take a little more time and energy, but it might be worth it so that I don't have to deal with you."

"I'm wounded, Detective." Keevers laughed again, and Austin thought about hanging up on him. His curiosity wouldn't let him. Keevers might be a bad guy, but he had a reputation for selling the truth.

"Not as much as you will be if you waste my time. I'm going to have to go to a lot of trouble to get the kind of money you're asking for."

"It won't be a waste of effort. I can tell you that."

"We'll see. Meet me at the west entrance of the Lost Woods at noon tomorrow. I'll bring the money for the information about Rinehart and the answer about the rest from my captain. You bring the list. We'll discuss the terms of our next deal then." He hung up on Pauly's sputtered protest.

He'd show. Pauly was nothing if not greedy and eager for a quick buck.

But ten thousand dollars was way more than he'd ever asked for before.

He dialed Slade's number, waiting impatiently while the phone rang. Once. Twice. Three times.

"Slade here."

"It's Austin."

"You're at the prison already?"

"Yes, but I haven't been in yet. I just got off the phone with Pauly Keevers."

"What kind of information does he have to offer? It better be good or he's not getting a dime," Slade growled, his voice gritty and a little worn.

"You okay, Slade?"

"Just tired of hearing the same thing from the doctors. No improvement. You'd think with modern medicine being what it is, they'd be able to bring someone out of a coma."

"You're at the hospital with your dad?"

"Yeah. Hold on. The nurse just walked in."

Austin waited, listening to the faint conversation, his fingers tapping his thigh, his gaze on the brick facade of the prison. Camden West was somewhere on the other side of that wall, and Austin was anxious to pick the guy's brains.

"I'm back. Sorry about that," Slade said.

"No problem."

"Tell me about Keevers."

"He says he has some big information to share. He wants ten thousand dollars for it."

Slade whistled softly. "That's a lot of money."

"Exactly."

"Did he say what kind of information it is?"

"You know Pauly. He was vague and slightly full of his own importance."

"We can't pay that kind of money if we don't know what we're paying for."

"I set up a meeting with him for tomorrow. He's going to bring me a list of Rinehart's associates."

"How much for that?" Slade asked.

"Three hundred."

"Good. You pay him that. Ask for more information about the other. He's not getting another cent until he tells us what we're paying for. Pass that message along for me, and let's see what Keevers says."

"Will do." Austin disconnected and jumped out of the SUV. Time to interview Camden. See what Rinehart's good friend had to say.

Twenty minutes later, he realized Camden wasn't going to say anything at all. He stared into the man's pockmarked face, tried to read something in his blank eyes and dead expression.

"You're telling me that you don't know anything about who Rinehart was hanging with in the weeks before his death?"

"Said it ten times already, Detective. Not going to change my story to make you happy."

"You might want to change it to make yourself happy, Camden. Rinehart is dead. His folks are going to bury him next week."

Camden flinched at the words. A chink in his armor, and Austin was ready to hammer into it, see if he could break him down.

"Here's the deal. Nothing you tell me about your old friend can hurt him, but it might help you. The way I hear it, you're wanting work privileges. You help me out, and I might be able to help you."

Camden's eyes widened, but he didn't take the bait. "I told you that I don't know nothin'."

"You're lying. You know something. You and Rinehart grew up together. You were like brothers. You shared booze and drugs. You can't tell me that he didn't let you in on his secrets."

"You're right. We were like brothers, but that doesn't mean I know all his business." His gaze skirted away.

"You know it all, and you know who he was working for when he died. Are you going to let his killer go unpunished?"

"The way I hear it, you pulled the trigger. Doesn't that make you his killer?"

"I pulled the trigger, but the person who paid your friend to steal a police captain's dog and kidnap a seven-year-old is responsible for Jeb's death."

"Let's say I agree. Let's even say that you're right. Me and Jeb were like blood, and I want to do right by him." Camden leaned in close, his eyes yellow flecked with brown, his breath reeking of onion and old food as he whispered, "But I got a wife and two kids. Another few months, and I'm up for parole. I want to go home to them. Not be buried ten feet under and never seen again."

Austin's pulse jumped at his words, at the fear in his eyes. "We can offer protection if you need it."

"No one can offer that. Not for me. Not for my family. Not if I talk, and I'm not going to."

"Tell me what you know, Camden. I promise you, I'll put in a good word with the parole board, and I'll make sure your wife and kids are safe until you're released. As soon as you're out, we'll relocate your family. Set you up in a nice little house, help you start a new life." Austin sweetened the pot, sure that Camden wouldn't be able to resist.

"You ask me about anything else and I'll talk, but I'm not talking about the guy who hired Jeb. Sorry, Detective. I'm done." He stood and shuffled to the door, motioned for the guard who stood on the other side.

Austin nodded, and the guard opened the door, led Camden away.

The interview hadn't gone the way he'd hoped, but Austin had learned something. Someone *had* hired Rinehart, and whoever it was had the ability to terrify hardened criminals.

The Boss?

The more Austin learned, the more convinced he became that there was a puppet master pulling strings in Sagebrush.

Who?

Why?

He had to find out if he was ever going to close the case and bring Rio home to Slade and Caleb. Had to solve it if he was going to protect Brady.

And he was. He had no other choice.

Slade was his boss, his friend, a man he respected and admired. He couldn't fail him.

He couldn't fail Eva and Brady, either. As much as he had wanted to stay emotionally distant, as many times as he'd reminded himself that he shouldn't get too involved, he'd already broken every rule he'd made for himself. Already fallen into the depth of Eva's eyes, looked into Brady's face and seen a child who needed him. A dangerous thing, but he couldn't seem to back off from it. Couldn't seem to change direction.

Wasn't even sure that he was supposed to.

God's plan. Not his. That's what Austin had always wanted. What he'd sought every day for years. Sometimes it was difficult to know where his will ended and God's began, to find that place where his desire to control things, to make things happen was superseded by the knowledge that God was the master planner, the creator of every opportunity.

He sighed and pulled away from the prison, his thoughts swirling like mist on a lake. The truth was that, aside from his work, he didn't know where his life was heading. Didn't know what direction he was going. Only knew that eventually God would lead him to the place he was supposed to be.

Chapter Twelve

"Can I go outside, Momma? *Please?*" Brady's wheedling tone drilled its way into Eva's skull and settled there, pounding behind her eyes and in the base of her neck. She popped the lid on a bottle of aspirin before she answered, swallowing two pills down with a gulp of cold, black coffee.

Patience.

She needed it.

Two days trapped in the house with her grumpy son, and she'd had about all she could take of him and of herself.

"Brady, you know that the doctor said you need to rest for the next few days. Resting doesn't mean going outside in the cold." She kept her tone light despite the fact that she'd answered the same question a half a dozen times.

"It's not cold. The sun is even out." Brady pressed his face to the living-room window, the scratches on his cheek and the bruise on his forehead stark reminders of his reasons for being grouchy. He hadn't slept well in the hospital. Wasn't sleeping well at home. Eva wanted to change that, but no amount of comforting words seemed to help.

"Forty degrees is cold, and that's what the thermometer on the back deck says the temperature is."

"Can I go look?"

"You know you can't."

"But—"

"No more arguing."

"Okay. I guess I'll just play with my Legos." He sighed dramatically and went to the plastic bin he'd left on the coffee table. He dumped the bin on the floor, sorting through the blocks with such intense concentration, Eva smiled.

"What are you going to build?"

"A doghouse."

"For Lightning?" She looked at the big, white stuffed dog that Arianna had given him.

"For Justice. When Austin brings him over—"

"They might not have time to stop by today. You know that, right?" It had been a full day since they'd heard from Austin, and Eva wasn't disappointed about that.

Much.

She frowned, rubbing the knot in the back of her neck.

She wasn't disappointed *at all*.

As a matter of fact, she was relieved.

The last thing she needed was one more complication in her already complicated life. She glanced at the flashing light on the answering machine. Dozens of friends had called since Brady's release from the hospital. So many that she'd begun screening her calls and letting most go to voice mail. She appreciated her friend's concern, but she and Brady both needed some quiet time if they were ever going to begin to heal.

"They will come, Momma. Austin said they would."

"Sometimes things come up. Emergency things."

"Austin will come," he insisted.

"Right. It's lunchtime. How about we make some macaroni?"

"I'm still building my doghouse. Hey, you know what?"

"What?"

"If Justice can't fit in it, we can use it when we get our puppy."

"I never said we were going to get a puppy."

"But you like Justice. We could get one just like him."

"Sweetie—"

"I'd take care of him. I'd feed him and take him for walks—"

The doorbell rang and he jumped up, nearly stumbling in his haste to get to the door.

Eva pulled him up short. "Wait."

"It's Austin. I know it is!"

"We always look before we open the door." She glanced through the peephole, saw Daniel Heppner standing on the porch. Letter carrier and a deacon at Eva's church, he'd been working the same route for three decades, his grizzled face and bright smile a comforting sight.

So why did she feel slightly disappointed?

She opened the door. "Daniel! How are you?"

"I was just going to ask you the same thing. Quite a to-do you've had around here."

"It's definitely been a long couple of days."

"Sounds like it. I couldn't believe it when I saw the story on the news the night Brady was kidnapped. Went out to the woods and joined one of them search parties."

"That means the world to me, Daniel."

"Shouldn't. We didn't find him. You and that detective did that all by yourselves."

"It was Austin's dog who found me. Justice is the best dog ever!" Brady exclaimed, and Daniel smiled down at the boy.

"A bloodhound, right? Saw him on the news, too. You know, when I was your age, I had myself a bloodhound. Me and my dad used to use him for hunting. Name was Mule 'cause he was a stubborn old dog, but I sure did love him."

"Momma is thinking about letting me get a bloodhound in the summer."

"I never said that, Brady."

"Every boy needs a dog, Eva, and a bloodhound is as good a dog as any."

"See, Momma?" Brady beamed, and Eva didn't have the heart to tell him to forget his dream. What was the harm in it? Besides, maybe they would get a puppy in the summer. A little bloodhound with Justice's hangdog face.

"We'll talk about it."

"That's good news, young man. When a mother is open to talking, it means she's almost convinced. Now, I've got to give you what I came with and get back to my route." He held a package out to Brady.

"It's for me?"

"Your name is right on it, son, and I don't know any other Brady Billows."

"Thanks!" Brady took it. "Can I open it, Momma?"

"After Daniel leaves." She took the package from her son's hands, frowning at Brady's name scribbled across white wrapping paper. "I wonder who it's from."

"Can't say, but I can tell you that it was sent overnight from San Antonio yesterday."

"Strange. We don't know anyone from there."

"Lots of people know you, though. At least they know of you and your son. Stories have been running on the news all over Texas. Even had a cousin in Houston call to ask if I knew your boy. Wanted to know how he could pray for you." He glanced at his watch. "Now, I really do have to be on my way. It's me and Agatha's thirty-fifth anniversary, and if I'm late for lunch, it might be our last."

"I don't think she'll kick you to the curb for being a few minutes later." Eva laughed.

"Not when she sees the diamond ring I bought her. Seeing as how she's put up with me for so long, I figured she deserved it. Hope she likes it. Took me nearly a month to find the perfect one."

"She's going to love it." Eva smiled, her heart giving a little twinge of longing. She'd once dreamed of having the kind of relationship that Daniel and his wife had. She'd thought she could find someone she could love wholeheartedly and who would love her the same way. A friend, a lover, an ally during the good times and the bad. When Rick had walked into Arianna's Café, smiled into her eyes and told her she was the most beautiful woman he'd ever seen, she was sure that he was the answer to those dreams.

She couldn't have been more wrong.

"You make sure you ask her about the ring on Sunday, okay? She'll want to show it off. One carat of sparkling diamond and a pretty gold band. Of course, it can't compare to the beauty of the woman who will be wearing it." Daniel winked, and the little ache of longing in Eva's heart became a full-blown throb. "Enjoy your package, little Brady. See you tomorrow!"

"See you, Big Daniel," Brady replied.

Eva closed the front door, slid the bolt home and carried the package into the kitchen, studying the scrawled name and address for several minutes. Nothing out of the ordinary except that she and Brady didn't get packages in the mail; they had no family or friends in San Antonio and...

Nothing.

But unease snaked its way around her heart and squeezed tight.

"Can I open it, Momma?" Brady reached for the package.

"Not yet," she said, grabbing his hand, reluctant to even have him touch it.

"But Daniel said it's for me."

"It's addressed to you, that's for sure, but we don't know who it's from."

"Maybe they put a note in the box."

"Maybe."

"If we open it, we'll know."

"Right." She held the box to her ear, feeling like a fool, but unable to make herself remove the tape that held the paper in place.

"What are you trying to hear?"

"Nothing. I'm just being silly." She pulled at the tape, slowly peeling back the paper and revealing a shoe box.

Nothing remarkable about that.

The lid was taped closed, and she slid her finger under the edge, ran her fingernail through one piece, her heart racing, her mouth dry with fear.

Over a shoe box wrapped in white paper.

"Is it shoes?" Brady edged in closer as she cut through another piece of tape.

"If it is, they're not your size." She slid her fingernail through a third piece of tape, and Brady frowned.

"The bottom of the box is all messy, Momma."

"Is it? She turned the box, saw an oily stain there.

"Do you think there's food in it?"

"I don't know, but I think maybe we should have that police officer who's sitting outside come in and take a look."

"Why? Do you think there's something bad in there?" Brady's eyes widened, and he stepped back.

"Not really." But she could not make herself break through the last few pieces of tape and remove the lid. "Come on. You can work on that doghouse while the police officer checks things out."

She led Brady into the living room and opened the front door.

"One. Two. Three." Austin slapped the hundred-dollar bills into Pauly Keevers's hand, doing his best to avoid looking into the snitch's triumphant face. If he looked too long, he might be tempted to do something he'd regret. Like shove a fist into Pauly's smiling mouth. Much as he wanted the information, he hated using a criminal to get it.

"Pleasure doing business with you, Detective." Pauly's gleeful tone did nothing to improve Austin's mood.

"I wish I could say the same."

"I guess you being a police officer makes it tough to pay a guy like me. Think of it this way, though. You got what you needed and saved the city time and money in the process."

"Always a businessman. Right, Pauly?"

"Exactly. And if you think about it even more, you might even agree that we're in the same business. We both bring bad guys down. I just happen to—"

"Be one of them?"

Pauly's laughter scared several blackbirds from a nearby tree. "Man, you kill me, Detective! Now, you've got your information, and I've got a little spending money. I guess it's time to say goodbye."

"Not so fast." Austin grabbed Pauly's arm. "You said you had some other information for sale."

"I changed my mind."

"Too bad. My captain says we may be willing to pay. It all depends on the information."

"Like I said. I changed my mind," Pauly insisted, but there was no mistaking the hunger in his eyes. The greed. It gleamed dark and sharp, and Austin had every intention of taking advantage of it.

"Ten thousand is a lot of cash, Pauly. Way more than the three hundred you're clutching."

"True." Pauly glanced at the three bills and frowned.

"A guy like you could do a lot with ten thousand dollars, and it's not like anyone would know that you were the one who provided the information." Austin pressed the advantage, Pauly's reluctance making him more interested than ever in finding out what he had to offer.

"You know how to make a guy think, that's for sure. But there's only one thing I like more than money."

"What's that?"

"Me."

"You're scared." Not a question, but Pauly sniffed, his dark eyes flashing.

"Cautious. So how about you give me a little time to decide how much information I want to share? I'll get back to you in a few days."

"Sorry. We either do the deal now, or we don't do it at all."

Pauly scowled, but he didn't refuse. "Tell you what. I'll give the captain something to think about. After we've all had some time to mull things over, I'll give you a call. Just warning you, though. *If* I decide to talk, it's going to cost a couple of thousand more than the price I already named."

"You're getting greedy, Pauly."

"I've always been greedy." Keevers grinned, but his shoulders were tense, his hands fisted.

"What do you want me to tell the captain?"

"You tell him there's been stuff going on in Sagebrush for years. Little things, but they're all connected to something way bigger."

"That's too vague. Give me something more or the deal's off."

"We haven't agreed to a deal, Detective," Pauly said, but the bait had been set, and he was already in the trap. They both knew it. Keevers might love himself, but he would never turn down the kind of money that they were talking about.

"Enjoy your three hundred, Pauly." Austin started walking away, knowing before the other man called out that he would.

"You want to give him something to really sink his teeth into? Tell him that the Billows murder, the two bank heists last year and the O'Reilly missing-persons case are all related," Pauly said as Austin opened the door of the SUV.

"You have proof of that?" Austin knew about the cases Pauly was referring to. He'd actually worked the O'Reilly case. A high school football coach who'd been accused of dealing drugs, Mitch O'Reilly had disappeared two days before he was scheduled to appear in court. Austin and Justice had been called in, but they'd never found the coach or his body.

"I've heard talk."

"From who?"

"I can't tell you that, Detective. Bad for business. As for proof, that's more your expertise than mine."

"We're not paying ten thousand for speculation." Austin's cell phone rang. He ignored it. Didn't want to lose the thread of the conversation or give Keevers a reason to walk away.

Pauly shrugged, his eyes filled with hunger again, his gaze sharp and just slightly amused. "You asked for a list of Jeb Rinehart's recent associates. You've got it. Now I'm heading out. I've got things to do. Money to spend. I'll give you a call when I have time."

"Give me a call in the next twenty-four hours or don't bother calling at all."

"I'll keep that in mind." Pauly swaggered away, and Austin let him, his mind humming with possibilities. He was on the scent of something big, and he didn't want to let it go. Wouldn't let it go. First, Brady's information about The Boss. Now, Pauly's assertion that several major crimes were connected.

A puppet master pulling strings.

He'd thought it before.

Knew it now.

All he had to do was find exactly what he'd told Keevers that he needed—proof.

He checked his cell phone as he climbed into the SUV, frowning as he read Captain McNeal's number.

He hit redial, waiting impatiently while the phone rang.

"It's about time," Slade growled.

"I was in the middle of my meeting with Keevers. What's up?"

"I just arrived at the Billows's house. Jackson and Titan have been called in."

"A bomb?" There'd be no reason to call in Jackson and his black lab otherwise, and Austin's blood ran cold at the thought.

"We're not sure. Brady received a package in the mail. Something about it made Eva nervous. She called in the patrol officer who's outside her house. He was concerned enough to call dispatch and ask for backup."

"I'm on my way." He sped from the entrance of the woods, branches of low-hanging trees brushing the top of the SUV as it bounced over the rutted road. Justice whined impatiently, sensing Austin's tension and adrenaline. Probably hoping they were going to work.

"Sorry, boy, it's Titan's turn," he said, keeping his tone

easy and neutral. Justice picked up on body language and vocal cues, and Austin kept that in mind when working with the bloodhound. Still, he couldn't control his body's reaction to stress, his rapid heartbeat and wildly racing pulse. After the kidnapping, they'd been expecting another overt attempt on Brady's life and had planned accordingly. Police patrol. Twenty-four-hour guard.

It hadn't been enough.

Brady could have died.

Eva could have, as well.

He scowled, pressing on the gas and shooting onto the highway, sirens blaring, nerves humming, everything inside shouting for him to hurry.

It took twenty minutes to get to Eva's neighborhood. Oak Street had been cordoned off, and a patrol officer checked Austin's ID and waved him through the barricade.

Several police cars were parked in Eva's driveway, and curious neighbors stood in a yard three houses up.

Austin grabbed Justice's leash and opened the hatchback. "Want to go visit Brady?"

Justice whined, his nose twitching with enthusiasm as he jumped to the pavement. No orange vest, so he knew he wasn't on the job, but he seemed to recognize Eva's house, his tail wagging rapidly as they walked up the porch stairs.

"I'm glad you made it, Austin. The captain has been asking for you." Valerie walked toward him, her coppery-red hair in a high ponytail, her uniform pressed and crisp.

"I got here as quickly as I could. Any response from Titan?"

"He alerted. Slade called in the bomb squad and escorted the Billowses to his place. He should be back in a couple of minutes. I'm clearing the block. You want to give me a hand?"

"Sure." But what he really wanted to do was head over to Slade's, make sure that Eva and Brady were okay.

"Thanks. I'll take the east end of the street. You handle the west," Eva suggested.

"What about Jackson? Is he still inside?"

"He's already gone back to the station. He's calling San Antonio P.D. Wants to see if they'll send a man out to the post office that the package was mailed from. The Feds will be involved, too, of course. We'd better get moving. The captain wants these houses cleared before the bomb squad arrives." Valerie smoothed a hand over her hair and shoved her hat back on as she hurried toward a group huddled in a neighbor's yard.

Austin led Justice in the opposite direction, the truth of what had almost happened pulsing through his blood. A bomb mailed to a seven-year-old child? What kind of person did something like that? Then again, what kind of person climbed into a kid's window during the dead of night and kidnapped him? Not the kind Austin wanted out on the street. That was for sure.

He'd already been feeling the pressure of time passing, the quick tick of the clock marking the minutes since Rio was stolen and Brady kidnapped. It seemed louder now, the beat of his heart echoing the passing moments, reminding him that each second that went by without a perp in jail was another second that Brady remained in danger and that Slade and his son remained separated from the German shepherd that they considered part of their family.

He knocked on the door of Eva's neighbor, his gaze flickering to a spot up the street. Slade's house. Eva and Brady tucked safely away inside of it.

Only no one could be safe if bombs were being used.

Explosives could destroy houses, buildings, cars.

Take out an entire block if enough of them were used.

"Yes?" The door opened a couple of inches, and he turned

his attention to the elderly woman who peered out from the crack in the door, her blue eyes wide behind thick lenses.

"Detective Austin Black with the Sagebrush Police Department. Are you the only one home?" he asked as he flashed his badge and tried to refocus his energy and thoughts.

He *would* find the person responsible for the bomb.

First, though, he needed to clear the block.

Chapter Thirteen

A bomb.

A real bomb that could have exploded. One that might have killed Brady. The thought made Eva dizzy, terrified her in the same guttural way that finding Brady's empty bed had.

She paced Slade's living room, wishing that she could grab Brady, get in her old, battered station wagon and drive until they reached a place where no one knew them.

The problem was, she didn't know how far she'd have to go to outrun the danger that seemed to be stalking her son. A hundred miles? A thousand?

"Eva, why don't you sit down? Pacing isn't going to change things." The police captain set a large plastic bin filled with cars in front of Brady. "These are Caleb's. I'm sure that he won't mind if you play with them."

"Thank you," Brady said, his eyes wide with surprise and awe. He had toys, but not large bins full. Eva didn't have the money for them. Most days that didn't bother her. Today, watching Brady dig through the toy cars, Slade's retired K-9 partner lying beside him, his head on Brady's leg, it made her heart ache.

"No problem. Now, if you two will excuse me. I've got to get back to your place. Officer Lawrence will stay with you until I get back."

"What about Austin? Can't he stay with us?" Brady asked, looking up from a car he was rolling along the floor.

"Austin should be arriving shortly. I'll ask him to stop in when he has time." If Slade was surprised by Brady's request, it didn't show. He just grabbed his coat and nodded to the taciturn officer who stood near his front door. Average height and build with flashing black eyes and a fierce scowl, he looked about as happy to be standing guard as Eva was to be pacing Slade's living room.

Someone tapped on the front door, and it swung open. Crisp air tinged with rain drifted in as Austin stepped into the room with Justice.

Austin.

Eva hadn't known that she'd been waiting for him until he appeared. Hadn't known how much she'd craved having him near until he walked toward her.

"Austin! Justice!" Brady jumped up, flung himself at Austin's knees.

"Brady, don't." She tried to dislodge him, but Austin brushed her hands away.

"It's okay. We're buddies, right, sport?"

"Yes. Guess what?"

"What?"

"There's a bomb at my house." Brady sounded fascinated and terrified, and Austin must have heard both in his voice. He crouched so they were eye to eye.

"I heard about that. There are people over at your place taking care of it. When you go home, you don't have to worry about it anymore."

"Maybe someone is going to send me another one."

"If someone does, your mom will call for help again. Just like she did this time." He straightened, his attention on Slade. "The bomb squad just arrived."

"Good. I'm heading back over. You want to come with me or stay here?"

"I'll stay."

"Put yourself to good use and interview the witnesses, will you? I'm leaving Officer Lawrence as extra insurance. We can't afford to lose our primary witness."

Primary witness?

Brady was more than that, and Eva wanted to say it. Wanted to tell Slade what he could do with his extra insurance and his house and his son's bucket of cars.

She kept her silence as he walked outside. Kept it as he closed the door. Kept it because it wasn't his fault that her life had fallen to pieces.

"Get any hotter and steam is going to start pouring out of your ears," Austin murmured, his lips brushing her hair as he steered her to the sofa. "Sit. You're pale as paper."

"I'm naturally fair." But her migraine was back and her stomach was sick, and every time she thought about the package that she'd almost opened, her knees went weak.

She collapsed onto a nicely cushioned sofa. So much better than the Goodwill store special that she'd bought the day she'd signed the mortgage on her little house. She tamped down envy, reminded herself that she was working toward her goals. That before she knew it, she'd have her degree and the job she wanted somewhere far away from Sagebrush and all its horrible memories.

"Are you doing okay?" Austin sat beside her, his scent wrapping her up in warmth and comfort and familiarity. Although she'd only known him for a few days, it felt like she'd known him for a lifetime.

Terrifying.

So was the look in his eyes, the depth of his gaze. The way looking at him felt like looking at every dream she'd ever had.

"I'm fine."

"You don't look fine," he said quietly.

"How is someone supposed to look after a bomb is mailed to her son?" She focused her attention on Brady, on Officer Lawrence, on the floor. On everything and anything but Austin.

"Probably a whole lot like you. About ready to fall over," he responded, and she couldn't help smiling, couldn't stop herself from looking right into his handsome face.

Big mistake.

Her heart throbbed, her breath caught.

Pull yourself together. He's just a man.

Right. *Just* a man.

One who'd acted like a hero and who treated her son like he mattered and who Eva could almost believe in.

Almost.

"Don't worry. I'm not planning to collapse."

"Glad to hear it. Much as I'd like to sweep you off your feet, I'm not sure either of us would want me to have to sweep you up off the floor."

"Neither of those things is going to happen."

"We'll see. Do you mind if I ask Brady a few questions?" He changed the subject, and she let him, because trying to continue it would make it seem as if she cared one way or another.

She didn't.

Shouldn't.

But maybe the thought of being swept off her feet wasn't

quite as awful as it had been a week ago. Especially if the person doing the sweeping was Austin.

"He's really shaken. It might be better for him if you waited." And better for *her* if Austin left.

"Then I guess we can get started on your interview. How about we go in the kitchen?" He pulled her to her feet, and a million butterflies took flight in her stomach.

"I'd rather not leave Brady alone."

"I'm not alone, Momma. Justice is with me," Brady said as he rolled a police car in front of the bloodhound's nose. The dog sniffed it, licked Brady's cheek and settled into a heap of fur beside him.

"I know, sweetie, but—"

"He'll be fine, ma'am. I'm here to keep an eye on him," Officer Lawrence said, speaking up for the first time since he'd arrived.

Not the best timing, in Eva's opinion.

"Right. I guess it's fine, then."

"Great. This shouldn't take more than a few minutes." Austin pressed a hand to her lower back, his palm burning through her T-shirt, the heat seeping through her skin and into her blood, burning her cheeks and her heart.

She felt like a schoolgirl with her first crush. Only she wasn't a girl, and she knew exactly where crushes could lead.

"Go ahead and have a seat." Austin gestured to the dinette set that sat in a corner of the room, and she perched on the edge of a chair.

"You've got a little color back in your cheeks. Feeling better?" Austin dropped into the chair across from Eva, studying her face as she quickly braided her hair and unbraided it again, the silky gold strands sliding through her fingers.

She seemed fidgety and tense, her gaze skittering away from his, her foot tapping on the tile floor. "I'm not sure there's much that I can tell you, Austin. The box was delivered by our regular mail carrier, and I know that he'd never hurt Brady."

"It was postmarked San Antonio, so we've got no reason to believe it didn't come from there. I'm curious as to what made you suspicious of it, though."

"I already told Officer Lawrence—the bottom of the box was seeping something. That seemed odd. Plus, I don't know anyone in San Antonio." She drummed the table with her fingertips, still not meeting his eyes.

"You don't have to be nervous around me, Eva." He covered her hand, and she stilled, her gaze finally settling on him.

"I'm not."

He quirked a brow. "Then why all the fidgeting?"

"I have a lot of energy?"

"Nice try, but I'm not buying it. Want to try the truth, instead?"

"Sure. Why not? Here's the thing, Austin. I've been swept off my feet before, and I don't want to be again." She sighed, pressing her fingers to the bridge of her nose and closing her eyes briefly. When she opened them, he was struck again by their beauty, the soft green mistiness of them, the quiet stillness in their depths.

"My comment about sweeping you off your feet was a joke, Eva."

"Was it?" she asked, and he couldn't give her anything but the truth.

"Yes, but there might have been a grain of truth in it."

"Austin—"

"You're a beautiful, intelligent woman and you're a wonderful mother. That combination is hard to resist."

"Yeah. I've been fighting men off for years." She smiled, walked to the window that looked out over Slade's backyard.

"Then you know that no one can sweep you off your feet unless you want to be swept."

"I was kidding about fighting men off. It's just been me and Brady since the day he was born. That's the way I've wanted it."

"Is it the way you still want it?" he asked softly.

"I...don't want to get hurt again. That's what I know. I don't want Brady to be hurt. He's a little boy with big dreams and a wide-open heart. I want him to stay that way for as long as he can."

"You can't protect him from hurt, Eva. It's part of life. You can't make your childhood better by making his perfect, either."

"I'm not trying to. I'm just trying to give him the best possible life he can have. I'm trying to make sure he has the kind of love and security I didn't. There's nothing wrong with that."

"I never said that there was. I'm just saying that you can't give up your possibilities because you're afraid of what will happen to Brady if you go after them. As long as he has your love, he'll be just fine." He urged her around so they were facing each other. Tears glittered in her eyes, but they didn't fall, and he wondered if she ever cried, ever allowed herself to feel whatever it was that simmered in the depth of her gaze.

"I thought you needed to ask me some questions." She moved away, sat at the table again, her face pinched and hollow.

"Has Brady been talking about the kidnapping?" If she wanted to change the subject, he'd comply, but they weren't finished with the conversation. Not by a long shot.

There was something about Eva that called to him, some part of her heart that seemed made for his. He couldn't deny that any more than he could allow himself to push for something she didn't seem to want.

"No. I think he's been trying to forget it. Maybe even pretend it didn't happen. Then the package came, and he's right back where he was a couple of days ago—terrified."

"I'm sorry for that, Eva. I wish I could make it all go away, but I can't."

"You're a hero, but not a superhero, huh?" she said, and blushed.

"I don't have a cape tucked away in my backpack that I can take out and use when I need to swoop in and rescue my friends, that's for sure."

"Too bad. If you did, you could break out the cape, and Brady and I could hitch a ride out of town."

He met her eyes. "You're thinking of leaving?"

"Just thinking that it might be safer to go than to stay."

"Go where?"

"I don't know. I could drive east or head north. I'm sure that we could find a nice quiet little town to hole up in."

"You know that won't protect Brady, Eva," he reminded her. "It'll just take you both away from the people who want to help you."

"Maybe, but I just want so badly for him to be safe."

"He will be. I promise you that."

A shadow crossed her face. "Don't make me promises, okay, Austin? Everyone who ever has just ended up disappointing me."

"Then they were all too foolish to know what they'd be losing out on when you walked away."

"And you're not?"

"I guess that will be up to you to decide," he responded, lifting her hand, his thumb trailing over her red and cracked knuckles.

For a moment, Eva went perfectly still, her eyes wide with surprise.

"I—" She stood, nearly toppling the chair in her haste. "If we're done, I think I'd better go check on Brady," she said, and then she ran from the room.

Eva figured that she could run from the room, the house, the town, the country, but there was no way she could run from the way Austin made her feel. His words were still echoing in her head as she plopped down beside Brady, scratched Justice's silky ears and tried her best to quiet her rioting heart.

"Are you okay, Momma? Your cheeks are all red," Brady said, his big, blue eyes shadowed with anxiety. With everything else that had happened, he didn't need anything more to worry about, and she hugged him close, pressed a gentle kiss to his bruised forehead.

"I'm fine."

"Then why are your cheeks red?"

"Because—"

The front door opened, and Slade walked into the house, his dark hair mussed, his expression grim. "The bomb squad is finished. An evidence team is over at your place, but I think it's safe for you and Brady to go home."

"Did they detonate the explosives?" Austin asked as he strode out of the kitchen. The question was for Slade, but his gaze was on Eva.

"Yes. The bomb was rudimentary at best. Probably put together by someone who downloaded instructions off the internet."

"Then it wouldn't have done much damage?" It's what Eva wanted to believe, but Slade shook his head.

"It might have been rudimentary, but it still would have done plenty of damage. Come on… I'll walk you two home. What time does your shift end, Officer Lawrence?"

"Another hour."

"You want to accompany us, then?"

"Sure. I'll wait outside until you're ready." The officer stepped outside, the door closing softly behind him.

"Why don't you let me escort them, Slade? I'm parked over there, anyway," Austin offered.

"Sounds good. When you're done, I'd like you to come to the station. I'm calling a meeting of the K-9 Unit. We need to discuss what you found out from West and Keevers, and we may as well do it as a group," Slade said.

Too bad, because spending more time with Austin wasn't something Eva should be doing. Not if she wanted to guard her heart.

"Let's get those cars cleaned up, Brady," she said, tossing a handful of cars into the bin, her cheeks still too hot, her heart still beating wildly.

"I'll give you a hand."

Austin. Of course.

His shoulder brushed hers as they worked, his scent masculine and compelling.

"Done!" She threw the last car in the bin, grabbed Brady's hand. "Let's go."

"Are we in a hurry?" Austin asked, opening the door and letting her step out ahead of him.

"I'm just anxious to get home."

"Tired?"

She sighed. "It's been a rough couple of days."

"Things will get better." He shortened Justice's leash. "Hey, sport, you want to help me walk Justice back to your house?"

"Really? Sure!" Brady's smile looked like Christmas morning and birthday presents all rolled into one.

"Put your hand here." He helped Brady slide his hand through the loop in the leash, and Eva's heart melted into a puddle of longing so deep she thought she might drown in it.

This was what Brady had been missing.

What he probably hadn't even known he'd wanted until Austin had walked into their lives.

What would happen when he walked out?

"I wish you wouldn't—" she started to say, but couldn't finish. Couldn't deny Brady a few minutes of excitement because of her own insecurities and fears.

"What?"

"Nothing important."

"Good." Austin grinned, urging her up the street.

She could feel the weight of a dozen eyes. Her neighbors, watching as the good-looking police detective escorted her home. No matter that another officer was a few feet ahead of them, never mind that a bomb had been discovered in a package addressed to Brady. In their minds, they'd have her married off to Austin by the next morning, and there wasn't a whole lot she could do about it.

"Keep frowning like that and you'll have wrinkles before you're thirty," Austin chided as they walked up her porch stairs. Crime-scene tape dangled from the railing and flapped in the cold breeze.

"A gentleman wouldn't mention such a thing."

"Who said that I'm a gentleman?" He took the leash from Brady's hand, ruffled his hair. "Thanks for the help, sport. I'll see you later."

Don't tell him that, she wanted to say. *Don't lead him on and disappoint him.*

But Austin touched her cheek, his fingers gentle as a butterfly's kiss. "See you later, too."

She heard the promise in his voice, saw it in his eyes, and she couldn't find it in herself to say anything at all.

Chapter Fourteen

Austin had never been big on meetings. He preferred action to words and would rather be out following a scent trail with Justice than sitting in a conference room sipping coffee and listening to the team discuss the details of a case. A necessary evil, that's how he thought of them. Today, though, he was hoping that the meeting would turn out to be way more than that.

Things were escalating, the bomb an indication that the person who'd kidnapped Brady was getting desperate. That desperation could only lead to more aggressive attempts on Brady's life. The Special Operations K-9 Unit needed to shut the guy down and lock him up before that could happen.

Guy?

Guys.

The brown-haired kidnapper and The Boss.

Austin snagged a cookie from a plate someone had set in the middle of the long table and bit into it as Slade McNeal entered the room and took the seat between Lee Calloway and Parker Adams.

"It looks like we're all here, so I'll go ahead and get started. I have some information to share, and then we'll let Austin and Lee give us their updates." Slade scanned his five member team.

"Information? You mean about the bomb that was mailed to Brady Billows?" Lee Calloway asked.

"We're still working our San Antonio angle, Lee. This has got to be something different," Jackson Worth responded, his dog Titan shifting under Jackson's chair as his handler spoke.

"Right. I got some news a couple of minutes ago, and I'm hoping that it'll help bring this case to a close." McNeal paused. You've heard of Dante Frears? He's an old war buddy of mine."

Austin had heard of him. As a matter of fact, he'd hung out with Slade and Dante on a couple of occasions. A well-respected member of the community, Dante had wealth, power and the kind of good-old-boy charm that had won him friends all over Sagebrush.

"There aren't many people in town who haven't heard of him, Slade. What did he call you about? Does he have information that will help our investigation?" Lee asked.

"Not directly, but he's willing to help us get it. He's offering a twenty-five-thousand-dollar reward to anyone with information that leads to Rio's recovery."

"That's a lot of money," Parker said.

"Hopefully it will be enough to motivate someone to step forward. We need Rio on the force, and I need him home. Caleb isn't doing well with this new loss." Slade didn't talk much about his personal life. The fact that he'd mentioned his five-year-old son hinted at big problems.

"If there's anything I can do to help, let me know. I'm pretty good with kids," Valerie offered.

"Thanks, but the only thing that is going to help Caleb is having Rio back. Now, let's get to our next order of business. Any change with Jane Doe, Lee?"

"She's unconscious, and the doctors don't know how long that will last. Her fingerprints aren't in the system, and so far, no one has reported her missing. Until someone does, we're walking in the dark."

"How about you, Austin? Did your meeting with Camden West pan out?"

"Not even close. He wouldn't talk. Didn't even bite when I mentioned the possibility of early parole and relocation."

"Do you think he's trying to protect someone?" Slade asked.

"I think he's trying to protect himself. He's afraid of someone, and so is Pauly Keevers."

"I find that hard to believe. Word on the street is that Keevers is only afraid of God." Parker leaned back in his chair and frowned.

"I would have said the same about Pauly before I met with him today." Austin filled the team in on his meeting with Keevers.

When he finished, Slade stood and paced to the bank of windows on the far wall. "We've got problems, and they're not limited to Rio's theft. If Keevers's information is accurate and the crimes he mentioned are connected, there's a crime ring in Sagebrush, and it's been operating for years."

Everyone spoke at once after that, a hodgepodge of voices and ideas filling the room. Some members of the team thought Pauly was lying. Others were eager to pay Keevers the money he'd demanded for more information.

Finally, Slade raised his hand, and the group fell silent.

"I'm not sure what we're dealing with, but Pauly has never

sold us information that didn't pan out. Austin, when Keevers contacts you again, let him know we're willing to pay what he wants for the information."

Slade left the room and the rest of the team followed, their moods grim. No chatting or joking. With Rio missing, the team felt incomplete, and Slade's concern and anxiety were weighing on everyone.

"Want me to put the word out that you're in the market to buy information again? Get a little fire burning under Keevers?" Parker asked as they walked to their cubicles.

"We're better off waiting. I want Keevers to think he has the upper hand and is calling the shots."

"I hope he wants to call the shots soon, then. Whatever he knows has to be huge if he's worried for his safety."

"Worried or not, I'm hoping he talks," Austin retorted. "If there *is* a crime ring in Sagebrush, I want to take it down."

"I like the way you think, Austin." Parker grinned, but Austin didn't feel much like smiling.

Rio missing. Two victims hospitalized. A little boy in danger. Time ticking away, and Austin had more questions than answers.

He walked into the kennel, retrieved Justice and led him to the SUV. They'd been working long hours, and the bloodhound deserved some time to run and play.

Ten minutes later, he pulled up in front of his two-story Victorian. A pretty house, that's what the women who visited said. The guys couldn't have cared less about the gingerbread trim or the wraparound porch.

Austin cared.

He'd painstakingly restored them. Had done the same with the interior, refinishing the time-worn hardwood floors and the hand-carved railing that curved up the winding staircase. To Austin each of those things represented everything that he hadn't had when he'd been a kid, moving from low-income apartment to low-income apartment while his mother struggled to provide.

Permanence.

He'd needed it. Now that he had it, he wanted someone to share it with.

He frowned, unlocking the front door and letting Justice run inside ahead of him. If things had worked out with Candace, they might have had a child by now. The house might be filled with the scent of dinner cooking, the sound of a baby crying and the weight of Candace's disappointment.

Yeah.

Things would have been great until he couldn't be there for a birthday party, a dinner date, a movie night.

He pulled a meal from the freezer and shoved it into the microwave, not sure why he was thinking about Candace. He didn't miss her. Didn't wish things had worked out differently.

His cell phone rang and he answered as he took out the meal. "Hello?"

"Austin? It's Eva." She didn't have to tell him. A dozen years from now, he was pretty sure he'd still know exactly what her voice sounded like.

"Is everything okay?"

"Yes. I just…"

"What?" He took a bite of lukewarm pasta and thought that he should invest in some cooking lessons so he could eat better.

"How was your meeting?"

"Interesting. An old friend of Slade's is offering twenty-five-thousand dollars for information leading to Rio's return."

"That's incredible!" She sounded excited, and he smiled, imagining her twisting the end of her long ponytail, her eyes glowing.

"I'm working on a couple of other leads. Nothing I can talk

about right now, but I'm hoping we'll be able to find Brady's kidnapper soon."

"Me, too. I'm ready for our lives to go back to normal."

"What's normal for you, Eva? You're a mother, a waitress, a student. What else do you do with your time?"

"Nothing. I don't have time for anything else." She laughed. "What about you? Wait…don't tell me. Let me guess. In your free time, you climb mountains, hike trails and volunteer as a coach for a local football team."

"Not quite." It was his turn to laugh.

"Then what? Aside from convincing little boys that you can almost walk on water, that is."

"Brady doesn't think that."

"No, but he does adore you," she murmured.

"Is that the real reason why you're calling?"

She hesitated. "I just don't want him hurt."

"Why would he be?"

"Because when this is over, you're going to go back to your life, and Brady will be left with his. He may realize how big a hole there is in it."

"What hole?" He shoved his pasta away, looking out into the gray-blue evening.

"He's never had a father. He's never even had a man in his life aside from teachers. That makes the attention you're giving him even more special. Imagine how he'll feel when he doesn't have it anymore."

"You're assuming that he won't," he said, his tone sharper than he'd intended.

"You're upset," she said quietly.

"No. I'm insulted. I like Brady. He's a great kid. I'm not going to track down his kidnapper and then walk out of his life. Not unless you ask me to."

"I—"

"Tell you what. I'm right in the middle of dinner. How about we hash things out later?" He cut her off, not sure he wanted to hear what she had to say. If she told him to back off, he would, but he wouldn't be happy about it.

"What are you having? Anything better than leftover chicken noodle soup?"

"Does overcooked and then frozen pasta count as better?" He nudged a noodle with his fork.

"Tell me you're not really eating that."

"I am. Got it out of my freezer and stuck it in the microwave right before you called."

"That's not healthy eating for a guy who leads such an active life."

"Careful, Eva. Keep talking like that and I might get the impression that you care."

"I never said that I didn't."

"But you don't want to."

"Brady isn't the only one who I think is going to be hurt when this is over." She sighed. "Listen, I've got some cod in the fridge. Why don't you come by, and I'll make it. We can have salad with it, and chocolate chip cookies for dessert."

"Keep tempting me, and I might just take you up on the offer."

"I want you to. I owe you. If it weren't for you and Justice—"

"I don't want your gratitude. If that's what this is about, then I think I'll stick to my pasta."

"I… It's not."

"In that case, what time will dinner be ready?"

"Give me an hour to clean up the kitchen and the rest of the house, then I'll be ready to cook." She hung up, and Austin dumped the pasta into the trash can.

An hour, and he'd be eating dinner with Eva and Brady,

sitting at the table in their little kitchen, feeling like part of something bigger than himself. That's what friendship and family did. They offered a connection that made a single person become something more.

Eva and Brady's faces flashed through his mind.

He could build something with them. He knew it. Build it, nurture it, make it into something better than any of them could have on their own.

He wanted that more than he wanted to be safe.

Wanted it more than he wanted to protect the pieces of his heart.

Prayed that Eva wanted it, too, because finding her and Brady was like finding a puzzle piece that had been missing for far too long.

A perfect fit?

Austin didn't know, but he thought he'd be a fool not find out.

Chapter Fifteen

She shouldn't have invited him for dinner.

Didn't know why she had.

Or maybe she did.

She liked having Austin around, felt his absence when he was gone.

If Brady was in the throes of hero worship, *she* was in the throes of something far worse.

"Idiot," Eva muttered as she pulled the cod out of the fridge and salted it liberally. She'd pan sear it, serve it with a nice Caesar salad. Feed everyone, and then send Austin away.

Simple as that.

Only nothing seemed simple when Austin was around.

When he was with her, all the promises she'd made to herself, all the things she'd sworn she'd never feel again were right there, telling her that she'd been a fool to ever think she had control over any of them.

The doorbell rang, and Brady shouted excitedly.

"He's here, Momma! Austin is here!"

"I'm coming." She dried her hands on a dish towel, peered out the peephole. She knew who she'd see, but her heart jumped, anyway.

Austin.

She opened the door, stepped back so he and Justice could enter.

"Sorry we're late. We had an errand to run."

"Actually, you're right on time. I was just starting the fish. I'll make the salad after that. We should be able to eat in about fifteen minutes," she said as Brady patted Justice's head. The bloodhound's tongue lolled out in ecstasy, and she was sure there was a smile hidden beneath his jowls.

"Maybe sooner if we use this." Austin pulled a large salad from a brown paper bag. "I thought having it premade might speed up the process."

"You're that hungry?"

"Starving." Austin smiled, his eyes deeply shadowed, his bomber jacket hanging open to reveal a black T-shirt. She wondered what it would be like to lay her head against his chest, hear his heart beating steadily beneath soft cotton and warm flesh.

Stop!

"I'd better get the fish started, then." She turned, and he snagged her belt loop, pulled her back.

"Hold on. I brought something for Brady. I thought you might like to see it, too."

"What?" Presents? She didn't like that, and she thought that she'd have to tell him. Make it clear that she didn't want him to buy her son's affection. It wasn't like he didn't already have it. As a matter of fact…

He pulled a fluffy, white stuffed dog from the bag.

No. Not quite white. The fake fur was a little dingy, but not dirt-encrusted like it had been the last time she'd seen it.

"Snowflake!" Brady took the dog, hugged it to his chest.

"I thought you took that as evidence," Eva said.

"I did, but the forensic team couldn't find anything but mud on it, so I got Slade's permission and signed it out of the evidence room."

"Thank you, Austin! This is the best present ever!" Brady threw himself at Austin, his thin arms wrapping around Austin's broad shoulders. Seeing them together made Eva's heart ache.

She'd always wanted this for Brady. A male influence. Someone her son could look up to. A father figure who could fill the spot that Rick had left. She'd wanted it but had known that going after it could only lead to hurt. Hers *and* Brady's.

So what had she done?

She'd invited Austin for dinner, that's what.

She sighed, heating the pan and laying the fish in it.

"Need any help?" Austin moved up behind her, his chest so close to her back that she could feel his heat through her shirt. She wanted to turn into him, slide her hands up his arms and into his dark hair. Wanted to let herself believe that one moment could lead to another and to another until they'd built hundreds of moments together.

"You can grab some plates from the cupboard." Anything to put some distance between them.

"You're uncomfortable." He opened the cupboard, pulled out three mismatched plates.

"Why do you say that?"

"You're gripping that spatula like you're afraid it's going to jump out of your hand."

"Right." She loosened her grip.

"Momma? Is dinner ready?" Brady padded into the kitchen, Justice right behind him. They looked cute together. The sweet little boy and his furry companion.

Maybe getting a puppy in the summer wasn't such a bad idea. "Soon. Why don't you help Austin set the table?"

She let them work and talk while she finished the fish, plated it and the salad, poured ice water into plastic cups. Did everything the same way she'd done it a thousand times before. Only this time, Austin was there, his gaze following her as she moved around the kitchen, sat in her chair, reached for Brady's hand and for his.

"Do you want to pray, Austin?"

He offered a simple prayer of thanks. Nothing flowery or overwrought. When he was done, he squeezed her hand gently. "This looks good. Thanks for inviting me."

Her cheeks heated at his praise, and she dug into the fish, tried not to think about the fact that they were sitting at her little table together.

Like a family.

Only they weren't.

She finished her fish, but it tasted like sawdust, her heart pounding so frantically she thought she might be sick.

This hadn't just been a bad idea.

It had been a horrible one.

By the time everyone finished eating and she'd tucked Brady into bed, she felt frazzled, her nerves raw.

She poured coffee into two mugs, handed one to Austin, doing her best to avoid his gorgeous eyes.

"What's wrong, Eva?" He took the mug from her hand, cupped her jaw so that she had no choice but to meet his eyes.

"I wish none of this had happened. Not Brady witnessing a crime. Not him being kidnapped. Not the bomb. Not..."

"Us?"

"Is there an us, Austin? Or is this just a game we're playing until it's over and we find out that we've both lost."

"I don't play games."

"That's what Brady's father told me a couple of days before I found out he was married," she said, and regretted it immediately.

"Let's get one thing straight, okay? I'm not Brady's father, and if I were, I wouldn't be living in Las Vegas while you raised my son," he bit out.

"I know. I'm sorry. I guess that I've just always figured that if I could fall for someone like Rick once, I could do it again."

He searched her eyes. "So you decided not to let yourself fall at all?"

"Something like that."

"How old were you when you met him?" Austin asked.

"Eighteen. He walked into Arianna's Café and started spouting a bunch of pretty phrases. I was convinced he meant them. Convinced that we'd get married and have a beautiful house and beautiful children and live happily ever after. Too bad my Prince Charming turned out to be a toad."

"I'm sorry, Eva. You deserved better."

"My mother said the same thing when I found out that I was pregnant. I think she was relieved that Rick didn't want to leave his wife and make a life with me. She was terrified that I'd end up married to someone just like my father. *You deserve better,* she'd said. Funny that she thought that about me and not about herself."

"Not so funny," he murmured, his hand slipping from her jaw and sliding under the hair at her nape, his palm raspy and warm and altogether too wonderful.

"Austin, this isn't a good idea."

"No?"

"No." But she was leaning into him, her hands on his chest, her fingers curled into the fabric of his shirt, every cell in her body yearning for him in a way that she had never yearned for Rick. Had never yearned for anyone.

"I'll stop if you want me to, Eva. I'll walk away and let you and Brady go on the way you were. Just say the word, and I'll go home."

She couldn't.

Didn't.

And his lips touched hers, gently, easily. No pressure. No demands. She wanted so much more, and she slid her hands into his hair, pulled him closer. She yearned for *this,* for him.

She lost herself in the sweetness of the kiss, the gentleness of his touch, her heart thundering wildly, her body humming with need.

"Momma! Help me!" Brady's desperate scream cut through the moment, his terror making Eva's knees weak, her body fluid and loose.

Justice barked. One quick sharp burst of sound that seemed to be coming from Brady's room.

"Brady!" Eva tried to run, but Austin pulled her back.

"Stay here!" he shouted as he ran into Brady's room, his heart pounding double-time, his muscles tight with fear.

Brady seemed to be half asleep, sitting in the middle of his bed, his white-blond hair sticking up in every direction.

That's the first thing Austin noticed.

The second thing he noticed was Justice, his paws resting on the window frame, his nose pressed against the glass. Hackles raised, body stiff, he growled long and low, the warning raising the hair on the back of Austin's neck.

"Did you see something, boy?" He touched the dog's head, and Justice dropped down, his body relaxing as if whatever he'd seen was gone. Austin scanned the area beyond the window. Purple dusk had turned to pitch-black night, deep shadows shrouding the yard. No moonlight. Just darkness upon darkness.

"Brady!" Eva skidded to a stop next to the bed, her face pale, her eyes filled with fear. "What's wrong?"

"He was trying to get in the window. I saw him, Momma. He was coming to get me again." Brady threw himself into her arms, and she sat on the edge of the bed with him, her hair just a shade darker than his, her lips still pink from Austin's kiss.

"Who was trying to get you, sweetie?" She smoothed Brady's hair.

"The man with the brown hair."

"Maybe you were dreaming," she said, but her gaze jumped to the window, then settled on Austin. "Do you see anything?"

"No, and neither does Justice," he said, because the blood-hound lay relaxed and at ease near his feet. Someone *had* been there, though. Austin didn't say that. Not in front of Brady. The poor kid was already scared enough.

"See, Brady? Everything is okay. If it wasn't, Justice would be barking and growling."

"But I saw him, Momma. I really did. Justice growled, and I looked, and he was right there," Brady insisted, but he sounded tired, his eyes drifting closed as he leaned against Eva.

"Whatever you saw is gone now. Go to sleep, sweetie." She eased Brady onto his pillow, covered him with a thick, blue blanket, kissed the fading bruise on his forehead and motioned for Austin to follow her into the hall.

His hair was mussed from her hands, his eyes blazing. The feel of his lips was still warm on hers. She wanted to throw herself back in his arms and tell him how scared she was. Wanted to listen as he told her everything would be okay.

She wrapped her arms around her waist instead, glancing into the room. Brady lay still and silent. Probably sound asleep again.

"Justice saw something, didn't he?" she whispered.

"Yeah."

"Could it have been a deer or a mountain lion? Maybe a bear?" That's what she wanted it to be. Any one of those things would be better than the alternative.

"Justice doesn't growl or bark at animals. I'm going to take him out back. I'll knock when we're finished."

"Austin…" She didn't know what she wanted to say, her thoughts lost in the swirl of dread that filled her mind and drove everything else away.

"It's going to be okay, Eva." He cupped her shoulders, his palms warm through her T-shirt, his gaze steady. She'd spent her life wondering what it would be like to have someone she could really depend on. As she looked into Austin's eyes, she thought she finally knew.

"I hope you're right."

Austin did, too. He squeezed Eva's hand, dropped a kiss on her forehead. "I'll be back as soon as I can."

Austin hooked Justice to his lead and led him out the back door, using his flashlight to illuminate the dark edges of the yard.

Justice snuffled the ground as they moved toward Brady's window. The bloodhound paused there, huffing deeply as he nosed the grass.

"What do you smell, boy?" Austin crouched near the house, studying the packed earth beneath the window. No footprints visible, but that didn't mean no one had been there.

"Something going on out here? I saw a light and thought I'd better check things out." The patrol officer who'd been sitting guard out front walked around the corner of the house. Older than Austin by a couple of decades, he had the confident walk and the straightforward air of someone who knew his job and did it well.

"Brady thought he saw someone looking in the window at him."

"If he did, the person didn't walk around from the front of the house."

"It would have been easy enough for someone to cut through the back neighbor's property without being seen. It's black as pitch out here," Austin replied, and the patrol officer nodded.

"True. Did your dog alert?"

"He saw something."

"How about I dust for prints? See if we come up with anything on the sill?"

"Sounds good. I'll see if Justice can pick up a scent and track it. I'll radio in if we find anything. Seek," he commanded.

Responding immediately, Justice inhaled deeply, his body trembling with excitement as he raced through the neighbor's backyard and onto the street beyond it.

Chapter Sixteen

Midnight and still no sign of Austin.

Exhausted, Eva paced the living room for another hour and finally gave up her vigil. She changed into flannel pajamas and climbed into bed next to Brady. He seemed to be sleeping nightmare free, his body limp and his breathing deep. Good. After a couple of restless nights, he needed his sleep.

Eva did, too, but she couldn't make herself relax enough to drift off. Every creak of old wood, every groan of wind in the eaves reminded her that someone might have been stalking the house just a few hours ago.

Stalking Brady.

Please, God, let the police find the second kidnapper soon. Please keep Brady safe until they do, she prayed silently.

Brady whimpered in his sleep, and she smoothed his hair and kissed his forehead, finally giving up on the idea of rest. She went to her room and dug through her dresser drawer. Her mother's Bible was there. Unlike the hardcover Bible Eva usually read from, her mother's was soft, worn leather and still held just a hint of the cheap perfume that Tonya had worn every day of her life for as long as Eva could remember.

Eva carried it into the living room and flicked on the lamp, the soft, golden glow chasing away the darkness and some of her fears. She pulled back the curtain, making sure the patrol car was sitting at the curb.

Still there.

And still no sign of Austin.

He'd said that he'd stop back in when he was finished his search, so where was he?

Had he been attacked? Overcome? Injured?

She tried to push away the thoughts. It didn't do any good to speculate. But she couldn't seem to help herself. She kept imagining his body lying bleeding and broken somewhere. Imagined him in desperate need of help with no one to turn to.

"Stop it!" she hissed, settling on the couch and curling up under the afghan Mrs. Daphne had given her for Christmas. She felt cold to the bone, her body aching with it, her teeth chattering. If she hadn't been completely terrified by the thought, she'd have walked into the backyard and grabbed a couple of pieces of firewood from the pile, started a fire in the fireplace.

She *was* terrified, though, so she stayed put, pulling the afghan closer and letting the Bible fall open, knowing exactly which passage it would fall to. Isaiah 40:31.

But those who hope in the Lord will renew their strength. They will soar on wings like eagles; they will run and not grow weary, they will walk and not become faint.

The words were underlined and highlighted, the page stained with years' worth of tears that had flowed because

Tonya had married a criminal, a rake, a liar, a thug. Tears that had fallen because she'd felt trapped by her commitment and the love that had made her weak.

So many tears.

Eva's first memory was of her mother crying. She'd been five or six and peeking out of her room after Ernie stormed from the trailer. She could still remember the knot in her stomach as she'd watched her mother pick up the shattered plates and the old clock that Ernie had destroyed. Tonya had been young. Maybe twenty-four, but she'd moved like an old woman, bending slowly as if every bone hurt. When she was done, she'd pulled the Bible from its hiding place under the couch cushions and lowered herself into the old rocking chair, tears pouring down her face, her lips moving as she read words that should have comforted her.

Eva didn't want to be that woman, rocking to the rhythm of her sorrow. She didn't want to be so in love with someone that she lost every bit of who she was.

She wanted a love that built rather than tore down. A relationship that made her better rather than worse.

She wanted the dream she'd had when she was a kid. The happy home and the loving husband.

Someone knocked on the door, the soft sound pulling Eva from the past. Austin. She didn't have to look to know it was him. She swiped her hand over the Bible's wrinkled page, trying to wipe away the memory of her mother's tears, her hand shaking, her heart beating hard and heavy as she walked to the door.

She felt sick with the memories of her mother, tired in a way that she hadn't been since she'd found Tonya lying in a pool of her own blood, her hand reaching for her husband's. Even in death. Even after she'd given the last bit of what she had for him.

Eva opened the door, crisp winter air gusting in and cooling her heated cheeks, her heart leaping as she looked into Austin's eyes.

If anyone could ever be her happily-ever-after, it was him.

The thought whispered into her heart, lodged there and she couldn't deny it.

"Sorry it's so late. I wouldn't have knocked, but I saw your light go on, and I thought you'd like an update," Austin said quietly as he unhooked Justice's leash and stepped inside.

"I was up waiting for you, so you don't have to apologize." Her voice sounded gravelly and thick with the tears that she didn't want to shed.

Tears for her mother.

For herself.

Tears for the things that could have been if Tonya had only been strong enough.

"Are you okay?" he asked gently, pulling her into his arms and pressing her head to his chest.

She knew she should back away, deny herself the comfort that he offered, but she wanted to stand there with him almost as badly as she wanted to take her next breath. Her hands slid beneath his coat, her heart thudding painfully, her breath coming in a quick dry sob.

"Eva?" He eased back, looked into her face. "What is it, honey?"

"Why can't you be a horrible person, Austin? Why can't you be untrustworthy and mean? If you hated children and kicked puppies and chewed tobacco, it would be so much easier to walk away from you."

"Who says you have to walk away?" He smiled a little, running a knuckle down her cheek, sliding it over her bottom lip.

"Me."

"Why?"

"Because I'm a coward."

"You aren't even close to being that." He pressed a gentle kiss to the palm of her hand, closed her fingers over it, and her entire body shuddered with longing.

"You're wrong. I'm the biggest coward in the world." She dropped onto the couch, pulled the afghan close. It wasn't nearly as warm as Austin. "Did you and Justice find anyone?"

"We tracked a scent trail for a few miles, but lost it close to downtown."

"So someone really was looking in Brady's window?" She hadn't wanted to believe it, but she couldn't say she was surprised.

"Yes, and there's more. We pulled a print from the windowsill. There was a match for it in our database. That's why I was gone for so long."

"You have a name?"

"Don Frist. He has a rap sheet a mile long. Mostly petty crime, but he was in jail last year on drug-possession charges. I pulled his mug shot. He's our second kidnapper."

"You're sure?" She grabbed his hand, didn't even realize she was holding on to him until his thumb ran across her wrist, the sweeping caress sending heat through her blood.

"Positive. He's the guy I saw in the Lost Woods. We have a warrant out for his arrest. All we have to do is find him."

"What if he comes back before you do?" The thought of him skulking around the house, searching for a way inside, made her stomach churn.

"We've upped police presence in the neighborhood and put a patrol car on the street behind yours. That will make it more difficult for him to access your yard through the neighbor's."

"Difficult, but not impossible."

"No." He paused, ran a hand down his jaw. "Eva, there's something else."

"Go ahead."

"Frist's fingerprints matched some that were pulled from your parents' home after their murders."

"Are you saying that he killed my parents and now he's after my son?" She stood so quickly, she felt dizzy, stars dancing in front of her eyes, darkness sweeping in so unexpectedly that she would have fallen if Austin hadn't grabbed her waist and held her steady.

"Sit back down, Eva, before you pass out."

"I'm not going to pass out." But she sat, anyway. Just in case. "Now, will you please tell me what's going on? Did Frist murder my parents?"

"Aside from the fingerprints, there was no evidence to link him to the crime. He was questioned after his prints were found, and he had an airtight alibi."

"What alibi? A friend vouching for him? A glimpse of him at a bar somewhere?" She sounded bitter and angry. She *felt* bitter and angry. Two years she'd been waiting for a suspect to be named and someone to be arrested, and the police had had Frist's fingerprints all along.

"He was at a wedding in Maine, and he had photos and plane tickets to prove it. He said that his fingerprints were at the crime scene because he was a friend of your father's."

"My father didn't have any friends." He'd had people who he used and people who used him, but no friends.

"The investigating officer thought there might be a criminal connection between the two of them, but that didn't mean that Frist was the murderer."

"It didn't mean he was innocent, either."

"No, but there were other fingerprints at the scene. A couple of sets that were identified. A couple that weren't."

"Why is this the first that I'm hearing of it?" she asked sharply.

"I can't answer that, Eva. I wasn't the investigating officer. If I had been, I'd like to think that I would have been a lot more forthcoming with you."

Her eyes bore into his. "You'd like to *think* it?"

"It would be easy for me to say that I would have been, but sometimes information is kept from the family of the victims out of compassion or concern."

"Right." She walked across the room, tried to wrap her mind around everything he'd told her. "You don't have any proof that Frist murdered my parents, but you do have proof that he was at my house and that he kidnapped Brady. He'll at least pay for that."

"Right, and we're looking for more. We're waiting for a judge to issue a search warrant. Once he does, we'll go into Frist's house and see what we can find."

"In the meantime, Brady is still in danger."

"And will be until we can bring Frist in. I think you need to consider bringing in a tutor while all this is going on. Having him at home rather than school will make it easier for us to protect him."

"A tutor for how long?" she asked.

"For as long as it takes to find Frist."

"That could be months, Austin, and I can't take any more time off work. Arianna has already made it clear that I'd better show up on Wednesday. If I don't, I'll lose pay, and I can't afford that."

"Don't worry. Everything is taken care of," he told her.

"What do you mean?"

"Slade and I agreed that Mrs. Daphne couldn't be Brady's babysitter while you work. We'll have a police officer take over until all this blows over."

"Blows over? You make it sound like a thunderstorm." She

sighed, and he smiled, lifting the Bible from beside her and letting it fall open in his hands.

If Tonya had met him, she'd have thought he was exactly the kind of man Eva deserved.

The thought made her eyes burn and her chest tight.

"Yours?" he asked, and she knew he was looking at the tearstains, the underlined words, the pain.

"It was my mother's."

"What was she like?"

What *had* Tonya been like?

When Eva thought of her, all she saw were tears.

"Sad."

"Because she couldn't escape her marriage?"

"She could have left Ernie if she wanted to. She had a degree in elementary education. I found that out after she died. She had plenty of qualifications and the intelligence to make a life for herself and for me. She chose not to."

"Because she loved your father?" he asked.

"Yes, but Ernie didn't love her. He didn't have it in him to love anyone. If he had, maybe things would have turned out differently."

"Eva..." He touched her arm, and she felt a moment of yearning so deep that it shook her to the core.

She didn't want to need him.

Didn't want to need anyone, but being with Austin made her forget all the reasons why. "It's late, Austin. You'd better go."

He didn't argue. Just set the Bible back into place, smoothing a hand over the worn cover like a final benediction before he walked to the door.

"I'll call you as soon as I hear anything about Frist."

"Thanks." She put her hand on the door handle, but he

pulled it away, wove his fingers through hers so that their palms were pressed together.

"Just one more thing before I go."

"What?"

"This." His lips grazed hers, the touch so light and un-expected that she didn't feel it until it was over. Didn't ac-knowledge it until he was gone, the door between them, the thundering pulse of her blood sloshing in her ears.

She touched her lips, felt the warmth that lingered there.

A kiss that took nothing and gave everything, that's what he'd offered, and she'd taken it because she hadn't had the strength to turn away.

She sighed and turned off the light, grabbing her mother's Bible as she walked to Brady's room.

Chapter Seventeen

Spending five days housebound with an energetic seven-year-old was enough to drive any mother to the brink of insanity, Eva thought as she poured cereal into Brady's bowl and tried to explain why he still wasn't ready to go back to school.

At least it was Wednesday. Her first day back at work.

She was happy to be getting out of the house. Not so happy to be leaving Brady at home. Even if she was leaving him with a police officer.

"But, I *am* ready to go back to school, Momma. I caught up on all the work I missed and everything," Brady told her as he spooned up a bite of cereal.

"I know you feel ready, Brady, but you can't go back until the police find the man who took you. Until then, they want you to stay home where they can keep their eyes on you."

"But *you're* going to work. Why can't I go to school?"

"I *have* to work or we won't have money to pay the bills. You can miss a couple more days of school. You're smart enough to get caught up."

"But can't I come with you, Momma? We haven't gone anywhere in days and days."

"Not today, but as soon as Austin says it's safe, I'll take you to Arianna's for pancakes."

"Okay." He sighed and poked at the cereal. He'd slept restlessly the past few nights, still plagued by the nightmares he'd been having since the kidnapping. But his eyes weren't as deeply shadowed, his cheeks not as gaunt.

"Maybe after we have pancakes, we can go to the park. You can invite a few of your friends over and we'll all go together."

"That would be fun, I guess."

"You guess? You've been asking me to take you to the park for months." She'd been too busy working and going to school and doing all the things that she'd thought would make their lives better to bring him before. Now she realized how quickly everything she'd been working for could disappear, and she wanted to make sure that she spent time having fun with Brady while she could.

"I don't know if I want to go to the park."

"We can go somewhere else, then." She ruffled Brady's soft hair, knowing that he was as scared to go out as he was anxious to leave. She felt the same, torn between the need to get back to her life and her fear that something worse would happen to Brady once they ventured out again.

"You know what I really want to do, Momma?" He shoved the nearly full cereal bowl away.

"What?"

"I want to go for a walk with Austin and Justice. If we went for a walk with them, we'd be safe."

"That sounds nice."

Really nice.

So nice that she was tempted to call him up and ask him if he wanted to do it right at that very moment.

She pressed her fingers to her lips, sure she could still feel the heat of his kiss, realized what she was doing and let her hand fall away.

So silly to be pinning dreams on him.

Especially when he hadn't been back to visit since Don Frist had been fingered as the second kidnapper. He'd called, though. Quite a few times, just checking in and giving updates. Talking about work and asking her about school and about Brady.

Normal mundane conversations that had made her heart soar and her pulse sing.

"Will you call and ask if he'll come take me for a walk, Momma?"

"You know he's busy, Brady. He's trying to catch your kidnapper."

"Why is everyone busy but me?" he whined.

"You'll be busy soon enough. Your tutor is coming today, remember?"

"I don't want a stinky old tutor—"

"Brady Billows! That is an awful thing to say when the school has worked so hard to find someone to teach you at home."

"Sorry, Momma."

"Just make sure you don't call her stinky and old again," she chided, "Especially not when she's here. If you do, that puppy we've been talking about won't happen for a long time."

"I won't say it to her or anyone else. Promise."

"Good." She kissed his head, shoved his bowl back in front of him. "Eat."

"Mrs. Daphne always makes me waffles and eggs when I don't have school."

She sighed. "I'm not Mrs. Daphne."

"Is she coming over today?"

"No, but there *will* be someone else with you besides the tutor."

"Who? A police officer?"

"I think so."

"Will he have a gun?"

"I don't know, Brady. How about we just wait and see?"

"I hope that he *does* have a gun, but what I really want is for him to have a dog like Justice. Then I'll have someone to play with all day."

"That would be fun." Eva poured coffee into her mug, searched the refrigerator for cream that she knew wasn't there. No milk, either. She'd used the last on Brady's cereal.

"I could even take the dog outside—"

"No."

"Just in the backyard."

"Brady, I mean it. If you go outside, I'm going to have to take all your Legos away for at least a week."

"Okay. I won't go outside. But I *can* play with the dog, right? I can take it into my room?"

"We don't even know if there's going to be a dog, but if there is, and the officer says it's safe, you can play with it." Eva went into the bathroom to run a brush through her hair, scowling at the reflection in the mirror. She wasn't one to spend much time worrying about her appearance, but there were days when she'd love to get her hair done, maybe paint her nails, put on a little makeup. Today was one of them. Dark circles under her eyes, pallid complexion, she looked like a before ad for a cosmetic procedure.

She pulled her hair into a high ponytail. Comfy shoes for all-day walking, a slight hint of blush and gloss and she was ready. She just needed Brady's bodyguar—*babysitter* to arrive.

"Momma! Someone is ringing the doorbell!" Brady hollered, and she grabbed her purse, rushed to the door and opened it.

"Next time, you might want to ask who it is first," Austin said as he and Justice walked in. Dark windblown hair, his jaw stubbled by several days' growth, he looked good. Really good.

"I was just on my way out. I'm opening the diner this morning," she said.

"That's why I'm here."

"You're not…"

"What?" His smile said it all. *He was.*

"Austin, you said a police guard. You didn't say it was going to be you."

"I don't trust anyone else with Brady's life," he said, and her heart melted, every bit of her resistance melting with it.

"You're staying with me, Austin?" Brady said, and he sounded like he'd just won the lottery.

"I sure am. Want to go get those blocks you like to play with? I'm thinking we should build something giant today."

"Really? Mrs. Daphne never plays with me!" Brady ran to Eva and gave her a kiss goodbye before disappearing down the hall.

"You've made his day," Eva said, still not sure how she felt about it.

"And you've made mine. You look beautiful this morning." He tugged her close, gave her an easy hug that should have been friendly and felt like so much more.

"I'm a mess. Between a sleepless night and not much time to get ready, I—"

"You're beautiful. End of story."

"Austin—"

"Better get going, or you're going to be late. Based on what I saw when Arianna visited you at the hospital, I'd say that won't be a good thing."

Eva nodded, but she couldn't bring herself to walk out the door.

"You know I'm going to take good care of him, right?" Austin framed her face with his hands, smiled into her eyes, and every cell in her body strained toward him.

"I know."

"Then why are you hesitating?"

"He's my son. He's everything to me."

"I know, and I'll protect him with my life if I have to. Now go to work, before I do something that I won't regret but that you might." His gaze dropped to her lips.

Her cheeks heated, her pulse raced, and she seriously considered throwing herself right into his arms.

She left instead.

He closed the door, and she heard the bolt slide home.

Locked out of her house.

Well, not quite. She had the keys.

She could go back inside if she wanted to, but Austin was right. She had to get to work. Arianna expected her to be there to open the restaurant, and if she was late, there'd be trouble.

She didn't need that any more than she needed the mess she'd found herself.

Austin at her house, protecting her son while she went to work?

It smacked of domesticity, made her feel soft and vulnerable, but not nearly as scared as she thought she should be.

That was probably a bad thing.

She glanced at the house as she pulled out of the driveway, imagining Austin and Brady side by side on the floor, building a doghouse or a police car or a trap for the bad guys Brady kept dreaming about.

She wanted so badly to go back.

Not because she didn't trust Austin. Not even because she

was worried about how much of a fixture he was becoming in her life.

She wanted to go back so that she could watch them together, be part of the laughter and fun. Be…

What?

A family?

Such a strange thing to think, but she couldn't seem to stop herself. When Austin was around, she felt lighter, the weight of some of her responsibilities shifted to his broad and steady shoulders.

That should scare her.

It really should.

So why was she smiling?

Humming along with the radio?

Acting for all the world like a woman who was falling in love?

Love?

She didn't believe in it. Not the kind that lasted, anyway. Not for her.

But just like the happily-ever-after she'd given up believing in, if love were ever going to happen for her, it would happen with Austin.

She frowned, shoving the thought away.

Brady was happy and well protected when he was with Austin. She believed that, and for now, that was all that really mattered.

Chapter Eighteen

Babysitting was a piece of cake compared to chasing down clues and following up on leads. Austin scowled at his computer screen. Eight hours at Eva's place, and seven at the office, and he still had nothing to show for his day.

Unless he counted the block jail that he'd built with Brady. He took a sip of lukewarm coffee.

Five days after Brady's kidnapper had been identified, and Frist was still free. Too bad, because Austin would have loved to have personally locked the guy up and thrown away the key.

He tapped his pen against his desk, eyeing the evidence list and the case file. With a twenty-five-thousand-dollar reward on the line, it seemed like someone should have come forward with information by now, but the silence was deafening and the case seemed to be grinding to a slow halt. Even Keevers hadn't followed up on his promise of big information.

Justice whined from his place beneath the desk, and Austin patted the bloodhound's knotty head. "Sorry, boy, this is about as exciting as it's going to get tonight."

"Are you still here, Austin? It's a little late, isn't it?" Slade walked toward him, his steps brisk. Past midnight and they were both at the office. Obviously, neither of them were happy with the progress that was being made on the case.

"I spent most of the day at the Billowses, and I wanted to do a little work here before I went home. See if I could make heads or tails of the information we've gathered."

"And?" Slade pulled a chair over.

"Until we find Frist, we're at a standstill."

"At least he hasn't gone after Brady again."

"*Yet.* He's gone to ground, but that doesn't mean he's out of the picture for good."

"Any contact with Keevers?"

"He hasn't called. Parker said that he's been quiet on the street, too."

"Scared?" Slade asked, and Austin shrugged.

"Could be. Or maybe he's just hoping that if he holds out a little, we'll be desperate enough to go higher on the price."

"I cleared up to fifteen thousand. Any more than that, and we're going to have to pass." Slade snagged Frist's mug shot from Austin's desk. "Have we posted this on our website?"

"Yes."

"And at the post office?"

"Yes. He's been all over the news, too. So has the information about the reward Frears is offering. I'm surprised no one has stepped forward yet."

"You and me both. With that much money on the line, it seems like we should have dozens of rats crawling out of their nests to feed."

"You know why people get quiet, Austin?" the captain set the photo down again. "Fear. And if people around here are afraid, they must have a reason."

"The Boss?"

"That's what I'm thinking. I want to know who he is. I want to know what he's doing in our town. How long he's been here. What crimes he's responsible for."

"Who works for him?" Austin offered.

"That, too. Dante called me this afternoon."

"Yeah?"

"He wanted to check on Caleb, and he wanted to know if we've had anyone come forward with information." McNeal scrubbed a hand across his face. "I hated to tell him that we haven't."

"It could still happen, Slade. We're early in the game."

"We're nearly a week into the game, Austin. Rio has been missing that whole time. I'm afraid if we don't find him soon, we never will."

"We're going to find him. I won't give up until we do."

"I'm glad to hear that, but you know the statistics. A case not solved within the first forty-eight hours is less likely to ever be solved. The longer the case remains open, the less chance of it being resolved."

"That doesn't mean—" His cell phone rang, and he grabbed it, motioning for Slade to give him a second while he answered. A few minutes past midnight was an odd time for anyone to be calling, and his heart raced with the possibilities.

"Austin Black."

"Hey, Detective, long time, no talk." Pauly's smooth voice oozed through the receiver, and Austin smiled, mouthing the name to his captain.

"Maybe a little too long. I thought you were interested in some cash, but the offer might be off the table now," he responded.

"Now, wait just a minute, Detective. You take the offer off the table, and you may never find that missing dog."

"What are you talking about, Pauly?" Austin straightened in his chair, motioned for Slade to lean in close to the phone.

"I've heard some whispers about your captain's missing partner, and I thought that maybe you could sweeten the pot to get access to them."

"How sweet do you want it?"

"Just throw in a couple thousand more. Let's make it an even twelve, and I'll tell you everything I know."

"Twelve thousand is a lot of money, Pauly."

"What I know is worth every penny of it."

"We'll see."

"So, it's a deal?" Keevers pressed.

Slade nodded.

"It's a deal."

"Just so we're clear, if the information I give you leads to the mutt, I want the twenty-five-thousand-dollar reward."

"If it helps us find Rio, you'll get the twenty-five thousand, too."

"That's what I wanted to hear. You have that twelve for me?"

"I can have the cash tomorrow." He glanced at Slade who nodded again.

"Good. Meet me at the same place as last time at two in the morning. Don't bring anyone with you, and don't tell anyone but your boss that we're meeting. Not anyone, Black. Otherwise, I might have to leave town, and we'll both be left with nothing."

Keevers disconnected, his words ringing in Austin's ears. He'd sounded scared, and that wasn't like Pauly. As much as he played both sides of the fence, Keevers had never seemed overly concerned about getting caught. Now he was issuing warnings, trying to protect himself.

"That was...interesting," Slade said.

"He sounded nervous."

"I thought the same. Let's hope the information he's offering is as worth it as he's claiming."

"He's never failed us before."

"I know. And I've got to admit that this is getting my blood flowing. Hopefully, it will also breathe some new life into the case. I'll expect to hear from you as soon as your meeting is over."

"You know that you will," he promised.

"Good. Now, how about we both pack up and get out of here?" Slade retreated into his office, and Austin shoved the file into the cabinet, turned off his computer and stretched the kinks out of his back.

"Come on, Justice. Let's go home," he said.

Justice lumbered up from his spot beneath Austin's desk, stretching his long, sturdy body and shaking off the last vestiges of sleep, his jowls slapping back and forth with the force of the motion. Austin scratched the sensitive spot beneath his chin, grinning as the bloodhound nudged his hand for more.

"Sorry, boy. We've got to get going." He attached Justice's leash and led him out into the silent parking lot.

Sagebrush was quiet this time of night. Most reputable establishments closed; most people locked away in their homes. A small city with a rural vibe, it wasn't the kind of place where people partied until all hours of the night. Sure, there were dives and bars where those who wanted to could lose themselves until the sun came up, but those places were few and far between.

That was one of the things Austin loved about this town.

He crated Justice and started the SUV, pulling out onto the deserted road and driving toward home. He hadn't been there since morning when he'd left to go sit with Brady. He'd stayed at the Billows's place listening to Brady's home tutor go over addition with carrying and how to write a friendly letter until Eva arrived home at five. She'd been harried and tired, thanking him absently as he'd rushed out the door. They could have been an old married couple, moving in synch, plugged into each other's lives but somehow distant.

Could have been, except that they weren't married.

Weren't even a couple.

Not in the truest sense of the word.

There was something there, though, their relationship both exciting and fresh and easy and familiar. He'd never experienced that with a woman before, and the power of it had him thinking about Eva way more than he probably should be.

He pulled up in front of his house, the windows dark and uninviting. He should have remembered to leave a light or two on. Not because he feared the dark, but because it made coming home seem so much less lonely.

"Come on, boy. I think lack of sleep is starting to get to me." He let Justice out of the crate and walked to the front door. A box sat on the stoop. Cardboard. Maybe two by three feet and a half foot tall. He hadn't ordered anything, and the box didn't look sealed or sent. No address label. No tape. Nothing.

The hair on his nape stood on end, and he tugged Justice back as the bloodhound tried to nose the box. "Stay!"

The dog subsided, his nose lifted into the air, his body straining forward as if he were desperate to get to the box. Justice wasn't trained in explosive detection but he had a great nose, and whatever was in the box was exciting him.

"Stay!" Austin ordered again, then moved toward the box cautiously. He had no reason to believe he'd be the target of an attack, but better to be safe than dead.

A white envelope rested between the box and the door,

and Austin opened it carefully, letting a slip of paper fall into his hand.

Someone had scribbled across the front:

You were probably too busy to eat dinner. I thought I'd better feed you so you're not stuck with overcooked pasta again. E.

Surprised, he opened the box flaps and pulled out two large plastic containers. He wasn't sure what was in them, but whatever it was smelled good. His stomach rumbled, and Justice whined. Obviously, he was hungry, too.

"Come on. I think it's time for both of us to eat." He carried the box into the house and set it down on the table, fed Justice and let him out in the backyard.

He knew what he shouldn't do. Call Eva and thank her. Especially not at this time of night. He glanced at the clock. This time of *morning*.

He was tempted, though.

Too tempted.

His cell phone rang as he opened up the first container.

"Black, here," he said as he poured thick stew into a bowl and shoved it into the microwave.

"Did you get the food, or did the coyotes drag it away before you got home?"

His heart pounded at the sound of her voice. "I just got it and was thinking about calling you. I thought it might be too late."

"I thought the same thing, and then I started worrying that maybe something had happened to you, and that's why you hadn't…"

"Called to thank you for the food?"

"Yes, but I didn't mean for it to sound like I *expected* you to thank me. It's just… Okay. Maybe I did mean it to sound that way. What I mean is, you're always so polite, and I couldn't imagine that you'd… Never mind." She sighed, but there was a smile in her voice, and he imagined her pale cheeks flushed with embarrassment, her eyes glinting with humor.

"I'm glad you called, and you know it's never too late, right? I'd be happy to answer the phone any time of day if you were on the line."

"Keep sweet-talking me, Austin, and I might have to make pie the next time I bring you dinner."

"What kind?"

"Apple?"

"My favorite." He pulled the stew from the microwave, set it on the table, wishing he were at Eva's house, sitting in her tiny kitchen, looking in her eyes rather than talking to her on the phone. "The stew looks great. When did you bring it over?"

"I asked Mrs. Daphne to drop it off. Now, of course, she thinks we'll be married by fall." The phone clicked, the soft sound repeating twice.

"Is someone trying to call you?" he asked.

"Yes."

"I can let you go—"

"No!" she nearly shouted, and Austin frowned, his hand tightening on the phone.

"What's going on, Eva?"

"I don't know. Probably nothing. It's just, we've been getting phone calls all afternoon. Whoever it is hangs up as soon as anyone answers. It's silly, I know…but it's bothering me."

"Aside from the call you just received, when did you get the last one?"

"Just before I called you."

"And how many calls do you think you've gotten altogether?" he demanded.

"At least one every hour since I got home."

"And you're just now letting me know?" Austin dropped

his empty bowl into the sink and paced to the window. Bright moonlight poured onto the yard, painting it in shades of gold and gray. A beautiful winter landscape, but that didn't mean that danger wasn't lurking somewhere in it.

"It seemed like a silly thing to bother you about."

"How about from now on, you let me decide whether or not something is too silly to bother me with?"

"That would kind of defeat the whole purpose of me vetting things so that you can rest."

"I don't need rest, Eva. I need to make sure you and Brady are okay. I'll be there in ten minutes."

"You can't—"

He hung up.

No amount of arguing on her part was going to keep him from driving to her place. Hopefully, once he got there, they'd figure out that there was nothing more to the calls than a wrong number or a persistent solicitor. Somehow, though, he didn't think that was going to be the case.

Chapter Nineteen

She probably shouldn't have called Austin.

She *definitely* shouldn't have called him.

But Eva had been nearly asleep when the phone rang for what seemed like the hundredth time. She'd been drifting into a nightmare where Brady was missing again, and she'd grabbed the phone, confused, still riding the waves of fear. She'd pressed the receiver to her ear, heard nothing but the soft sound of empty air. There'd been something awful in that emptiness, as if the person were right outside the window, watching as she lay in bed.

The thought had been horrifying, and she'd found herself reaching for her cell phone and dialing Austin's number. She hadn't wanted him to come over. She'd just wanted to hear his voice, ask if he'd gotten the food that Mrs. Daphne had dropped off, pretend that her life was normal and easy and that Austin would always be a part of it.

"And so what if he isn't? You'll go on, and you'll be fine," she whispered as she drew back the living-room curtain and looked outside. Moonlight drenched the street in gold, but clouds moved across the horizon. Rain coming, and she could almost feel its energy in the air.

Or maybe that was her own energy.

Restless.

Anxious.

Scared.

The police car sat where it had been all day, the officer offering a quick wave as he caught sight of Eva. She could have flagged him down, had him come in and check things out.

She hadn't.

She knew what that said about her. Knew what it meant.

She couldn't make herself care, though.

Maybe she wouldn't have Austin in her life forever, but having him there now was wonderful.

Lights flashed behind the curtains, and she knew he'd arrived. She didn't wait for him to ring the doorbell or to knock, just opened the door and stepped out onto the porch, standing in the dark while he got out of his car. He ran up the porch stairs, and it felt as though he was coming home.

Her throat clogged, her eyes burned, and she let him pull her into his arms, let her head rest on his chest. Felt his heartbeat beneath her ear.

Felt as if she was exactly where she was supposed to be.

"I'm really sorry, Austin. I shouldn't have called," she said, looking up into his face.

"Of course you should have. Let's go inside and see if we can figure things out." He took her arm, his hand warm against her cool skin, his fingers sliding along her elbow and leaving a trail of fire in their wake. She took a deep breath, trying to clear her mind, but all she managed to do was fill it up with more of Austin. His darkly masculine scent, the clean crisp fragrance of soap and winter air.

He went to the phone, lifting it and scrolling through the last few calls. "An unlisted number, but we should be able to find out where it came from. Did you let the answering machine pick up at all?"

"Once I realized that someone was calling and hanging up, I let it pick up every time except the last." She sat on the couch, her muscles aching from a long work shift and too many hours hunched over schoolbooks.

"Mind if I listen?"

"Knock yourself out, but he didn't leave a message."

Austin pressed play, cocking his head to the side as he listened to empty air. Finally, the last message ended. "He's persistent. I'll give him that."

"Maybe it's a solicitor," she suggested.

"Calling so frequently? I don't think so."

"I'd say a bill collector, but the only debt I have is my house mortgage, and I always pay that on time."

"You're grasping at straws, hoping this isn't connected to Brady's kidnapping." It wasn't a question, but she answered, anyway.

"I'm not grasping. I'm just trying to find a reasonable explanation."

"The only reasonable explanation I can think of is that someone is trying to get under your skin. Maybe force you into making a move that will get you out from under police protection."

"Well, he's definitely managed to get under my skin, but I'm not going to do anything stupid because of it."

"Glad to hear it." He smiled, and the butterflies in her stomach took flight. Again. "I'm going to call this in. See if we can get a bead on where the phone call is coming from. Maybe our perp has finally made a mistake, and we'll be able to bring him in."

"I'll start some coffee. I don't know about you, but I could use some."

"Decaf?"

"If you want." She walked into the kitchen while he made his phone call, plugging in the coffeepot, but keeping the light off. She didn't want to wake Brady.

"We're set. Hopefully, we'll have the phone traced by first light." Austin walked into the room, his voice as quiet as his footsteps. Of course, he'd be thinking about Brady sleeping just down the hall. That's the way Austin was, always thinking about others, planning around them. It made him difficult to resist.

Maybe even impossible to resist.

Did she even *want* to resist him?

She turned away, focusing her attention on the coffee and the cup she was pouring it into. "Want some milk or cream? Mrs. Daphne ran to the store for me. We were running low on supplies."

"Black is fine." He took the mug and sat at the table, his long legs encased in dark denim, his feet in scuffed cowboy boots. Masculine. Strong. Sitting right there at her kitchen table, and Eva wanted to stand behind him, rub the tension from his shoulders, let her fingers slide through his dark hair.

"Cookies?" Her voice was husky, her hand shaking as she pulled a package from the cupboard.

"I think I'll wait and have more stew when I get home."

"You're still hungry?" she asked, telling herself that she wasn't going to offer to heat something up for him, that she'd already done her part by making double what she normally would for dinner and sending Mrs. Daphne to Austin's house with it.

"No, but the stew was so good, I want more."

"I have plenty in the freezer." She started to open the

door, ready to do exactly what she'd said she wouldn't, but he grabbed her hand, tugged her so that she was standing between his legs.

"I'm fine." His hands were on her waist, his eyes dark pools that she couldn't seem to look away from.

Didn't even want to try to look away from.

She touched his hair, her fingers trailing through the silky strands. "I like your hair."

"I like you." He stood, his hands sliding up her back and down again.

"Austin…"

"You look beautiful today. Have I told you that?"

"Yes," she whispered, because she had no breath in her lungs, no thoughts in her head.

"Good, because I think that if I live to be a hundred, I'll never forget how you look right now."

"In a flannel robe with my hair scraped back in a braid? I *want* you to forget it."

"It's not going to happen. You know why?"

"No, but I think you're going to tell me."

He laughed, but his eyes were somber. "You're the only woman I've ever known who hasn't cared that the only time we can get together is late at night or early in the morning, the only woman who hasn't needed full makeup and nice clothes to feel confident. That makes you exceptionally beautiful to me."

Just centimeters separated them, and she put her hands on his chest, not sure if she wanted to push him away or pull him closer.

"You terrify me, Austin, because when you say things like that, all I can think about is just how long I've been waiting to meet someone like you."

"Good," he murmured, his lips grazing the tender flesh behind her ear.

She melted against him, her hands sinking into his hair as their lips met. Every thought, every fear, every caution flying away. She felt raw and open, vulnerable and tender.

A tear slipped down her cheek. Just one tear, and she couldn't stop the rest from falling. They spilled down her face, soaking into Austin's shirt, her body stiff and aching from the effort to stop them.

"Shhh," he whispered.

"I'm sorry."

"Don't be."

"I *am*. I've ruined a perfectly good moment." She sniffed, stepping away from his arms, lifting her coffee cup and trying to sip the warm brew.

"*Perfectly good?* I was thinking it was a little better than that."

His comment surprised a laugh out of her, and she brushed the last of the tears away. "Don't be so wonderful, okay, Austin? It will only hurt more if you walk away."

"I think I told you that I don't plan to do that."

"Does anyone ever plan to?" She sighed.

"What are you really afraid of, Eva? Because I don't think it's me."

"Rick—"

"Don't." He raised a hand, cutting off the words before she could speak them. "I'm not him. I already told you that. If you still can't accept it, maybe it's best if I walk away now."

She should let him go.

It would be easier on both of them.

A quick break now, before they fell any further.

He took a step, and she touched his shoulder, let her hand fall away as he glared into her face. "What?"

"You want to know the truth? I'm terrified that I'll turn

out like my mother, sitting in a rocking chair, crying for a guy who never loved her. I'm afraid that I'll waste my life on someone who wouldn't waste a second on me. I'm afraid that all the things I want are going to tie me to something that isn't good for me, and I'll wind up dead in a pool of my own blood, Brady crying over my body."

"That's a lot of fear for someone who says she has faith." He raked a hand through his hair, took a sip of coffee.

"I do have faith. In God. Not in myself."

"Maybe you need to have it in both. And in me. I'd better go. It's late, and we both have busy days tomorrow." He walked out of the kitchen, left her standing there, the taste of his lips still on hers, the heat of his touch still pulsing wildly through her blood, the sound of his words echoing in the empty place in her heart.

Chapter Twenty

Tall trees loomed black against the night sky, the Lost Woods beckoning as Austin parked his SUV near the west entrance and jumped out. Keevers stood next to a small Jeep, his shoulders tense.

"You're late," he said as Austin approached.

"Getting the kind of money you asked for takes time."

"But you do have it?"

Pauly Keevers wasted no time getting to the point of the clandestine meeting. His eyes gleamed in the darkness, his face taut and tense with nerves or excitement. Austin couldn't decide which the snitch was feeling. He wasn't sure it even mattered. One way or another, he planned to get what he'd come for.

"Only if you have the information we agreed to exchange it for."

"Let me see the cash. *Then* we'll talk."

"You don't hold all the cards here, Pauly, and we're going to do things my way," Austin responded.

"Hey, I'm willing to play it your way. I just want to make sure this is worth my time."

"It is." Austin flipped open the narrow briefcase he and Slade had filled with cash just an hour ago. Twelve thousand dollars was a lot of money to pay for information that might lead nowhere, but it wasn't much at all if it led to Don Frist or Rio.

"Wow-wee, Detective. That sure is a pretty pile of cash. I'm glad you came prepared to deal." Pauly whistled under his breath.

The Lost Woods rustled behind him, dozens of animal eyes staring out from the shadowy underbellies of the trees. Pauly didn't seem to notice. He was too busy eyeing the money in the case. Probably trying to count it.

"I wouldn't be here if I wasn't. Now, how about you give me the information, so that we can make our exchange, and we can both be on our way?" Austin snapped the briefcase closed, and Pauly flinched.

"Okay, but remember, you didn't hear this from me. As a matter of fact, you never even spoke to me."

"Isn't that the way it always works?"

"Yeah, but this time it has to work even better. I don't want anyone knowing. Not cops. Not friends. No one."

"No problem."

"Okay, then. Here's the deal. There's a crime syndicate working under the radar in Sagebrush. Been there for years, pulling jobs like that big bank heist a few years back. You remember the one? A hundred thousand dollars stolen?"

"I remember." Austin hadn't worked the case, but he'd known about it. A teller had been murdered during the robbery, and the local news had run the story for weeks.

"I don't know much about the syndicate, but the guy who

runs it is called The Boss. Rinehart worked for him. So does Frist."

"You know an awful lot about an organization you're not involved in," Austin said as he ran through the details in his mind. So far, everything Keevers said coincided with what they knew.

"I know what I hear, and I've been hearing things for years. I hear about a drug deal and The Boss is mentioned. Bank robberies are mentioned, and The Boss's name is whispered. The guy has been throwing money around and using it to grab more money."

"Be more specific, Pauly. I can't go anywhere with hints and vague references."

"You got a pen?" Pauly didn't wait for Austin to pull out his notebook. He started listing several major crimes that had never been solved. Bank heists, murders, pharmaceutical thefts.

"Are you sure this is all related to The Boss?"

"As sure as I am that you're standing in front of me with a boatload of cash."

"If he's got so much money to throw around, why aren't you working for him?" Austin eyed Pauly, wondering if the information was something fabricated to throw Sagebrush P.D. off Frist's tail.

"No way would I get involved in a scheme with a guy like The Boss. Not even if he paid me a hundred times what you've got in that case."

"I thought you'd do anything for cash."

"Not deal with a guy like him. He has a reputation for making sure people don't talk. The way I hear things, he'd kill his own mother if she got in the way of something he wanted."

"I'm guessing you know a few people who got in his way," Austin prodded.

"Ernie Billows for one," Pauly confirmed with a nod. "Look what happened to him and that pretty wife of his."

"You're saying The Boss killed them?"

"*Had* them killed. I don't think The Boss likes to get his hands dirty."

"Why kill Ernie?"

"Guy was threatening to go to the police with some syndicate names if he didn't get paid more for a job he'd done. The Boss made sure that he didn't get the chance."

"Any idea who the hit man was?"

"I have an idea, but it'll cost you more."

"Then how about you just tell me about Rio. Where is he?"

"That, I can't tell you. I do know this. The Boss hired Frist and Rinehart to take the captain's dog. I heard that straight from the horse's mouth."

"Which horse?"

"Rinehart. A couple hours after the dog was taken, I was behind Arianna's Café finishing up a deal. You know the place?"

"Yeah." Austin didn't ask what kind of deal it was. Knowing Pauly it could have been anything from exchanging information to exchanging drugs for money.

"So, I'm back there and I hear someone coming. Thought it might be one of your guys, so I hid behind the Dumpster. That's when I realize it's Rinehart and Frist. Both are steaming mad and arguing over finishing some job they've been paid to do. Frist says he wants nothing to do with it. He's done. Rinehart says that he'd better not cross The Boss or he'll wake up on the wrong side of eternity. Frist says that he got the dog, and that's all he was paid to do."

"And?"

"That's it. I didn't hear anything else, and I didn't put two and two together until I heard the story about the missing dog and the missing kid. That's when I figured that they must have been talking about nabbing Rio and finishing off the job by getting rid of the boy."

"You should have been a police detective, Pauly."

"Funny. Now, how about my money?"

"Not yet. Why does The Boss want Rio?"

"I hear that he lost something really valuable out here in the wilderness, and the captain's dog is the only one who can find it. Now, how about that cash?"

"One more thing before I hand it over to you, Pauly… Where's Frist?"

"That I can't help you with. He's still in town. I know that, but he's lying low. Don't know if he's more afraid of The Boss or the police. Probably The Boss. If I were him, I would be." He shuffled his feet impatiently. "Now, the money, Detective? We did have a deal, after all."

Austin knew Pauly well enough to know they were finished. He wouldn't get any more information out of the snitch, and that suited Austin just fine. Slade and the rest of the K-9 Unit were back at the station waiting for Austin to return with the information, and he was anxious to bat the stuff around a little. See what they could make of it.

"It's yours." He thrust the briefcase into Pauly's waiting hands.

"And there may be more if you get Rio back, right? You find the dog because of something I told you, I get the 25K reward. That's what you said on the phone, and I'm holding you to it."

"See you, Pauly."

"Now, wait a minute, Detective," Pauly sputtered.

Austin ignored him.

He had bigger fish to fry.

He climbed into his SUV, mulling over Pauly's words.

A crime syndicate made sense and meshed with what the K-9 Unit had already begun to suspect. Like every other city, there'd been crime in Sagebrush over the years. No one had ever connected any of it to an organized effort, though.

But there *was* something bigger going on.

The bank heists alone had netted someone close to a million dollars.

Austin wanted to know who that someone was, and he wanted to see him taken down.

He *would* see him taken down.

Now that they knew what they were dealing with, the Special Operations K-9 Unit would respond the way they always had. They'd come together, work toward the common goal, and eventually, they'd put The Boss behind bars where he belonged.

The first step to doing that was finding Frist.

They had to track him down and keep Brady safe while they were doing it. From the sound of things, The Boss wasn't eager for them to succeed. He'd sent Frist and Rinehart to silence Brady, and that hadn't worked.

Would he come after Brady himself if Frist were taken into custody?

Based on everything Austin knew, he didn't think so. The kingpin of a crime syndicate didn't get where he was by being stupid. Brady was the sole witness to Rio's theft. The only people at the scene had been Rinehart and Frist. Once both men were out of the picture, there would be no need to dispose of the boy, because he wasn't an inherent threat to The Boss.

He was still a threat to Frist, though.

The guy must be in panic mode, trying to find the quickest way out of the trouble he was in.

Austin frowned, glancing at the clock on the dashboard. It

was late. Just past two, but he knew Eva would be up study-ing. He shouldn't call.

But knew he would, anyway.

He waited until he reached the police station, then dialed her number.

She picked up on the first ring.

"Hello?" she said, her voice breathless.

"Did I wake you?"

"No. I was studying."

"I thought you would be," he said softly.

"Just like I thought you'd be the only one who'd call my cell phone at this time of the night."

"You mean aside from your crank caller?"

"I haven't gotten one call from him since yesterday."

"That doesn't surprise me. We were able to track the cell signal to a prepaid phone that someone threw in a trash can downtown."

"Any fingerprints on it?" she asked eagerly.

"You're getting pretty good at this detective stuff, Eva."

"Hardly." She laughed, but he could hear the tension in her voice. "What are you really calling about, Austin?"

"I'm worried about you and Brady."

"Haven't you always been?"

"Yes, but things feel different tonight."

She released a sharp breath. "Because you met with the snitch?"

"Yes."

"I guess you're not going to tell me anything that he said?"

"I can't. Just be careful, okay? Stay inside. Don't make your-self or Brady an easy target."

"I'm going to take that to mean that you're no closer to finding Frist?"

"We're not, but he's not the only one I'm worried about,"

Austin admitted. "There may be something bigger going on than we first thought, and there may be some very dangerous people who are willing to play for keeps."

"You mean Rinehart and Frist aren't?"

"I mean they weren't the ones calling the shots."

"Be careful, then, Austin. I'd hate for anything to happen to you."

"The feeling is mutual."

"And keep me posted about Frist, okay? Brady is going stir-crazy being locked up inside all the time."

"What about you? Are you going stir-crazy, too?"

"With my crazy schedule? Hardly."

"Too bad," he murmured.

"Why do you say that?"

"I was going to offer to come over after my meeting and take you for a walk in your backyard."

She snickered softly. "That sounds...dangerous."

"You and me and a moonlit night? It definitely would be."

"What moon? It's about to rain." She laughed, the sound husky and warm. He felt it to his core, imagined her hair sliding through his fingers, the feel of her lips against his.

Soft.

That's how she'd felt in his arms, and he wanted more of it. More of her.

"If it rains, we'll just sit inside and have some coffee. I can even help you study."

"That sounds even more dangerous."

"Then maybe we'd better wait until the sun comes up," Austin suggested, and Eva wasn't sure if she was more relieved or disappointed.

"Tomorrow, then? I have the day off." And Brady would be awake and a welcome distraction. Definitely a good thing when it came to being around Austin.

"Sure. I'll be there around ten. See you then."

She smiled as she hung up, because that's what Austin did to her. Made her comfortable and happy in a way she hadn't been in a very long time.

She shoved her cell phone into the pocket of her jeans, grabbed the book that she'd been studying and turned off the living-room light. Talking to Austin had been the perfect end to her day, and she was ready for some sleep.

She changed into pajamas and walked into Brady's room, standing over his bed and touching his soft hair as she prayed for him. From the day he was born, all she'd wanted was to give him the life he deserved. It's what she'd been working toward for years. She'd wanted her love for her son to be her focus, wanted him to always feel secure and safe in her heart. She'd worried that bringing a man into her life would change what she'd worked so hard to build.

Truth was, Austin *had* changed things.

He'd made them better, his presence opening the world up for Brady, giving him a taste of what it meant to have an honorable man in his life.

But what if it didn't work out?

What if the things she and Austin felt were fleeting rather than permanent?

Could she risk Brady's heart?

Did she even have a choice anymore?

Brady loved Austin and Justice. Eva saw that every time the two showed up to babysit and every time they left. No matter what happened between her and Austin, that bond had to be maintained.

She sighed, touching Brady's hair one last time before leaving the room.

Maybe this was what faith meant—plunging headfirst into

the water without knowing how deep it was, trusting that no matter what, things were going to be okay.

Letting go of the past to grab on to an unknown future.

She'd always thought that she couldn't do any of those things because of Brady. Now she thought that she *must* do those things *because* of him.

She went to the living-room window, pulled back the curtains and stared out into the night, her thoughts spinning so fast that she knew she'd never fall asleep.

Since her parents' murders, she'd had her life planned out. She'd made sure that everything went according to that plan. No veering from the course she'd set. No getting distracted or taking the chance that she'd make a mistake. She'd been sure that was the way God wanted it, had convinced herself of that.

Maybe she'd been wrong.

Maybe all this time, all this fighting to make things be the way she'd thought they should be had gotten in the way of allowing God to make things into what they were meant to be.

Her chest burned with the thought, her mind going back to the kiss she and Austin had shared mere hours ago. The heat of it had lingered long after he'd gone, but it had been the comfort he'd offered when she'd cried that Eva would never forget. The sweetness of his words, the gentleness of his hands, the comfort of his arms. She'd wanted to stay there forever. Such a foolish longing, but it hadn't felt foolish. It had felt like finally coming home.

Rain began to fall, splashing against the window and roof, sliding into puddles on the ground. She really needed to go to bed. She really did, but she stood for a moment longer, staring out into the night, imagining a future with Austin in it.

Something shifted in the darkness, a shadow moving along the sidewalk, heading toward the police cruiser parked beneath the streetlight.

A dog?

No. A child. Very small. Maybe three or four. Out in the rain. Alone. Shocked, Eva ran to the door, turned off the alarm, was almost down the porch steps when the patrol officer got out of his car.

"Go on back inside," he called. "I'll check things—" He crumbled to the ground, his body a heap of dark cloth and pale skin.

She ran toward him, heard a soft pop, fell back, breath gone. Thoughts gone.

Get up. Get in the house. Get to Brady.

She struggled to her feet, stumbled up the porch stairs. Footsteps pounding behind her. On pavement. On grass.

Go!

She fell into the house, red streaking the white door as she fumbled with the lock. Blood pounding in her ears, sliding down her arm. Head swimming as the lock finally found its home.

Something slammed into the door, the impact reverberating through the wood. Through Eva. She scrambled back, blood dripping onto hardwood, staining the receiver as she lifted the phone and dialed 911.

Chapter Twenty-One

Please, God, let me get there in time. The prayer screamed through Austin's mind, matching the screeching frenzy of sirens as he raced down Oak Street. He had to make it in time. There was no other option. No other acceptable outcome.

Please, God.

He pulled the SUV into Eva's driveway, his blood running cold as he jumped from the vehicle, saw the door hanging open. No alarm. Eva must have turned it off at some point.

Please.

"Austin! Hold up!" Slade shouted, but he didn't wait. Couldn't. Not with Brady and Eva's lives hanging in the balance.

He entered the house silently, easing in through the open door. Darkness. Silence. No sign of a struggle. Nothing but wet footprints tracking across hardwood. Drops of blood on Eva's throw rug. His pulse raced, but he moved slowly, following the sound of rain and wind into the kitchen and the open back door. Something lay in the threshold. Brady's little stuffed dog. Austin left it and walked into the yard. More darkness, rain splattering onto the wet grass, the sound hushed and expectant.

Someone called out, the cry cut off abruptly.

Austin pivoted, running in the direction of the sound. Around the side of the house, skidding to a stop as he caught sight of dark shadows writhing on the ground.

"Freeze!" he shouted, but he didn't pull his firearm. Couldn't risk a shot when he didn't know where one person began and the other ended.

"Austin!" Brady called, and every muscle in Austin's body tensed, every nerve jumping as he turned, saw the little boy running toward him, bare feet splashing in puddles, pajamas clinging to his skinny frame.

"No. Brady, don't!" Eva tried to yell, but the words barely escaped. She clawed at the hands squeezing her throat, stealing her breath. There. Then gone. The scent of alcohol and rage lingering as her attacker pulled out a gun, aimed.

"No!" The words tore from her throat, cold rain falling onto slick grass, sliding down her frozen cheeks. She tried to grab the man's legs, pull him off balance, but her body refused her brain's commands.

A sharp quick report sliced through the darkness, and something warm and heavy landed on her chest and stomach. She wanted to scream, but she had nothing left. Wanted to shove the weight away, but she could only slide deeper into darkness.

"Eva!" Austin's voice carried through the blackness, faint, but so insistent, she couldn't ignore it.

"I'm okay," she mumbled, forcing her eyes open, looking into his face. How had she not realized who he was the first time that she'd seen him? How had she not looked into his face then, and known that she was seeing forever?

She blinked, clearing her eyes and still seeing what he was.

What he could be. If she allowed it. She wanted to tell him that, reached out to touch his cheek, but the words didn't come and her hand seemed glued to the muddy ground.

"Brady?" she managed as he lifted her hand, squeezed gently.

"He's safe."

"Where...?"

"With another officer." Austin looked over his shoulder, said something to whoever was behind him. Slade maybe, but Eva couldn't see the details through the thick mist of pain.

"That man... Don Frist—"

"Alive, but he's going to wish he weren't."

"Did—"

"No more talking, Eva." He touched her lips, his fingers as cold as the pouring rain, but somehow warm, too.

"Ma'am?" An EMT shoved in next to Austin and leaned over Eva, his fingers probing her wrist.

"I'm okay," she said, because it had to be true for Brady's sake.

"You will be." He pressed something to her shoulder and waves of pain rolled over her, chasing away every thought. Darkness again, and then she was moving, floating across golden fields and green grass, blue sky above. No. Lights above. Bright and yellow, Austin's face so close she could feel his breath on her cheek, see flecks of silver in his eyes.

"Hang on, Eva. Brady needs you. *I* need you," he growled, the fear in his voice matching the cold erratic thud of her heart.

I need you, too, she wanted to say, but he was gone before she could, the ambulance sirens screaming as she slipped away again.

Hours later. Days? Eva didn't know, just heard the quiet beep of a machine, smelled the faint metallic scent of dried blood and antiseptic. She tried to sit up, but pain shot through her shoulder and down her arm, blinding her and stealing her breath.

"Brady," she whispered, because he was her first thought.

"He's fine. One of our K-9 officers is with him in the waiting room." Austin stepped into view, his hair damp, his jaw dark with stubble. He had been her second thought, but not by much.

"How are you feeling?" He brushed hair from her cheek, his palm resting there.

Like she'd been run over by a truck, but she couldn't get the words out. Just covered his hand with hers, pressing his palm more firmly to her cheek. She held on tight. Afraid that if she didn't, she'd float away again.

"That good, huh?" he asked.

"I need to see Brady."

"They won't let him in the ICU."

"I need to see him, anyway, and he needs to see me. He needs to know that I'm okay. Then I need to find someone to take care of him while I'm at the hospital. I need—"

"You were shot and the bullet came within an inch of your heart. What you need is to rest and recuperate. I'll take care of everything else."

"I think you're too good to be true, Austin," she whispered, and he smiled, his eyes soft.

"I'm sure you won't be saying that in another year or two or ten."

"Will you still be around in ten years?"

"Do you want me to be?" His hand slipped from her cheek, skimmed her shoulder, wrist and palm. Pressed close to hers, their fingers linked as if it had always been that way. The two of them facing the world together, a combined force working to protect Brady and provide the best for him.

Could it really be that easy?

Or would it all fall apart as quickly as it had happened?
She couldn't know, but she had to try.

"I want you around for as long as you want to be here."

"Good, because I'm thinking forever sounds like the right amount of time." His lips brushed hers, light and gentle as a butterfly's wings, and her eyes burned with a hundred dead dreams and a million new ones.

A tear slipped down her cheek, and Austin brushed it away. "Don't cry, Eva. Everything is going to be okay."

"I know," she said, but everything she'd ever wanted was right there beside her, and he was so steady and wonderful and sure that the tears just kept coming.

Austin brushed more tears from her cheeks, looked deep into her eyes. "I'll be right back."

She wanted to tell him not to go, but he was gone before she could. Out the door and away, the soft beep of the machine and the quiet hiccup of her breath the only sounds in the room.

Minutes later he was back, Brady in his arms, a nurse running behind him. "Detective, you can't bring him in there—"

"He's her son, and she wants to see him." Austin walked across the room, set Brady down beside the bed. "You'll be careful, right, sport? Your mom is delicate, and we don't want to hurt her."

"I'm not delica—"

"I'll be careful. Hi, Momma. Are you really okay?" Brady's chin quivered, and she knew he was trying hard not to cry. She wanted to pull him onto the bed, hug him close, but pain shot through her chest as she reached for him. She touched his face instead, looked into his blue eyes. She'd almost lost him, but he was there, whole and healthy and safe.

"I am now that I know you are."

"I was so scared, Momma. I thought the bad man was

going to kill you." Brady started crying in earnest, and Austin lifted him, patting his back and murmuring something she couldn't hear. Eva watched them together, her eyes growing heavy, the nurse's protests fading. She'd been on her own for so long. There'd been no one else that she trusted as much as she trusted herself to care for Brady. She hadn't thought there would ever be anyone that cared about her son as much as she did. She'd been wrong. Austin could. Did. Would.

The mattress dipped as someone sat on the edge of the bed, and she opened her eyes, looked into Austin's handsome face. Brady lay against his shoulder, eyes closed and body limp as if he'd given everything he had to those last tears and was ready to sleep for hours.

"He needs to be in bed," she said.

"He needs to be with you more."

"The nurse—"

"Agreed that this was best for both of you."

"He's going to get heavy."

"He could never be that." Austin took her hand, squeezing gently. "So how about you do what your son is doing and get some rest? We'll both be here when you wake up."

"I'm glad," she responded, linking her fingers with his again, letting the warmth of his touch, the sweetness of his smile carry her into sleep.

Epilogue

Ten days later

"Are they going to be here soon, Momma?"

"*He*. Not they. You know that Austin can't bring Justice into the hospital," Eva responded as she dropped a pile of get-well cards into the flower-print overnight bag that Mrs. Daphne had lent her.

"Let me do that, dear. You're still looking peaked, and I wouldn't want you to wear yourself out before you even get home." Mrs. Daphne took the bag from Eva's hands, her blue-white curls bouncing as she scooped up an oversize flower arrangement and tottered across the room. She placed both on a cart the nurse had wheeled in, setting them next to several other flower arrangements.

"It looks like you have everything," she said. Mrs. Daphne had brought Brady to visit after school and had decided to stay when she'd heard that Eva could finally go home. A good thing, as something as easy as packing an overnight bag seemed too much for Eva's convalescing.

She eased into a chair, wincing as the muscles in her shoulder and chest protested.

"Are you okay, Momma?" Brady hovered next to her, and she tried to smile. He'd been through a lot, and it had taken its toll. Nightmares, anxiety, fear. The counselor had assured Eva that those things would get better in time.

"I'm fine, sweetie. I'll just be happy to get home."

"When did your young man say he would be here?" Mrs. Daphne asked, patting an errant curl into place.

"Around two."

"Well, then, he *will* be here at any moment. While we're waiting, though, I thought I'd get Brady some juice from the cafeteria. He didn't have his snack after school, you know."

"That's fine."

"I'd rather stay with you, Momma," Brady touched her hand, but he didn't cling to it like he had in the first days after she'd been shot.

"If you want to stay, you can. But I'm feeling a little thirsty, too, and I was thinking that if you went, you could get me some juice."

"You're *really* thirsty?"

"I'd *really* like some juice." Because the counselor had said the best way to help Brady was to offer him opportunities to prove to himself that he was safe, that Eva was safe, that everything was the way it had once been.

"Okay. Orange or apple?"

"Orange, of course." She watched as Brady skipped from the room with Mrs. Daphne, then leaned her head back against the wall. Exhausted.

"I think I'm going to have to stick a little closer to your

side." Austin's voice cut through the haze of the half sleep Eva had fallen into, and she opened her eyes, smiled.

"Why's that?"

"I leave for a few hours and you wear yourself out." He kissed her gently, the warmth of his lips filled with promise.

"I'm okay. Just resting for the ride home. Brady is a little chatterbox today."

"He's excited that you're finally coming home. Where is the little guy?"

"He went to get juice with Mrs. Daphne. Why?"

"We've had some new developments in the case. I wanted to fill you in while he wasn't around."

"What developments?" She straightened, her heart beating a little faster as she looked into his midnight-blue eyes, saw the concern there.

"Frist is talking."

"That's good, right?"

"Yes, but some of the things he's saying concern you."

"He killed my parents, didn't he?" She'd been hoping for a confession or at least some kind of proof that Frist was responsible. With the future stretching out in front of her, she wanted to close the door completely on the past. Finding her parents' murderer was part of that.

"No, but he says he knows who did. He gave us a name. Charles Ritter."

"I've never heard of him."

"He's a lawyer. A successful one. According to Frist, he is also affiliated with The Boss. Frist says he's middle management. One of three people who may know who The Boss is. According to Frist, Ritter was asked to kill your father as a test of loyalty. Your mother just happened to be—"

"At the wrong place at the wrong time?"

"That's what Frist says. Ritter isn't talking at all. He's lawyered up, but his prints matched some found at your parents' place, and he had a handgun in a safety deposit box. It's the same caliber as the murder weapon."

"So, it's finally over?"

"It is." He brushed strands of hair from her cheek, his fingers gentle and light.

"What about Rio? Has Frist told you where he is?"

"He says he doesn't know. He left him in a crate in an alley downtown. That's the last he saw of him."

"Do you believe him?"

"I don't know. The way I see it, a guy who was desperate enough to use his niece to bait a police officer wouldn't hesitate to tell a few lies to save his own skin."

"Is the little girl finally back with her parents?" Eva could still see the child walking down the sidewalk, tiny and alone, the image etched so deeply in her mind that she didn't think she would ever forget it.

"Not yet. CPS is investigating. Frist's brother knew that Frist was wanted by the police and still let him take his daughter for the night. That's something Child Protective Services is taking seriously."

"Do you think she'll ever be returned to her family?"

"I'm not sure, but I do know one thing."

"What's that?"

"I love you, and I'm glad Frist didn't take you from me."

"I love you, too," she whispered.

"You're not kissing again, are you?" Brady asked as he and Mrs. Daphne walked back into the room.

"I wish," Austin laughed. "You ready to take your mom home, sport?"

"Yep!"

"Then we'd better give her this." He took a small jeweler's box from his coat pocket, and Eva's heart jumped.

She met his eyes. Saw everything she felt reflected there.

Hope.

Love.

Joy.

"I know what this is!" Brady shouted as he took the box from Austin's hands. His cheeks were flushed, his eyes wide with joy.

"My goodness! What in the world?" Mrs. Daphne edged in close.

"It's the ring Austin bought, Momma. He showed it to me last week, and I've been keeping the secret all this time. And it was really hard." Brady opened the box, took out a beautiful diamond solitaire and handed it to Austin.

"Austin..."

Austin pressed a finger to her lips, cutting off her words. "Let us finish. We worked really hard on the presentation. Ready, sport?"

"Yes."

"Okay. Let's do this thing." Austin took Brady's little hand in his big one, both of them dropping to one knee.

"You are my heart, Eva, and I want to spend the rest of my life with you. Will you marry me?"

"And adopt Justice? Because he wants to be part of the family, too," Brady added, and Eva laughed, joy spilling out in tears that slid down her cheeks. She didn't bother wiping them away as she reached for Austin, allowed him to help her to her feet. She looked into his eyes, felt the truth of his love and said the only thing she could.

"Yes!"

★ ★ ★ ★ ★

DETECTION MISSION

Margaret Daley

To Shirlee McCoy, Sharon Dunn, Valerie Hansen,
Terri Reed and Lenora Worth

The Lord also will be a refuge for the oppressed,
a refuge in times of trouble.
—*Psalm 9:9*

Chapter One

Who am I?

She bent over the bathroom sink in her hospital room, cupped her hands and splashed some cold water on her face. As though that would suddenly make her remember who she was. She studied herself in the mirror and didn't recognize the person looking back at her. That revelation only intensified the panic she'd been struggling with ever since she woke up from a coma yesterday. Her fingers clenched the countertop.

Earlier, the nurse had brought her a few toiletries since she didn't have any. After brushing her hair and putting it into a ponytail, she stared at the red gash, recently healed, above her eyebrow. She closed her eyes and tried to recall how it had happened. The screech of tires echoed through her mind. The sensation of gripping a steering wheel made her hands ache. She looked down at them, her knuckles white.

A car wreck?

A sound coming from the other room invaded the quiet. The sudden intrusion kicked up her heartbeat. She moved toward the door, putting her hand around the knob. But when two deep male voices drifted to her, she stopped and pressed her ear against the wood to listen.

"Where is she?"

"Who?"

"The patient who belongs in this room."

"I don't know. I'm here to clean her room. She wasn't in here when I arrived."

The sound of the two men talking about her sent her pulse racing even more. Why? It seemed innocent enough. But she couldn't calm the pounding against her chest. Her breathing shortened. One of the voices was familiar. But how could that be? The only interactions she'd had since she'd regained consciousness were with women. She eased the door open an inch and had a pencil-narrow view into the room.

"I can come back another time. You'll have to ask the nurse where the patient is." The guy who was there to clean her room shifted back and forth while holding a plastic bag in one hand and a dry mop in the other.

The other man, just out of sight to the left, said, "I will." That was the voice she'd heard somewhere before this. She wished she could see him.

Instead, she examined the features of the custodian with a beard and dark-slashing eyebrows over a piercing gray gaze. Although he was a complete stranger there was something about his frosty eyes that scared her. She eased the door shut and leaned against it.

Fear from somewhere deep inside her swelled to the surface. She couldn't get a decent breath. She tried to search her mind for any clue to who she was, to the man with the familiar-sounding voice. A voice with a rough edge to it.

But what bothered her the most were the custodian's gray eyes. Why? Did she know him? Someone from her past? Then why couldn't she muster the strength to go out there and demand to know who she was?

Of course that conundrum led to lots of other baffling questions.

Like…how did she end up in the hospital?

And were the police interested in her? The nurse last night had told her they would be glad she had awakened, that they needed to talk to her. Why? She knew nothing. At all. Her mind was a blank.

A suffocating pressure in her chest made it difficult to breathe. A sense of danger pressed in on her. According to Nurse Gail, the police had found her in the Lost Woods several weeks ago. She'd been hurt and disoriented. After she was brought here to the hospital she'd slipped into a coma from a head injury. No one knew how she'd received that wound.

But why hadn't anyone reported her missing? Come forward to identify her?

Tears flooded her eyes. She squeezed them shut, refusing to give in to crying. From somewhere she sensed she'd given up doing that a long time ago.

A knock at the bathroom door caught her by surprise. She gasped, then went still, hoping the person went away.

"Are you all right in there?"

She stiffened at the sound of that familiar voice. Words jammed her throat.

"Ma'am? Are you okay? Should I call the nurse?"

"Who are you?" she finally managed to ask, her voice wobbly.

"I'm Lee Calloway with the K-9 Unit of the Sagebrush Police Department." Something in his tone conveyed a concern, urging her to leave the relative safety of the bathroom. Was he the cop who found her? Was that why he sounded familiar to her?

Laying her trembling hand on the knob, she turned it and opened the door a few inches. "Sagebrush? Where is that?" The large muscular man, resplendent in a dark navy blue police uniform, stepped back. The sight of his badge riveted her attention. Sweat coated her forehead.

"In Texas, southwest of San Antonio."

Texas? Did she live here? Maybe someone knew her, had come forward to identify her after all. "Who am I?"

The corner of his mouth hiked into a lopsided grin. "That, ma'am, is one of the questions I'm here to ask you."

"One?" Again she stared at the badge for a long moment before she lifted her gaze to take in his face. For a few seconds, she lingered on his mouth curved in that smile. She tore her attention from his lips and tracked upward until she connected with his dark brown eyes. "You don't know who I am, then?" She'd hoped that was why he was there.

"No, ma'am. When we apprehended you, you didn't have any ID on you. At the time you kept babbling you didn't know your name."

"I still don't," she whispered more to herself, but he heard her.

"We ran your fingerprints, but there wasn't a match in the database. And from our inquiries around Sagebrush, no one knows you here…and you weren't reported missing."

She moved into her hospital room. Aware of its suddenly small dimensions, she kept herself near the door to the corridor. "You said you apprehended me. Am I under arrest?" As she asked that question, she couldn't believe she would be. It didn't feel right—in her gut. She couldn't be a criminal, could she?

"As far as we know, you have done nothing wrong, but we found you in the Lost Woods running from someone or something. You couldn't tell us anything about that. You were scared, had a nasty gash on your head, cuts and bruises all over you. You lost consciousness shortly after I found you. Do you remember anything about that?"

She took in his features—short, sandy-brown hair, piercing dark eyes with long lashes, a dimple in his left cheek when he smiled. A vague memory tugged at her. His face looming over her. "Did you chase me?" Behind her eyes a hammering sensation grew as if the stress of trying to remember was taking its toll on her.

"When you saw me, you ran, and I went after you."

"Why did you chase me?" she asked.

"We believe you might be a witness to a crime that occurred in the Lost Woods."

"I am?" Trying to think overloaded her mind, a blank one with only shadowy figures wavering, never staying long enough for her to really see them.

"We were looking for a seven-year-old, Brady Billows, who went missing."

"I don't know him. Did you find him?" The thought of a child in danger pushed all her problems into the background.

"Yes, he's safely home with his mother now. That ended well."

"That's good," she said with a sigh.

Exhaustion spread through her the longer she stood. The officer was between her and the bed. But if she didn't sit down soon, she would collapse. She moved to the side, intending to skirt around him, when his cell phone rang.

He answered. "Calloway here." His calm expression evolved into a frown that grooved lines into his forehead. "I'm on my way. I'll meet you there." He returned his cell to his pocket. "Sorry, there's been a development in the Lost Woods. I'll come back later."

She flattened herself against the wall to allow him to pass her in the short hallway to the door. "A development? What?"

"Nothing you need to be worried about," he said, and left the room.

Then why was she worried?

Lee Calloway drove toward the west end of the Lost Woods where the patrol officer and witness were waiting. From what the dispatcher had told him, there might be another crime committed in the woods on the outskirts of Sagebrush.

The same area where he found the woman in the hospital room several weeks ago, running as though someone was after her. As far as the police were concerned she was a Jane Doe. What had happened to her? Why was she running in the woods? Who was she running from? Did she know anything about the boy's kidnapping?

He didn't like mysteries. Probably why he became a cop in the first place. He was always trying to get to the bottom of things. Would he be able to with this beautiful, mysterious woman or would she remain an enigma? The doctor had said she could have amnesia when she woke up, and that certainly seemed to be the case. She might recover all her memory or part of it, but some people never did.

Had her head injury been the sole reason she couldn't remember, or was it more than that? Some kind of psychological or physical trauma beyond the obvious wound she had sustained? The coma she slipped into was caused by the head injury, according to the doctor. But how and why did she receive it? Still no answer to that question.

Lee parked near the trailhead into the Lost Woods where the police officer and a young man dressed in a jogging suit waited. When Lee climbed from his SUV, he went to the back and lifted the door. Kip, his black-and-white border collie who worked as a cadaver dog, sat with his tail sweeping back and forth.

Lee rubbed him behind his ears, one of his favorite places to be scratched. "You ready to work?"

Kip barked.

Lee hooked the leash to his dog's halter. "Then let's go."

Kip jumped from the back of the vehicle and trotted next to Lee as he covered the distance to the patrol officer.

"What do we have here?" Lee asked, assessing the young man who kept darting glances toward the woods a few yards away.

The patrol officer started to say something, but the jogger interjected, "I decided to run in a different part of the forest today. I won't do that again. In fact, I may never run here again."

"What did you find?"

"Blood, lots of it. I tripped on a root, stumbled and fell. That's when I saw it."

"Show me."

The jogger shuffled his feet nervously. "It's a ways in."

"Fine."

"I'll stay back. Another K-9 team is coming to help in a search if it's needed," the patrol officer said.

Lee nodded in agreement and then followed the young man on the path.

"These woods used to be safe. There was a shooting here not long ago. A kidnapped boy found here. What's happening in Sagebrush?"

"That's what I aim to find out." As well as the whole Sagebrush special operations K-9 Unit. Their captain's father had been beaten and was still in the hospital, unresponsive. On top of that, Captain Slade McNeal's dog, Rio, was stolen at the same time and hadn't turned up. Something big was going down in here. According to Pauly Keevers, a snitch, a major crime syndicate was operating in town so low under the radar that no one knew who The Boss was or the second-in-command. Both used ruthless tactics to get their way.

"I fell over there." The young man stopped on the path and stepped around some brush. "There's the blood."

Lee stooped to examine a pile of dead leaves caught against the trunk of a tree. Dried blood caked them. He peered up at the man. "Thanks. I'll take it from here."

"Do I have to stay? I need to get to work soon."

"Does the officer have all your contact information?" Lee asked.

"Yes, he does."

"Okay, then…you're free to go. Just let the officer know I'm setting up a search."

As the young man jogged away, Lee rose and took Kip off his leash. If there was a body to be found, his cadaver dog would find it. And from the indication of the amount of blood loss, there very likely was a body somewhere. Kip put his nose to the ground and set out. Lee kept him in sight as his border collie went to work.

Ten minutes later, Kip stopped and barked. When Lee approached his dog, he stood next to a spot of disturbed ground, his head down, staring at the churned earth.

"What have you found?"

Kip barked again, his gaze still trained on the dirt.

Lee put on some latex gloves, stooped and began to dig carefully. From his dog's behavior, something dead was buried here. When he saw a piece of blue fabric, he ceased.

"Good boy," Lee said, as he always did whenever his cadaver dog found a body, then he scratched Kip's favorite place before rising. "I'm calling this in." He rotated in a slow circle, searching the area for any other signs of another grave.

Pulling out his cell, he placed a call to the station to report a body being found. Then while he waited for the crime-scene techs to show up, he checked the surrounding area in case there was another body. There were several low-level criminals missing, including Pauly Keevers who had assisted them recently. Was the body Kip discovered one of them? And could there be other graves in the woods?

Her lungs burned from lack of air, but she couldn't stop running. He'd catch her. Branches clawed at her, scraping across her skin. Stinging. A tree limb slapped against her face. The darkness of an approaching night crept closer, disguising the terrain and making her path difficult.

Instead of slowing down, she increased her speed. The sound of him crashing through the woods behind her filled her with terror. The pounding of her heart outpaced the pounding of her strides.

Then her foot landed in a hole, and she stumbled, flying forward. The hard impact with the ground knocked what little breath she had from her. The cold earth welcomed her.

The crush of leaves and snap of branches echoed through the trees. He was coming to get her. Kill her this time.

She scrambled to her feet and started forward when a body slammed into her...

She jerked, raising her arms to strike him. All she encountered was air. Warm air. Not cold. As the nightmare evaporated, her eyes popped open. She was still in the hospital, and the custodian from earlier today stood at the side of her bed with a plastic trash bag in one hand.

His frosty eyes on her, he inched closer.

A scream welled up inside her. Clamping her lips together, she fumbled for her call button and pushed it while scooting as far to the other side of the bed as she could.

"Ma'am, I didn't mean to wake you up."

"You didn't?"

"You were thrashing around. I was going to put up your railing so you didn't fall out of the bed."

She peered down at his other hand without the trash bag and noticed it was clasped around the bar. "I'm fine. Just a bad dream."

The door opened and the young, redheaded nurse called Gail came into her room. "Is something wrong?" The nurse looked from her to the custodian.

She couldn't think of anything to say to Gail, especially when the man who caused her to push the call button was standing nearby. "I—I—was wondering when the doctor would be by. I thought he would be here by now." Even to her it seemed like a lame reason to bother the busy staff.

The custodian stepped away from the bed, picked up her trash can and emptied it into the plastic bag.

The nurse didn't say anything until after he left the room. "Did he bother you? He's relatively new here and may not know all the procedures."

"No, not really." Some of the tension siphoned from her once the man was gone. "I had a nightmare and woke up with him in my room. It scared me, I guess. I pushed the button without really thinking." She curled her hands until her fingernails stabbed into her palms. Why did everything frighten her?

The nurse gave her an empathic look. "Are you recalling anything that happened to you?"

Remembering the nightmare, she almost said yes, but she didn't really know what was real and what was…fear of the unknown. She shook her head. "I still don't remember who I am."

Gail slid her hand into her pocket. "I have something of yours. I was going to give it to you when I brought your medicine later." She withdrew a gold heart locket and passed it to her. "You were wearing it when you came into the hospital. I put it in a safe place so when you got better you could have it. It's beautiful. There's a name carved into it."

"There is?" She took it from the nurse and held it in her palm.

"I hope it helps you to remember. Sometimes an object will spur a memory." Gail started for the door but paused before leaving. "I'll make sure the other member of housekeeping assigned to this floor will take care of you. She's an older woman. You might feel more comfortable with her."

As the nurse left, she stared at the locket with intricate etching in it. She opened it and saw a picture of a young woman with long blond hair, probably around eighteen. *Heidi* was engraved in the other side. Touching her own blond hair, she wondered if this was a photo of her. From the vision she'd seen earlier that day in the mirror, it could be.

What did she call herself? Jane Doe? That didn't sit well with her. It made her seem like she was nobody—not worthy of a name. That, more than anything, bothered her. She couldn't form any kind of picture in her head of who she was. Did she like steak, going to the movies, reading books? What were her likes? Dislikes? The black hole her memories were lost in terrified her.

She made her way to the bathroom again to study her reflection and then reexamined the photo in the locket. There were similarities in what she saw in the mirror and the woman in the picture. Was it her when she was younger? How old was she now?

Is Heidi my name?

"Heidi," she said, and liked how it sounded. A sense of comfort surrounded her. She needed a name, and Heidi could be it.

Just the effort of walking into the bathroom sapped her energy, especially after spending the day wondering why the police officer had left her bedside to go back to the Lost Woods where they'd found her. Leaving the bathroom, she nearly ran into Officer Lee Calloway, dressed in casual clothes, not his uniform.

He stepped back to let her pass him. "The nurse said you were up."

"Yes." She stated the obvious because she didn't know what else to say. As she shuffled toward the bed, she felt his dark gaze on her and, surprisingly, it didn't bother her. She needed answers and hoped he could tell her more about his finding her. Maybe something would trigger her memory.

He stood back while she perched on the side of the bed. "I wanted to ask you some more questions."

"I still don't remember who I am, but the nurse gave me a locket she'd kept for me with a picture inside it and the name Heidi engraved on it."

"Is the picture of you?"

She flattened her palm to show him the necklace that she'd gripped in her hand. "It might be when I was younger."

His fingers grazed across her skin as he picked it up and opened it.

A tingling from his touch zapped her, further surprising her.

He studied it, then her. "Maybe. Or a member of your family? A sister? Your mother?"

"I don't know, but I'm going to use the name. I need one, and it's better than Jane Doe. I'm pretty sure it isn't my daughter." She attempted a smile, and the gesture seemed alien to her. "I'm probably between twenty-five and thirty."

Again, he scrutinized her. "If I had to guess, closer to twenty-five."

When was her birthday? Where was she born? Questions she couldn't answer flowed through her mind in a steady stream until she had to shut them down or scream in frustration. "What do you need to ask me? I'll help if I can." She really hoped she could. This officer was being so nice to her.

"Describe the man you saw in the woods."

"I saw a man in the woods?"

"When I found you hiding, you said something about a man." Lee pulled out some photos. "See if you can recognize the one you were talking about." After spreading out four pictures, he pointed to each one. "Take your time. Study them."

She examined the four men, and nothing clicked for her. "I don't know them."

"So you haven't seen these men?"

She shook her head. "Not that I remember."

He held up one of a dark-haired guy with a thick neck and bushy eyebrows.

"No. Maybe." The bushy eyebrows niggled her memory for a few seconds but nothing concrete came to mind. "I don't know." How many times had she said that since she woke up?

"This one?" Lee indicated another man, red hair with thin lips.

"No. Nothing."

She laid her finger on the man with the bushy eyebrows. "Who is he?"

"Don Frist."

"Could he have been chasing me before you saw me?"

"I don't know. We didn't see him pursuing you. But you were definitely running from something or someone."

"Where is this man?" She examined him again, wanting to be able to identify him—to know someone.

"In jail."

"What did he do?"

He has quite an extensive rap sheet...which includes kidnapping Brady Billows."

"The little boy you told me about this morning? I don't understand why anyone would harm a child." The idea that someone would kill or hurt a little boy knotted her stomach. Did she have a child? The more she thought about the question, the more she didn't think so.

"I agree. But Brady will be fine, thankfully. He was scared but between his mother, Eva, and Detective Austin Black, another K-9 team member, he'll be safe."

"Did he find the little boy?"

"Yes and he will soon be his stepfather."

A happy ending. Relief unraveled the knots. "I'm so glad." Peering down, she touched her left ring finger, but there was no sign she'd ever worn a wedding band. For some reason she felt in her heart she loved kids. Not liked. Loved.

"Do you remember something?"

"Yes. I love children."

"Do you remember if you have any?"

"I don't think any of my own. It doesn't feel like it. I don't think I'm married." She held up her ringless finger on her left hand.

"Maybe you worked with children."

"Could be."

"That could help us find where you're from. Contact friends and family."

"No" tumbled from her mouth before she could stop the word.

Chapter Two

The panic that invaded Heidi's voice made Lee wonder if she knew more than she was letting on. "You don't want us to look for your family and friends? Don't you want to know who you are?"

She dropped her head, staring at her lap. "Yes, of course, but..."

"But what?"

When she lifted her gaze to his, her beautiful brown eyes shimmered with tears. "Why was I running through the woods? How did I get hurt?" She touched her forehead. "How did I get this gash?"

"You think someone is after you?"

"I don't know." With a deep sigh, she settled back against the raised bed.

"So you don't want us to put your picture out and see if anyone knows you?"

She kneaded her fingertips into her temples. "Not right

now. I'd like to try and remember who I am first. I just can't get past..." Nibbling on her bottom lip, she averted her eyes.

"Why you were running as if someone were after you?"

She nodded. "Earlier today, I had a dream—no, nightmare. Someone was chasing me and it looked like I was in a wooded area. He caught up with me and—" she connected with his gaze "—and he was trying to kill me. What if that's true? What if that's why I was running when you saw me?"

"The only two men we know were in the woods were these two I showed you." He pointed to the redheaded man. "This guy is dead." Then he tapped the photo of the guy with the bushy eyebrows. "Don Frist is in jail. If they were after you, you're safe."

But why would they have been after her in the first place? All the police's quiet inquiries around town about her identity had hit a dead end. No one knew her and there wasn't anyone fitting her description missing in Sagebrush. But could there have been a third man in the woods that day? They'd thought there might have been. Would she be able to tell them if she remembered?

"Give me a chance to recall first. The doctor said my memory could come back at any time."

He didn't want to tell her he'd already told his captain he was going to do some checking in the surrounding towns. He could still do that quietly, go through the police in those towns, and check their missing-person's reports. For some reason he felt responsible for her. He'd captured her in the first place, when she tripped and fell while he chased her. She'd hit the ground hard. He'd always wondered if that was what had caused her to lose consciousness. "Have you talked to the doctor today?"

"Not yet, but last night he told me he wants to make sure

the swelling has gone down. If so, he thought I could leave here in a day or so."

"Where are you going to go?"

Her light brown eyes widened. "I don't know. Did I have a purse with me?"

"No, but you had some money stuffed in your jean pocket."

"How much?"

"Four hundred in twenties."

Surprise flitted across her lovely features again. "Where did that money come from?"

"Good question. I don't suppose you remember?"

She shook her head slowly.

"As far as the police are concerned, it's your money and will be returned to you. I can bring it to you tomorrow."

She met his eyes. "Will you wait until I leave here? I don't want to keep that much money here."

"Fine. In fact, Heidi, I'll take you where you want to stay. Unless you have somewhere else to go, we would like you to stay in Sagebrush at least until you remember. In case you recall something about the men in the woods that day." He paused. "Don Frist will stand trial, and if you could testify to his presence or that you saw him with the young boy, that would be great."

Her forehead creased. "What if I don't remember?"

"Don't worry about that. I don't like taking on extra worrying because it's a waste of time. I figure I'll leave the future in God's hands. He's very capable of taking care of it."

"Any suggestions about where to stay?" she asked.

"I'll check around and see what I can come up with."

"I appreciate it, but I don't want to cause you a lot of extra work…"

Her vulnerability poured off her and ensnared him. "It's

not. I know a few people who know a few others. We'll find somewhere for you to stay."

Her smile reached deep into her eyes and lit them. "I don't know why you're doing this, but thank you. I don't know where to turn."

"My pleasure, Heidi. Now I'd better leave you to get some rest. I'll be back tomorrow afternoon to see when you'll be released from the hospital."

He strode from her room and headed for his SUV in the parking lot, his dog poking his head out the window. The second Lee opened his door, Kip barked, peeking his head over the front seat and licking him on the cheek.

"Glad to see me? I wasn't gone long." He started the engine and rolled up the window. "Lie down. We've got a mission. To find Heidi a place to stay."

The next day Lee paused in the doorway of Molly's kitchen at his boarding house, a large Victorian home near downtown, a block off Sagebrush Boulevard. He took in a deep whiff of her coffee, the best in town. Two things that appealed to him about the place besides its quaint atmosphere were its owner, Molly Givens, like a second mother to him, and a large fenced backyard for Kip.

At the sink rinsing some dishes, his landlady glanced over her shoulder. "Did you bring your mug?"

"Yep. Wouldn't pass up an opportunity to have some of your coffee. It sure beats what I make myself."

"It smelled like you were brewing burned rubber. Here, pour yourself a big cup. I certainly don't need to drink any more. Doctor's orders. Watching my caffeine intake."

Lee filled his travel mug, relishing the aroma wafting from the glass carafe. "I seem to remember you talking a few weeks ago about fixing up those couple of rooms on the third floor and taking in another boarder. Are you still interested in doing that?"

The kindhearted older woman dried her hands and faced him. "What are you up to?"

"I know someone who needs a place to stay while she recovers."

"Recovers from what?"

"She was injured. A head trauma. She has amnesia. She can't even remember her name."

Molly quirked a brow. "That lady you found out in the Lost Woods?"

"Yes, but it's not common knowledge. How'd you find out about her being here?" He should have realized if anyone knew what was going on in Sagebrush, it would be Molly. She didn't have to work, but she'd been lonely after her husband died five years ago, and she'd opened her second floor for two tenants. She was a people person and couldn't see living in a huge Victorian house by herself. He'd been glad he'd snatched up the first apartment, and shortly after that another coworker had taken the second one available. Mark Moore, a fellow police officer who worked the graveyard shift, lived across the hall from him.

"Lorna Danfield spilled the beans. We're good friends. From church."

"Oh, yeah, I forgot. Lorna was the one who reminded me of your empty third floor. I should have remembered you two take care of the flowers for church." Lorna was the secretary at work and was always looking out for the officers and dogs that were in the K-9 Unit.

"I've been talking of doing something. Now is as good a time as any. When will your lady friend be getting out of the hospital?"

Lady friend? That made what he was doing sound like more

than someone helping another. And that was all this was. After his breakup with his fiancée, Alexa, eight months ago, he certainly wasn't ready to jump into a relationship beyond casual. "I'll find out today, but I think in the next day or so."

Molly blew out a deep breath. "There's a lot of work to do in a short time."

"I think I can get some of the guys from the unit to help. We could work on it in the evenings."

"And if she gets out before that, I have a spare bed in my apartment."

"If she stays for a while, I don't know how far her money will stretch to cover expenses." Lee dumped two spoonfuls of sugar into his coffee.

"That's okay. She's in need."

"Thanks—I knew I could count on you. She feels alone."

"I can imagine." Molly set her hand on her hip. "Well, maybe not really. I'm who I am because of my memories. It would be awful not to remember anything."

"Some people might like a clean slate."

"A do over? As far as the Lord is concerned, every day is a new beginning in His eyes. He forgives and forgets."

Lee shifted under the intensity of Molly's gaze.

"Let what Alexa did go, Lee."

"She wasn't who she appeared to be. I'm a cop. I'm trained to read people. She had me totally fooled."

"The only one you're hurting is yourself."

"How am I supposed to just forgive and forget?" he ground out. "She slept with another man and is having his baby. We were talking about getting married the whole time she was seeing this guy—a fellow cop."

"At least Dan works on a different shift."

"Yeah, but we still run into each other." Lee glanced at the clock over the stove. "I've got to go. Work calls."

"You might have a hard time pulling Kip away from Eliza this morning. They've been playing and chasing each other around the backyard."

"I think Kip has his eye on the Malinois. They both like to herd and try to with each other."

When he stepped outside, he spied the two dogs lying together under a maple tree. Kip saw him, jumped up and hurried toward him. Eliza, Mark's dog, raced toward him, too. She looked similar to a small-size German shepherd with tan fur and a black muzzle. He greeted Kip in his usual manner, then patted Eliza.

"Gotta leave your girlfriend, Kip. We've got a job. We're heading for the Lost Woods. Captain wants us to start a grid search of it, see if we can find any more bodies. Several people are missing."

Kip rubbed up against Eliza, yelped once then loped toward the gate. With one last glance at Eliza, her head tilted, her ears perked forward, Kip barked again as though to tell him to get moving. There were times he felt the dogs they worked with understood every word they said to them. As they were all highly trained and intelligent, he wouldn't be surprised if they did.

"Sorry, girl, gotta take him to work," Lee said before jogging toward his dog.

In the driveway he opened the back of his SUV for Kip. "We have to make a quick stop at headquarters, then to work."

Kip lay down, putting his head between his two stretched out legs, his tail wagging.

"I figured you'd go for that. See all your buddies."

Ten minutes later, Lee snapped a leash on Kip and they entered through the back of the one-story red brick police station where the K-9 Unit was housed. Lorna Danfield, the secretary for the K-9 Unit, sat at her desk near Captain Slade McNeal's office.

When Lee covered the distance to her, Kip planted himself right next to her chair and waited for her to acknowledge him. She finished a call then turned to lavish attention on Kip. He loved it and always liked spending time with her.

"Is the captain in his office?" Lee asked while his partner enjoyed Lorna's pampering.

"Yes, he's expecting you. I'll take care of Kip while you go inside."

He started to leave, rotated back and said, "Thanks for the suggestion about renovating Molly's third floor for our Jane Doe. I mean for Heidi."

"She remembered her name?"

"No, but she has a locket with that name in it so that's what she's decided to call herself."

"That poor dear. I'll have to pay her a visit once she settles in at Molly's."

"I haven't asked her to move in yet. I will today after work. She may have other plans."

"Where's the young lady going to go? She doesn't know who she is or know anyone." Kip bumped Lorna's hand, and she scratched behind his ears.

"True, but she might not appreciate a stranger coming in and planning her life."

"Or she'll appreciate it because she doesn't know what her options are right now." The secretary nodded at Lee. Go see the captain. I hear you're gonna have a busy couple of days."

"Yeah, a thousand-acre wooded area will take some time to cover properly. With the discovery of Ned Adams's body, Captain thinks there could be others out there. With all that has happened lately connected to the Lost Woods, it could very likely be a burial ground for those others like Pauly Keevers and a couple of low-level criminals like Adams."

"If any dog can find a dead body, it'll be Kip."

He winked. "You're just partial, but I agree with you."

Lee knocked on his captain's door then stuck his head into the office. "You wanted to see me?"

"Yes, I know you heard Pauly Keevers is missing. No one has seen him in the last three days. Normally with someone like Keevers I wouldn't be overly concerned. He's been known to go off drinking and disappear for days. I hope that's the case here."

"But you don't think it is?"

Slade shook his head. "I wanted to emphasize how important it is we find Pauly. The chatter in the criminal community is that he was killed for talking to the police. Now no one is talking. With Adams's body found in the Lost Woods, people are wondering who else is out there. Adams wasn't a snitch but he worked for Charles Ritter."

"The lawyer who was arrested for being involved in the murder of Eva Dillows's parents?"

"That very one. I'm sending Austin and Justice with you to search the woods. Austin has something of Pauly's that he'll give Justice to track him while you look for any other buried bodies. Austin has already checked Pauly's hangouts in town yesterday afternoon. As I said, no one has seen the man in several days. Justice had his scent leaving Pauly's apartment but lost it at the street."

"Maybe he got into a car."

"Pauly doesn't own one so it was someone else's. Where did they go? We owe Pauly. He gave us our first big lead about what's going on with Rio's kidnapping and my dad's beating."

"Just so you know, I'm asking our Jane Doe—who will be going by Heidi—to stay at Molly's boarding house. That way

I can keep an eye on her and maybe help her remember what happened to her." He exhaled slowly. "It could be connected to this case. She was there that day Brady was found. What did she see? We still think there's another guy out there involved in the kidnapping."

"Good thinking. Let me know if she agrees." The captain picked up his pen and scribbled something on the paper in front of him.

"I'm asking a couple of guys from the unit to help me fix up Molly's third floor for Heidi over the next few nights. You're invited. Six tonight. I'll supply the pizzas."

"I'll be there. Give me something else to think about other than this case, my missing dog and my dad still in a coma. At least Heidi came out of hers. Maybe that means Dad will soon."

When he left the captain's office, he peered at Kip and knew how he'd feel if anything happened to his dog. They were partners. He'd feel the loss. At least Slade had Rio's sire to fill in the gap. But that still wasn't the same.

Using the grid pattern, Lee followed Kip, on a long leash, in the Lost Woods. So far, nothing. Austin and his bloodhound Justice hadn't found anything, either. He paused for a few seconds to get his bearings and scanned the tall trees that shaded the forest floor as if it were late afternoon. Up ahead a ray of sunlight streamed through the foliage as though pinpointing one spot.

His cell rang. He pulled it off his belt and answered, "Calloway here."

"I found a wrecked car on the outskirts of the woods on the north side by the highway," Austin said, then gave him the coordinates.

"I'm not far. I'll be right there." Lee hung up and noted his position on his GPS, then set out in a jog toward the area.

Ten minutes later, he arrived at the dark green Buick sedan, which was partially covered by branches and greenery. The front end was smashed. One tire was shredded as though there had been a blowout. The air bag in the driver's seat had gone off, lying limp now, a fine white powder all over the place. From the small ditch it was halfway lodged in, the car sat at a thirty-degree angle.

"Someone tried to hide it." Detective Austin Black came around from the other side.

"That's what it looks like to me. Have you called in the license number?"

"Yeah. It's registered to a William Peterson from San Antonio. Where is he? Was it a stolen car? Captain is sending out a couple of crime-scene techs to process it, maybe they'll be able to pull some fingerprints. Then we can tow it to the police impound." Austin hesitated. "He wants us to continue our search. Do you think this was one of the kidnappers's cars? That this Peterson is involved in the crime syndicate?"

Or was this how Heidi ended up in the woods that day? "Maybe, but if so, why would he leave it here in light of what went down in the woods a couple of weeks ago? It could have just been abandoned by Peterson. It looks pretty damaged, and it's an old car. He might have decided to walk away from it." As he said that to Austin, Lee kept picturing Heidi pushing open the driver's door that was still ajar, then stumbling out. Disoriented. Hurting from the wreck. That would explain her injuries. "Maybe our mystery woman is connected to this car." But why would she attempt to hide it?

"That thought already occurred to me, and the captain is looking into it."

"If she's tied to this car and Peterson, I'd love to be able to tell Heidi some good news," Lee said. "At least give her a name and some facts about her life. Maybe be able to contact family and friends."

"She's going by Heidi?"

Lee nodded at his teammate. "Yeah, she didn't want to use Jane Doe."

"I don't blame her. So she hasn't remembered anything?"

"No. Do you see any evidence in the car?" Lee approached the vehicle, careful not to disturb any footprints. But with the dense leafage on the ground, he didn't see any.

"Not from the passenger's side."

Lee peered inside from the open driver's door and spied a cloth stuffed between the seats. After donning gloves, he reached in and pulled out a bloodied cloth. "Whose blood?"

"Maybe William Peterson?"

Or Heidi? Did a car wreck cause her injuries? It fit. Lee took out an evidence bag and dropped the cloth in it, then pulled out his cell and called the captain to report the development.

Will the name William Peterson mean anything to Heidi?

"You staying until the crime-scene techs show up?" Lee asked Austin.

"Yeah. No use both of us standing around waiting. But I thought it might be a good idea to have Kip check this area in light of the car being found. Something might have gone down here."

"I agree. We'll work our way out from here, then resume our search where we left off when you called."

An hour later, Lee determined the area surrounding the car was clear of any dead bodies and trekked deeper into the woods to the last place Kip and he had searched. He gave his dog a long lead on his leash and Kip went to work, nose to ground. As the border collie went back and forth through the forest, Lee kept thinking about the car Austin had found and couldn't help wondering if it was connected to Heidi. As soon as possible, he would delve into William Peterson's life and see if Heidi and Peterson knew each other, because even if she didn't remember who he was, there could be a link between the two.

As the door to her hospital room opened, Heidi tensed, scrunching the sheet up in her hands. Nurse Gail entered with her medicine she needed to take. Heidi drew in a composing breath, causing pain to stab through her chest. One of her ribs had been cracked and was healing, but it still hurt her when she inhaled too deeply. The list of her injuries from minor to major only confirmed something bad had gone down right before the police found her.

"Hi, how are you this afternoon? The earlier shift told me the doctor is releasing you if your lab work comes back okay." Gail gave her the little cup with her pills in it, then poured her some water and handed that to her.

"Yes, that's what he said to me, but…" *What am I going to do? Where am I going?*

"But? Are you concerned about not being well enough to leave?"

"No." She'd examined the dark recesses of her mind until she had a headache. "I'm not sure what to do next."

"I can understand that, but officer Calloway called earlier when you were down in X-ray to see if you were going to be discharged today."

"He did?"

"Sorry I didn't get the message to you sooner. This has been a busy afternoon. He's coming right after work. He has a place for you to stay, at least temporarily."

In the darkness that surrounded her, there was a ray of light. "He mentioned he would ask around."

"When Lee says he's going to do something, he does."

Maybe they were in a relationship. Gail was an attractive redhead about Lee's age. "You've known him long?"

"We went to school together. He's a good friend of my husband, Harry. He's a trainer at the K-9 Training Center next to the police headquarters. Harry got Lee interested in becoming a K-9 officer. He was a natural. Lee is like Harry. They're big animal lovers."

Did she have a pet in her other life? Was it left alone because she wasn't there to take care of it? "I remember hearing barking in the woods."

"You do? That's good. It was probably the K-9 Unit searching for Brady. By the time Lee found you, the kid had been rescued." Gail lifted the tray of medication she had. "I need to make my rounds."

Heidi scanned the almost-bare hospital room with no flowers or cards. It hammered home how alone she truly was. Even sitting in bed, she had little to think about other than trying to remember and meeting a dark screen. It would be good to get out of here and try to build some kind of life for herself while she waited for her memory to return. *If it returned.*

The least she could do was try to make herself presentable to one of the few people she knew. Maybe she should dress. She went to the closet and checked its contents. A set of clothes was hanging up. They must be hers, but she didn't remember them—buying them or wearing them.

Inside the bathroom, she quickly donned the jeans, which fit her perfectly, and the gray fleece sweatshirt. The small amount of energy she expended dressing herself tired her out. Apparently she wasn't going to bounce back as fast as she wished.

When she came out of the bathroom, she glimpsed a movement out of the corner of her eye right before a beefy hand covered her mouth and nose.

"The third time is the charm. Good thing I'm a patient man."

The deep voice of the custodian penetrated her panic-filled mind.

Chapter Three

Lee ascended the stairs to the hospital's second floor two at a time. He'd hoped to be here earlier, but Austin and he had stayed a little longer in the Lost Woods because reporting the wrecked car had delayed their search. But almost a third of the area had been covered, making for a long day. They didn't find anything other than the Buick, which might or might not be linked to the kidnapping. To Heidi.

No scent of Pauly in the forest or another grave, however, had been found. He counted that a good day. Pauly could still be alive, passed out drunk somewhere they hadn't looked.

He caught sight of a custodian going into Heidi's room at the other end of the hall. Several staff members rushed toward him, passed him and went into a patient's room nearby. A code blue sounded over the intercom. A nurse hurried with a cart. Lee stepped out of the way and slowed his pace.

I won't be a victim, screamed through Heidi's mind as she twisted and pummeled her attacker. That managed to increase the constriction about her. Finally she went limp, dead weight, which threw off the custodian. He stumbled forward, still holding her, but the hand about her mouth slipped.

"Help. Help," she yelled.

His hand clamped again over her mouth. "You'll pay for that."

The door crashed open, and Lee charged into the room, his gun drawn. "Let her go. Now." He aimed his weapon at the man's head.

"I could snap her neck."

"And you'll be a dead man. Is that what you want? Right now you'll be charged with assault. If you hurt her, you'll be dead."

Through her haze of terror she heard the man's heavy breathing. She felt his sweat drip on her, the roughness of his hand. The scent of his body odor as though he hadn't showered recently assailed her, gagging her.

The hammering of her heart thundered through her mind. She focused totally on Lee before her, a fierce expression on his face, his feet braced apart, both hands on the gun, steady, pointed toward her attacker. Seeing Lee dressed in a uniform accelerated her fear even more as though she'd faced a police officer before with a gun aimed toward her. Was she a criminal?

Slowly the man released his grip on her. She closed her eyes for a few seconds. When he dropped his hand from her mouth, she hastened away from her attacker—away from Lee. She collapsed against her bed, clutching the sheets.

Lee hurried to the assailant, put him up against the wall and handcuffed him. Then he reached into his pocket, withdrew his cell and placed a call to the police station. Taking her attacker by the arm, Lee pulled him to the chair nearby and shoved him down.

"Stay put," Lee said to the six-foot man then approached her. "Are you all right?" His gaze skimmed over her briefly before he returned his full attention to his suspect.

"Yes." The word came out on a shaky breath. She glanced down at her hands trembling and sat on the bed, tucking them under her legs.

"I have a patrol officer coming to take this man in. Once he leaves, I want to do some checking here about—" he flicked his gaze to the name badge on the guy's custodian uniform "—Gus Zoller."

Her assailant glared at Lee. "I ain't talking."

"That's your prerogative."

Dazed by all that had happened, Heidi dug her teeth into her lower lip and studied the man. His icy gaze nipped at what little composure she had left. If she could remember, she might know if he was someone she knew—had a reason to try and kill her. But she couldn't answer that. There was nothing about him that seemed familiar except his eyes. Should she say something to Lee about that?

She glanced at her rescuer and as long as she kept her gaze on his face she was all right, but when she looked down at his badge and dark blue uniform, her throat closed, her stomach clinched. Frustration swamped her. She had reactions to certain things and didn't understand where they came from. Did she have something against the police?

"Still doing okay?" Lee asked, his gaze trained on Gus Zoller.

"Yes. Thank you for being here." Her voice still quavered, but she was regaining her composure.

"I'm not sure if I'm glad I was late or not. If I had come earlier, he might not have attacked you."

"But he would have waited until later. He's been in here before."

"Other than yesterday morning?"

"Yes, yesterday evening."

Lee's glare drilled into the man. "What happened?"

"I woke up from a bad dream, and he was hovering over my bed. I panicked and pushed the call button."

"Obviously a good thing you did. Why didn't you tell me?"

She gestured toward Gus. "Because he said I was thrashing around and he claimed that he was putting up my railing. I woke up punching the air, so I thought he was right."

"That must have been some dream."

"You know how dreams are. Often weird with strange things happening." She hoped that was the case because her nightmare had scared her. Not knowing what was real or not real only heightened that feeling.

The door swung open and a patrol officer came inside, "Is that the suspect you want me to take down to the station?"

"Yes. I'll be down later to have a little word with him. Book him on assault, for starters."

"Will do." The officer grabbed hold of the man and pulled him to his feet.

When her assailant left, some of the tension in Heidi drained away. She dropped her head and inhaled a deep breath. "I wanted to ask him why he was trying to kill me. What have I done to have someone after me?"

"That's a good question. One I intend to find the answer to. I'll be asking the man later and will see if I can't convince him to tell me why."

"Please do. It may help me figure out who I am." Even if she discovered something bad, this not knowing was driving her crazy.

"I'm going to talk to the staff and personnel about the suspect. I'll be back in a little while."

"Please...don't leave me alone."

Lee gave her a reassuring look. "You aren't alone." He walked to the door and motioned for someone to come into the room. "This officer will be standing guard. While I'm gone, I'll have the doctor make sure you're still all right to leave the hospital."

"Thanks." She lay back against her reclined bed and closed her eyes, trying to picture anyone from her past.

The same dark screen mocked her. She'd never felt so alone in her life. She didn't have to remember her past to know that was true.

After paying human resources and hospital security a visit, Lee caught his friend Gail in the hallway coming from the room where there had been a code blue earlier. "What happened?"

"Someone unplugged that man's life support, and he crashed, but thankfully we revived him and he's fine now."

How convenient for Gus that everyone was in Room 253. Planned or a coincidence?

The nurse looked around him. "Why is an officer standing outside Heidi's room?"

"One of your custodians assaulted her."

Alarmed, Gail pushed forward. "Is she all right?"

Lee stopped his friend. "She's fine. Just confused and scared. I asked her doctor to check her out before she's discharged from the hospital."

"Who was it?"

"Gus Zoller. What can you tell me about him? Any reason you can think of why he would do this?"

Her forehead creased, and she slowly shook her head. "It doesn't make any sense. He's new here. He started in January. But he always did his job and was pleasant to the patients when he interacted with them."

"Was he friendly with anyone? Another staff member?"

"No, come to think about it. He kept to himself. Did his job and went home."

Lee nodded. "If you think of anything else that might explain why he went after Heidi, call me."

He continued toward Heidi's room with the information he'd received on Gus from human resources. Later tonight after he interviewed the suspect, he intended to check his apartment out.

When he entered the room, he found Heidi lying on her bed, staring at the wall. "Are you sure you're all right?" Lee brushed his gaze over her cheeks, which were still drained of color. He couldn't blame her for being jittery with anyone she saw. She didn't know what happened to land her in the hospital. Who was a friend? Who was a foe? Her aching despair spiked his protective instincts.

Heidi nodded slowly.

"Did Gail tell you I found a place for you to stay?"

"Yes."

"I live in a Victorian boarding house run by Molly Givens. She lives on the bottom floor and another police officer lives on the second floor in an apartment across from me. Molly has wanted to open up her third floor for another tenant. It doesn't require a lot of work so a group of my friends are going to put the finishing touches on it over the next several nights."

"The doctor said I could still leave today," she informed him. "And after what just happened, I want to get out of here."

"I don't blame you. I can keep an eye on you at the house so there isn't a repeat of this afternoon. Molly has a spare bedroom downstairs for you to use. Your place should be ready for you to move into in two days. Are you okay with that?"

"Are you sure Molly is all right with it?"

"Meet Molly. You'll see she's fine about you staying. Like I said, I'll feel better if you're nearby." He smiled gently. "Mark, my neighbor, works the graveyard shift. He'll be around while I'm working if you run into a problem. I'll be there at night."

Her eyebrows slashed downward. "I hate not knowing what's going on. I don't feel like I'm the kind of person who made someone angry enough to want me dead."

"This has to be hard on you, but I'll help you find answers. I know you feel alone, but you aren't now." He couldn't shake from his mind the haunted look he glimpsed a few times on her face.

Tears glistened in Heidi's eyes. "Why are you doing this for me?"

"Several reasons. First off, I'm a cop. I became one to help others in trouble. And you're most definitely in dire straits. Also, I want you to remember. You might be able to help us with what's been going on here in Sagebrush."

"What's going on?"

"Last month Captain Slade McNeal's father was almost beaten to death. He's still in this hospital. Like you, he slipped into a coma. My captain's K-9 dog was stolen at that time. Brady, the seven-year-old who lives down the road from Slade, was kidnapped because he witnessed both the beating and Rio's abduction. I know how I'd feel if something happened to Kip. My dog is my partner. We've been through a lot together."

"I think I like dogs."

The vulnerability in her expression chipped away at his declaration he was through with women after Alexa. "In a while you'll find out. There'll be two dogs at Molly's. Besides Kip, Mark's pet is an ex-K-9 dog—Eliza, a Malinois."

"Why would someone take your captain's dog?"

"We're working on that," Lee said, not wanting to reveal to Heidi what Pauly Keevers had told them—that Rio was taken to find something valuable in the Lost Woods. "In addition to Slade's father being hurt, his dog stolen and young Brady Billows being kidnapped, a number of lowlifes have disappeared. One turned up dead in the Lost Woods the other day.

"Who?"

"Ned Adams? Have you ever heard that name, seen him?" Lee showed her a photo of the dead man.

She shook her head. "Was he a criminal?"

"Yes, he was dealing drugs and working for another man we have jailed and awaiting trial. He was shot execution style. Someone is making a point. Something big is going on here, and no one is talking."

"But you said you've checked around here and I'm not from here. At least you don't think so."

"True, but you may know something about what happened in the Lost Woods that can help us."

"You think that's why that man came after me?"

"Maybe, especially since you woke up and could possibly remember and talk. Speaking of which...do you know a man named William Peterson?

"You found another dead body in the woods?"

"No, but we found Peterson's car wrecked at the edge of the woods, not far from the highway. He lives in San Antonio, but his neighbors said he left on business weeks ago and wasn't expected back for a few more days." He cleared his throat. "SAPD checked with his employer, and he never showed up to see any of his business clients. He's a sales rep for a manufacturer. When his daughter hadn't heard from him, she filed a missing-person's report."

"You think I know him?"

"It could explain your injuries." He showed her a driver's license photo of Peterson, a fifty-two-year-old with balding dark hair and a plain face.

She examined it for a long moment then scrubbed her hands down her face. "I don't know. The name doesn't sound familiar at all. Nor does his picture look familiar." Frustration, mixed with concern, marked her features.

"Don't worry. It might not have anything to do with you." He wanted to touch her and comfort her, take the strain from her expression. He kept his arms at his sides. "I'll go see if the doctor has signed your discharge papers while you get dressed."

"Speaking of clothes, I need to go by a store and pick up some extra items. What you found me in is all I have."

"There's a Super Mart not too far from here. We'll stop there, then maybe Molly or Gail can take you shopping when you get settled in."

"I can't believe all these people came to help fix up this place for me," Heidi said, standing back from the group painting and preparing the hardwood flooring to be refinished. "I should be helping."

"Didn't anyone tell you that you just got out of the hospital a few hours ago? You're to rest. Isn't that right, Gail?"

Lee's friend stopped taping the floorboard and looked up at Heidi and him. "I'd better not see you lifting a finger tonight. Consider this your welcome-to-Sagebrush greeting. It's got to be better than the first one."

"Yes. Hands down."

Heidi's laughter floated across the room, drawing a couple of his friends' attention. Lee liked the sound, light with a musical quality. He hadn't seen her smile and certainly not heard her laugh much in the short time he had known her, but for some reason he wanted to make that his mission, to see and hear more of that.

"I thought you were resting downstairs." Lee touched her elbow and led her toward the exit to the three-room apartment.

"I was getting bored. Resting is all I've done for the past few weeks." Heidi leaned closer to him, her fresh scent of apples and cinnamon instantly reminding him of his childhood home at Christmas. "Molly went into the kitchen to make some sweet tea for y'all and see to her chocolate chip cookies. I snuck up here when she left."

"You said y'all. Maybe you're from the South. You have a faint accent."

She cocked her head and stared off into space for a long moment. "I don't know. I like the sound of cold sweet tea even though it's the first of February."

"I can't say it gets that cold here in southwest Texas in the winter." He guided her toward the third-floor landing. "It's not that I wouldn't love for you to join us. I just don't want you to overdo it."

"I have to admit I'm tired. You would think after resting and sleeping so much I wouldn't be. My body isn't wanting to cooperate with my mind, which would like to be upstairs with y'all pitching in, especially with how nice Molly has been."

He descended the stairs with Heidi next to him. "Tell you what. Come join us about seven when the pizza is being delivered. Until then, take a nap."

"All I can promise is I'll rest. I'm tired, not sleepy." At the bottom of the steps on the first floor, she turned toward him. "I can find my own way back to Molly's spare bedroom after I see her in the kitchen."

"You're going to go in there and help her?"

She pointed to herself innocently. "Who, me?"

"Don't answer. I don't want to know you aren't resting. See you at seven, and I'll introduce you to the folks you don't know."

She headed for the kitchen while he went back upstairs. He hadn't had a chance to talk with Gail. She'd gotten off work late and arrived here as soon as her shift ended. Not three minutes afterward, Heidi had come into the room. He didn't want her involved at this time.

"Is she going to behave herself and take it easy?" Gail asked when he entered the first room in the new apartment.

"Probably not. She may not know it, but I have a feeling she has a stubborn streak."

"I call it determination. She went through an ordeal and is alive. Someone wanted her dead in the woods attacked her earlier today." Gail pursed her lips. "I can't believe Gus Zoller tried to hurt her. On my floor. Bold. Desperate, maybe. So why go after Heidi unless she knows something?"

"That's what I'm thinking. I've talked to everyone but his supervisor in housekeeping. She had already left for the day, and I wanted to bring Heidi here."

"Mrs. Hanson is a tough one, but all you have to do is flash that great smile of yours and that badge, and you won't have any problems."

"Mrs. Markham, are you flirting with my friend?" Gail's husband joined them, with beige paint in splotches all over his clothing.

Looking her husband up and down, Gail fisted her hand and planted it on her waist. "Harry Markham, I declare I've never seen a man so messy except when it comes to the dogs. Everything has to be neat and precise with them."

Harry flicked his brush at his wife.

Her eyes grew round when she saw the paint spatter her shirt. "Good thing for you this is an old blouse." But as Gail said that, she pushed the brush he held upward into his face.

"I'll leave you two to work this out," Lee said and crossed the room to continue painting the far wall with Mark and Slade.

"I don't get it. I would have thought by now we would

have a flood of leads to run down with Dante Frears coming forward and offering $25,000 for any information on the whereabouts of Rio and the person responsible for my father's beating." Slade finished his section and moved to the next one.

Lee picked up his brush and dipped it into the paint. "Give it time, Captain. I can't imagine someone passing up that kind of cash for long. Someone's gonna come forward. We're going to find your dog and get the person who hurt your dad."

"The criminals in town are scared and keeping their mouths shut, especially with Keevers's disappearance. And now that we found Adams's body in the woods, they are even more nervous. Who has them so afraid?" Slade applied his long strokes to the wall. "You would think we'd be aware of some criminal with that kind of power."

"Maybe it's a cop, and he's got all the bad guys quaking in their boots," Mark said with a chuckle.

Slade laughed. "Yeah, I'd like to be able to make the criminal element in Sagebrush quake with fear."

Was that the person that had Heidi so frightened? Lee thought back to her reaction a couple of times when she looked at his police badge on his shirt. She'd tensed. Did she know more than she was letting on? His gut told him no, but he'd been all wrong about a beautiful woman before and ended up hurt.

Mark Moore, his neighbor across the hall, glanced toward him. "I think you're smart, Calloway, keeping our mystery lady close. Easier to keep an eye on her. She could be involved in all of this."

"Why do you think that?" Lee's hand tightened about the brush. "Someone tried to kill her today."

"She was in the woods that day the police found Brady. She could be part of the crime syndicate. Others have gone missing. Ned Adams, a petty criminal connected to Charles Ritter—

one of the three middle managers in this crime syndicate—ended up dead. Maybe he angered The Boss. Maybe The Boss is cleaning up loose ends. The only others found in the Lost Woods were the two kidnappers. What was she doing?"

Lee bit back his response, *Running for her life.* There was a slim possibility she was involved, but he didn't doubt she had amnesia. It would be hard to fake that lost look or the scared vibes pouring off her. Someone was after her. He wasn't convinced it was someone in the crime syndicate. Besides, she wasn't from around here. "She's in trouble. I think a crime was committed against her, not the other way around."

"If not the kidnapping, then what about the wrecked car and the missing man?" Mark retorted. "Maybe she had something to do with William Peterson, instead."

Lee's protective instinct welled up in him. "Haven't you heard of innocent until proven guilty? I'm counting on you, Moore, keeping an eye out for her while I'm at work."

His neighbor attacked his section with angry strokes. "Sure. But I get to tell you I told you so if she proves to be involved."

Lee ground his teeth together and again kept his mouth shut. It was a good thing he and Moore worked on different shifts.

Slade jumped into the fray. "I've talked with the police chief. I want both of you to watch our mystery woman. Someone did go after her today. She may still be in danger, and until we know for sure, we need to protect her. I still think she knows something about what happened in the woods the day Brady was found." He glanced at Lee. "Have you talked with Zoller yet?"

"I'm going to after you all leave. I want the man to stew for a while. Maybe then he'll be ready to talk. He wasn't earlier."

His captain frowned. "I hope so. We don't have many leads to follow."

★ ★ ★

Later that evening, Heidi sat at Molly's kitchen table. "Those cookies smell great. Are you sure I can't do anything to help you?"

"Nope, other than help me take this upstairs to the workers. I want you to rest and take it easy." Molly used her metal spatula to remove the last batch of chocolate chip cookies from the baking sheet. "The pizzas should be here any minute. We should be ready. Are you hungry?"

Heidi's stomach gurgled. "I wasn't until I started smelling the cookies. I might just go right to them and skip the pizza."

The landlady glanced toward her. "You must have a sweet tooth."

"I guess so."

"You wouldn't know it from the looks of you. You're thin and petite. Almost frail."

"I haven't eaten much in weeks. A forced diet you could say."

Molly patted her rotund stomach. "I need something. The doctor says I should lose at least fifty pounds. I just don't know how and when they crept up on me. But then you wouldn't know anything about that."

Heidi looked down at herself. Was that the case? She concentrated on thinking about what she might like to eat. Chocolate chip cookies. That was a definite, but what else?

The doorbell rang.

"Will you get the pizzas and head on upstairs? I'll follow with the tea and glasses."

"Sure," Heidi said, but the thought of opening the front door to a stranger—and most everybody was one right now—constricted her chest as she made her way to the foyer. The pain from her healing rib cage intensified. She inhaled a series of shallow breaths, but her palms sweated as she reached for the handle and pulled the door toward her.

"Don't, Heidi," Lee said from behind her.

Chapter Four

Heidi grasped the knob and started to push it closed when she glimpsed a young teenage boy, holding large boxes. She relaxed as Lee came up beside her.

"Four large pizzas for Lee Calloway," the delivery boy said, glancing back and forth between her and Lee.

"I'll take them." Lee withdrew some money from his pocket and handed it to the guy. "Thanks." After she shut the door, he continued, "I don't want you to open the door for anyone you don't know."

"That narrows it down to almost everyone besides the people here tonight."

"Exactly. You were attacked earlier today. We don't know why. To be on the safe side I want you to stay close to this house and not go anywhere alone. If neither Mark nor I am here, I'll have a patrol car drive by a few times an hour or park out front until we figure out what's going on."

"I'm a prisoner?" she murmured more to herself, the idea

not frightening her as much as not knowing what was going on and who was after her.

"Not exactly. But you'll need to use caution. We don't know what's going on."

We. That one word comforted her more than she thought possible. It also felt alien to her, as if she'd been alone in the world before Lee Calloway had taken an interest in helping her. From what Molly had said, Lee was a thorough, highly respected police officer. *Thank You, Lord.* The thought surprised her in how freely it came to mind. A natural response from her that was there in spite of her lost memory. She remembered asking the Lord's help in the hospital room when she was attacked. Was her faith important to her?

"Let's take this upstairs. The crew is restless and hungry." Lee started for the steps.

Heidi watched him, his movements economical and full of self-assurance. She liked what she saw so far concerning Lee, but she wouldn't kid herself. Their relationship was strictly professional. He thought she knew something and intended to keep her alive long enough to find out what.

Lee took the chair across from Gus Zoller in the interview room at the police station. Lee didn't say anything for a long moment, but he stared at the man with a beard and gray eyes. For a few seconds Zoller kept his gaze trained on Lee, then he dropped his glance away from Lee and peered at the table between them. A tic twitched in the man's lean cheek.

"Why did you attack Jane Doe?" Lee asked, keeping the information about the name she was going by to himself.

Zoller shifted in his chair but remained silent.

"Who hired you?"

Still nothing from the man.

"You'll be charged with attempted murder. It'll be an open-

and-shut case. We'll also be looking into whether you pulled the plug on the life-support machine of the patient in Room 253 in order to create a diversion while you attacked Jane Doe. You can either make this hard on yourself or easy."

"I ain't talking. Bad things happen to people who do." The man lifted his gaze, stabbing it into Lee. "My mama didn't raise no dummy."

"So you're willing to go to prison for a long time rather than make a deal with us. We can protect you."

Zoller cackled, its sound almost desperate. "Sure you can."

"What does Jane Doe have to do with what's happening in Sagebrush?"

"I want a lawyer." The suspect pressed his lips into a thin line.

"Fine. You're the one that'll be rotting away in prison." Lee shoved back his chair and rose. "Not smart."

As he left the interview room, questions bombarded him. Who had everyone so scared? Did someone want to quiet Heidi because she witnessed something in the woods? Or was she involved somehow? Again that didn't feel right to him, but then Alexa had fooled him. Maybe he wasn't the best person to read a woman's motives.

After telling an officer on duty about allowing Zoller to contact a lawyer, Lee hurried to his SUV with the warrant to search Zoller's apartment in hand. Although Mark was at the house, Lee didn't want to be gone too long, but it was important to check out Zoller's place.

Fifteen minutes later, Lee parked in front of a three-story apartment building in an area that was above a custodian's pay scale—unless he was paid to take care of problems. Tomorrow he would dig into Zoller's background and financial information. Maybe he could find out who hired him by following the money trail.

The manager of the building took Lee up to Zoller's apartment on the third floor and let him in. Lee waited until the older gentleman left before swinging the front door open and moving into the dark apartment. Letting the light from the hallway illuminate the entrance, he ran his hand along the wall by the door, found the switch and flipped it up. Nothing. He tried it again. Still nothing.

The hairs on the nape of his neck stood up as Lee pivoted in the darkness while putting his hand on his gun. A split second later a large bulk slammed him back against the wall near the open door. His head jerked back then forward. The air swooshed from his lungs, and pain spread through his chest. The switch dug into his back as his assailant used his body to pen him down.

The attacker's face loomed inches away from Lee. The pressure on his torso trapped the breath in his lungs. The dim lighting from the hallway shone briefly on the man's craggy face as Lee used all his strength to shove the large man away. Before Lee could reach his gun, his attacker slammed his fist into Lee's gut, then brought up his right one and clipped his jaw, a ring packing an extra punch.

The world spun before Lee's eyes as the man raced from the apartment. He began to slump toward the floor, caught himself and staggered out into the hallway. The sound of a door shutting down the hall drew Lee's attention in that direction. An exit sign glowed. He stumbled forward. His vision blurred, and the corridor tilted at an odd angle. Lee reached out with his hand and touched the wall to steady himself.

Taking in a deep, stabilizing breath, Lee made his way toward the exit at a more sedate pace than he would have liked. By the time he reached the door, he had his bearings back and increased his speed. But he kept his hand on the wall as he descended to the first floor and pushed through the door that led outside. To the left was the street. To the right the back of the building and the parking lot for the tenants. He hurried toward the front. An empty street with his lone SUV parked along the curb greeted him.

Rotating around, Lee retraced his steps and continued toward the parking lot. As he rounded the apartment building, he spied a white Taurus making a left turn and speeding away. He couldn't make out the license-plate number.

He gritted his teeth and went farther into the parking lot to check it out in case that wasn't the assailant fleeing the scene. A dozen cars sat before him. He walked around to verify no one was hiding.

A dull throb pulsated in his head. His jaw ached. He grazed his fingertips over it and came away with blood. Probably the ring cut him. More irritated than anything, he trudged back into the building and found the manager's apartment again.

The older man's eyes bulged when he peered at him. "What happened?"

"There was someone in Zoller's apartment. He attacked me and fled."

"We have a few cameras around the building. Maybe he was caught on tape."

"Where are they?" Lee demanded.

"The stairwell on both sides of the building and the lobby."

"I'd like the tapes from all three." Something good might come out of this.

"It feeds into a room in the basement. I'll go get them."

"I'll come with you." Lee wasn't about to let anything happen to the one lead he might have to the perp in the apartment. "Then I need to go back up to Zoller's apartment. The light is out in his place when you go in."

"The whole apartment?"

"Don't know."

"I'll check the circuit breaker and see. It's in the basement, too."

As Lee followed the manager, he placed a call to Molly. "I'll be home later than I thought. How's Heidi?"

"She's sleeping, finally."

"Mark's still there?"

Molly chuckled. "Yes. Don't worry about us. I know how to take care of myself."

"Molly, these people mean business."

"I have a gun and I know how to use it."

"You do?" he asked in surprise.

"Yes. My husband used to go to the shooting range. I went along and learned how to fire a gun. I got so good that I made more bull's-eyes than he did the last couple of years before he died." She blew out a breath. "And don't forget, Kip's keeping us company. A very good watchdog. What's going on? Anything else besides Heidi being attacked today?"

Lee stopped outside a small room in the basement and turned away from the manager. "Yes. I was jumped tonight when I arrived at Zoller's apartment."

"Are you okay?"

"Yes."

"What in the world is happening in Sagebrush?"

"That's what I'm determined to find out, and I feel Heidi knows something she doesn't remember right now."

"The poor child. She's all alone. Well, at least she has you and me. When she's ready, hopefully she'll remember."

"I hope that it is in time. Is your alarm system on?"

"Yes, you and Mark have drilled it into me to set it every night. But you know it's not state of the art. I might need to look into a better one. At least in the meantime, I have two cops and a couple of police dogs living here."

"I've got to go. I'll stop by your apartment when I'm

through here." Lee stuck his cell back in his pocket and went into the room to retrieve the tapes.

After getting the security videos he needed, Lee waited while the apartment manager checked the circuit breaker.

The man frowned. "Someone flipped the breaker off for that apartment. I'm resetting it so you can see in there."

"Thanks." Lee made his way up to Zoller's place, and this time when he went into the apartment, he drew his gun, prepared, even though he felt the assailant was long gone. In the bright light from the small foyer, Lee surveyed the ransacked living area and called the station for assistance. This was going to take longer than he'd hoped.

Sleep evaded Heidi. She prowled the guest bedroom in Molly's apartment. Lee was interrogating the man who attacked her. Did Gus Zoller know her? Why was he trying to kill her? Was he the man in the woods from her nightmare? Maybe Lee would have some answers to her questions. She hoped Zoller's capture meant she wasn't in any more danger. But the thought didn't bring any comfort. Chilled, she rubbed her hands up and down her crossed arms.

She looked around the room—unfamiliar like everything she looked at lately—and decided to see if Molly was still up. She had mentioned she didn't usually turn in until eleven or twelve.

Heidi found Molly in her living room, reading a thick black book. The older lady smiled at Heidi and set her Bible on the small table next to her on the couch.

"Don't stop because of me." Heidi hung back in the entrance, not sure what to do.

"I always have time for you. Couldn't sleep?"

Heidi moved to the other end of the sofa and sat. "I tried, but I kept thinking about Lee interrogating Zoller. There's so much in my life I don't know. At least I want to know what the man said to Lee."

"He should be back soon. He called a while ago and said he was checking out the man's apartment and would be back after that."

Silence fell between them, and Heidi stared down at her lap, searching her mind for something she could talk about. Why did she remember who the Texas governor and the President of the United States were? The capital of Texas was Austin. The surrounding states are New Mexico, Louisiana, Arkansas and Oklahoma. And yet, she remembered nothing about her personal life.

"I can't even begin to imagine what you're going through, Heidi, but you will remember what you need to."

She lifted her gaze to Molly, the woman's features set in a calm she wished she felt. "How can you say that?"

"It's just a feeling I have. I like to look at life in a positive light. I can't control a lot of things, but I can control my attitude."

"I can't even tell you what my attitude toward life is." Heidi gestured toward the black book on the table. "I can't tell you if I've ever read the Bible. What my favorite food is. But after this evening, I'll say pizza is in my top five."

"True, you don't know much about your past right now. That doesn't mean you can't decide how you want to approach your life now regardless of your past."

"What if I never remember?"

"Then you have a chance to start over fresh," Molly said. "There are people out there who would love to be able to do that. God placed you here for a reason."

"That's what you think?"

The older woman nodded. "I used to struggle against everything, then I started looking at what was happening to me from different perspectives and found things that were positive about every situation."

What in the world was positive about not remembering who she was? About having someone want to kill her, and not knowing why? About what caused her nightmare?

Molly chuckled. "I know. I sound like Mary Sunshine, but I don't stress like I used to. My blood pressure is manageable, and for years it wasn't."

"But you know who you are."

"And you know who you are—" Molly touched her chest over her heart "—in here where it counts."

A beeping sound filled the air. Kip came to his feet near the apartment door.

Molly grinned. "That's Lee." She pushed to her feet. "But I'll check just to make sure."

When she went to a table, pulled open a drawer and withdrew a gun, Heidi's eyes grew round. She instinctively fisted her hands, poised and ready to fight or flee.

Molly cracked her door open and peeked out, then glanced back at Heidi. "It's him." She stuffed the weapon into her dress pocket and stood to the side as Lee entered.

Heidi's gaze riveted on the cut along his jaw about two inches long with dried blood. "You're hurt. What happened?"

His mouth cocked up at one corner. "Let's just say the welcome mat wasn't laid out for me at Zoller's apartment."

"I thought he was at the station." The panic she'd experienced fighting the man earlier swamped Heidi. She flexed her hands then curled them into tight balls again.

"He's locked up. Someone ransacked his place, and I interrupted him. We fought. He fled before I could have a little chat with him."

"Who?" The one word came out in a breathless rush. There was another man involved in this mess she was caught up in.

Lee eased into the chair across from Heidi. "Good question. Fortunately, I got a brief look at him. I'll meet with the police sketch artist and see if I can come up with a picture. After I do, I want you to look at it. Maybe you'll recognize the man."

"Me? I don't see how." Heidi gritted her teeth, wishing she could say something different.

Kip parked himself next to Lee, who greeted him with a rubdown. "Still, it's worth a shot. Besides, I want you to know what the man looks like."

"In case I run into him, too?" She shivered, thinking about another person out there targeting her. Why? What could she possible have locked in her mind to cause someone to want her dead? She massaged her temple as though that would bring the information to the surface and put an end to her terror.

"Yes, he could be the person who hired Zoller."

"Sure, anything to find out what's going on."

Lee glanced toward Molly putting her gun away in the drawer. "I want you to look at the picture, too." A frown twisted his mouth. "You do have a permit for that?"

"Of course. I'm a law-abiding citizen. Contrary to others in town." Molly took her seat again on the couch. "Why would someone ransack Zoller's apartment?"

"To cover up a connection with Zoller? To retrieve something Zoller had? It could be a hundred different reasons, and Zoller isn't talking."

The memory of Zoller's piercing eyes sent fear through Heidi. Maybe she knew Zoller in her old life. There had to be some connection for her to react so vehemently to his cold, gray eyes. Like a few other instances, she felt it deep down in her gut. "Why do you think Zoller was hired to kill me?"

"Because of his reaction when I asked him who hired him. He's protecting someone."

The man in her nightmare? Another shudder snaked down her spine.

"Which means you'll have to be extra careful. My captain wants Mark and me to keep an eye on you, and if we can't, to pull in another officer. Right now you're our best lead to figuring out what's going on in Sagebrush. Who The Boss is."

"The Boss? You think I know who he is?" How? Why? The idea she might alarmed her.

"Don't know. But someone wants you dead for some reason. You need protecting."

The idea someone like Lee would protect her gave her a sense of security in the midst of all that was going on.

Lee turned his attention to his landlady. "Molly, this place is as good as any we have, but I don't want you caught up in the middle of this. We can leave—"

"Hold it right there, young man." Molly held up one finger. "First, I can take care of myself. Second, no one has a beef with me. Third, you'll be here protecting Heidi. Fourth, I care what happens to her."

"Okay. I get the point. We'll secure this place. I'm also going to have Kip stay with you, Heidi. He's a great watchdog."

A vision of a black-and-white border collie wagging his tail when she met him made Heidi smile. She must love dogs. The feeling Kip had produced in her was one of warmth. Was there a dog somewhere waiting for her to return home? "He's adorable," she raved, fastening her gaze on the animal now lying at Lee's feet.

"And good at his job. He thinks of himself as tough and macho, so don't say that in front of him again or he'll get an idea he should act—" Lee dropped his voice to a faint whisper "—adorable."

A laugh bubbled up in Heidi, and she got the feeling she

hadn't laughed much in recent years. Maybe she didn't want to know about her real life.

"I need to get his water bowl from my apartment, otherwise he'll try drinking out of the toilet." Lee stood.

Heidi rose, too. "I'd like to go with you."

One of his eyebrows arched.

"The more I know the layout of this house the safer I'll feel," she offered as the reason she wanted to accompany him.

"Fine."

"That's my cue to go to bed. It sounds like tomorrow will be a busy day." Molly made her way toward the short hall that led to the two bedrooms.

Out in the large foyer of the Victorian home, Heidi stopped Lee's progress toward the staircase by clasping his arm. She immediately dropped her hand to her side and stepped back. "I can't put Molly in danger. Tomorrow I should go to a hotel or something."

He shook his head. "That's not necessary. I'll be back here after work tomorrow to finish up the third-floor apartment so you can move in there tomorrow evening. You'd be safer upstairs than at some hotel. I can control this place better. And, besides, the person is after you, not Molly."

"Strangely, I'm comforted by that fact. I don't want anything to happen to her because of me."

"I'm not going to let anything happen to you or Molly. I can't imagine what you're going through right now, but I want to help as much as I can."

His declaration reinforced she wasn't as alone as she'd felt when she'd first awakened in the hospital. "I'm going to help you fix up the apartment tomorrow afternoon. That's the least I can do."

"Only if you promise not to overdo it. Okay?"

She nodded, her throat jamming with emotions that overwhelmed her at the man's kindness. The sense she hadn't received a lot of that lately disturbed her further. But why had she reacted to seeing Lee in a police uniform, especially when she saw his badge? What if she was somehow involved with The Boss whom Lee was looking for? What if she was a criminal? She delved into the dark recesses of her mind and couldn't answer those questions. She didn't feel like a criminal, but could she trust her feelings?

With one corner of his mouth tilted up, he gazed down at her. "We're gonna figure out what's going on so you'll be safe."

What if I did something wrong? The question begged to be asked, but Heidi couldn't bring herself to say the words. She wanted to trust Lee. He gave her every reason to trust him, but when she thought of him as a cop, she remained quiet.

He grazed his fingers across her forehead. "I know you're worried, but look at it this way—no one tried to kill you until you woke up. That means you know something they want to keep quiet."

So all she was to him was a lead he had to protect so he could find out what she knew. That thought shouldn't upset her, but it did. "I don't know anything. I don't know how many times I have to say that to get people to understand that."

"But you're awake and talking. They figure it's only a matter of time before you do say something."

"All I remember is running in the woods." Her nightmare invaded her conscious mind. "I—I…" She recalled slamming into a man. A tall, muscular man.

"What, Heidi?" Lee came nearer, laying his hand on her shoulder, his closeness demanding her attention. "What have you remembered?"

"I was being chased by someone in the woods. Maybe you? Maybe one of those two men you showed me pictures of after I regained consciousness? Maybe someone else? I don't know, but I do know I collided with a man over six feet tall with a broad, muscular chest."

"Do you remember what he looked like?"

A vague picture began to materialize in her mind. "I remember..."

Chapter Five

"I remember touching his arms and thinking he works out."
Which sent her into a frenzy, trying to get away from the man
as fast as she could. Another memory edged its way forward.
Heidi had known someone who prided himself on keeping
physically fit. The man in the woods? The guy who attacked
Lee tonight?

"That might fit the guy in Zoller's apartment tonight."

"I don't want anyone hurt because of me." The past few
days overwhelmed her, and tears swelled into her eyes. One
slipped down her cheek.

Lee brushed it away, one hand cradling the side of her head.
"The police are going to work as hard as we can to make sure
that doesn't happen again."

Another tear rolled down her face. Crying seemed foreign
to her, and yet she couldn't stop the flow. Lee wrapped his
arms around her and pulled her against him. The warmth of
his embrace seeped into her, and she tried to stop crying. But

it was as if all her emotions burst through a tight barrier and exploded from her.

"I won't let anyone hurt you. I promise."

His whispered words soothed her troubled soul, and for a few seconds she believed what he said. Then reality hit her. She pushed back from him, swiping her hands across her cheeks. "You can't do that. You don't know if you can."

He frowned. "You're right. Let me rephrase what I said… I will do everything humanly possible to keep you safe." His scowl slowly evolved into a smile. "Let's get Kip's bowl." He held out his hand to her.

She took it and mounted the stairs to the second floor. After retrieving what he came for from his apartment, Lee started back to Molly's place.

"What if Kip doesn't want to stay with me? What if he doesn't like me?" Heidi asked as they approached Molly's.

Lee chuckled. "I doubt that'll happen knowing my dog." When he opened the door, the dog in question was dancing about the foyer, his tail wagging.

Kip took one look at Heidi and wiggled his body toward her, nudging her hand with his head.

"I don't think that's gonna be a problem," Lee said, kneeling next to the border collie.

Heidi did likewise and received a big, sloppy lick on her cheek.

"That's about all I can remember about the man who jumped me last night at Zoller's." Lee paced behind the woman who was the resident sketch artist for the police. "I know it isn't much to go on, but maybe someone will recognize him."

He watched her put the finishing touches to the drawing of a man with thick eyebrows and a nose that must have been broken several times. He didn't have a sense of the man's hair because he'd worn a hoodie that shadowed his features. But in the brief time he'd been able to focus on his attacker's face, Lee had zeroed in on the nose and eyebrows that were almost a continuous line across.

"He had dark brown eyes."

The sketch artist shaded in the eyes then presented the drawing to Lee. "Anything else?"

"No, even on the surveillance tapes a lot of his face was hidden by the hoodie. Thanks." Lee took the paper from her and headed to Lorna's desk. "Can you have this reproduced and passed around to everyone? He's the guy who attacked me at Zoller's apartment last night. Is Zoller's lawyer here yet?"

"Yes, about ten minutes ago. They're in the interview room waiting for you." The secretary reached for a piece of paper in a folder and gave it to him. "This just came in about the car you found yesterday in the Lost Woods. One set of finger-prints was identified— our Jane Doe's on the steering wheel, various places like the stick-to-shift gears and the driver's-side door inside and out. There are some others, but they're still trying to match them."

He remembered the police taking her fingerprints in hopes of identifying her. Nothing had turned up. "Anything else with the car?"

"Not yet. It's only been a day. They're still running some tests."

"Thanks, Lorna. You're a jewel." Lee made his way toward the interview room.

He relished another round with Zoller. He needed answers, and hoped with Zoller's lawyer's advice that he would receive some. When he entered the room, the two men ended their quiet conversation. Zoller slouched back in his chair while his lawyer, Walter Smithe, straightened and looked at Lee.

"When I went to search your apartment last night, I was

attacked. Someone ransacked your place. What were they looking for?"

Zoller shrugged. "How should I know? Did you ask your attacker?"

A cocky edge leaked into Zoller's words and attitude, inflaming Lee's anger. He shoved it down. He didn't need to lose his control. "He escaped, but not for long. Then he can join you in your cell."

Zoller slanted a glance toward his lawyer who shook his head. "Can't help you. I wasn't there."

"Did you have a search warrant, Detective?"

Lee produced it for the lawyer. "We do everything by the book. I wouldn't want him walking on a technicality when we have him solid for attempted murder."

The man slid the warrant back to Lee. "My client doesn't have anything else to say to you. He's willing to admit to assault against the patient, but there was no intent to kill her."

"Not according to her." Lee wished he could also charge his suspect with attempted murder of the patient who had his life support system unplugged, but there was no evidence linking Zoller to that—at least right now.

"It's his word against hers. Up until yesterday, Mr. Zoller has been a model citizen. The woman insulted him, and he overreacted. I'll be talking with the DA. This interview is over."

Lee ground his teeth and pushed to his feet. "If you know what's good for you, you'll cooperate with the police."

Zoller dropped his gaze. "You heard Mr. Smithe. Your Jane Doe isn't the woman she claims. She provoked me." The man lifted his chin and stabbed Lee with a hard glare.

Unless he could convince Zoller to disclose who hired him and whatever else he knew, he had reached a dead end until he located his attacker from last night. Someone had to talk. This uncanny reticence worried him.

Lee left the interview room and told the officer to return the prisoner to his cell, then he headed back into the main room. Slade stood at Lorna's desk, looking at the sketch he'd given the K-9 Unit's secretary.

His captain peered up when he approached. "I haven't seen anyone who looks like this. Circulate the sketch. Maybe someone else has."

"Captain, I need another officer to watch Heidi when Mark or I am not available. After last night I don't think she should be without full-time police protection until I find the person who hired Zoller."

"Is he talking?"

"No. He lawyered up."

Slade grimaced. "Who's representing him?"

"Walter Smithe."

"Oh, great. How does a custodian have the money to afford Walter?"

"Maybe The Boss hired Zoller to kill Heidi."

"Possibly. I don't get the impression he dirties his hands with the small stuff. But who knows? We don't know much about our Jane Doe or for that matter, the man behind the crime syndicate."

Lee swallowed back the words to defend Heidi. The captain was right. They didn't know anything about Heidi and her possible involvement in what was going on in Sagebrush. But his attacker last night might know. He intended to focus his attention on finding that man.

"Who do you want on the roster to help you and Mark?"

"Valerie. I think Heidi could use a woman about her age to protect her."

"Fine. She may be able to help her remember. With the two

attempts connected to Heidi, I agree we need to have someone around at all times. How's Molly with all this?"

"Mad at whoever is doing this to Heidi. Molly has taken
her under her wing. Did you know Molly has a gun and says
she can shoot, very well?"

Slade chuckled. "Yep, I've seen her on the shooting range."

"Why am I the last person to know that my landlady is a
gun-toting woman?"

"I'll let Valerie know. She'll need to start filling in for you
tomorrow because I need Kip's expertise to finish the search
of the Lost Woods. You and Austin have over two-thirds of
the area left. Pauly Keevers is still missing, and I'm concerned
he's buried out there like Ned Adams."

"With Adams dead and Keevers missing, no wonder no
one is talking. I'll get with Austin and we'll start first thing
tomorrow." He raked a hand through his hair. "The rest of
today I'll be at Molly's. I'm finishing the apartment upstairs
so Heidi can move in tomorrow after the floor dries."

"She's going to stay in the apartment by herself?"

"No. Kip will be with her at night while I'm guarding the
one way up to the apartment."

Slade eyed Lee. "It sounds like this is personal."

"It is. Someone attacked me, and I don't take kindly to that.
That was the man's first mistake. I'll find him."

Lee left the police station with a copy of the sketch to show
Heidi and Molly. He panned the street, eager to return to
Molly's boarding house. Mark was there, but his dedication
to Heidi wasn't the same. He felt better when he was protecting her himself.

Halfway to his SUV his cell rang. He answered it, surprised
it was Gail at the hospital. "What's going on?"

"When housekeeping was cleaning the room Heidi was
in, the woman saw something that looked odd," his friend

replied. "She came and got me. I think it's a bug and I don't mean the insect kind. I didn't touch it, and neither did the lady from housekeeping."

"I'll be right there."

Lee climbed into his car and headed for the hospital. A bug? Interesting.

When he arrived at the nurses' station on the second floor, Gail finished writing something in a chart then came from behind the counter.

"It looks like something I've seen on T.V.," she said as she walked toward the room Heidi had stayed in the day before. "What I'm going to show you isn't something the hospital has in the rooms."

Inside, Gail bent over and pointed to a small black box attached to the underside of the bed.

After putting on gloves, Lee scooted under the listening device, disconnected it from its power source and carefully removed it, then placed it in an evidence bag.

Gail wrote on a pad, *Is it safe to talk?*

"It was a room transmitter and hooked into the electricity used to power the bed. I essentially turned it off. I'll swing by the station and have it checked out. It could explain why all of a sudden Zoller was trying to kill Heidi. He probably planted it. When she woke from the coma, he must have been afraid she would start remembering and tried to silence her." A sudden thought came to Lee. "Is Patrick McNeal still in the same room?"

"Yes." Her eyes widened. "You don't think his room is bugged, too?"

"I'm checking."

Lee made his way down the hallway and within two minutes found a similar listening device in his captain's father's room. As Lee rose from under the bed, his gaze latched on to Slade's dad. All evidence of his severe beating had healed, but Patrick still hadn't regained consciousness and the doctors feared permanent brain damage.

"Someone was keeping tabs on both of them." What he didn't say to Gail was the implications of how desperate someone was.

After what happened to Lee the night before, Heidi had gotten little sleep. Every time she fell into a deep slumber and the nightmare began, she yanked herself awake and paced the bedroom in Molly's apartment. Once she'd paused at the window and parted the curtains to look outside. Dark shadows littered the area around Molly's place, and she could easily imagine someone lurking in their depths, watching.

The window in the bedroom she'd stayed the night before was only four feet from the ground. She folded her arms across her chest and inspected the newly finished apartment on the third floor—thirty feet to the ground from the few windows in the place. Would that be far enough up to keep her safe?

Heidi bent down and felt the floor. Still not totally dry. She'd hoped she could stay up here tonight, but she would have to wait until tomorrow.

A cold nose nudged her hand, and Heidi glanced down at Kip. "You back from visiting Eliza?"

The border collie barked.

"If only you could talk," she said with a laugh, scratching the dog behind his ears.

"I don't think we'd want to know what goes on in his mind. Remember he likes to find dead bodies."

Heidi glanced over her shoulder at Lee mounting the last step to the third-floor landing. A tall woman with long red hair came up behind him. Another dog—a black Rottweiler with tan markings and a bobbed tail—accompanied the lady.

"This is officer Valerie Salgado. She and Lexi are members of the K-9 Unit. When I'm searching the Lost Woods the next several days, she'll be staying with you. Kip's talents are needed for the task."

"So you really do think there are more dead bodies in the woods?"

"I certainly hope not, but we have to cover all bases."

Valerie crossed to Heidi with her arm extended toward her. "I thought I would stop by and meet you before tomorrow morning."

Heidi shook the officer's hand. Valerie's warm smile put Heidi at ease. While Kip and Lexi sniffed each other, Heidi said, "What's Lexi's specialty in the K-9 Unit?"

"Apprehension/protection. Which is perfect in your case."

"How long have you been with the K-9 Unit?"

"I'm a rookie, but I come from a long line of cops. It's in my genes. I know Molly is about ready to serve dinner so I'd better take off. I have to pick up Bethany from the babysitter."

"Bethany? Your daughter?" Heidi asked.

"No, my niece, but I'm her legal guardian now." Valerie started for the exit. "Just wanted you to know you'll be in good hands when this guy isn't here." She tossed a look toward Lee.

There was something about Valerie that Heidi liked. Her whole face lit up when she grinned, giving Heidi the impression she smiled a lot.

As the rookie and Lexi descended the staircase, Lee came to Heidi's side. "You all right?"

"Just wondering if I had any close friends in my other life."

"Do you?"

"Don't know." She gave him a wry look. "Maybe I should record that and play it when someone asks me a question."

"I thought I would ask and see if you answered without thinking about it."

"You do believe me about not remembering, don't you?"

"Yes," he said with only a second's hesitation.

That second bothered Heidi. "But you don't trust me."

"I don't trust many people. Truth is... I don't know you."

"That makes two of us." She sighed. "I don't know myself, either."

He put his hand at the small of her back. "Then you and I will get to know you together."

"It should be an interesting journey." She started down the stairs. "Now that you've enlisted Valerie to help you and Mark keep an eye on me, I get the feeling that you want a police officer here at all times. Why?"

"I'd rather be cautious than have something happen to you."

"Because of last night and the guy who attacked you?"

"Yes...and the fact a listening device was planted in your hospital room. Not to mention Zoller attacked you and he isn't saying a word about why or who else may be involved." He rubbed a hand across his face. "And there's no doubt in my mind that someone else *is* involved. He's either too scared to talk or protecting someone."

Heidi halted and swung around on the step. "How did you find a listening device?"

"Housekeeping discovered the bug, and Gail called me."

"Why didn't you tell me while we were working on the apartment earlier this afternoon?"

"I wanted to see what the tech guy said about it. Maybe see if it can be tracked."

"Can it?"

"No." His eyes softened. "I didn't want you to worry any more than you already are."

She put one fisted hand on her waist. "I don't want to be kept in the dark. I feel my whole life is that right now. Don't make it worse for me. I need to know everything."

Lee sniffed the air. "Molly fixed her beef stew. We'll start by seeing if you like beef stew and go from there."

Heidi stepped into his path. "Promise me you'll let me know what's happening with my case."

"If you'll let me know when you remember something, even something seemingly unimportant."

"Okay. Then I guess you should know I'm pretty sure I had a dog once."

"How do you figure that?" Lee asked as they headed toward the kitchen on the first floor.

"Being with Kip feels so natural to me. Like I had a pet before..." She shrugged. "I don't know... Before all of this." Sweeping her arm across her body, she indicated her new surroundings.

"But you don't know for sure?"

"No. I can't say I know anything for sure. I have feelings. Like a sense it was something I'd done or liked. What if I have to piece my whole life back together using that method?"

"Those feelings come from somewhere. Give yourself time to heal. A lot has happened to you in a couple of weeks."

"There's so much I don't know." She started to enter the kitchen but stopped when Lee clasped her shoulder. Turning, she met his gaze, seeing worry in the depth of his eyes. "What aren't you telling me?"

"We matched some of the fingerprints in William Peterson's car to yours. We got the results back earlier today."

"You have my prints? When did you get them?"

"We took them while you were in a coma to help us ID you. They aren't in any database."

She didn't know whether she should be angry they fingerprinted her without her knowledge, or relieved by the news no criminal database had a record of hers. "So I'm not a criminal," she finally said, deciding that was good news.

"Did you think you were?" The corners of his mouth twitched, and he pressed his lips together even tighter.

"What was I supposed to think? The police apprehended me running away from an area where a crime had gone down. Yeah, the thought had crossed my mind."

"Maybe you've been so good that you haven't been caught—until now."

Her mouth dropped open. "Seriously? You think that?"

His laughter burst from him. "No. I don't. I think you're a victim in all this."

He said it with conviction, which prompted her to ask, "Then where is William Peterson? Why was I in his car?"

"Two very good questions that I'll look into just as soon as I find the person behind your attack. My first priority is to keep you safe."

"My first priority is to remember who I am and why I was running in the woods."

"Then we'll work together. I think if you figure out those two things a lot will fall into place."

The idea of them being a team sent a wave of calmness through her. A sense that he would keep her safe followed that peace. And for some reason she couldn't shake the feeling she hadn't felt safe in a long time.

Molly stepped into the doorway into the kitchen, drying her hands on her apron. "I don't know about y'all, but I'm hungry. C'mon, you can talk in here."

After Heidi sat at the table, Molly stretched out her arm and took her hand, then did the same with Lee. "Let's pray."

Lee clasped Heidi's other hand and bowed his head. "Father, please help Heidi to remember who she is and to keep her safe. Help the police solve what is going on in Sagebrush and bless this wonderful food Molly has prepared. Amen."

When his fingers fell away from hers, Heidi missed his

touch. There was an added comfort in it. Again, something she was sure she hadn't experienced in a long time. Did she want to remember a past that might be riddled with problems and tragedy? Maybe it was better she never did. A fresh start might be what she needed. Was that why she wasn't remembering?

"Molly, I want to help you around the house since you won't take any rent right now."

The older woman with salt-and-pepper hair shook her head. "I can't take money from you."

"I have that four hundred dollars."

"You need to keep that for emergencies. When all this is settled and you have your life back, we'll talk about paying rent."

"I need something to do. I can only sit around for so long."

"You've been through a trauma. Give your body time to heal." Lee spooned the carrots, potatoes and onions onto his plate, then passed the bowl to Heidi.

"I can't answer what I did in my old life, but I know I didn't lounge around. I worked and I enjoyed working. If I didn't, I have a feeling I would go crazy. You would be doing me a favor, Molly."

"I know what you can help me with. I'm making a quilt for a fund-raiser at church. Do you sew?"

"We'll find out, and if I don't, I'll learn. But I also would like to help with the cooking. From what I've seen I think I can do some of it, that I might have enjoyed doing it in my old life." The more she talked about herself, the more she felt her life was divided into two parts. Before the accident/trauma—she wasn't even sure what to call what had happened to her—and after it.

"Sure. I usually provide a breakfast each morning and sometimes either a lunch or dinner depending on Mark and Lee's schedules. Neither one likes to cook and I do." The landlady smiled. "It'll be fun to see what you can do. It might even help you to remember other things about your past."

"Speaking of remembering—" Heidi swung her attention to Lee "—can I see William Peterson's car? Maybe it will trigger some memory. Where did y'all find my fingerprints?"

"Driver's door. Steering wheel. The stick-to-shift gears."

"So I was driving it. Where are the keys to the car? Did I have any on me?"

Lee shook his head. "Four hundred dollars and nothing else. No purse or wallet. I'll take you tomorrow afternoon to the car impound. The vehicle's been processed, so it should be okay."

"Keys are probably in the woods somewhere since that's where you found the car." Molly slid her fork into her mouth.

"While I'm there tomorrow, I'll walk out from where the car was toward the place where you were first spotted and see if I can find them. I'll use a metal detector."

Heidi rolled William Peterson's name around in her mind, trying to picture him other than from his driver's license photo that Lee showed her. She couldn't.

"What do you expect to find seeing the car tomorrow?" he asked.

"I don't know what I'm looking for. Anything to help us figure out what happened. William Peterson lives in San Antonio. How did I end up here in his car? Where is he?"

"I have a call in to the police in San Antonio to check with his friends and his work, Boland Manufacturing. I should hear something pretty soon."

"San Antonio is a few hours away. Why don't you go check in person?" Molly halved her roll and buttered each part.

"I can't until after I complete my search of the Lost Woods. Kip works best with me, and I need to be near to help protect Heidi."

"What if we both went?" Heidi proposed. "Maybe I know

this guy somehow. If that's the case, seeing where he lives and works might help me. Is there anything in his car that might explain my presence in it?"

"We found a bloody cloth in the car tucked down between the seats. One of the blood types is yours. We're running DNA because there were two blood types."

She glared at him. "Is there anything else you're not telling me?"

"I didn't say anything because it might not be yours. You're type O+, which is the most common blood type. The other blood type we found is B+."

"And you didn't want to worry me. Quit protecting me. I'm not that fragile. What if the wreck caused the cuts and before I got out…"

"Yes?" Lee cocked an eyebrow.

"If I tried to stop the bleeding after the car went off the road, where did the other blood come from?"

"Exactly. You had a number of injuries all over you. Some the doctor said were caused by something like a wreck, others appeared more like from a beating." Did she run into someone in the Lost Woods who beat her but somehow she got away? Or did William Peterson?

"What blood type is William Peterson?"

"Don't know. Trying to find that out."

A dull throb pulsated behind her eyes. "There are so many questions and no answers." She massaged her temple. "Lee, please let me accompany you to San Antonio. I'll be safe with you. If no one knows about the trip, then the person who wants me dead won't know where I am."

Lee nodded reluctantly. "I'll have to run this by my captain. If he gives the all-clear, we'll go after I complete the search of the woods."

The prospects of actively doing something to find out what

happened to her gave her hope she would recover her memory and regain her life. "Good. Until then I'll help you, Molly."

Lee's cell phone rang. He dug it out of his jean pocket, looked at the caller and rose. "Hello," he said as he strode from the kitchen.

"Probably the station," Molly said gently. "He always does that when they call. He takes his job very seriously, you see. I think that's why he's so upset about what's happening to you. He feels responsible for you, and that you were attacked in the hospital."

"He had no idea someone was going to try and kill me," Heidi protested.

"Still. He blames himself. If he'd been just a little earlier, you would have been fine."

"We wouldn't have known someone was after me if I hadn't been attacked."

The sound of footsteps returning wafted to Heidi as she picked up her sweetened iced tea. Molly placed her forefinger against her lips and looked toward the entrance.

"Why the frown, Lee?" the older woman asked.

"Gus Zoller was released on bail a while ago."

Chapter Six

The glass slipped from Heidi's numb fingers and crashed to the tile floor, shards flying everywhere. Lee hurried to the table and began picking up the broken pieces.

"I'm so sorry, Molly," Heidi said and bent over to help.

Molly snorted. "Accidents happen and believe me, I'd have done the same thing if I'd found out the man who tried to kill me was out of jail." She got up and moved to the closet, withdrawing a broom and dustpan. "Y'all move before you cut your hand."

Flashes of the assault yesterday zipped through Heidi's mind. And the man responsible was walking around free. She rose and fled the kitchen.

She heard Molly say, "Go."

The next thing Heidi realized, Lee was right behind her. "I'm not going to let him hurt you again. The DA was going to push to keep Zoller in jail without bail. But when the judge set a high bail amount, I thought that would be enough to keep him there." He blew out a frustrated breath. "I should have realized how wrong that thinking was, especially since Walter Smithe's services don't come cheap."

Her stomach roiling, Heidi glanced over her shoulder. "You don't have to follow me. I'm not leaving. I'm going upstairs to my apartment."

"You can't. The floor isn't dry."

Heidi halted with one foot on the first stair. "Oh, that's right. I forgot."

"C'mon back to the kitchen," he said softly. "Molly told me she made her one-of-a-kind pecan pie. She has won cooking contests with this recipe. Add a scoop of vanilla ice cream and—"

"I'd be five pounds heavier," Heidi said with a laugh.

"I like hearing you laugh. You should do it more often."

"It's sad it doesn't feel natural to me, as if I don't laugh a lot." She released a long sigh. "I don't think I want to remember what my life was like. I know you need me to for your case but—"

He put two fingers over her lips and said, "Shh. I want what is best for you, and ultimately I think knowing about your past is important to you moving on." He inched closer. "But only when you're ready to deal with it."

Right now her past was unimportant—not when she peered into the kindness in his dark chocolate eyes. "I'm not sure what I'd do without you. I feel lost."

His fingers combed through her hair, his hands framing her face. His gaze smoldered as it skimmed over her features, lingering on her mouth, her lips parted slightly as she drew in stabilizing breaths. But she couldn't get enough. His look robbed her of rational thought.

She swallowed several times, trying to drag her attention away from him. In the short time she'd come out of her coma, he'd been here for her. Made her feel safe. What would happen when her real life intruded? Who was the man in her nightmare? Why was he trying to kill her?

Lee lowered his head toward hers and all she could focus on was his mouth inches away from her. The feel of his breath teasing her lips open, the rough texture of his palm against her cheeks, the scent of him—a hint of Kip mingling with the fading aroma of the beef stew all converged to overwhelm her senses to let down her guard totally.

The sound of paws clicking against the hardwood floor invaded the quiet of the foyer. The next thing Heidi felt was a cold nose against her hand at her side, urging her to pet Kip. When she didn't move fast enough to pay the dog some attention, he barked once.

She laughed. "He's most persistent."

"He's learned not to give up when he's on the trail of something," Lee whispered close to her mouth, then sighed and pulled back.

"Is that how his partner is?"

"Afraid so." His lips quirked into a half smile. "Molly must have let him in. When he's ready to come in, he's persistent there, too, until someone obliges."

"Probably figured there was some beef stew left over for him."

"And he'd be right. Molly has been known to sneak him some people food when I'm not looking."

Molly appeared in the hallway. "Anyone for dessert?"

"Sure," Lee immediately answered while Heidi continued to pet Kip. "How about you?" He glanced at her.

"When I grew up, I couldn't eat dessert until I'd finished my whole dinner. I'm afraid I left some on..." Heidi straightened.

"You remembered something from your childhood?"

"Yes, and I'm sure it's right." She grinned. "But I'm not

a little girl anymore. I make my own decisions. I've decided pecan pie with ice cream sounds perfect."

"We're coming, Molly." Lee put his hand at the small of Heidi's back, and they headed for the kitchen.

Heidi tried to focus on where that tidbit from her childhood had come from, but when she searched her mind, all she found were dark holes and no other sense of who she was.

The next day in the Lost Woods, with Kip sitting next to him, Lee stood over another grave, now empty. He'd prayed this wouldn't be the outcome of Keevers's disappearance. He'd hoped they would find him alive somewhere.

The crime-scene techs and the ME had just left with Pauly Keevers's body. At least they knew what had happened to Keevers. He was shot execution style just like Ned Adams. From the condition of the body it was probably not long after he disappeared, but the ME would tell him a more accurate time of death after the autopsy.

Any way he looked at it, finding Keevers's body an hour ago answered some questions but posed more. Did the same person kill both Adams and Keevers? He wouldn't be surprised if ballistics came back saying both were murdered with the same gun.

Is that same person behind Zoller and his attempt on Heidi?

Kip barked, pulling Lee from his thoughts. So many questions. Few answers.

"C'mon, boy. We need to get back to the station. It's been a long day."

Half an hour later, Lee dragged himself into the police station. He'd deposited Kip over at the training center so he could fill out the paperwork on finding Pauly Keevers's body. On his way back to the station, he'd swung by Zoller's apartment building, looking for the man's pickup in the parking lot. It was gone. He didn't like not knowing where the suspect was at this moment. Heidi was protected with Valerie, but the unknown factors always ate at him.

He liked to control his surroundings—well, as much as he could. But especially lately, he realized how little control he had. He had command over his reactions but not over others' actions. He looked at Dan Harwood's desk across the room. His ex-fiancée had given birth to Dan's son six weeks ago, and he had to see Dan's family pictures of Josh up on the bulletin board in the break room whenever he went in there. Mostly he avoided the room.

Why be constantly reminded of his past romantic failure? If truth be known, he had been glad Kip had interrupted that heated moment between Heidi and him last night. Otherwise he would have kissed her, and that would have been a mistake. He'd thought he'd known Alexa and he hadn't. With Heidi he knew he didn't know her. She didn't even know herself.

He was running late. He needed to get the report finished and on his captain's desk. Lee sat down and began filling it out. Thirty minutes later, he completed it and gave it to Lorna, then he crossed to the back door. The training center for the canines was behind the police station. A minute later he entered it and came to a halt a few feet inside.

Alexa stood with Dan, showing her new baby to Harry Markham and Kaitlin Mathers, two of the trainers. Kaitlin's enthralled expression fixed on Josh's tiny features. Lee knew of Kaitlin's love of children—he shared that same love. And the woman he'd wanted to have those kids with was only a few feet away, holding another man's baby. Alexa slanted her gaze toward him and stiffened. Dan peered at him and then immediately looked away.

"I'd better be getting home," Alexa said, taking her baby back from Kaitlin. "I'm sure you all have work to do."

"Actually, I was heading home. I'll walk with you two." Harry grabbed a set of keys from his desk and accompanied the couple who avoided eye contact with Lee as they passed him in the suddenly small training center.

"Kip's out back. Sorry you came in on that." Kaitlin's voice pulled his attention back to the reason he'd come to the center. "He still had some energy to run off. I hear he did good today in the woods."

"Yeah, he found another body buried much like the other one."

Kaitlin brushed a stray lock of honey-blond hair off her face. "Are you through searching the area?"

"We pushed to really get as much done today as possible. Tomorrow, Austin and I should be through. We still have about a third of the woods left."

"I hope you don't find any more bodies," she said.

"Me, too. Kip might be a cadaver dog, but I celebrate when he doesn't find a dead person."

Compassion gleamed in her hazel eyes. "But every family needs closure. Kip gives them that when he finds their loved ones."

Lee trailed Kaitlin to the back of the training center where Kip was waiting for him, his tail wagging. No doubt his partner heard him talking to Kaitlin.

"What are you going to do when we have social occasions for the precinct?" Kaitlin asked as she unlocked the gate.

Kip pranced out and jumped up on Lee to greet him as if his dog knew he needed some attention in that moment. "Be civil."

"That wasn't what I was asking. I know you'll be that. You were engaged to her eight months ago. Now she's married to another man and had his child. I know your desire to have a family. You can't tell me it doesn't hurt."

"It did, but Alexa and I weren't meant to be together." He sighed. "I would have hated bringing a child into this world and discovering that a little late. I have a peace about what happened."

She patted his upper arm. "There's a woman out there for you. Don't give up looking."

As Lee took Kip from the training center, Kaitlin's words rang in his mind. He wasn't in any hurry to find a woman. Alexa and he had known each other for several years and dated for a good amount of that time seriously before becoming engaged. And still he hadn't known her like he should have. That realization chilled him in the cool February air.

"You have a way with dogs. Lexi took to you in no time." Valerie sat in the chair she and Heidi had just carried into the renovated third-floor apartment.

The dog in question came to Heidi to be scratched along her back. She wiggled when Heidi hit a certain spot, her bobbed tail vibrating in excitement. "I've been discovering that with Kip and Eliza. I wonder if I have a pet somewhere. If I do, I hope someone is taking care of it." For a few seconds an image of a small, white bichon pranced across her mind, tail curled, big, brown eyes dominating her face. "Cottonballs," she whispered.

"What?" Valerie leaned forward.

Heidi blinked. "I think I had a bichon. At least at some time in my past. Her name was Cottonballs."

"You're remembering?" Eagerness took hold of Valerie's face. "That's great."

The image faded and nothing else came to mind. "I'm not sure. Maybe it's wishful thinking."

"Or maybe it's the first of many memories to come."

"A bichon named Cottonballs is hardly evidence to discover who I am," Heidi said wryly.

"No, but the next memory may be something to help us find out."

Closing her eyes, Heidi plowed her fingers through her hair and willed another image to materialize in her mind. Nothing. She pounded her fist against the arm of a chair she sat in. "It won't come. Since I woke up, I've been trying to remember."

"Maybe you're trying too hard. Don't think about it...just enjoy the moment. You get a chance to get to know yourself without the baggage from your past."

"I hadn't thought of it that way." She stared out the living room window. "I didn't realize it was so late. Shouldn't Lee be home by now? Do you think he found another body in the woods?"

"It's a big area. He told me he wanted the search completed by tomorrow so he may be pushing to get as much done as possible. He said something about taking you to San Antonio after that. Do you think you're from there?"

"No, I don't like big cities." As soon as the sentence left her lips, Heidi clasped her hand over her mouth. "I did it again. I can't tell you why I feel that way about big cities, but I know it's true."

"Sagebrush is about as big a town as I want," Valerie said.

"What's the population?"

"About sixty to seventy thousand."

"Give or take a thousand or two," a deep male voice said.

Heidi swiveled around to find Lee in the open doorway. "Where's Kip?"

His eyebrows rose. "No, 'Hi, honey, I'm glad you're home'? Instead, only concern for my dog." He covered the distance between them. "He's downstairs eating. Nothing comes between him and his dinner—not even a pretty lady."

Valerie rose. "Which is my cue to take my hungry dog home and feed her."

"No problems?" Lee asked as he passed the rookie cop.

"We had a bit of trouble getting the large coffee table through the doorway, but other than that it has been quiet." In the hallway, Valerie turned back. "Oh, by the way, we left the heavy pieces of furniture for you and Mark to haul up here. Mark said he'd help you first thing tomorrow morning before you go to work and he gets some shut-eye."

"So he's finished with testifying in court today?"

"Yeah. It only took a day. Not too bad. See you, Heidi." Valerie waved, then disappeared down the stairs.

"I like her. As you can see, we managed to move most of the furniture and items Molly had in here back except for the mattress, couch and chest of drawers. I'm sharing the kitchen downstairs since there isn't a full one up here." She paused. Molly told me this used to be the nursery and this area was the playroom with the bedroom through there, but she and her husband never had any children, so slowly over the years it became a storage place. I get the feeling she thinks of you as the son she never had."

"The feeling is mutual. She's filled a hole in my life since my parents are both dead."

"I'm sorry to hear that. My mom's gone, but my father is alive."

Surprise brightened his eyes. "He is? Where?"

She thought about what she'd said, again trying to force herself to remember. "I don't know, but I feel I have a father somewhere. This is the second time today that I've had a flash-back. Earlier I told Valerie I had a dog, at least once in my life."

He smiled. "This is great. The doc said you might remember all at once or slowly."

"Or never."

"But you are beginning to so I'm optimistic you will continue. Did you recall anything when Valerie took you to see Peterson's car in the impound?"

"No. Not from lack of trying. If my fingerprints hadn't been in it, I would say I didn't have anything to do with the car, but fingerprints don't lie."

"True, fingerprints are a tangible piece of evidence, but I wouldn't worry. You know what the car looks like. You might remember something later." He turned toward the door. "I'll go downstairs and clean up. Molly said dinner would be on the table in half an hour."

Heidi jumped to her feet. "Oh, I've got to finish what I cooked for tonight."

"You did dinner?"

"Part of it. Nothing fancy. I made cornbread salad to go along with the chili Molly fixed, and I made a dessert."

"Dessert. Two days in a row."

"Molly said I needed to put some pounds back on my body."

"What kind of dessert?" he asked with a grin.

"Peach cobbler. She had some peaches she canned last summer. They were perfect for the recipe."

"So you like peaches?"

"Anyone in their right mind would love these peaches, but yes, I seemed to have a hankering for fruit—all kinds." Heidi strolled toward the small hallway outside her apartment. "In some ways, it's kind of fun discovering what I like and don't like."

Lee's eyes flickered with interest. "What don't you like?"

"Coffee. I'm sure Molly's is great, but I couldn't stand the stuff. Now sweet tea is totally different. Love it."

"Take it from a coffee drinker…hers is wonderful. Anything else?"

"I'm impatient and a perfectionist. At least when it comes

to sewing a quilt. I wanted to help Molly, but I'm not so sure I helped her much with the quilt she's working on."

"So sewing isn't for you?" Lee halted at the door to his apartment.

"No, not at all, but I need something to do and it is for a good cause—helping children in need."

"You like children?"

"Yes."

"No hesitation. How do you know?"

"I just do. When you were talking about Brady in the hospital, I thought about it and I knew. It made me wonder if I worked with children."

Lee unlocked his door. "Do you think you could have some?"

"I don't think so. For one thing, I wouldn't go off and leave a child of mine. I'm not from around here so that means I came from a ways off. Besides, I wasn't wearing a wedding ring. I even checked with Gail about that when I came into the hospital."

"You weren't wearing one when I found you in the woods, and you were pretty tan. You lost some of that while you were in the hospital, but I was looking for any evidence that might help me find out who you were." His gaze fixed on her left hand, her ring finger. Had Heidi ever been in love? Had she been hurt or betrayed in the past? Like him?

"I'd better go and help Molly. See you soon," she said into the silence that suddenly hovered between them.

Lee watched Heidi as she descended the stairs to the first floor. In the short time since she had awakened, she was remembering more and more. Would she recall enough in time to help them find out what was going on in Sagebrush? Would she get to a point and stop? But mostly he wondered what she would remember—what kind of life did she have before she was hurt? The woman intrigued him. She was handling having amnesia a lot better than he would have.

As he entered his apartment, his cell went off. The number was blocked so he couldn't tell who the call was from. "Hello."

"Officer Calloway?"

"Yes?" The voice sounded familiar.

"I want to talk."

"Zoller?"

"Yeah," the caller rasped out.

"I can meet you down at the police station."

"No! I'll be at your place in fifteen minutes." Fear coated each word. "I'll come to the back door of Molly's."

Before Lee could tell him no, the man clicked off. He didn't want the man near Heidi. He'd talk with him outside. Instead of taking a shower and changing, Lee checked his gun and then headed downstairs to the kitchen. He walked to the back door and brought Kip in.

"I thought you were changing," Heidi said as she set the table.

"I want you two to go to Molly's with Kip. I have someone coming to see me."

Molly stirred the pot on the stove. "Who? Dinner is almost ready. Have the person stay. I have plenty."

"No."

His landlady's forehead crinkled. "Who's coming to *my* house?"

"Zoller, and I'm meeting with him outside in the backyard. I'm not inviting him inside."

A fork clinked to the kitchen table, and Heidi's mouth fell open. "How could you bring the man here?"

"He hung up before I could say no. Besides, I heard fear in the man's voice. His information might help, especially if he can tell us who hired him to attack you. This could end soon."

Molly turned the burner on the stove down to low. "Let's go, Heidi. I'll get my gun. You'll be all right."

As Heidi left with Molly, all Lee could see were her large brown eyes growing even wider.

When a rap came on the back door, Lee hurried to answer it. He squeezed through the small opening. "What do you want to tell me, Zoller?"

The man lifted his right hand, something white clasped in it.

Heidi paced the length of Molly's living room, biting her thumbnail. She hated not knowing what was going on between Lee and Zoller. For a few seconds, memories of Zoller going after her in the hospital inundated her. "I don't like this one bit. What if Zoller is laying a trap?"

"Lee can take care of himself."

If something happened to Lee because of her, how would she forgive herself? He'd already been attacked trying to protect her. "I'm sure he can, but—"

A gunshot pierced the air.

Heidi dropped to the floor.

The blast of a shot sounded at the same time Zoller collapsed onto the stoop. A bullet whizzed by the left side of Lee's head and lodged in the doorjamb behind him. Blood spread outward from a hole in Zoller's chest. Drawing his gun, Lee ducked back into the house. After he flipped off the light in the kitchen, he went to the window in the alcove and peered out between the blind slats. Darkness blanketed the backyard, no sign of any movement.

The shot came from the right and from the angle of the bullet hole in Zoller and the one in the doorjamb, at an upward trajectory. The top step of the stoop was about four feet from the ground. That meant the killer—he had no doubt Zoller was dead from the direct hit to the man's heart—hid behind the bushes near the side of the garage.

"Lee, are you okay?" Heidi's voice came from the direction of the entrance into the kitchen.

"Yes, stay back and call 911." He didn't want to take his eyes off the backyard long enough to make the call.

"Do you need my help?" Molly asked. "Should I guard the front of the house?" Kip's bark accompanied the last question.

"Molly. Heidi. Get back into the apartment with Kip." He heard Heidi in the background talking to the 911 operator. "Help is on the way. I think the killer got what he wanted." If someone tried to come in through the front door, a beep would go off to indicate it was opened. He should be able to make it to the hallway before the assailant reached Molly's.

"Zoller?" That one word from Heidi wavered.

"Yes. Now do as I say."

The sound of their footsteps faded, and a door slammed shut. Lee kept his gaze glued to the area where the shot came from, just outside the six-foot chain-link fence. Most likely the killer was long gone because if he'd been after him, he would have been dead a second after Zoller. Lee had been wary of Zoller but hadn't been expecting a sniper to shoot the man right in front of him.

In the distance, the sirens reverberated through the air. A few minutes later, police officers flooded the backyard and the front bell rang. Lee strode to the foyer and opened the front door.

Mark charged into the house. "I was at the station when the call went out. I didn't want to use my key and get mistaken for an intruder. Anyone hurt?"

"Gus Zoller was killed on the back stoop. A shot to the heart."

His neighbor hurried toward the kitchen. "What did he want here?"

"To meet with me, but someone didn't want him talking to me." Behind him the door to Molly's apartment creaked open. Lee glanced back and glimpsed Heidi with Molly next to her peeking out into the hallway.

"It's safe. Four officers are searching the backyard," Mark tossed over his shoulder before entering the kitchen.

That was all either lady needed. They bridged the distance to Lee.

Heidi put her hand on his arm. "Are you sure you're not hurt?"

He nodded, touched more than he cared to admit by her concern.

"We both hit the floor when we heard the shot," Molly said with a chuckle. "I don't think I've moved that fast in a long time. I'm gonna ache tomorrow morning."

Mark came in from out back. "Zoller is definitely dead. I took the bullet out of the door frame. Maybe ballistics can tell us something about the gun used. One of the officers found where the shooter must have stood."

"By the bushes near the garage?"

"Yep. The ground was damp. There are footprints there. The crime-scene techs will take a casting. Looks like a man's cowboy boot, size twelve or so. The right heel has a chip out of it."

"So all we have to do is check every man's boot in the area for a chipped heel."

"I know…a long shot. But it'll help put the man at the scene when we do find him." Mark glanced from Heidi to Molly and then back to Lee. "I'll take care of the crime scene."

Nodding, Lee headed for the back door. "I'm taking a look at Zoller. He had something in his hand."

He squatted near Zoller's body. The man's right arm stretched out from his side. A white piece of paper stuck out of Zoller's fisted hand. Lee took a pair of gloves from Mark and then carefully pried his fingers open until the note was exposed.

He picked it up by the corner, and in the flood of light from the security lamp, he read, "Kill him, Blood."

Mark looked at the note Lee held. "Blood? What's that mean? Is it a name?"

Lee shrugged. "This must have been what spooked him into calling me."

"Is this to Blood or from Blood?"

"Don't know. When we find the shooter, we'll ask him." Lee slipped the note into an evidence bag Mark held open for him.

Lee caught Heidi standing in the door, her eyes wide, the color drained from her face. "You okay?" he asked as he closed the distance between them.

Backing away from the door, her attention fixed on him, she shook her head. "Who would call themselves Blood?"

"I'm sure that isn't his real name," he said, not really having a response to her question but wanting to alleviate her fear. "The note might have fingerprints on it. Maybe ones besides Zoller's."

She stared straight ahead at his chest. "There's been so much death. This isn't the first dead body I've seen. I saw another," she murmured in a monotone.

"When?"

For a moment she didn't reply. His concern increased the longer she was silent. He clasped both of her hands, feeling their trembling, and cupped them between his.

"Heidi, when did you see a dead body?"

"Recently. When I spied Zoller on the stoop, another body flickered in then out of my mind. Not him." She lifted her glistening eyes to his. "But I don't know who, where or when."

"Maybe it's connected to why you were running in the woods. You could have come upon someone killing Adams. When I found his grave, it was clear he'd been dead a few weeks. I'll know more when I get the autopsy. Pauly Keevers's death was more recent but the same gun was used in both murders. Probably the same killer."

Heidi shuddered.

Lee wrapped his arms around her and pulled her against him. "I'll protect you. I'm not going to let anything happen to you."

His gaze connected with Molly's. Worry etched deep lines in her forehead.

"I'm putting this food up for right now. Later if anyone wants to eat, they can heat the chili up in the microwave. I suggest we move to my living room," she said over the voices drifting to them from the backyard. "I for one need to sit down."

Lee slung his arm over Heidi's shoulders and then Molly's. "It sounds like a great suggestion. Mark will let us know when the crime-scene techs are through."

"Will you have to leave and go to the station?" Heidi asked as they moved toward the foyer.

"No."

She released a long breath. "Good."

He looked down into her face, and he could tell she was shell-shocked. He couldn't blame her with all that had happened to her the past few days. The realization only reinforced his desire to protect her and get to the bottom of what was going on in Sagebrush.

★ ★ ★

"So the gun that killed Zoller was the same one used in the deaths of those two men whose bodies Kip found in the woods?" Heidi shifted toward Lee in his SUV nearing the outskirts of San Antonio on Saturday.

"Yes. The ballistics report came back late yesterday afternoon confirming it. The bullets matched in all three murders. Same gun."

"From what I remember the Lost Woods is a beautiful place. It's a shame so much darkness has shrouded it lately."

Lee nodded soberly. "It's gotten more dangerous ever since a teenager was shot dead in the woods five years ago."

"Did you catch the person who killed him?"

"No. Daniel Jones, sixteen years old, fled into the woods with 30 grams of crack cocaine. Daniel had been arrested before for dealing. Captain McNeal pursued him, and when the teenager pointed a gun at him, the captain shot him in the thigh." He grimaced. "But someone else shot the boy in the heart. The bullet used by the sniper was untraceable. The case went cold."

"Those poor parents. They never had any closure on their son's death."

"That's the really sad part in all of it. There wasn't a father around and Daniel's mother committed suicide the night she heard the news about her son. The captain was devastated by the events."

The thought of losing a child slowed her heartbeat to a throb. "So someone out there got away with murder—with killing a child."

"Yes. We think it was Daniel's supplier, trying to shut the teen up before he gave him up. We never found out who Daniel's dealer was. Since then, the Lost Woods had become

a haven for criminals. They use it to hide and for various illegal activities."

"If you know that, why can't y'all do anything about it?"

"We make periodic sweeps through there, like what Austin and I finished yesterday, but they always seem to be one
step ahead of us. We've rarely found anything going down at
the time we're there."

Heidi faced forward, the traffic becoming heavy as they
entered the city. "I'm no expert, but I have watched police
shows on T.V. It sounds like you have an informant tipping
the criminals off to what you're doing."

Lee slanted an amused look at her. "How do you know you
watch police shows? Another memory?"

"No, but Molly loves them, and while I stayed with her,
I caught a couple. I didn't care for them. They aren't always
realistic."

"How do you know that?"

His question made her pause. "I don't know. Just a feeling.
You haven't considered someone might be telling the bad guys
what y'all are going to do before you do it?"

"I know most of the people I work with, and they are good
people."

"Good people can be bought off. Money has a way of cor-
rupting. Some folk worship money like a religion. It's everything to them. That and the power money brings to them."

"So true. That's why I decided to become a cop rather than
a veterinarian. You don't become a cop for the money."

"Why did you?"

"To help others. To make Sagebrush a safer place for people
to live." He tossed her a grin. "To put the bad guys in jail."

"That's the way I feel about working with children. You
don't get rich in the sense of money, but you do in other
ways. The personal satisfaction can't be measured in monetary

terms." As her words tumbled out, she knew this was another memory worming its way to the surface.

"You worked with children? Doing what?"

She closed her eyes and tried to picture herself working with kids. She saw herself reading a book to a circle of children. "I read to them. At least I think I did. I'm not sure where the feeling comes from, but I'm sure I had something to do with kids. Maybe I worked in some kind of school, a library, day-care or..." She captured the memory and tried to expand it, but she met with a blank slate—even the strong sense of caring for children evaporating. "I don't know. Maybe I'm just grasping at anything that sounds remotely possible."

He stopped at a red light. "I can picture you working with kids. Your voice is soft and easy on the ears. Reading to them makes perfect sense."

The compliment flushed her cheeks with heat. Their gazes linked across the small expanse of the car. "Thank you."

"For what?"

"For saying that." In that moment she realized she hadn't heard many compliments. What kind of life had she had before this? Was she purposely not remembering because she had such a horrible life she didn't want to remember?

Someone honked a horn. Still, Lee didn't look away.

She smiled and wrenched her attention from his face to the stoplight. "I think they want you to go before the light changes to red again."

He chuckled and started across the intersection. "You're a distraction."

"Sorry about that."

"Oh, don't be sorry. It's a pleasant distraction."

Again, warmth infused every pore of her at his compliment and stayed with her until he pulled into William Peterson's driveway.

"Does this place look familiar to you?" Lee asked.

"No. Not even a vague sense I've been here before. Have the police gone through his house?"

"Yes. His daughter is meeting me here and letting us inside. She wants to get to the bottom of what has happened to her dad. Until we found his car, no sign turned up for weeks concerning him." Lee climbed from his SUV. "With all that Kip has been doing lately, he's probably content to be in Molly's backyard with Eliza today."

"I'm not so sure about that. You didn't see that puppy-dog look he gave you when we drove away."

"He's just playing you. He'll be happy outside with his girlfriend." He scanned the peaceful street.

As they made their way toward the porch to sit and wait for the daughter, an older woman popped up on the other side of the hedge that separated Peterson's property from hers. "He's not there. He hasn't been around for a month. The police suspect foul play. Such a shame. William is a nice man, always willing to help me if I need it."

Lee turned toward the woman, dressed in a jogging suit.

"I was tying my tennis shoes when you drove up," the neighbor said to the surprise on Lee's face. "I usually go for my morning walk about this time." She checked her watch. "Well, I'm a little late today since it's around eleven."

"Mr. Peterson's daughter is meeting us here." Lee headed toward the older woman, probably around sixty. When he reached into his pocket, she backed up, her eyes round and wide. "Ma'am, I'm a police officer from Sagebrush, Texas."

The neighbor stopped her backpedaling and actually moved forward to look at Lee's badge. "Did you find William?"

"No, but we found his car outside Sagebrush."

"No sign of him?"

Lee shook his head.

Heidi watched the exchange as Lee tried to get as much information about the missing man as he could from the neighbor.

"William has never been this popular when he was home. First a man came to see William about a month ago, then the police and now you. You all wanted to know about what kind of man William was. Well, I'll tell you what I told them. He was a good neighbor. Minded his own business. No loud noises coming from his house late at night. I'll sorely miss him."

"So you think something's happened to him?" Lee asked.

The older woman's eyebrows rose. "Don't you? Isn't that why you're here?"

"I'm here to meet with his daughter."

Peterson's neighbor snorted. "I told that other man William was a loner. His life was his work and his family."

"You've mentioned this other man twice. He wasn't with the San Antonio Police?"

She shook her head.

"No, at least he didn't show me a badge or say he was."

"Why was he here?"

"He said he found William's wallet and wanted to return it. I said I'd take it, but he didn't give it to me. Actually I never saw it, but he asked who were the closest people to Mr. Peterson." She shrugged. "I mentioned his daughter and the people he worked with at Boland Manufacturing. Of course, William is on the road a lot because he's on their sales staff."

"What did this person look like?"

Heidi approached Lee and the neighbor as Lee continued the interview.

The woman glanced at her. "Are you police, too?"

"She's assisting me," Lee explained, returning the lady's attention to him. "Do you remember what the man looked like?"

"Sure I do. My mind is like a steel trap. It's getting better with age, not worse." She tapped her chin, her gaze slanting upward. "Let me see. His nose was big like a fighter I once saw on T.V. and he had thick dark eyebrows. I know men don't want to pluck theirs but he needed to. His hair was blond. It was long and tied back with a leather strap."

Lee pulled his cell out and clicked on a picture. "Did he look anything like this?" He showed the neighbor the photo of the sketch of the man who had attacked Lee in Zoller's apartment.

She took the phone and studied the picture. "Maybe. His eyes were narrower, which made his eyebrows stand out even more. His mouth was thinner, too." She gave him the cell back. "But it could be the same man. Is he a criminal?"

"A person of interest. Has he been back since last month?"

"No. Ah, I see Mary Lou is here. You might ask her if the man came to see her."

Heidi swung around as a petite woman with long blond hair and brown eyes exited a car and quickly closed the distance between them, her features stamped with surprise.

Probably a mirror of Heidi's own expression. Because the young woman coming toward her looked a lot like Heidi.

Chapter Seven

At first glance at the woman approaching him, Lee thought he was seeing Heidi—but the closer Mary Lou came, the more he could tell them apart. Yes, they had the same straight long blond hair, hanging loose about their shoulders. Their bodies were slender and petite and their features had similarities. But there were differences. Mary Lou's eyes were blue, not brown. Her mouth was thin and her chin had a cleft in it.

Could Heidi be related to Mary Lou, therefore, to William Peterson?

Next to him, anxiety vibrated off Heidi. The woman stopped a few feet from them, and her gaze skimmed over Heidi. Silence stretched to a long minute while each assessed the other.

"Do you know me? Are we related?" Heidi asked in a shaky voice.

Mary Lou tilted her head and squinted her eyes. "No. We do look somewhat alike, but I've never seen you before."

"Have you seen this man?" Using his cell, Lee showed her the photo of his attacker at Zoller's apartment.

"I'm not sure. A man came to see me a month ago wanting to contact Dad. I told him he was away working and he'd have to get the schedule from his company."

"So you didn't know his schedule?" Lee slipped his phone back in his pocket.

"Actually, I did. The man caught me outside working in the yard. I wouldn't have opened my front door to a stranger, especially someone who gave me the creeps. I wasn't about to tell him where my dad was."

"When was the last time you heard from your father?"

Mary Lou's eyes shone with unshed tears. "He called me as he was leaving town. What I don't understand is how his car ended up in Sagebrush. That isn't near one of his stops. His first stop was Midland."

"That's what we're trying to piece together. How did he usually drive to Midland?"

"Part of the way on I-10, then up through San Angelo. But sometimes, something would catch his fancy and he'd take a different route. He loved to drive and didn't care if it took him a little longer to get to his destination."

"So you don't know the direction he went?"

Mary Lou swallowed hard. "No."

"May I take a look around your dad's house? Maybe there's something in there that'll help us figure out what route he took to Midland. And hopefully that'll bring us one step closer to finding your dad." Lee slid a glance at Heidi who stood rigid beside him, the hard line of her jaw conveying her frustration and confusion.

"When he didn't check in with me or the company, I looked around his place but didn't see anything. But you're welcome to search for it yourself. You might see something I didn't think was important. All I want is my dad back." William Peterson's daughter headed for the porch.

Lee shifted toward Heidi. "You okay?"

"I just want answers for this woman. For me."

"I know. We'll keep looking until we find them." When he said those words to Heidi, he realized the commitment he was making to her went beyond his duties as a police officer. If something happened to William Peterson outside of Sagebrush, it wasn't in his jurisdiction. But he felt what happened to William Peterson was closely tied to Heidi somehow.

At the end of the day, Heidi climbed from Lee's SUV and walked toward Molly's house. "I had hoped the trip to San Antonio would produce a lead to William Peterson's whereabouts."

"We didn't completely come up empty-handed. We now know where Peterson went on his way to Midland." Lee unlocked the front door and held it open for Heidi to enter first then hurried to turn off the alarm system. "I just wish I could have followed the lead instead of turning it over to the sheriff of Tom Green County."

"It's comforting to know there are people who'll mail a man's wallet back to him with his money still in it."

Pausing at the bottom of the staircase, Lee frowned. "Yeah, but the fact Peterson didn't have his wallet doesn't bode well at all. I'm afraid something bad has happened to him."

Heidi remembered the fear that had crept into Mary Lou's face when she'd opened the package she got from her dad's mailbox right before they left. According to the daughter, she'd checked the mail the week before, so the package had arrived three or so weeks after her father disappeared. "I hope not. I like Mary Lou. It was scary how much we looked alike—at least when I saw her walking toward me. I thought I might have found some answers to who I was."

Lee started up the steps. "I'll look into Peterson's family background and make sure there isn't a connection."

Heidi stopped on the staircase. "You don't trust what Mary Lou said?"

"I don't trust easily. I've learned to check out what people say. In my line of work you have to."

"I can see that. Some people aren't who they seem to be," she murmured, convinced she'd found out the hard way the truth behind that statement.

"The sheriff will let me know what he finds out from the man who returned the wallet."

"Sagebrush is hours away from Tom Green County. Did I drive William Peterson's car here by myself? Or was Peterson with me? If so, where is he now?" She sighed impatiently. "You haven't even found the keys yet…"

"Looking for a set of keys in the Lost Woods is very different from a dead body. We may never find them. The good news is we didn't find Peterson dead in the woods."

Exhausted by the long day on the road, Heidi leaned back against the banister, her head throbbing with tension and unanswered questions. "Where's Molly? I'm surprised she didn't meet us at the door, wanting to know what we discovered."

"This is the night she goes to her quilting group. They meet once a week at a member's house. I'm sure I'll be quizzed the minute I see her."

"Unless it's soon, I'll be in bed." Heidi finished her climb to the third floor. "This tired body isn't used to being on the go for over twelve hours straight. I didn't get my nap today."

At the top, Lee took her hand and drew her around toward him. "You'll be your old self in no time, but it does take the body some time to get back its stamina after a trauma. Take it from someone who knows."

"How do you know?"

"Three years ago, I was in a serious car accident. I stayed in the hospital a week and was on leave for several months recovering. Molly is the one who kept me sane. She's wonderful. I owe her a lot."

"Me, too." His nearness shredded what composure she had after a long day with still no answers of how she'd ended up in Sagebrush driving William Peterson's car. "Could he be alive but hurt somewhere near here after the accident?" she asked out loud, voicing her concerns that had been in the back of her mind during the return to Sagebrush.

"I guess it's possible. But why hasn't anyone come forward?"

"I don't know." She pressed her fingers into her forehead to try to ease her headaches.

He grasped her other hand and held them both up between them. "We're going to find the answers."

"Why can't I remember? I want to remember." For days she'd half thought she didn't want to know, but now she realized she needed to find out what happened to her and who she was. Mary Lou needed closure. *And I need peace.*

"I know this was a tough day. No answers. But I think we're a little closer to the truth." He released her hands and brought his up to frame her face. "This can seem overwhelming at times, but take one step at a time. You're remembering pieces of your life. More will come."

"How do I know if what I think I remember is right? What if it's all a lie? A joke I played on myself."

"No. Nothing in your body language when we talk about what you remember conveys that feeling to me."

"Maybe I'm just good at hiding my true feelings," she murmured.

"Hiding feelings and lying are two different things. I often hide mine. I don't open up much to others." He bent closer toward her, his warm breath caressing her face. "Relax. Don't try to force the memories. They'll come when you're ready."

His lips hovered an inch away from hers. She wanted him to kiss her. She wanted to feel like she belonged somewhere. That she wasn't just some nameless person with no past. With no one to care about her. Loneliness deluged her, and she found herself raising up on her tiptoes to kiss him.

The second their mouths connected he took command of the kiss, deepening it. His hands delved into the strands of her hair, holding her head still as his lips ravished hers. For a moment it didn't matter that she was Heidi with no last name. Lee made her feel special, cherished, totally feminine.

He pulled back all too soon. Although only inches apart, she felt bereaved. But the tickle of his breath fanning her lips left her quivering in his embrace. Wanting more. Needing to feel she mattered to someone. She grasped onto the wonderful sensations still cascading through her.

"I'm sorry, Heidi. I shouldn't have kissed you. I'm guarding you. You don't need this added complication to your life."

"I understand. I'm fine." The words came automatically before she could process what she was saying because she really didn't understand all that was happening to her. She stepped to the side and back, breaking any connection between them. "It's been a long day and..." She was going to tell him she wanted to soak in a hot bath to help ease the tension from her, but decided he didn't need to know that.

He rotated toward the staircase. "I'll go get Kip from the backyard. I'll be right back."

"Don't hurry. I have a few—things to do first. I'm not going to sleep right away."

He grinned. "Call me when you're ready for Kip. I'll make sure he's worn out so he won't demand too much attention."

"That's great. Give me thirty minutes."

She let herself into her apartment, recalling the kiss as she moved toward the bedroom. After slipping off the light coat Molly had given her, she walked toward the closet to hang it up among the meager items of clothing she had. She needed to buy a few more soon.

When she opened the door, thoughts of that hot bath enticing her to move faster, she absently reached inside for a hanger. She touched something solid, muscular—like a shoulder.

Panic flew through her at the same time a large hulking man barreled into her.

"Kip, the lady wants a few minutes, so it's just you and me. How about we play catch?" Lee picked up the tennis ball and threw it the length of the big backyard. His border collie took off with the lightning speed he was known for. Not even half a minute later, he pranced back with his prize clutched between his jaws.

Kip sat in front of Lee, cocked his head and dropped the ball at Lee's feet. "I know I neglected you today, but I figured I'd give you some quality time with your gal. I hope you used it wisely."

Kip barked.

"I don't know if I did. I kissed Heidi. Not sure I should have. She's confused enough without me adding to it." Lee again sent the toy sailing through the air.

A few yelps accompanied Kip's chase. When his dog trotted back for more, Lee tossed the ball and Kip retrieved it several more times.

He should be upset with himself. But he wasn't. He'd enjoyed the kiss and Heidi had, too, if her response was any indication. Her fervor had matched his. He turned toward the house and glanced up at the third-floor window to Heidi's bedroom.

What was she doing up there? he wondered. Not that it was any of his business. He decided to give Heidi a little more time to herself before taking Kip up to her apartment to stay with her.

His dog bumped his hand at his side. Barking.

The man drove Heidi into the bed, the back of her knees hitting its side. For a few seconds she relived Zoller's attack, then she latched on to the face of her attacker. Thick eyebrows that ran together and a large, crooked nose dominated her vision for that split moment in time. The same man who had assaulted Lee.

Somewhere deep inside, her rage shoved her panic away. She wasn't going to let this man win. She was tired of being a victim. Clutching him, she dug her fingernails into his biceps, fighting to remain on her feet.

But he was too strong, too large. He dwarfed her, forcing her back onto the bedding, his body covering hers. The sensation of being caged beneath a man flooded her with panic again. His huge hand over her mouth and nose smothered her. Her heartbeat thundered in her ears. Her breath trapped in her lungs. She plummeted her fists into his back, but it didn't seem to affect him.

He cackled. "I like a good fight. Too bad I don't have time to dally before killing you."

Fear entwined with her panic, overwhelming her to the point she froze.

"Ready for dinner?" Lee asked Kip.

Kip replied by racing to the back door, planting his behind on the stoop and waiting for him.

With one last glance toward the window, a sigh escaping between his lips, Lee jogged to the small porch and let his dog inside. Kip lodged himself at his bowl while Lee went to get the sack of dry dog food.

When he came out of the walk-in pantry, Kip was gone. Lee put the bag on the floor and looked around. *Where is he?*

A series of barks echoed through the house.

Blackness swam before Heidi's eyes. The pressure on her chest along with her attacker's hand over her mouth and partially over her nose made it almost impossible to draw any air into her lungs.

I can't give up, slowly drifted through her thoughts like a heavy fog snaking through the swamp.

Lord, I really need You again. Help me.

When the man shifted to bring more force down on her, she used that second to bite down on the fleshy part of his palm. Surprise widened his eyes, and he jerked back.

She let out a scream while frantic yelping reverberated through the apartment.

The noises from above propelled Lee into action, running for the stairs and taking the steps two at a time. Kip continued to bark. He could hear his dog attacking Heidi's door.

When he hit the third floor, he slowed his pace a fraction in order to pull his gun out of his holster and open the door.

Before he had his weapon drawn, the door crashed open and the man he had been looking for plowed right into him, using his forearm to bowl him over. Lee fell back against the hardwood floor. The assailant raced down the stairs.

"Take him down," Lee called out to Kip as he scrambled to his feet.

He rushed into Heidi's apartment, the sounds of his dog

attacking the man driving him even faster to check on Heidi, then go after her assailant. He had to make sure she was okay first.

Halfway into her place, Lee glimpsed Heidi grasping the doorjamb into the bedroom, the color gone from her face, her whole body shaking.

"I'm okay," she choked out. "Get him."

"Call 911." He pivoted and flew out of the apartment and down the steps.

A whelp, followed by a whine, unnerved Lee and propelled him even faster. The front door opened and slammed as his feet landed on the bottom floor.

Kip lay on his side, but when he saw Lee, he wagged his tail and struggled to stand.

"Stay." Lee gave him the signal. "Guard Heidi."

Lee hurried from the house, catching a glimpse of the attacker as he rounded the hedge at the side in the yard. He spurred his pace, going as swift as he could push himself. The man would not escape again. He would get him and bring him to justice.

Thirty feet away, the man sprinted toward the end of the block. Lee pumped his legs faster, determined to catch up.

Twenty feet away. Heidi's assailant turned down an alley that ran between two houses. Lee urged every bit of speed out of him. His lungs burned. Pain radiated from his chest.

He reached the alley and plunged down the darkened lane. A back porch light illuminated the area halfway down. The man he was after dove into a car. The sound of it starting pushed Lee to bridge the gap between them.

Fifteen feet away. The flash of the headlights came on, blinding Lee momentarily.

Almost within reach the car surged forward. Lee planted his feet, bringing his gun up and squeezing off a shot at the windshield. But the sedan kept coming at him. He leaped to the side, catching a glimpse of the license plate number as the man sped out onto the street, going to the left.

After putting his weapon into his holster, he withdrew his cell and called the station to report the number and description of the car—a beat-up white Taurus, the same as the one leaving the parking lot at Zoller's apartment.

Her legs shaking, Heidi made her way to the third-floor landing. She dragged in deep breaths of air. Her chest hurt with the effort. Where was Lee? Kip? She slowly descended the staircase, gripping the railing to steady herself.

When she reached the top of the steps on the second floor, she spied Kip sitting at the bottom facing the front door, which was wide open. She quickened her pace to the dog. Kip's focus stayed glued to the entrance. She sat on the bottom stair, feeling safe with Kip at her side. She owed the border collie—and Lee—her life.

The sensations of the man pressing into her chest and holding her mouth and nose would haunt her. Not being able to breathe. Not being able to move. She shivered and plastered her crossed arms to her body.

Kip stood.

"What's wrong?" Heidi pushed to her feet, her heartbeat hammering against her rib cage.

Then she saw Lee mounting the steps to the porch. Kip's tail wagged, but the dog stayed at her side.

When Lee came through the entrance, Kip limped toward his partner. Lee stooped and examined his dog's front paw.

"What happened to him?" Heidi asked as she bridged the distance to them, sirens resonating through the night air.

"He tried to stop the assailant."

"That man was huge."

"I guess about six and a half feet. But this time I got a good look at him and the license plate on the car he's driving."

"I got a good…" An image of her attacker flashed into her mind, but it wasn't from when he was trying to kill her in her bedroom. It was from the woods. A picture of him standing over a body, staring down at the dead person, a shovel in his hand, drove all other thoughts from her. "I know why he wants me dead. I remember him from the woods."

The sound of running footsteps intruded. The red and blue flashing lights drew her attention toward the open door.

Lee caught her gaze. "We'll talk later. I want this man found now." He stood and faced the police entering the house.

Heidi knelt and put her arms around Kip while Lee talked to the officers. She tuned them out and pulled up the scene from the Lost Woods when she stumbled upon a man digging a grave. Was it one of the graves Lee found? Or was there another man buried out there?

Chapter Eight

An hour later, Heidi sat on Molly's couch while she was in the kitchen preparing her some herbal tea to help her sleep. Nothing would help her sleep. Every time she closed her eyes, she visualized the man who attacked her, with a shovel in his hand, digging a grave. Three police officers guarded the house—one in the house and two outside. All had dogs so evidently they were part of the K-9 Unit.

Molly carried a tray into the living room and placed it on the coffee table, then took a seat next to Heidi. "This will make you feel better. Nothing is better than this special tea blend I have for calming your nerves." The landlady poured the brew into two cups, adding sugar to both of them. "When my husband died, I drank this every night to help me sleep. I lived on it for months." She passed Heidi's tea to her. "Wow, just listen to me chattering away. I get that way when I'm upset."

Whereas she went silent—another tidbit Heidi realized about herself. She sipped the special blend, its flavor subtle yet smooth. She didn't have the heart to tell Molly nothing would help her relax—not until she saw Lee again and she knew Kip was all right.

"I don't understand how that man got into your apartment. The alarm was left on except when I had the cable company out here. My reception was going in and out yesterday and this morning. Someone came out this afternoon. That was the only person in the house and that serviceman has been here before on a call."

"Did the cable guy fix your problem?"

"Yes, he said one of the lines to the house was faulty. He replaced it."

Could that have been deliberately done in order to get someone into the house? Or was her assailant watching and waiting for an opportunity?

Molly lounged back, drinking her tea. "You said something about remembering some of what happened in the woods the day you were found?"

"Yes, I was wandering in the woods, dazed, when I came upon a man—the one who attacked me—burying a dead body. I tried to sneak away, but I stepped on a twig. He heard, looked up and saw me. I ran. He came after me."

"What happened then?"

Heidi closed her eyes and pictured the scene. Visions of vegetation all around popped into her mind but nothing else. It was like she'd hit a green wall. "I don't know."

"Why were you dazed?" Molly asked.

"My head was bleeding. I had blood on my hand when I touched my forehead."

"How did it happen?"

Heidi shook her head. "I guess I was driving that car Lee found in the woods. It must have been from the wreck, but I don't remember." Her voice rose several levels as frustration pounded at her. She needed to remember. *God, please help. I know I've turned to You before, that You've been there for me.*

Molly laid her hand on her arm. "Honey, it will come to you. Look at how much you've remembered since you came out of your coma. Forcing it doesn't help."

Calmness descended over Heidi as though a cloak of peace encased her. "I hope Kip is okay."

"Lee will make sure of that. He didn't think his leg was broken, but an X-ray will show one way or another."

"So many people have been hurt because of this man." She wouldn't be safe until he was caught.

"Lee was going to join the search once he took Kip to the vet. I've never seen Lee so determined to put an end to what's been going on."

The last look Lee had given her before departing had radiated his fierce resolve to see justice done. If anyone could help her it would be Lee.

Listening to his police radio, Lee drove the streets of Sagebrush, trying to figure out where the assailant would go to hide. The police and sheriff had moved fast to shut down all roads leading out of town. He'd identified the man as Keith West from his DMV photo. His mistake was driving his own car to kill Heidi.

At an intersection, Lee glanced at Kip stretched out on the backseat. The vet had given his dog a clean bill of health as far as anything broken. No fractures showed on the X-ray, but his leg was bruised and swollen a little. According to the doc, Kip would be better soon. The vet gave his partner something to help that along.

Recalling his conversation earlier today with Heidi about the criminal activity in the Lost Woods, especially in the past few years, Lee directed his SUV toward them. He would canvas the east side while he called it in to have some other officers check the other ways into the woods. There were a handful.

An hour later, after going down one dirt road after another, he made a hundred-eighty-degree turn at another dead end. As he did, his headlights shone briefly on something white. A surge of adrenaline zipped through Lee as he called in his location, asking for backup. When he started to climb from his SUV, Kip perked up, his tail wagging.

"No, boy. You have to stay here. I'm not taking a chance of making your injury worse. I'll wait for reinforcements."

Ten minutes later as Lee stood at his car, scanning his surroundings and listening, the sound of a car coming down the road toward him bounced off the trees around him. Valerie parked next to his vehicle and both she and her dog joined him.

Lee pointed toward the white vehicle about ten yards off the road, hidden partially by the dense woods. "That's got to be West's car. Since he couldn't drive out of town, he must've decided to find a place to hide until we give up the search."

"And these woods are a perfect place to do that. How's Kip? I heard about him getting injured."

"He'll be all right. The medicine the vet gave him and some rest will help. That'll be the hardest part of all of this—trying to get him to rest."

Valerie chuckled as she peered at the back window where Kip looked out. "He's a workhorse. All our dogs are. Let's put Lexi to work. We'll start at the car and see if we get a scent she can follow."

"I wonder if he's holed up in the cave system where Brady was found. West was in the woods that day and may have a connection to the kidnapping besides the other two men we know of. I want to catch him alive and get him to talk."

Wearing his night-vision goggles, standard equipment for the K-9 Unit for cases like this, Lee led the way to the vehicle. At the car, Valerie opened the driver's door and let Lexi smell the seat. She snatched a jacket thrown across the front seat, lying against the passenger's door. Lexi sniffed it and then went to work. Lee followed the pair as the Rottweiler, nose down, hurried through the underbrush. The trail stopped at the mouth of the cave. Lexi sniffed the ground, picked up the scent and headed away from the entrance. Toward the road where Lee and Valerie had parked their cars.

Barking pierced the night quiet. Ferocious sounding. Kip. Lee flat-out ran toward his SUV, his gun drawn. Keith West would not hurt his dog again. He broke through the brush onto the road. A man fled down it toward the edge of the woods.

Over Kip's yelping, Lee called, "Valerie, make sure Kip is all right. I'm going after West. He isn't getting away."

"Go. I'll follow in a sec."

Sprinting after West, Lee spied the man plunge into the thick vegetation, more like a tangle of bare branches. Lee stayed right on him, gaining slowly. The limbs scratched at him as he went after West. The man stumbled through the brush into a small clearing. Pivoting he pointed a gun at Lee and pulled the trigger.

His quick reflexes took over. As the gun blasted the air, Lee lunged to the side and rolled on the ground. He came up, aimed his gun and shot West in the arm. The attacker's gun dropped to the earth while he clutched his injured limb.

"Lee, are you okay?" Valerie asked, coming up behind him.

"Fine." Lee rushed West and kicked his gun out of his reach, then stood over the man with his weapon fixed on his chest. "Don't even think of moving." As much as he needed West alive, fury rampaged through Lee, urging him to shoot if the man dared to move.

As Lee stared down at West through the eerie green of his night-vision goggles, West's hate-filled eyes focused on him as though his glare could drill a hole right through Lee. At least with this man's capture, Heidi would be safe.

Heidi prowled Molly's living room, trying to ignore the worried look on her landlady's face. She would feel much better when Lee was back safe. Remembering the huge size of the attacker, goose bumps rose on her skin. She rubbed her hands up and down her arms.

"He'll call when he has news," Molly said, peering up from working on a section of a quilt. "Why don't you try lying down in my spare bedroom? I'll wake you up when I hear from Lee."

"No, I can't sleep. I don't care how tired I am."

"The nice police officer out in the hall told me they put up roadblocks all around Sagebrush. He won't be leaving unless he walks out of here. His information and photo have been put out on the T.V. and radio. They'll catch him soon."

"What if they don't? I'm scared to even close my eyes."

"Sit down here—" Molly patted the couch next to her "—and rest. You haven't been out of the hospital long. You need to heal."

"I know, but I feel like I have a large bull's-eye on my back. At least now I know why that man was after me."

"Yes, and because of you, he won't be getting out on bail like Gus Zoller. I can't see a judge letting a murderer walk the streets, especially since the ballistics also matched the bullet that killed Keevers and Adams. That's two murders Keith West was involved in."

Because exhaustion seeped through her, Heidi sank onto

the couch and collapsed back against the cushion. "I don't know what I would have done without you and Lee. I feel so alone." She hated the pity party she was throwing for herself, but vast unanswered questions still plagued her, even though she had remembered a few things from her past.

Molly covered her hand with hers. "Dear Heavenly Father, please show Heidi she is never alone with You in her life. That You walk beside her through the difficult times as well as the good ones. You're there to shoulder her burden and help her through her troubles. Amen."

Tears crowded Heidi's eyes as she listened to Molly's prayer for her. Each word soothed her anxiety. "Thanks. I feel in my other life I believed in the Lord. What you said comforts me. When I think of God it seems natural, like something I did a lot." Her hand beneath Molly's curled into a ball. "But I have to even piece together my faith."

Her friend cocked her head and examined Heidi. "Do you really? Don't you know everything you need is in here?" She touched the place over her heart. "When you have time, borrow my Bible and read it. It'll come back to you." She picked up her copy on the coffee table and placed it in Heidi's lap. "Keep that."

"I can't. You read it all the time."

"I have others."

As she ran her fingertips across the bumpy surface of the black cover, that peace she'd glimpsed earlier surrounded her. "Thanks. This means a lot to me."

"Then you've made this old lady happy."

"Old? Since when?" Heidi murmured.

"My arthritis is acting up. Must be some weather system going through."

"Where I live they need rain badly."

"Where's that?"

Heidi delved into the depths of her thoughts, but a name of a town wouldn't materialize. "I can picture a small adobe house, but I don't know if that is where I live."

"That could be anywhere in this part of Texas. And this state is a big one. But you remember another bit of information. That's a good sign."

But was it real or wishful thinking on her part? Was it something she wanted, not had? Heidi started to say something when a knock sounded.

Molly gasped. Rising, she hurried to the door and inched it open, then flung it wide. "We've been waiting for you to return. Tell us what's happened."

The sight of Lee entering the apartment accelerated Heidi's heartbeat. Tired lines grooved his forehead, but he was in one piece. Before he shut the door, Kip limped into the room, immediately making his way to Molly then Heidi.

Heidi scratched him behind his ear and on his neck. His tail moved from side to side. "It's so good to see you, Kip." She rubbed her cheek against his fur. "What did the vet say?"

"He should be good as new in a day or so."

"Praise the Lord," Molly said, taking her seat again. "Did you catch Keith West?"

"Yes. Valerie was my backup and is taking him to the emergency room so I could come by and tell you two what happened."

"He was hurt?" Recalling how he hurt her should make her ecstatic the man was suffering, but she wasn't. "Will he be able to talk, help you with the case?"

"One of my earlier bullets in the alley grazed him across the cheek. That should be patched up in no time, but I had to shoot him in the arm. They may keep him overnight. As soon as I can, I'll be interviewing him. Probably tomorrow morning." He released a wary breath. "I'm going to the hospital to see to securing the man. I want you to identify him as your attacker tomorrow. I don't want to see him out on bail. He assaulted a police officer, which should make the case even stronger."

"You need some coffee to take with you. That stuff at the hospital isn't good." Molly stood. "Heidi might be able to help strengthen your case against Keith West. I'll leave, and she can tell you what she remembered in the woods."

Lee's gaze linked with hers. "You remember?"

"Some things. Seeing Keith West again helped." Heidi went on to describe what she saw in the woods the month before. "Maybe that can help you get him on murder."

"Did you get a good look at the person he was burying?"

"No. All I thought about was getting out of there."

"Will you be able to show me where you were? Or the general location? Pauly Keevers wasn't killed until recently so West couldn't have been burying him. But if it was the place where I found Ned Adams, great. If it wasn't, that means there's another one out there that we haven't found."

Heidi crinkled her forehead. "But wouldn't Kip have found all the graves?"

"Only if I had him in the right vicinity. The woods are a thousand acres. Although I did a grid-by-grid search, it's possible there were some areas I missed."

"I'll do whatever I can to help this investigation," Heidi promised. "I don't want Keith West out of jail."

"Then in the next couple of days, we'll work to nail him."

Molly returned with a travel mug that she gave to Lee. "Are the police officers going to leave?"

"Until we figure out what's going on, I'm leaving one in the foyer and one patrolling the grounds. At least for tonight. Also Kip will stay with you two."

"Great. I'll go get some coffee for the offenders. I made a whole potful. It'll probably take me a good ten minutes or so."

Lee chuckled, a grin spreading across his face. "Subtlety isn't one of your strong suits."

Molly waved her hand in the air. "Carry on."

His gaze bound to Heidi's, Lee waited half a minute after the door closing sounded in the living room before shortening the distance between them to almost nothing. His arms entwined about her and tugged her near.

"Tell me what happened upstairs."

For a few seconds, his softly spoken command didn't register on her brain because she responded to his cozy proximity with an opposite reaction than she'd displayed with her assailant. There was no desire to fight for her freedom. Instead, she nestled against him, drawing in his scent, his warmth.

"He was hiding in my closet. I went to put my jacket up, and he came at me. His presence totally took me off guard, but something deep inside me kicked in and I wasn't going down without a fight. He tried to smother me with his hand."

"He was in your closet?" His mouth twisted into a thoughtful look. "I wonder how he got in without being noticed."

"The television was giving Molly some problems so a cable man came out to fix it this afternoon. Maybe then?"

"I'll take a look around before I go to the hospital, but I think the threat is over. I'll also check with the cable company to make sure they actually sent a guy to repair Molly's T.V. reception."

"She knew the man who came to fix the problem. He'd been here before."

He shrugged. "But West might have snuck in while the cable repairman went in and out of the house."

"Will this end everything?"

"It should. I'll make it known you've already talked to me

about identifying West in the woods burying a body. After I check on him, we'll go through his place. I need to find the gun used on the men found dead in the woods and Zoller. It wasn't the one on him. That will cinch the case against West."

"Good." A long sigh escaped her lips. "I want this over with so I can focus on getting my life back."

"Will you stay here?"

The question surprised her but shouldn't have. She hadn't thought much about what she would do next. "I don't have anywhere to go. Do you think Molly would mind? I could get a job and finally start paying rent."

"Ask Molly, but knowing her, I have a feeling she would insist you stay here. She's taken a liking to you."

The prospects of looking for a job and facing the world without her memory restored should concern her, but for some reason, cuddled in his embrace, it didn't. "I'm remembering some. I think I'll recall more with time." She hoped, because how could she totally move on with her life with her mind like Swiss cheese.

"I'd better go, but tomorrow I want you to ID West, then, if Kip is up for it, go with me to the woods either in the afternoon or the next day."

She smiled. "Whatever works for you. I'm not going anywhere."

"Good, because I'd like to get to know you when you aren't running for your life."

The words sent her heart soaring. "That'll be nice," she whispered right before Lee planted a kiss on her mouth, quick but mind shattering.

When he parted and strode toward the door to the hallway, she wanted to go after him, insist he stay. But he needed to work on the case against West. Her gazed remained fixed on the entrance a long moment after he left. Again, she wondered if it was a good thing for her to remember her old life. Something deep inside her kept shouting no.

The next morning, Lee sat across from Keith West in the interview room at the police station, the suspect's shoulder bandaged, his arm in a sling. A police officer stood behind West to prevent him from moving if he tried. So far the man hadn't asked for a lawyer. Why?

"We've got you connected to three murders, the last being Zoller. The gun used in those murders was found at your house under a floorboard. You should have gotten rid of it, but frankly, I'm glad you didn't. Its presence at your place only strengthens the case against you. I have a witness that puts you in the woods with a shovel and a dead body, digging a grave. The person you tried to kill last night will testify to that. And let's not forget that when I chased you from the crime scene yesterday, you tried to run me down with your car." His lips flattened. "The list just goes on and on. You won't be getting out of prison until you're an old man if you live that long. A lot of people connected to this case have ended up dead."

West glared at him, but from the shudder that wracked the man's body, Lee could tell his words had made the desired impact.

"However, if you talk, we can protect you," Lee continued. "We want the person behind what's been happening in Sagebrush. We want The Boss."

"If I talk, I want the deal in writing from the DA. Not a word until then. I'm prepared to tell you who I'm working for. I'll need to be protected from the get-go. You know what happens to people who talk. Most have ended up dead. I don't want to be among them."

"Finally, a criminal who's smart."

West shrugged. "I look out for number one above all. If I'm going down, so is the guy who pays me."

Loyalty obviously wasn't in this man's vocabulary, but Lee wasn't complaining. "I'll get back to you with the paperwork after the DA signs off on it. Until then you'll be guarded."

Lee left the interrogation room to make arrangements to protect West and to let the captain know about the deal. Slade would work with the DA while Lee went to the Lost Woods with Heidi to check the location of where she saw West burying a body. If there was another in the forest, that might impact the deal the DA would make with West.

Lee threw together a photo array for Heidi to make an ID of the man who attacked her, then headed to Molly's, finally feeling they were progressing toward discovering who The Boss was. Was West one of the three middle managers in the organization? From Don Frist, one of the men who kidnapped Brady, they knew there were three of them. Charles Ritter, a crooked lawyer, who was jailed last month, was definitely one of them. He wasn't talking, but he would be prosecuted for the murders of Eva Billows's parents. Periodically Austin, as the arresting officer, would have a little chat with Ritter. But each time he had refused to talk.

When Lee arrived at his Victorian boarding house, he parked behind Valerie's car. She and Lexi were guarding Molly and Heidi. Both he and the captain thought that Heidi was safe now that West was sitting in jail. Although that didn't mean Lee wouldn't keep an eye on Heidi and be there to help her, she could start rebuilding her life with no worries someone else was coming after her.

Lee found Molly, Heidi and Valerie talking in the kitchen while Molly was baking a cake for a ladies' group. "I've come to the rescue, Heidi." He signaled for Kip, sitting at Heidi's feet, to come to him. As his dog made his way across the room, he was relieved Kip was no longer limping. "Captain wants us to check out the Lost Woods. See if we can find the place where you saw West."

A frown slashed her eyebrows downward. "Like I said last night—I'm happy to help. But my few memories of that place aren't good."

He strode to her and offered her his hand. "Then it's time to change that. It might help you remember everything that happened that day. If we can find the area, you might be able to recover more memories beyond the day in the woods. That will be a step toward recovering your old life."

She fit her hand in his. "That's what I'm afraid of."

Valerie rose. "I guess my services are no longer needed today."

"Thank you, Valerie, and I think I'll take you up on the offer to go shopping with me since I'm not familiar with Sagebrush."

"Great. I can show you the best places to get some clothes for a reasonable price. How about this Monday? I'm off then."

"Sounds good. I'm going to be looking for a job soon."

As Valerie and her dog, Lexi, left, Molly opened the oven and took out the cake pans. "I have a friend who's the head librarian at Sagebrush Public Library. She's been complaining to me she's losing one of her best workers at the end of next week. I'll give her a shout-out about you. That is if you want a job at the library."

"What about the documents I'll need to have a job?"

"You can work that out. There are provisions for people who have amnesia." Lee flicked a glance at his watch. "Ready to go?"

She nodded.

Lee started for the exit. "Good. The quicker we find the

place you saw West digging a grave, the quicker this will all be over with."

"I like the sound of that." Heidi followed him.

At the front door Lee paused and shifted toward her. "We'll start at the place where Peterson's car was. Then we'll head to the area where Ned Adams's gravesite is. Hopefully it'll be the one you remember and that will be the end of it."

"That's a good plan. Maybe going the route I did that day will help me."

As Heidi strode toward his SUV, Lee's cell rang. He opened the door for her, noting the caller was his captain. "What did the DA say?"

"I haven't talked with him yet. He's unavailable until the end of the day. His wife said she would let him know the second he got home."

"I'll be back at the station later, then. It'll give me time to search with Heidi."

When he clicked off, she asked, "Is there a problem?"

"No, just a delay. Happens all the time. Things don't move as fast as I wish they would."

"That's life," she said with a chuckle.

That laugh stayed with him as he put Kip in the back, then rounded the rear to the driver's side. He wanted to hear that sound more. The circumstances of how she came into his life made him wonder how much she had laughed in the past.

When he slid behind the steering wheel, he opened the folder he had with the photo array and passed it to Heidi. "Do you recognize the man who attacked you last night in any of these pictures?"

Without any hesitation, she pointed to Keith West. "That's him. I won't forget him anytime soon—that is, barring any unexpected head traumas."

"Good. We have the right man. Later I'll have you do a

formal ID at the station. I just wanted to make sure. Making sure we cover all our bases with this case."

"Gladly. I don't want to hear that he's back out on the street like Zoller."

"That won't be happening." At least Lee hoped that was right. The way the past couple of months had been going, he wasn't as sure as he used to be. Sagebrush was a medium-size city that, up until a few years ago, had been a nice place to live and raise a family. But with the rise in the crime rate, that wasn't true anymore. He wanted his town back.

Heidi looked around the area on the edge of the Lost Woods where Peterson's vehicle had been. "It doesn't look familiar, but then the car isn't here."

"Okay. It was worth a shot to see if you remembered anything. Let's head to the gravesite." Lee gave a signal to Kip to head into the woods.

As Heidi walked behind Lee on the narrow path with Kip on a leash in the lead, she said, "I'm glad to see he's back to normal. I don't want anything happening to Kip. He's special."

"I agree. He more than earns his keep. All the dogs in the K-9 Unit do. When we aren't working a case here in Sagebrush, we are often working with some of the police forces or the sheriff around here. Our unit has a stellar reputation." A shadow crossed his face. "The captain's dog, Rio, was the best of the best."

"And he's still missing?"

"Yes, not a hint where he is. Pauly Keevers told us Rio was taken to locate something in these woods, but we haven't found anything other than the two dead bodies and Peterson's car. Those aren't reasons to beat up an old man and steal the captain's dog. Besides, those incidents happened after Rio was taken."

"I would think if you took a police dog, you'd better have a good reason."

"Exactly. We haven't figured out what yet. It might make our jobs easier if we knew what the kidnapper wanted Rio to look for." Lee veered off the path and delved deeper into the vegetation.

Heidi's heartbeat kicked up a notch. Sweat beaded her forehead and upper lip. She'd been in this area before—running, afraid, not sure if she would live or die. Breathlessness assailed her lungs. She stopped, putting her hand over her chest, and inhaled gulps of oxygen-rich air.

"You okay?"

She locked gazes with Lee a few feet in front of her. The kindness and caring in his expression eased the panic attack. She wasn't alone. She had the Lord by her side. She had Lee. "I'm fine." Taking a step then another, she advanced toward him until he clasped her hand.

"I know this is hard. What went down that day in the woods had its impact on a lot of people in Sagebrush."

"Let's do this and then get out of here."

He cupped her hand between his. "If this isn't what you remember, we'll come back out another day and see if you can help me find the location. Maybe when West talks, he'll tell me and I can leave you out of it."

"If I can help, I will. I owe you."

"I could say the same thing. We're where we are on the case because of you."

Her stomach flip-flopped at the smile he gave her. It encompassed his whole face and reached deep into his eyes.

Lee led her the remaining fifty feet and pointed to the ground where the earth had been disturbed about seven feet by four. "Is this the place?"

Heidi didn't have to rotate completely around, but she did

to make sure. "Yes." She gestured at an area about fifteen feet away behind a large tree. "I stopped there to catch my breath and saw him with the shovel. I was thinking of asking for help until I got a little closer and stumbled upon the dead body."

"Good. At least there isn't someone else out here buried."

She bit her lip. "We hope."

"Yeah, I'm being optimistic. Must be your influence."

"Mine?"

"I've seen what you've been facing, and you're determined to move forward and get your life back. I like that attitude." He clutched her hand again. "Let's go. I want to get something to eat before I go back to the station to have a little discussion with West."

"You know what sounds good right now? A thick juicy hamburger with lots of French fries."

"I've got the perfect place. I'll call Molly and let her know we aren't eating at the house tonight. You'll love the food at Arianna's."

"Sounds good."

By the time they reached the outskirts of the Lost Woods near where Lee had parked his SUV, the sun began its descent behind the tall trees, casting shadows. Heidi glanced back at the dimly lit forest. Goose bumps streaked down her body. Creepy, especially when she thought of what she had seen in the woods, what Lee had found.

Out of the corner of her eye she caught a movement—a dog and a man. "Is someone else from your unit out here?"

"No, I don't think so. Why?"

"I just saw a large German shepherd running through there—" she indicated the place to the left of the path they had used "—and a man was running after the dog. Probably just a jogger or something. Maybe they're trying to get through before it gets dark."

He leaned toward her. "You say a German shepherd. What color?"

"Mostly black with tan markings."

"Which way?"

She pointed in the direction behind her to the left.

"Get to the car, lock the door. Kip, go with her." Thrusting his keys into her hands, he gave the command to Kip to guard Heidi, then dashed toward the area she'd indicated.

He turned and backpedaled. "Go now, Heidi. That dog might be Rio. That man may be the one who had him stolen. Remember they were looking for something around here."

She hurried toward his SUV, Kip right beside her. After climbing into the backseat with the border collie, she locked the doors, then peered toward where Lee was going. He was gone and the dark shadows grew. She put her arm around Kip. "It's you and me." The quavering in her voice mirrored the trembling in her hands.

Lee chased after the man with the German shepherd. Although it was dimly lit in the woods, there was enough light for him to follow the guy's trail. The medium-size man kept looking back then increasing his speed.

Even though he was dressed in his uniform, Lee shouted Rio's name several times and, "Police, stop!"

The man, wearing dark pants and jacket, ignored him and darted to the left into the denser part of the forest. Slowly, Lee gained on the runner. He lost sight of him in a thick stand of trees with lots of underbrush on the ground.

The few glimpses of the dog reinforced his thought the German shepherd might be Rio. Why else would the guy be running from him when he'd identified he was police? What was he hiding? Adrenaline fed him and spurred him even faster.

Suddenly, Lee came out into a small clearing where the

lighting was brighter and the man stood with his feet planted apart, his arms at his side stiff with hands fisted. Emitting a low growl, the German shepherd sat beside the runner.

Lee slowed then came to a stop twenty feet from the pair. The closer he came to the dog the more he didn't think it was Rio and opened his mouth to tell the guy he'd made a mistake.

But before Lee could, the man said, "Sic him."

The German shepherd lunged to his feet and raced toward Lee, teeth bared, a low growl coming from the animal.

Chapter Nine

With few options and no time, Lee unhooked his police-issued canister of pepper spray and squirted a stream at the charging dog. It hit its mark and the German shepherd came to a halt. It began rubbing itself on the ground.

The guy spun around and fled. Lee went after the man who commanded his dog to attack him, forcing Lee to protect himself. Anger fueled him. Within a few feet of the runner, Lee leaped forward, tackling the man to the ground. Before the perp had a chance to react and fight, Lee slapped handcuffs on him and yanked him to an upright position.

"What were you thinking? It's a good thing I didn't pull my gun and shoot your dog. You're under arrest."

"For what? I have a right to defend myself."

"I'm a cop. I'm dressed as one, and I identified myself to you. You don't have a right to use a dog like that."

"You ran after *me*," the man shouted, his face beet red.

"If you'd stopped like I asked, I'd have explained why." Frustration churned Lee's stomach. "C'mon. I need to take care of your animal. You obviously couldn't care less about your dog."

Heidi bit her thumbnail and absently patted Kip while waiting for Lee. He'd been gone for close to half an hour. Worried, she kept her focus on the place where he'd disappeared into the stand of trees. What if that was the person who'd kidnapped Rio and he ambushed Lee? She hadn't heard any gunshots. But there were other ways to take someone down.

As Lee emerged from the woods with a man, a patrol car pulled into the parking area as well as a van with writing on the side that was hard to read. Heidi scrambled from the SUV, leaving the door open for the light to illuminate the area around the vehicle.

In the dimness, she glimpsed the grim set to Lee's jaw. He handed off the man to the police officer, said a few words to him then turned his attention to the man approaching him from the white van. Lee gestured toward the woods. While the guy dressed in a brown uniform pulled out his high-beam flashlight and a gallon jug of water then started toward the forest, the patrol car backed out of the parking area and Lee crossed to her.

"Who's that?" Heidi asked, nodding in the direction of the man trudging into the woods.

"Robert Crane, the animal warden. He knows where the dog is and is getting him. I had the German shepherd's owner, that bozo who the officer took away, put a leash on his dog and tie it to a tree. Robert will take care of the animal and rinse his face with water. That'll help the dog."

"It wasn't Rio?"

"He has similar coloring, but no. The owner brings the dog out here to hunt for his food. I'm not sure the man feeds the animal other than what he gets for himself. On closer inspection the dog was too thin. He decided to sic the German shepherd on me to give him a chance to escape. I'm having Robert Crane go to the man's house and take a look around. He may have other abused animals there. I've got the feeling that poor dog isn't the only one."

"You have a very interesting career. Finding dead bodies, chasing men, rescuing a dog."

Hr grimaced. "Not before I had to use pepper spray on the dog to stop him from attacking me. But Crane will take good care of the animal. In the meantime, I have a shop owner who's looking for a watchdog at night. This one could be one with some retraining. I'm sure I can get Harry to do that."

"You're going to find him a home?"

"That's the least I can do for the poor dog. He's going to be much better off after tonight. I don't understand why people have pets if they aren't going to take care of them properly." Lee shut the passenger door and made his way to the driver's side. "I'll drop Kip off at Molly's, then one hamburger dinner coming up."

Heidi's stomach gurgled. "I'm famished."

Lee chuckled. "That makes two of us."

Later that evening, Lee faced West in the interrogation room as the man read through the paperwork on his deal. Interestingly, the suspect still didn't have a lawyer to represent him. "Do you want your lawyer to look it over?'

"No."

Lee lifted a brow. "Why not?"

"It's hard to tell who to trust in this town."

"Yeah, I've noticed that can be a side effect of crime."

West snorted and placed the paper on the table. "It seems in order."

"It's only good if the information you give us is useful."

"It's useful if you want to know who's behind those two snitches' deaths." West signed the document.

"And Zoller's?"

"I hired Zoller to do a job and he messed it up. Got himself caught. I don't tolerate a job half-done."

"It seems to me you got yourself caught, too."

West curled his lips into a sneer. "Do you want the info or not?"

"Please, spill your guts." Lee gripped the sides of his chair to keep from launching himself across the table. This menacing hit man had tried to kill Heidi.

"I was hired by Blood to take care of Adams and Keevers—and find a way to know what was going on in the hospital rooms of Jane Doe and Patrick McNeal. If they woke up, I needed to keep close tabs on them because if they started to remember what had happened to them, I was to take them out. Did you have anything to do with the missing listening device in McNeal's hospital room?"

Lee grinned. "Yes. I'm afraid I did."

"I hired Zoller, who had access to both of them, to plant the listening device in their rooms, and if they began to recall things about their *accident*, then to take care of them."

"Do you normally subcontract?"

"When it's needed, yes. It would look strange if I was discovered hanging around the hospital. Not so with Zoller. He needed the money. I had some I could give him."

"You're just a regular nice guy." Lee leaned across the table. "So this Blood is The Boss?"

A cackle rippled from West. "No way. No one knows who's The Boss, at least that I know. I think he only interacts with a second-in-command."

"Is that Blood?"

West shrugged. "I doubt it."

"Who's Blood and what does he have to do with The Boss?" The frustration from earlier returned full-force.

"Blood's real name is Andrew Garry. I'm pretty sure he's in middle management in the crime syndicate."

Lee leaned forward. "Like Charles Ritter?"

"Yes."

"Who else? I hear there are three of them."

"Can't help you with that," West said flatly. "Each one of them had their designated area and specific people they worked with. I worked for Garry, tidying up little messes that developed."

"Do you know anyone else in the organization?" Lee demanded.

"No, I worked directly with Garry."

Lee rose. "You'll be taken to a secure location while we check this information out."

Later, with an arrest warrant in hand and a photo ID of Andrew Garry, Lee and Austin headed for Garry's home with their dogs while another team took Garry's real estate office downtown. Lights from several of the rooms in the large two-story house alerted Lee the man might be home. Austin rang the bell while Lee looked inside Garry's large window. Cushions were slit and tossed from the couch and chairs. Books from a built-in bookcase cluttered the floor. The contents of the drawers in a desk joined the books scattered about the room that looked like it was a home office.

"He's been robbed or vandalized." He hurried to Austin and tried the knob. It turned. "This doesn't bode well."

Lee withdrew his gun and stepped into the foyer to a similar sight in every direction he looked. Motioning to Austin to take the right, he took the left side off the entrance hall and stepped into the home office. He made a circular pattern around the room, looking for any signs of Garry or the people who did this. As he moved through the office, glass crunched under his feet, the stench of liquor wafted to him. Bottles of alcohol in a minibar had been flung and shattered all over the place.

But no one was in the room.

Lee went back into the foyer and took the dining room and kitchen. The same damage occurred with the chaos in the kitchen even worse. No food item was left intact.

Austin appeared in the entrance. "The rest of the downstairs is just like this."

"Let's check upstairs. I'm calling this in." Lee pulled out his cell and let the captain know what happened at Garry's house.

"Is Garry there?" Slade asked.

"Not downstairs. We're on our way upstairs to check."

"I'll send backup. I haven't heard yet if he's at the office. So someone was looking for something. What?"

Lee took the stairs behind Austin. "If they were, they went overboard. Like they were making it look like vandalism."

"Like Eva's house?"

Lee glanced at his friend—who was engaged to Eva Billows—and said, "Yes. I'll get back with you, Captain." He stuck his cell back in his pocket and searched the rooms on the left side of the long hallway. All of them were ransacked. Whoever did this spent hours here. What was so important to risk doing that? Information about The Boss?

When Lee met up with Austin at the staircase, he shook his head. "Nothing but the same thing downstairs. No sign of Garry."

"Maybe the team will catch him at his office," Austin said, descending to the first floor.

"Or he was tipped off and has fled Sagebrush. Let's check the garage. See if his car is there."

A minute later, Lee stared at an empty garage, destroyed like the rooms in the house. "Our chance to question Garry

may be gone like the man. I'll have the night shift set up surveillance of the place in case he comes back here, but I'm not
holding my breath on it."

Heidi stood in the doorway of her bedroom, staring at
the bed where West had trapped her. The covers were still
messed up. She wasn't quite ready to return to her place on
the third floor until the man who hired West was behind
bars, too. She was thankful Molly had insisted she spend the
night again in her first-floor apartment. All she needed was
a change of clothes.

Her other two outfits were hanging in the closet. Where
West had charged out of and accosted her. The scene flashed
across her mind. The feel of his hand pressing into her mouth
and nose, cutting off her air supply, dominated her thoughts.

She only had five feet to the closet. She could dart across to
it, get the shirt and slacks and be back where she was standing in less than half a minute. But her feet remained rooted
to the floor. Another scene in another bedroom nibbled at
the back of her mind. She squeezed her eyes closed as though
that would block it. But sensations of helplessness, fear and
hopelessness flooded her.

No, not now!

Her eyes flew open. She was in Sagebrush. The past with
whatever happened was just that—the past. She sucked in one
fortifying breath after another until her heart rate had evened
to its normal pace.

Okay, I can do this.

Although the police protection was taken off her because
the threat was neutralized with West's capture, Lee still made
sure that Mark was going to be here while he was interviewing West. She appreciated that. Yet again, Heidi reminded

herself that she was perfectly safe and no harm would come to her by opening the door and getting her clothes.

The Lord is my light and my salvation; whom shall I fear? The Lord is the strength of life; of whom shall I be afraid? The Psalm came to mind, its words filling her with calmness.

She took first one step then another toward the closet. Before she knew it, she had her shirt and slacks in her hand and was back at the entrance into her bedroom.

Where had those verses come from? Again, she sensed her faith had been strong in the life she couldn't remember, that it had saved her in numerous ways. She turned away from the room and headed toward the third-floor landing. Maybe Molly would know which Psalm it was and Heidi could read all of it. She hurried down the stairs to the first floor at the same time that Lee exited Molly's apartment.

He smiled. "I was looking for you."

"The smile must mean you've got good news." Her pulse rate kicked up a notch. What she saw in Lee appealed to her. Commanding. Passionate about what he did. Protective.

"West gave up the man he worked for. It's only a matter of time before we find him."

"But you don't have him right now?" she asked with disappointment.

"He wasn't in his usual places—home or office—but police are watching for him." Although there were several feet separating them, the intensity in his gaze captured her and roped her to him. "West's employer has no reason to come after you. The only person your testimony could hurt is West. I have a feeling the man is scrambling to save himself." He closed the distance between them and clasped her upper arms. "It's over. You can walk the streets of Sagebrush freely."

Why did she feel it wasn't over?

"Tomorrow is Sunday. I hope you'll go to church with me and Molly."

"I'd love to," she replied, trying to sound upbeat.

"Then on Monday, when you're meeting with Valerie to shop, I'll take you to meet her and wait for you in the park downtown. Kip loves to play there with his Frisbee. Since that's my day off, too, I was thinking that once you're done shopping I could spend the afternoon showing you the area. If you're going to stay here for a while, you'll need to get acquainted with Sagebrush."

"I would like that." She held up the shirt and slacks she had. "When I went to get these, I realized the meager amount of clothes I have. If I'm going to look for a job, I need to have a few more, at least."

"Molly said you're staying with her tonight?"

She nodded. "I'm not ready to return to my apartment."

"When you are, I can have Kip stay with you at night for a while. He kinda likes you. Actually he isn't the only one. I'm glad you're staying in Sagebrush."

That earlier intensity returned to his look, luring her closer to him. She held her ground. There was so much uncertainty in her life. How could she give in to the feelings he created in her? "Where is Kip?"

Lee backed away a few paces, glancing at the hallway that led to the back of the house. "When I came home, I took him straight outside. He's probably ready to come in by now. He likes to be in the middle of everything going on."

That brief moment of connection vanished, and Heidi wondered if he would have kissed her again. Now she wished he had. *You can't have it both ways.* Maybe when her life settled into a normal routine, she could figure out what was going on between Lee and her.

Until then, she had to find a way to resist his considerable charm.

★ ★ ★

From across the street on Monday, Lee watched Heidi and Valerie meet up in front of Lace and Frills Boutique, a consignment shop Valerie assured her was very reasonably priced with some great clothes. His coworker was pushing a stroller with her niece in it. Valerie was the guardian of Bethany, who had been orphaned recently.

Heidi knelt in front of the eighteen-month-old, saying something to the baby. He remembered their discussions about children. Thinking about how they both loved them warmed his heart.

When Heidi rose, she held the door open for Valerie to push the stroller inside. He knew Heidi was worried about money, but once she started her job at the library, she should feel better. It was only a formality that she was meeting with Molly's friend at the library tomorrow or so Molly had told him this morning. Heidi's life was starting to piece together. She wouldn't need him as much, especially after she settled into a routine and made her own friends.

He should be happy about those prospects for Heidi. But deep down he wasn't. He liked feeling needed.

He had to keep his distance. She had a whole other life out there that she would eventually remember and go back to. After Alexa, he didn't want to be hurt again. And he'd probably see his ex-fiancée at the impromptu Valentine's Day party Molly had decided to throw on Friday, the fifteenth. According to his landlady, better late than never. But even worse than Alexa coming to the bash with her husband—because Molly was asking everyone associated with the K-9 Unit as well as other police officers at the station—was the fact that Valentine's Day was in a few days and he had a strong urge to get Heidi something.

To make her feel welcome. Yeah, sure. Who was he fooling? He cared about Heidi.

Kip trotted back with the Frisbee Lee had thrown across the park and dropped it at Lee's feet. His dog looked up at him expectantly, and when he didn't move fast enough to get the Frisbee, Kip barked.

"Okay, boy. I'll throw it a few more times, then I need to go shopping for a special Valentine's gift."

Kip barked again.

"Yeah, I know. I have no business doing that, but Heidi is all alone. I want to make her feel welcomed to Sagebrush." He hurled the plastic disc through the air, and his dog shot across the park after it.

Fifteen minutes later, Lee snapped Kip's leash on him and tossed the Frisbee in his SUV parked nearby. "Maybe the drugstore will allow you inside and you can help me pick out something. What do you think? A box of chocolates? A stuffed animal?"

His dog cocked his head and gave him a look like he was crazy.

"Okay. Those are pretty lame."

Lee set out down the sidewalk toward the Corner Drugstore at the end of the downtown area on the last corner before the residential section of the town started. Kip took up the lead, which was often his usual mode of traveling with Lee. He gave his dog an extra length of the leash so he could snoop when he wanted.

At a store a block away from their destination, Kip sniffed the front door as he had many others on their trek, but instead of moving on, he stopped and sat, then let out a series of barks. His sign that there was a dead body nearby.

Lee trotted forward, noting the building had a for-sale sign in the window, the shades drawn on the large plate-glass window. He tried the doorknob. It turned. Lee stepped through the threshold and paused, taking a few seconds to allow his eyes to adjust to the darkened shop.

Kip passed him and headed back toward behind the counter. Lee followed. His dog reached a closed door, probably to the office, and scratched on it. Lee opened it and moved into the room with a large desk and chair the only furniture. The stench of blood mingled with a musky, dusty smell.

Kip rounded the desk and sat. Lee followed and came upon a dead Andrew Garry, shot through the head, his blood pooled on the hardwood floor.

Carrying Bethany, Heidi left Lace and Frills Boutique a few steps in front of Valerie. Down the street, several patrol cars with flashing lights were parked in front of a building along with a coroner's van. She saw Lee outside on the sidewalk talking to his captain and knew in her gut that something was wrong.

Valerie came to her side and took her niece while Heidi grabbed her two sacks from the stroller. "It looks like there's been another death. That place has been vacant and for sale for the past few months. I know Andrew Garry has been aggressively trying to sell it. I need to check what's going on." She started forward.

"I'm coming. Lee is down there. He's my ride home." Lugging her bags, Heidi hurried after Valerie, pushing the stroller.

"I've got a bad feeling about this."

"Why?"

"I went to the Corner Drugstore last night and saw someone leaving that building. A woman. I thought she might be buying the place or had already purchased it. I'd heard rumors someone was looking at it."

"Who?"

"Not sure." Valerie increased her pace.

Heidi stood back from the scene while Valerie joined Lee and Captain Slade McNeal. With all these police she was sure it was a murder. Connected to the case Lee's been working on? She watched Lee talking, and his eyes softened when he glanced her way.

Lee disengaged from Valerie and his captain and made his way toward her with Kip. He smiled at her. "Valerie said your shopping trip was a success."

"I bought three more outfits, nothing too fancy or expensive, but they'll meet my needs." She gestured toward the building. "What happened?"

"I found Andrew Garry—the man we've been looking for the past thirty-six hours—dead."

"Murder?"

"A shot to the head."

"Do you need to stay?" she asked.

"No, the captain and Austin are processing the scene. Slade said this is my day off and to take it."

"Is this Andrew Garry the guy behind everything?"

"He was the man behind West and the killings of Adams, Keevers and Zoller. I don't think he's The Boss, just part of the crime syndicate." He gazed down at her. "The important thing right now is that you're safe and we're going to celebrate that fact today. Let's go."

"If you're sure?" She couldn't shake the feeling she wasn't safe until she dealt with her past—one that involved ending up in a wrecked car of a missing man. Where was William Peterson? How did she know him? *Did* she know him?

"I am. There have been enough deaths. I declare no business for the rest of the day."

"Sounds like a plan. What are we doing first?"

"Dropping Kip and your bags off at Molly's." He took her hand and urged her forward. "The rest is a surprise."

"I'm pretty sure in the past I didn't like surprises."

"Tough. You'll just have to wait," he said mysteriously.

"Am I dressed okay?'

He grinned. "Yep, jeans are great."

An hour later, standing in the barn at the ranch of one of Lee's coworkers, Jackson Worth, Heidi was faced with seeing if she knew how to ride a horse. Apparently, she did. When she sat in the saddle, the feel was familiar. When she guided her mare from the yard toward the dirt road that led to the back of the property, she knew how to do it. In the pasture, Lee kept his gelding next to her and set an easy gait.

"This is one of those days when you wonder if we're going to skip spring and go straight to summer. Winter and seventy-five degrees. I could take this every day."

She slanted her look toward him, the brim of his cowboy hat shadowing his eyes. His lazy drawl mirrored the gleam she glimpsed in his brown depths. "If I'm going to do too much of this, I'll need a hat like you have. This visor Molly loaned me just doesn't have the Western feel."

"If you stick around, it would be fun to do this on a regular basis. Jackson is always wanting me to come out here and help him exercise his horses. I used to do more, but in the past few years I've been pouring myself into my job. For a while, I was saving for a down payment on a house."

"Not anymore?"

"The need isn't that urgent anymore," he said gruffly.

"What changed?"

"The woman I was going to marry became pregnant with another man's child."

The tightness in his voice prompted her to slide a glance toward him again. "I'm sorry."

"No need to be. At the time last year when I found out, I was devastated. I couldn't believe Alexa would do that. I'm fine now. Me finding out and us breaking up were for the best. When I marry, it'll be because we are totally committed to each other. With my faith that's the only way I can go into a marriage. She obviously didn't feel that way."

"Are you sure you're over Alexa? I hear pain in your voice." Her gaze locked on his.

He lowered his head, the brim of his hat blocking the view of part of his face, but his mouth set in a firm, straight line. "Yes. I'm more disappointed than anything. We had dreams for the future, or so I thought. I think those dreams were more mine than hers."

"What dreams?"

"A house with some property for horses and children. I love kids. I wanted at least three. She wanted no more than one."

"And yet she had a baby."

"Yes—that hurt most of all."

"So how do you feel now with what happened between the two of you?"

"A family still is important, but now I'm a little leery of trusting. I'd known Alexa for a long time and look what happened." He chuckled ruefully. "Enough about me. I brought you out here for a change of scenery…and was hoping that in a more relaxed environment we could talk about *you*."

"Just as soon as I figure out who I am, we can talk."

"I didn't mean so much about your past. It's just that, your past. I'm more interested in your present."

"You are?" His last comment *intrigued* her.

"Yes."

She stared out into the distance. "But I don't really have much past, present or future. I feel like my life is in limbo."

"Have you thought about what you'll do if you never remember who you are?"

"I like the name Heidi. Now a last name is totally different. I'm not sure what to do about that."

"Give it time. It hasn't been that long since you got out of the hospital." He nodded encouragingly. "You're already starting to recall bits and pieces."

"Where are we going?" she asked, attempting to steer the conversation in a new direction.

"Somewhere special."

Up ahead, Heidi spied a small glade with some trees starting to leaf out while others were evergreens. When she arrived at the grove, the sight of a stream, the sound of rushing water over rocks, made her smile. Tranquil. Isolated. A haven in the middle of all the chaos her life was right now.

Lee dismounted then came to her to help her down.

She waved him off and slipped from the mare with ease. "I'm sure I've ridden before. Possibly many times."

"See…another piece of the past. And I agree no one would have ridden like you did without prior knowledge of how." He tied his gelding to a branch then took her reins and did likewise on another nearby tree.

"I don't know if I want to remember everything. I keep thinking about what the doctor told me—that all my injuries weren't from a car wreck and that I had injuries that were older than some. Like someone beat me."

Lee's eyes darkened with concern. "He did? Why didn't he tell me?"

"I didn't want him to tell anyone. I was—still am—trying to figure out how I would have gotten those injuries. What if William Peterson beat me up and I got away?"

"Then where is the man?"

She tried to think beyond what had happened in the Lost

Woods, but still came up blank. "Hiding? But then every-thing we've heard about William Peterson is how kind he is and helpful to others."

"The sheriff in Tom Green County as well as the San An-tonio police are still looking for him. No one who knew him could identify you. In San Antonio there isn't anyone missing that fits your description or picture."

Tension continued to build behind her eyes. She massaged her temples.

Lee covered her hands. "I thought we agreed not to talk business today. Time for that tomorrow. This is a day to relax and get to know each other. The time you've been at Molly's shows me that you're learning what you like and don't like. I want to hear about your discoveries."

Her heart swelling at his words, Heidi dropped her arms to her sides. "I'd like that. And I want to know more about the boy who lived down the road from here."

Lee grasped her and strolled toward the stream. "I'll regale you after lunch."

"Lunch?" She peered back at the horses. "Where's the food?"

A few more paces past a large group of bushes and Lee swept his arm across his body. "Here."

Heidi stopped, her gaze taking in the blanket spread out on the ground with a huge wicker basket at one corner and rocks holding the others down. The water flowed a yard away and a large tree, beginning to leaf out, shaded part of the area with the warm sun spilling through the partially bare limbs.

"I'm impressed." She grinned. "When did you do all this?"

"I brought everything out here before I took you to meet Valerie."

"What time did you get up this morning?"

He shrugged nonchalantly. "Early, but Kip loved coming

with me. He got to run across the pasture, chase birds and a couple of rabbits."

"That sounds like Kip. That is one thing I know I love— dogs. I wish I had one. Kip makes me feel safe. When I was sitting in the car Saturday night, I wasn't scared with him there."

"A trained dog is good protection." He tugged her toward the blanket. "I'm starved. Let's eat."

"When are you *not* hungry?"

"It's Molly's cooking. I don't see you turning her food down."

"I didn't eat for weeks." She sank onto the blanket. "I'm making up for that time."

"How are your cooking lessons coming along?"

"Good. That's another thing I've learned. I must have liked to cook. It feels so natural to me." She smiled softly. "I've enjoyed working with Molly. She's been so generous to me. I'm not sure how I'll ever repay her kindness…"

"Molly would be the first to tell you she'd more than happy to help." Lee sat beside her. "So are you moving back to your apartment tonight?"

"Yes… I need to. I'm tired of living in fear."

"I think you're doing the right thing," he said tenderly. "And I'll let you have Kip for as long as you need at night."

Emotions jammed her throat. She swallowed several times, then said, "Thanks. I appreciate that. I can't let what happened destroy my life. I need to move beyond all this." The fervent intensity behind her words surprised her for a second, then she realized it came from deep inside her. From her past she didn't remember.

"I agree. Dwelling on the past is not living. That's not what the Lord wants for us."

"I'm trying to depend on God. It isn't always easy, especially when you don't remember."

He lifted his hand and smoothed her hair back, hooking it behind her ear. "I know. I don't have the excuse you have, and I'm still trying to figure out how to do that. We can spend time figuring it out together."

Together. She wished that could be the case, but she didn't know who she was. How could she fall in love with such a gaping hole in her life?

He leaned toward her, cupping her head between his hands. When his mouth whispered across hers, she didn't care about who she might have been. These feelings he generated in her were all that mattered—at least for the time being.

Chapter Ten

Lee entered the kitchen at Molly's on Valentine's Day after putting in a long day at work. All he wanted to do was relax and enjoy his evening without thinking about work and the crime syndicate in Sagebrush. Every time he did, frustration knotted his gut.

"This is a test to see if you trust me." Lee held up the black blindfold.

Heidi turned from the sink where she was rinsing the lettuce and stared at the strip of material in his hand. "Can't you just take my word for it?"

He shook his head.

Heidi glanced toward Molly, who quickly averted her gaze and became focused on what she was stirring on the stove. Placing her hand at her waist, she said, "What are you up to, Mr. Calloway?"

"A surprise."

"You know how I feel about those."

Lee grinned. "C'mon. Don't be such a spoilsport. I promise you'll like my surprise."

When he approached her with the blindfold dangling from
his hand, she swung around and allowed him to tie it on her
head. Then he began leading her across the kitchen to the
hallway.

"Molly, you've been awfully quiet. Do you know what the
surprise is?"

"Yes. It's brown."

"Shh, Molly. I'm never going to tell you anything again,"
Lee said, tossing Molly a smile and a wink.

"A box of chocolate?"

"I'm not telling. You just have to wait." In the foyer he bent
close to her ear and whispered, "But chocolate is so mundane
and boring."

"But I like chocolate. You can't go wrong with chocolate."

At the front door, he leaned around to open it.

"Flowers? No, it can't be that. I've never heard of a brown
flower unless it was dead."

"Your powers of deduction are right on." After he swung
the door wide, he guided her across the threshold to the front
porch.

"Okay, where is my surprise?"

"Did anyone ever tell you that you're impatient?"

"Probably, but I can't remember. But if you don't take
off—" She reached up toward the blindfold.

Lee quickly untied it before she could. "There."

Heidi blinked at Harry Markham standing in front of her
holding a leash to a brown dog that was about two feet tall
and wagging its tail. "What is it?"

"A little bit of a lot of breeds," Harry answered. "But I've
been working with her and she's good at guarding and protecting. Lee thought you might like to see if you two are a match."

"To keep?"

Lee came around to face her. "Yes, if you want her."

"What's her name?" Heidi held out her hand for the mutt to sniff it.

"She answers to Abbey. I rescued her six weeks ago, but she needs a permanent home." Harry offered her the leash.

Heidi took it and squatted by the dog. Abbey immediately licked her on the face. "What a loving dog. I'd be thrilled to have her. But what does Molly have to say about all this?"

"She's fine with it. After all what's one more with two already here?" Lee quipped. "And Kip likes Abbey. I think Eliza may have some competition for my partner's affections."

Heidi looked up at Lee with the biggest grin on her face. "I love this present," she gushed while patting Abbey. "What made you think of getting me a pet?"

"When you told me about the memories of having a dog, seeing how you respond to Kip and then your comment yesterday about feeling safer with a dog."

"And if you remember your past and for some reason can't keep Abbey any longer, don't worry. I'll take her back and find her a new home." Harry started for the steps. "Now I'd better go. I have a wife to take to dinner."

His friend's comment reminded Lee of his own dream of having a wife and family. A pang zinged through him, leaving emptiness in its wake. To have that, he would have to trust a woman. Staring at Heidi and Abbey, he wondered if he could trust her. What would happen if she did recall her old life and she wasn't really who she seemed to be—a warm, kind, caring person?

He'd thought Alexa was caring and faithful and discovered she wasn't.

Heidi rose. "Are you sure Molly is okay with this?"

The older woman poked her head out the opening into

the house. "Yes, one hundred percent. If you can't keep her, I will. I figure one day Mark and Lee will each get married and move out. Then where will I be without Kip and Eliza around?" She stepped out onto the porch and greeted Abbey. "She's friendly. I think I see some German shepherd and collie and lab in her."

"Let's go introduce her to Eliza. Kip met her earlier today at the training center, but you never know how a dog will react on her home turf." Lee waited as Molly, Heidi and Abbey went into the house before following them.

In the backyard, Heidi kept Abbey on a leash while Kip and Eliza acquainted themselves with the new dog, sniffing and checking her out. Then he and Heidi walked Abbey around the yard and let her get to know the place.

"What do we do now?" Heidi stood at the bottom of the steps leading to the back stoop.

"Let her off her leash while we watch. We'll be here if there's a problem."

"Okay," Heidi said in a hesitant voice, then in slow motion she released Abbey. The dog immediately sat at Heidi's feet. She waved her arms. "Shoo. Go play."

With her big brown eyes, Abbey peered up at Heidi.

"I don't think she wants to play."

"Let's sit and see if anything happens," Lee suggested.

Heidi took the step next to him while Abbey stretched out her front legs and laid her head on top. "What kind of commands does she know?"

"Harry said you could come to see him in the training center tomorrow or Saturday, and he'll work with you and Abbey. She's been trained to protect and guard. Harry is very good at his job."

"Is that where the K-9 dogs are trained?"

"Yes. Kip stays there when I'm working on mundane tasks

like filling out paperwork and interviewing suspects. He's happier there. Although he does like to visit and get treats from Lorna, the secretary."

"Will she be here tomorrow night for the party?"

"Yes. She and Molly are good friends. She'll probably come over early and help set the place up for the party."

"How big is this party going to be?"

"Probably thirty or so. Everyone will come just for Molly's food. She knows how to feed her guests."

"I'm helping her with the food preparations. I know I've met some of your unit, but not nearly that many people." She gave him a "deer in the headlights" look.

He leaned back against a step, stretching out his legs and crossing them at the ankles. "You're going to charm them all."

"I haven't faced being in a crowd since the accident. I wonder if I'm an introvert or an extrovert."

Lee eyed her. "You know I've never thought about that."

"I can tell you're an extrovert," she murmured. "I've seen how good you are with people."

"I guess in my line of work it helps to be outgoing."

Heidi sighed. "It's really weird trying to decide what kind of person I am, and yet in other ways I innately know."

"Like loving children and dogs?"

"Yes, but that's easy. I hope Valerie brings her niece. I loved meeting her the other day. Bethany is adorable."

"She hasn't hit the terrible twos yet. Valerie's life certainly has changed lately with her sister dying and Valerie becoming guardian to her eighteen-month-old niece. Now the captain has ordered she be put on 24-hour protection because she saw the woman who might be Garry's killer." He paused for a long moment. "She left the scene of the crime about the time the medical examiner said Garry was murdered. Valerie doesn't like being watched one bit, but with all that has happened in the town lately, it's a wise decision on Slade's part."

"Maybe I should send Valerie a sympathy card. One person in protective custody to another. Except I'm free now." Heidi's smile twinkled in her eyes.

"It wasn't that bad, was it?"

"No, but limiting your freedom is never fun, even if it's for the best." Her grin widened. "I have to say, though, my jailer was what I heard one nurse at the hospital say was eye candy."

Cheeks flushed, Lee caught sight of Abbey lifting her head up. She watched Kip and Eliza running and chasing each other. Lee pointed to the dogs. "I wonder what Abbey is thinking."

When Abbey put her head back down and closed her eyes, Heidi chuckled. "That she can't be bothered with something like that. Maybe she's playing hard to get."

"Ah, one of the games men and women play."

"Well… I'm not touching that except to say I don't think I play those kind of games. In the past week I feel like I'm an open book. I don't know any other way to be."

Kip trotted up to him and dropped his tennis ball at his feet. "I think my dog is telling me to pay attention to him or else."

"What's the or *else?*"

"He'll nip me. Nothing that hurts, but he is persistent when he wants my attention."

"Not too far off from a child."

"Yeah." Lee picked up the ball and threw it.

As it sailed through the air, Abbey jumped up and raced after it at the same time Kip did. He reached it first and proudly picked it up between his teeth then pranced past Abbey. When Lee hurled it again, this time Kip slowed his pace and let Abbey retrieve the ball.

"Oh, boy, Kip has it bad. He let her have it."

"But not before he showed her who was boss."

Something in the tone of Heidi's voice—a hint of bitterness—pulled Lee's attention to her. A faraway look took hold of her for a moment. It was as if she'd recalled something from her past she didn't like. What secrets did she have locked in her mind? And how could he truly trust someone with secrets even she didn't know?

"I've been given the job of hostess while Molly is in the kitchen finishing up some last-minute food preparation. She might as well have said she was serving dinner. She's made a feast," Heidi said Friday evening as she hurried past Lee toward the foyer. "Do I look okay?"

"Hold up. You flew by me. I didn't get a chance to see how you look."

Heidi slowed to a stop and turned toward Lee. "This is one of the dresses I bought at the Lace and Frills Boutique. Valerie said it looked good on me."

Lee's gaze leisurely trekked down her frame, then drifted back up to her face. He whistled. "Yep, she is right. You'll turn every man's head tonight in that getup."

Heidi glanced at her dress—with small lilac and purple flowers on a white background. The close-fitting bodice and full skirt fell to just above her knees. "I'm not sure this is what I would have bought if it hadn't been for Valerie."

"Rest assured, you'll attract plenty of interest tonight."

Heat scored her cheeks. "That's not my intention." *I'm only interested in your attention.* Her eyes widened at that thought. She'd been trying not to think of Lee in a romantic way, but when he'd surprised her with Abbey yesterday, she couldn't stop her feelings from snowballing toward full-fledged love. No matter how much she told herself she couldn't fall in love with him until she got her life straightened out, she couldn't deny it any longer.

"What can I do to help you?" He closed the space between them, his fresh, lime-scented aftershave swirling around Heidi.

And roping her to him as though his arms had caged her against him. "Help me to remember everyone's names. There are a lot of people coming. I know Mark, Valerie, Slade, Harry and Gail. That's it."

"That's a great start. Don't worry if you don't remember everyone. They won't expect it since you're new." As the bell chimed, Lee skirted around her and headed toward the door. "I have a feeling you'll be a natural."

Heidi scurried after him. "Are the dogs okay out back?"

"The last time I peeked, Eliza was on one side of Kip and Abbey on the other. Man, he's got it made."

"You could always change his name to Romeo."

"No. That love story ended tragically." Lee swung the front door open wide.

Harry and Gail stood in the entrance. The nurse Heidi had become friends with in the hospital grinned and embraced Heidi. "You're recovering nicely."

"Thanks," Heidi said warmly. "It's nice to see you again."

For the next half hour, she and Lee stayed near the front door to welcome a steady stream of guests inside. It felt like an eternity until Heidi finally turned from letting the last couple into the party to scan the crowd milling between the living room in Molly's apartment, the common dining room and kitchen, and the large foyer. She leaned back against the door with a weary sigh. "Is the whole department here?"

"Not quite but almost all the dog trainers, the support staff and a good number of the police are here. How are you on the names so far?"

"That beautiful tall blonde over there is Eva Billows, soon to be Eva Black. The guy next to her is Austin, her fiancé and the partner to Justice, a bloodhound. They're the ones with the little boy, Brady, who was kidnapped last month." Her lips quirked. "I don't think I'll forget them since I stumbled into the middle of their search for Brady and then wound up in the hospital."

"Good point…" Lee nodded toward a man dressed in nice jeans with a white dress shirt and brown boots. "And who's the guy over there by Molly?"

"That's Jackson Worth, your friend who owns the ranch where we went to ride, and the woman between Molly and Jackson is Lorna Danfield. I'm glad to finally meet the lady who helped me get my job at the library. I've talked with her on the phone, but I wouldn't have imagined her with short curly blond hair."

"What did you imagine her looking like?" Lee asked with a chuckle.

"Medium, stocky, muscular like a pit bull. Molly described her as tough and a go-getter."

"That she is, but she loves dogs and will do anything for a friend. How about—?"

A knock on the door startled Heidi. She jumped away and whirled. "I thought everyone was here."

When she let the couple into the house, Lee stiffened next to her. Heidi slanted a look toward him. A fierce scowl lined his face.

"Hi, I'm Heidi. I'm helping Molly with the party." She offered her hand.

The man with dark hair and eyes shook it. "I'm Dan Harwood and this is my wife, Alexa."

Ah, now Heidi understood Lee's reaction to the pair.

"I'm glad you could come. Molly has a buffet-style spread in the dining room. She wanted people to eat whenever they were hungry." As she explained the setup, Heidi kept her attention directed at the man, but she felt the pierce of the woman's sharp gaze. When she shifted her focus to Alexa Harwood, Lee's ex-fiancée's full lips pinched together. "It's nice to meet you. I hear you recently had a baby."

Before Heidi could congratulate her, Alexa said, "I bet you did." She swiveled her piercing look at Lee, then clasped her husband's arm and practically dragged him away.

"Okay, that was a little awkward." The sudden tension evaporated the farther the pair distanced themselves from her and Lee.

"Molly didn't think they were coming."

"So you weren't prepared?"

"No," he bit out, the tension returning. "Excuse me. I want to check on the dogs and make sure they're still playing nice."

From Lee's reaction, she didn't think he was over Alexa. Suddenly the prospects of the party dimmed for Heidi.

Alone, she panned the foyer, and when she found Valerie, she made her way to her. "I thought you were going to bring Bethany."

"I was until my neighbor volunteered to watch her."

"Any clue who the woman was that left the murder scene?"

"No and I wish I could figure out why she seems familiar." The redhead sighed with frustration. "I've racked my brain, but I can't remember. If this is the way you feel all the time, I don't know how you do it."

"I've been trying not to force the memories anymore and get on with my life as it is now. Usually when I try to think of something, I end up getting stressed and nothing happens."

"Right. That's exactly how I feel right now," Valerie lamented.

"No doubt you'll think of where you saw her. Maybe when you least expected it."

"Where did Lee go? He didn't look too happy."

Heidi released a long breath. "He wasn't. You saw who

came tonight. He didn't think Alexa and her husband were actually coming. I think he still cares about her."

Valerie tilted her head and scrutinized her. "You like him."

"Does it show?"

"A little. You're like me—an open book."

"I'm discovering that. But I wish I wasn't. I don't want Lee to know how I feel. My life right now isn't really my own." Even surrounded by all these police officers, Heidi couldn't quite feel safe like she should. In her mind, she heard the ticking of an imaginary bomb that was about to explode. No matter how much Lee tried to reassure her she was all right now, she didn't totally believe that. And she didn't understand why.

"I could say that for a different reason. I never counted on being a mother anytime soon and certainly not like it happened. Bethany has to be my focus for the time being. Well, that and keeping myself and her safe. Good thing I have Lexi. Her specialty is apprehending and protecting. I may need that."

"I miss having her around. Did you hear I have a dog now?"

The rookie cop grinned. "Harry said something about it."

"Abbey's out back with Kip and Eliza. I'll show her to you."

Heidi and Valerie started for the kitchen when a cell phone rang. Everyone looked toward Captain Slade McNeal. He answered it, turned away for a few minutes and talked in a low voice. When he hung up and faced the partygoers, a smile as big as Texas greeted everyone.

"That was the hospital. Dad has come out of his coma. The doctor told me he is groggy but making sense. I hate to leave this wonderful celebration, but "

"Slade McNeal, if you didn't leave right away, I would think something was the matter with you." Molly marched to the front door and opened it. "Tell your dad hi from all of us and let us know when it's a good time to start pestering your father with visitors."

★ ★ ★

Lee stuffed his hands into his front jean pockets and stared out into the night. Kip, the reason he told Heidi he was coming outside, lay sound asleep with both females next to him. He hoped Kip fared better than he had with the opposite sex and having a long-term relationship. Why had Alexa come tonight? This was where he lived. She should have stayed away.

The sound of the back door opening and closing drew his attention to the person coming outside. He stiffened at the sight of Alexa. He looked away, but there was no place to go. The stoop was only six by six feet.

Alexa crossed her arms and blocked his escape into the house. "How many times do I have to tell you I'm sorry? I was wrong."

Her body language screamed the opposite of what she'd said. Lee gritted his teeth to keep his response inside.

"We need to work this out. You work with my husband."

Anger shot to the surface. "Maybe you and Dan should have thought about that before you got together. The least you could have done was break off our engagement before sleeping with him." He'd held his tongue for months, avoiding the pair as much as possible.

"I have no defense to that." She unfolded her arms and dropped them to her sides. Tears glistened in her eyes. "I hurt you. There's no way I can change that now. But I hope one day you'll forgive me."

She whirled around and hurried into the house at the same time Heidi and Valerie were coming out back. Alexa mumbled something Lee couldn't hear and pushed past the women. His gaze linked with Heidi's and an inscrutable look covered her usually expressive face. What had Alexa said to them?

"I wanted to show Abbey to Valerie," Heidi said in a strained voice, and descended the steps with Valerie.

As the two crossed to the dogs, Lee watched them without really seeing them. His mind swirled with emotions he needed to deal with because Alexa was right. He would see her from time to time. The situation as it was at the moment wasn't tolerable.

Why can't I forgive her, Lord? Why am I holding on to my anger?

Heidi and Valerie returned to the stoop with Abbey following the pair. Heidi petted her dog. "She's already protective. She sleeps at the side of my bed between me and the door. I think last night I slept the best I have since I woke up from the coma."

"She's cute." Valerie glanced from Heidi to Lee. "I'll leave you two. I have to call my neighbor to check on Bethany. I'm not used to this mom stuff yet."

"You'll get the hang of it in no time." Heidi stayed back while Valerie left.

Lee felt like he should say something, but what? "How's the party for you so far?" Lame, but what was his relationship with Heidi? Friends? More than friends? He knew one thing. He cared about Heidi…was attracted to her.

"Enlightening."

"How?" he asked curiously.

"First of all, the people you work with are great and incredibly supportive. They are all making me feel right at home. Which I appreciate since I don't know where my home is."

"Did you think they wouldn't be?"

"No, but I've been letting my feelings for you grow when I shouldn't."

He opened his mouth to ask why, but she held up her hand to stop his words.

"I realized after seeing you with Alexa that you still have issues with her that need to be resolved. I've been thinking lately that what we have between us is going somewhere. But

I guess I forgot more than my past. I forgot what it meant to become involved with a man who is on the rebound. You're still in love with Alexa and need to deal with those feelings before you can move on." She choked back a sob. "I have enough to cope with. I don't need to end up hurt, developing feelings for you that you don't return."

"Heidi, I don't…" His voice faded into the quiet. Maybe it was for the better that they gave each other distance. *Why can't I forgive Alexa? Why did I lash out at her?* Until he could answer those questions, he needed to keep away from Heidi—at least as much as he could, living in the same house.

She stared at him for a long moment, a sheen to her eyes. The look she sent him twisted his heart into a tangle of emotions. She pivoted and hurried into the house.

Leaving him with questions he couldn't answer. Leaving him with the knowledge he had hurt Heidi and hadn't intended to.

Chapter Eleven

"Well, what did you think of the church service and Pastor Eaton?" Molly asked as she steered Heidi toward the fellowship hall Sunday morning.

"Very inspiring. He gave me things I need to think about."

"We all need reminding about forgiving others. Holding grudges or anger only poisons the person keeping the grip on it."

All last night she'd wrestled with her covers, unable to sleep more than a couple of hours. She couldn't shake Lee's confrontation with Alexa Friday night—or his reaction to her presence when his fiancée left. She'd thought they were developing something special between them. She'd been wrong. At best he looked at her as a friend. Nothing more.

Then what did those kisses mean?

She didn't know. Maybe he was trying to use her to forget Alexa. Obviously, it didn't work. Now she needed to move on. Forget Lee as anyone other than someone who had helped her when she needed it.

She shored up her belief that she would eventually remember her past. Then she could put her life back together and take up her old life where she left off—wherever that was.

"Heidi?" Molly moved into her personal space. "Are you all right?"

She blinked, stepping back a foot. "Yes. Why?"

"Oh, I don't know. I've been asking you the same question for a minute. No response." Her landlady clasped her arm and tugged her away from the crowd pouring through the double doors into the fellowship hall. "Something is wrong. It has been since the party Friday night. You holed yourself up in your apartment yesterday except when you needed to take Abbey outside. What gives?"

"Just trying to figure out who I am."

Molly smiled at her. "You're a delightful young woman with a kind heart. That's who you are."

"There are times I feel like I'm being watched. That I need to always be aware of my surroundings."

"Everybody should be. That's being smart. Give yourself time to adjust after all that's happened to you. You wake up from being in a coma to find someone wants you dead and comes after you. But Zoller, West and Garry have been taken care of."

"I guess that's it." But she didn't hear much conviction behind her words. Surely in a couple of days she'll begin to feel more comfortable and secure.

"I'm so glad to have Patrick McNeal awake," Molly said. "I know how worried Slade was about his dad."

"I'm glad he doesn't have amnesia. There are times I feel like I'm in a large dark room trying to find my way around it."

"You'll find your way out of the darkness," Molly proclaimed softly. "The good Lord will see to it."

"I sure hope so." She scanned the people milling about, talking with each other or standing in line for the snacks and drinks served. Her gaze fell onto Lee, and she frowned. "I didn't see him come into the church." *Why didn't he sit by them like he had last week? Because he was protecting you then. Now he doesn't have to.*

Molly followed the direction Heidi was staring, then blocked her line of vision. "What happened at the party? I never saw Lee the last half. I know people were spread out all through my downstairs, but…"

"I think he left after he talked with Alexa."

"Oh."

"That's right. Oh. The conversation didn't go well."

Molly's eyes narrowed. "Is that why he went into work when yesterday was his day off?"

"I guess. I didn't see him yesterday. The only time I've seen him since the party is now—standing on the far side of the room with a ton of people between us."

Molly peered at Lee until his gaze connected with hers, then she waved him to her.

"Molly, why did you do that?"

"To get to the bottom of this. Alexa has done enough damage to him. It shouldn't continue."

Heidi leaned close to her landlady so no one else would hear and whispered, "It's simple. He still cares about her. He isn't over her. That doesn't leave any room for—others in his life. Now if you'll excuse me, I think the garden is particularly beautiful at this time of year."

As Heidi rushed away, she heard Molly say, "But it's winter. Most things are dead."

Just as her feelings for Lee were going to be when she convinced her heart he wasn't the one for her.

★ ★ ★

"Where is Heidi going?" Lee asked as he approached Molly in the fellowship hall.

"Do you care?"

"Of course I care," he retorted. "She's a friend. I feel responsible for her."

"Why? She isn't in any danger now that West is behind bars and Garry is dead."

"What kind of person would I be if I didn't care after all she has gone through? She doesn't know who she is or where she lived before this." And that was part of the problem. He'd started to have deeper feelings for her, and then he was reminded of the mistake he'd made with Alexa, a woman he'd known for years.

"What's going on with you and Alexa?"

He shifted uncomfortably. "What do you mean? What's that got to do with Heidi?"

"I heard about your conversation with Alexa Friday night. You haven't finished grieving for that loss."

Lee pulled her to the side. "Hold on there. I know it's over between us, and I wouldn't want it any other way."

"Then why are you so angry with her? Why haven't you forgiven her? Do you think you can truly move on without doing that?"

Lee looked around him. "Shh. Not so loud. I don't want the whole church to know my business."

"What are you intentions with Heidi?" Molly put her hands on her waist. "She has enough to deal with. You're sending mixed messages, and she doesn't need to try and figure them out right now. Remember she's trying to figure out who she really is."

"Is that why you insisted on Alexa coming to the party Friday night?"

She gave him a pointed look. "Your department is a close-knit one and what happened between you two has affected that. Dan should be able to bring his wife to gatherings without feeling uncomfortable."

"What about me? I'm not the one who went out and had an affair with someone Alexa worked with."

"I'm not saying what they did wasn't wrong, but I expect more from you." Molly glanced behind Lee. "Now if you'll excuse me, I see Lorna." She started toward her friend, stopped and said, "By the way, Heidi is out in the garden."

Lee watched his landlady thread her way through the crowd to Lorna. His teeth clenched so tightly his jaw ached. When she looked back at him, he stalked toward the door into the foyer, not sure where he was going.

He took several steps toward the exit to find Heidi in the garden. But he paused. What could he say to Heidi when he was so confused? He'd thought he'd moved on with Alexa. Now he wasn't sure.

His gaze latched on to the doors to the sanctuary. He needed answers. He strode inside to find a quiet place to lay his problem before God.

Heidi crossed her arms over her chest and wished she'd grabbed her jacket before leaving the church. She should go back in, but she didn't want to right now. Closing her eyes, she once again tried to picture what her life had been like before her accident. A small, white house with a porch faded in and out of her mind, never staying long enough for her to get a feel for where it was or any details that would help her remember more. What did it mean to her? What about the adobe house she'd remembered earlier?

The warmth of the sun disappeared. She opened her eyes to find clouds moving across it and obscuring it from her view.

Suddenly, she felt her life had been more like a cold, cloudy day with little sunlight and warmth. She shivered and hugged her arms even more to her.

From her vantage point on the bench in the middle of the garden she spied a man standing at a Jeep parked along the street. Tall with a broad chest, the man jiggled his set of keys and stared at her with an intensity she sensed across the distance. She fixed on the keys bouncing up and down. Fear edged into her mind. There was something about that action that caused sweat to coat her forehead while a chill encased her. She started to get up.

"Heidi, aren't you cold?" Lee asked, coming from around the corner.

Relief fluttered through her. Nodding, she slid her gaze toward the stranger beside the Jeep in the street. He was gone. Strange. Did she know him?

Lee slipped off his jacket and slung it over her shoulders, then sat next to her on the bench.

"What are you doing out here?" The sight of the man jiggling his keys stayed in her mind. Why did that action bother her?

"I came to find you."

"Why?" Heidi fingered her gold locket, rubbing her thumb over its surface.

"Because I owe you an explanation about Friday night."

"No, you don't. You owe me nothing. I'm the one who owes you for all you've done for me. You have a right to feel for and care about anyone you want. We'll just be friends. At least I think we are." Truth was, she didn't know anything right now. Again, she glanced toward the Jeep. Where did the man go? Her fingers tightened about the locket.

"Is something wrong?"

She peered back at Lee. "No, I'm fine. Just frustrated at myself for not remembering. I've recalled a small, white house with a porch and a swing on it." Swing? When did she realize it had a porch swing?

"Do you think it's where you lived?"

"Maybe. It could be my childhood home for all I know." She began to rise. "We should go inside."

"Stay for a moment."

She sank back next to him, suddenly no longer chilled.

"We're more than friends, Heidi. I care a lot about you… and I owe you an explanation about Alexa."

"Stop it. You don't. She's in your past. So you're angry at her for what she did to you. That's between you two." She shrugged. "No telling what's in my past. I'm probably upset at someone. How can I expect you to get over someone in eight months? I don't have the right—"

Lee clasped her upper arms and dragged her against him, planting a kiss on her mouth. Stunned, she didn't respond for a few seconds, then as before with him, she gave in to her feelings growing deep inside her. She sensed she'd never felt this kind of caring from a man before.

When he parted, his forehead touched hers while his hands cradled her face. "I figured out why I was still mad at Alexa. She has what I want—a spouse and a child. It isn't because I still love her. I was jealous that while I was hurt, she was getting what I wanted. When we became engaged, I'd thought I'd found what I wanted, but I knew something wasn't right even before I discovered Alexa was cheating on me with Dan. We'd known each other for several years, and yet we didn't really. Neither one of us truly shared ourselves with the other."

"It's not the amount of time you spend with someone. It's what you do when you spend the time with that person."

He cocked a grin. "I'm learning that. I don't know anything about your past, but I know the type of person you are. I see you with Molly, with Valerie's niece with Abbey and Kip. There are no barriers there. You're not trying to hide behind a facade of what you think others should see. You're you."

"That's because I don't know who I am," she said with a laugh. "What you see is what you get. You're learning as I'm learning who I am."

"But it's been a good journey. One I want to continue with you. I don't know where it will lead, but I do know we're not just friends."

"So what *are* we, then?"

"We're—dating. I'd like to take you out next weekend on an official date. I don't want to rush you. I know you've got a lot on your mind."

"I can't even tell you when I had a date last."

"I don't care," he murmured. "Ready to go back inside?"

"Yes, Molly is probably wondering where I am. We're meeting with the other ladies who are in the quilting group. She's determined to show me how to quilt. I think it's a lost cause. I don't know how many times I poked my finger with a needle. I think my forefinger has become a pincushion."

"Then don't do it." He rose and offered her his hand.

"I admire their work and wish I could quilt. I just don't think it's going to happen. I'm trying to do all kinds of things to see what I like doing."

"That's a good idea, but when you find you don't like doing something, then don't do it. Molly will understand."

Taking his hand, she stood. "I know. I'm going today to strictly be a cheerleader for their efforts. I like the women, and it's been nice getting to know them."

As Heidi walked toward the church entrance, she glanced over her shoulder at the Jeep across the street. It was gone, too. She'd been so intent on Lee she hadn't even noticed. He had a way of consuming her attention. Good thing she didn't have to be so attuned to her surroundings as she had when someone was after her.

Monday morning, Lee pulled up into the parking lot next to the Sagebrush Public Library, down the street from the police station. After turning the SUV off, he twisted toward Heidi. "I can pick you up after work. What time do you think you'll be off?"

"This isn't that far from Molly's. I'll walk home later today. I appreciate the ride, but I could have walked this morning, too."

He shurgged. "I was coming right by here on my way to work. This isn't out of my way."

"One of the first things I want when I get enough money is a car. I hate for you to feel you have to be my chauffeur."

"But I don't. I—"

She laid two fingers over his mouth. "I know, but I have to do this by myself. I need to learn to depend on myself. Ever since I've awakened from the coma, you've been there to help me, and I have appreciated that. Now it's my turn to figure out what to do."

"Have you always been this independent?" Lee asked without really thinking. "Never mind—"

"No, it's a good question, and one I wish I could answer. I hope so, but I don't know. Regardless, I want to be self-sufficient now."

"Then I'll see you at Molly's this evening. You can tell me about your first day on the job."

Heidi pushed the passenger door open. "See you then." When he started to leave the SUV to escort her to the library, she added, "I know where to go."

"Sorry. I forgot momentarily."

Lee watched her enter the building before backing out of

the parking space. "Kip, I'm gonna need you to bark when I try and do too much for her."

His dog responded with a bark.

When he parked next to the police station a minute later, he leashed Kip and walked him toward the training center. "Don't have too much fun without me. Desk work this morning on the case. I'm going to continue my search for who Heidi really is. Mostly phone work." His border collie peered up at him with a tilted head. "I know. Not my favorite part of the job, either."

He left Kip with Harry and strode toward the police station. A Jeep turned into the parking lot and slowed as it approached Lee.

A blond-haired man rolled down the window. "Can you give me directions to the Jefferson Inn?"

"Sure." Lee pointed toward Sagebrush Boulevard. "Go left and take this street through two stoplights. At the third one take a right. It's not far down on the left side of the road. It's a nice place to stay."

"Thanks."

As the stranger circled around and headed back to the main street through town, Lee remembered seeing the vehicle behind him when he drove into the parking lot next to the library. That guy was totally lost. He probably went through town and realized he'd gone too far.

As he entered the building by the back door, his cell rang. He quickly answered it when he saw the caller was from the San Antonio Police. "Calloway here."

"This is Detective Longworth in San Antonio. William Peterson's body was found in Tom Green County in an abandoned store along a back highway."

"What happened?" Lee ducked into an empty room off

the hallway, his gut clenching because he had a bad feeling about this.

"Beaten to death but the medical examiner thinks the official cause of death was strangulation."

He grimaced. "How long ago did this happen?"

"Estimated time of death was about a month ago."

Was Heidi somehow involved in this man's death? The second the question flitted into his mind, it left. Not the woman he knew. But she could have witnessed something. "Do you have any leads on who killed him?"

"Not much. The ME feels that the blows were inflicted by someone large and powerful and the bruises on the neck support that. Most likely a man or a woman with very big hands beat and strangled him. Some of the blows the man received cracked and broke bones, so not likely a woman."

Especially Heidi, who was petite with small hands. But still, did she know something about this man's death? Was that why she couldn't remember her past? More an emotional trauma now that she was physically recovering?

"I need to come interview your Jane Doe, the one you think might be connected to William Peterson's car found in Sagebrush."

"She still hasn't recovered her memory," Lee told the detective.

"I'm coming this afternoon. I have pictures of the area where William Peterson's body was found. They might help her recall what happened." The detective paused for a long moment. "This was a brutal murder. A lot of rage in it. She might know something and not realize it."

"Fax the pictures. Let me talk with her this afternoon, then I'll call you. She's gone through a lot since we were in San Antonio." Lee went on to explain what had happened in Sagebrush.

"Fine. I'll send them now with the autopsy report from the medical examiner in Tom Green County."

"Does it have the man's blood type in the report?"

"Yes, why?"

"There was a cloth found in the car with Heidi's blood type and an unknown person. DNA tests were being run on it, but the results haven't come back. You know how that goes."

The San Antonio detective sighed. "We spend half our time waiting on test results. I'll let the sheriff in Tom Green County know about Heidi. He's running the case and will probably give you a call later. At least I get to close out my missing-person's case. Not the way I want to, though."

When the detective hung up, Lee stared at the tile floor. He wasn't going to wait for a call from the sheriff. After he filled his captain in on the news of William Peterson's death, he'd give the sheriff a call. Heidi might be from that area. He would solicit the man's help in recanvassing the towns around there for any information on a missing woman of Heidi's description.

Later that afternoon, Lee passed the black Jeep—the same one from this morning—sitting in front of an office building several down from the library. The man must have found the person he needed to see. Lee turned into the parking lot and hurried into the building, wanting to catch Heidi before she left work.

The lady at the main desk directed him toward the children's section. Heidi sat in a chair with children in a semicircle around her, listening to her read them a story. He waited, watching her face lit with enthusiasm.

"The end," she said to the kids, a few immediately asking her to read another book. "Your parents are here to pick you up. This group will meet the same time on Thursday. Don't forget to take the books you checked out." She scanned the children as though counting them to make sure the right kids went with the right adult.

As the area emptied, Lee strolled toward her.

"You're so good with the kids."

She blushed. "I'm enjoying the job."

"I know you told me you could walk home, but I need to talk with you and show you some photos. I waited until you were through working today."

"Photos?" She picked up the story she'd read and reshelved it.

"Get your purse and jacket. I'll explain in the car on the way to the police station."

She stiffened. "This doesn't sound good."

He looked around, then leaned closer to say, "William Peterson's body was found yesterday."

She paled. "Murdered?"

He nodded.

"I'll be right back."

Lee lounged against a post while children rummaged for books on the shelves. By the time the dozen kids went with their parents, few stories were left. A prickling sensation danced across his nape. He glanced back but no one was there. He frowned, then saw Heidi exit a back room behind the counter and make her way to him.

Worry knitted her forehead, a solemn expression chasing away the earlier smile. "I'm ready. Are the photos at the police station?"

"Yes."

She stopped and rotated toward him. "Is this an official interview?" Tension vibrated from her.

He shook his head. "Peterson was killed by someone very big and strong. You don't fit that description." He wanted to take her into his arms and comfort her. This couldn't be easy for her.

"But what if I was there or I know something about it?" She tapped her temple. "All locked up in here."

"I'm hoping the photos will help you remember. I received a whole array from the sheriff in Tom Green County."

"He called you?"

"No, the detective on Peterson's missing-person's case. He faxed me some pictures, and I got some more from the sheriff."

Her face paled. "Photos of William Peterson?"

"Not ones you need to see."

"How bad was it?"

Lee blocked her exit from the library. "The person who killed him was strong enough to break his bones. That's strong."

"So he was beaten to death." A shudder shivered down Heidi.

"Technically, the cause of death was strangulation—someone with large hands." Lee took one of hers, laying it against his. He curled his fingers down over hers. "Ones much bigger than yours. So quit thinking you had anything to do with this man's murder."

"But I have a connection to the man. I don't know what, but I need to figure out what it is."

"*We* need to, so I'm going to walk you through what I know about what happened to Peterson." He entwined his fingers through hers and started down the steps.

"Where was he found?"

"In a deserted cafe/gas station on a back road. According to the sheriff, it doesn't have a lot of traffic. A couple's car broke down. When the husband went for help, he walked by the place and thought he would see if there was a pay phone somewhere around the store that still worked. He thought at first an animal had died in the building, but when he investigated it, he discovered Peterson." Lee opened his passenger door and then rounded the front of his SUV and pulled out of the parking lot.

"How long has the man been dead?"

"A month."

"About the time I arrived here in his car."

Lee nodded. "That's what I was thinking."

"And I'm not from around Tom Green County?"

"No one who fits your description is missing. I had the sheriff check last week and recheck again today. Actually, no woman is missing right now." He pulled into a space next to the police station. "I think it's time we put out an alert all over Texas and the surrounding states."

"Yeah, but what if the murderer finds out and comes after me? What if I witnessed Peterson's death and can ID the killer?"

Chapter Twelve

"Then I'll protect you as before. So far we've only had contact with law enforcement in the surrounding towns and counties, besides the sheriff in Tom Green County," Lee answered, pivoting toward her in the SUV. "If it will make you feel better, I'll drive you to and from work."

"Go back to watching my every move?" Heidi sighed, closing her eyes.

Lee clasped her shoulder. "Only if you want. We'll be cautious and alert."

The touch of his hand on her solidified his support through this new situation. From deep down she knew she'd never experienced the kind of emotions he stirred in her. "Fine. It was nice feeling free for a few days."

"You still are. Most likely whoever killed Peterson is long gone. And we don't even know if you witnessed the murder or even knew about it."

She looked him directly in the eye. "Then why did I have his car?"

He frowned. "I don't know, but we'll figure it out."

The fear and panic that had subsided when West was captured began to resurface. Heidi shoved it down. She wasn't going to let it rule her life. Molly talked about turning her problems over to the Lord. That was what she was going to do now. She was in a safe place with people who cared about her. Worrying would only add stress to an already strained situation. "I'm fine with whatever you think you should do."

"Good. I'm hoping the photos will help you. Not just the crime scene, but the area around it."

Fifteen minutes later, while Heidi sat at the table with the pictures spread out before her, nothing came to mind, no sense of recognition. Ever since Lee had shown her William Peterson's photo right after they'd discovered the car, she'd tried to remember seeing the man but couldn't recall anything. Now was no different.

Heidi's shoulders slumped forward, and her gaze suddenly fell on one picture to the right of her. A view of the left side of the building with a field stretching out behind it. A vision of her running as fast as she could flashed across her mind and disappeared. She tried to pull it back up but couldn't.

Tapping the photo, she said, "I was there. I think I was running from the store." Another image flickered in and out of her thoughts. She hugged her arms against her chest. "Someone was chasing me."

"Who?"

As she waited for another revelation, she curled her hands into fists. A hazy figure materialized in her mind. Vague. Wavering. "All I can tell is tall. Big." Tension left her rigid with her muscles locked in place to the point they hurt. Finally, she blew out a breath. "That's all. I can't remember anything else."

"That's a good start. What I think we should do is go to

the crime scene. Let you walk around and get a sense of the place. What day this week works for you?"

"Wednesday. I'm off that day. I hate to ask for a time off when I just started working there."

"Fine. Day after tomorrow will be perfect. I have some things I'll follow through with tomorrow, and that'll free me up to go on Wednesday. We'll get to the bottom of this."

Lee scooped up the photos and dropped them into a manlia envelope. "If you can wait a little bit, I'll put out the message about you to the law agencies in Texas and the surrounding states. The sooner we figure out who you are, the sooner you can get your life back. Maybe knowing who you are will nudge your memory."

Lee left her in the interview room, wondering about his statement concerning getting her life back. How could she expect a man to fall in love with her when she really didn't know who she was? That was something she'd been thinking for the past week. Now it appeared Lee was thinking that, too. He might care about her—even want to date her—but her past did matter to him whether he acknowledged it or not.

"I know it's troubling that the man's body was found, but it'll bring some closure to his family, at least." Molly handed Heidi a plate to put in the dishwasher.

"I know, but I feel I'm so close to recalling something and just can't. I even see a guy. Not clear, though."

"You helped Lee with the case here in Sagebrush. He'll help you."

The back door opened, and Lee came into the kitchen with Abbey and Kip following him. "I think these two would stay outside all night if I let them, especially if I agreed to stay, too, and throw the ball for them."

Molly dried her hands on a dish towel and hung it up. "You

timed that perfectly. We're through with cleaning up." She shifted her gaze from Lee to Heidi. "It's been a long day. I'm going to bed early tonight." Covering her mouth to hide a yawn, Molly shuffled toward the hallway.

Heidi yawned. "I have to agree with Molly. My first day on the job has worn me out."

"Good, then you'll have no trouble getting some sleep tonight. I was concerned with all that has happened that you might be too wound up to sleep."

"No. I'm exhausted." She patted the side of her leg, Abbey's cue to walk beside her. "I guess with having not worked for over a month that I'll have to build up my stamina."

"That makes sense." Lee trailed behind Heidi from the kitchen. "Where would you like to go on our date this weekend?"

Not lifting her foot enough, Heidi nearly stumbled on the stairs. She gripped the banister and steadied herself.

"You haven't forgotten about our date, have you?"

"No. I don't know what's around here. I'll let you decide." One less decision to make.

"I thought you didn't like surprises."

"I don't, so you'll need to tell me beforehand. Okay?"

At the second-story landing, Lee stopped in front of his apartment and said to Kip, "Stay." Then he started for the staircase to the third floor.

"I'm really all right. I know my way to my place. I know this has been a long day for you, too." She had to learn to take care of herself. She couldn't depend on Lee all the time.

The corners of his mouth hitched up. "It has, but I'll sleep better if I check out your apartment."

She swung around in his path. "Why? Do you think I'm in danger?"

He stared at her for a long moment, one shoulder lifting

in a shrug. "No. If someone was in your apartment, Abbey would have alerted you earlier."

"I'll see you tomorrow morning."

He crossed to her, cupped the back of her neck and kissed her, hard, full of pent-up feelings. "Good night."

Heidi watched him stroll to his door, glance back, then disappear into his apartment. She grazed her fingertips over her lips, imagining the touch of his mouth on hers all over again. Goose bumps rose on her skin. If their lives were normal...

Abbey nosed her hand. She looked down at her pet. "Sorry, girl. You caught me daydreaming. Let's go to bed."

Twenty minutes later, Heidi sank onto the covers and closed her eyes, sleep descending quickly.

Lee paced his bedroom, unable to go to sleep like he'd proclaimed. For the past hour the silence had mocked his attempts until he'd given up and gotten out of bed. He glanced down at Kip, who was watching him with his head resting between his outstretched legs.

"I know. No matter what I tell myself I can't seem to get her out of my thoughts. What secrets does she hold in her mind?" He could certainly understand if her subconscious suppressed what she'd witnessed if she'd seen Peterson being beaten then strangled.

But how would she be able to move on if she never remembered? It would haunt her, a barrier to any relationship she wanted to have. The cop in him needed answers; the man didn't care, so long as she was safe.

Staring at his bed, he decided to give sleep one more chance before he gave in and fixed a pot of coffee. The thought of him being forced to make the brew was enough to motivate him to get some rest. He closed his eyes, but all he saw before him was Heidi standing with her arms open wide, blood soaking her front.

He rolled over and punched his pillow.

Crash.

Lee flew out of bed, cocking his head to make sure he really did hear something above him in Heidi's apartment.

Another thump sounded, then something smashing against the hardwood floor.

He rushed toward the door to his apartment, only stopping long enough to snatch up his weapon and his set of keys. There was one to Heidi's place that she gave him after the shooting of Zoller on the back stoop.

He took the steps two at a time, Kip racing after him. In seconds he was inside Heidi's apartment. He signaled his dog to go into the bathroom off to the side while he crept through the dark toward Heidi's bedroom.

Suddenly, a figure came out of Heidi's room and flipped on the overhead light. He blinked at the sight of Heidi, her hair tangled, her eyes wide.

She stared at the gun he had aimed at her. He quickly dropped the weapon to his side.

"Sorry. I heard a noise like something crashing to the floor. I thought someone might have gotten in here, after all."

"I—I..." She gestured toward the room behind her.

Kip trotted over to Abbey coming out of the bedroom and sniffed her.

Her face ashened, Heidi folded her arms over her robe. "I remember. At least some of what happened that day."

"What happened in there?"

"I must have had a wrestling match with my covers and they won. The lamp on the bedside table did not. It's shattered along with the table on its side."

"You're bleeding." He pointed to her bare feet.

"I cut the bottom when I tried to pick up the pieces to the lamp."

"Sit. I'll find something to stop the bleeding, then you can tell me what happened."

While Heidi hobbled to the couch, she said, "There's a first-aid kit in the bathroom under the sink."

He found what he needed and sat next to Heidi, picking up her leg so he could tend to the bottom of her foot. After cleaning it out with hydrogen peroxide, he patted it dry, then checked to make sure no more slithers of glass were embedded in her skin before putting a bandage on the cut.

"Now tell me why you were wrestling with your covers."

"I saw the person who killed William Peterson in a dream."

Tension whipped through him. "Can you describe him?"

"He's about six and a half feet. Broad shoulders. Muscular arms. He limped."

"How about his face?" he asked.

"It was in the shadows, but the limp should help."

He met her eyes. "Could you see what was wrong with his leg?"

"Yes. I stabbed him with some scissors. It was bleeding."

"Tell me about the dream," Lee said, brushing a stray lock of hair out of her eyes and scooting closer on the couch.

"All I saw was his back because he had me by the arm as he dragged me toward the abandoned store after I tried to escape him. I knew if he got me inside he would beat me up, possibly kill me. He was so angry at me. Shouting over and over how worthless I was. He knew me. He wasn't a stranger." With shaking hands, she rubbed her eyes. "That's when William Peterson pulled up. He didn't like how I was being treated and wanted to help me. That was his mistake. The killer yanked me the last few feet into the dark store, turned toward me and hit me with his fist a couple of times. I blacked out. It happened so fast. Everything was a blur."

Lee took her quivering hands and held them. "Then what?"

"When I came to, the guy had William Peterson on the floor in the store and was pounding his fists into the man. I jumped on the assailant's back and tried to pull him off. Blood was going everywhere. He flung me into some shelving like I was a piece of trash he was throwing away. That's when he choked William Peterson to death." A sob escaped her throat and her eyes grew wide. "I saw a set of keys on the floor near the door and knew my one chance to get away was then or never. I grabbed the keys and flew outside to the stranger's car."

"And?"

"That's when the lamp shattered on the floor in the bedroom."

"Do you remember what happened after that?"

She shook her head. "I don't—want to. It was…" Her voice trembled to a halt, her teeth digging into her bottom lip. She swallowed hard several times before continuing. "That man can't find me. He'll kill me."

Lee kneaded his thumb into her palm, the action drawing her away from the memory of the nightmare and focusing her attention on him. "You don't remember how he knows you?"

"I think we were married once, and he was angry because I left him and filed for a divorce. I say that because he said divorced or not, he wouldn't remove his wedding ring. A court decree meant nothing to him."

She dropped her head, and when she lifted it again, tears shone in her eyes. One leaked out and rolled down her cheek. Lee's heart twisted. Any feelings he was developing for her had to be put on hold. That kind of past had to be dealt with. From her description of the man, he most likely abused her and kept her tethered to him through fear. He'd seen it enough as a police officer. Right now, all he could do was protect her and be a friend.

He drew her to him and enclosed his arms around her. "You're remembering more and more every day. It's only a matter of time before it all comes back to you. Our trip on Wednesday to the crime scene might be what you need. Maybe you lived somewhere in Tom Green County and someone will recognize you in person."

"No. I didn't live there." She pulled back and looked up at him. "I think I left where we lived to get away from him."

"Where?"

"Not around here. I don't even think in Texas."

He nodded. "Then quietly inquiring with the law-enforcement agencies in the surrounding states should give us something."

"I hope so. I don't like knowing a faceless man is out there wanting to harm me."

He gently lifted her chin and gazed into her eyes. "You have people who care here."

"I know." She smiled. "The best thing that happened to me is when you tracked me down in the Lost Woods."

"At least we now know how and why you had William Peterson's car and why both your blood types were on the cloth in his car."

She yawned.

"I can stay out here while you try and get some sleep."

"Are you kidding? No way am I closing my eyes again. My heartbeat is just now calming down." She disengaged from his tender embrace. "I'm going to make some tea and stay up." She glanced at a clock on a table nearby. "It's only a few hours to dawn. You go back and get some sleep. I'll be fine with Abbey and your apartment one floor below mine."

"Are you kidding?" he echoed. "I'm not going to sleep, either. I'm wide-awake now and could use a huge cup of coffee. Especially if I don't have to make it."

"That's one thing Molly didn't have to teach me. I know how to make coffee." Because *he* insisted she learn. "I'll make some for you."

"Perfect." Lee waved his hand toward Kip and Abbey sitting next to each other watching them. "I know it'll make Kip happy to stay."

She swiveled toward him, one hand on her waist. "How about you?"

"I don't think I have to answer that."

"Ah, yes, my knight in shining armor."

"My armor might be a little dented and tarnished. I'll go get some coffee." While Kip stayed, Lee hurried to the apartment and returned in record time. He didn't want to leave her alone.

"Not from my point of view." She strolled toward a counter where she had a hot plate, microwave and a few other cooking items off the living room and busied herself making the coffee and tea. After they were on, she asked, "So how should we pass the time for the next couple of hours?"

"Let's take turns answering a question the other asks."

"Sure, but you'll be at a disadvantage." She smiled. "I probably won't be able to answer very many questions."

"I know, but you might be surprised what comes out when you aren't thinking about remembering."

While Heidi retrieved two mugs from the cabinet, Lee re laxed back and observed her preparing the coffee. She didn't even ask him how he liked it, but she automatically fixed it the way he preferred with two scoops of sugar. Alexa always asked him one or two spoonfuls of sugar. Sometimes it was the little things that spoke volumes in a relationship.

★ ★ ★

"Captain, can I have a word?" Lee stuck his head into Slade's office midmorning on Tuesday, not long after dropping Heidi at the library.

"What's up?"

Lee came into the room and took the chair in front of his captain's desk. "I need tomorrow off. I'm taking Heidi to see the crime scene in Tom Green County." He went on to explain what she remembered from the night before.

"So she thinks she was married to the man who killed William Peterson. That makes it more important than ever to find out who she is. Some men can't let go even when something is over."

"I think Heidi will remember more when she sees the actual place where everything happened. For a time I wasn't sure she really wanted to remember what her past was. She even said that to me." He scrubbed a hand across his face. "She was afraid of what lead her to be in the Lost Woods that day I found her. Now she realizes she has to remember. There's a killer out there."

"Well, I hope you can figure it all out. Heidi helped us get one step closer to bringing down this crime syndicate in Sagebrush. Keep me informed."

Lee rose. "Will do, Captain."

At his desk Lee started making his calls. When he talked with a police detective in Santa Fe, he got a hit.

"We got a missing-person's report two days ago on a Lucy Cullen. She taught at a private school in the south part of the city."

"She's been missing for over a month. Why did it take them so long?"

"She called into work saying that her mother was critically ill. She asked for some time off while she went back home to Louisiana to care for her. Her mother didn't have anyone else. They granted it."

"Over the phone?"

"That's the way it sounded to me, but after a month they got worried when they didn't hear from her." The detective cleared his throat. "They tried the number she gave them several times, but no one ever answered or called back when they left a message. Finally, they were concerned something else was going on."

"Can you fax me the picture you have of her? Has anything been done on the case?"

The Sante Fe police detective snorted. "It hasn't been a high priority. We have a missing child that's taking our full attention."

"I understand. Send me any details you have. I'll let you know if our Jane Doe is your missing Lucy Cullen."

"Great. It's always nice closing cases."

Lee hung up, strolled to the break room to refill his coffee and returned in time for the fax to come through. When he saw the photo of Lucy Cullen, Heidi stared back at him. He'd found out who she was. Now he had a starting point to find out more about her. He put in a call to the principal of the school where she worked.

The only clue the man had where Lucy Cullen might have gone was Louisana. Even if the killer had forced her to make the call, maybe the place was a clue.

Heidi rolled the cart through the main room in the library, filled with patrons, toward the adult-fiction section. Clasping several books, a little boy, probably about four, ran toward the counter in the back, dodging his mom who chased after him. The child glanced over his shoulder at his mother and collided right into Heidi before she could get out of his way. Knocked back against the cart, she set off an avalanche of books sliding to the floor.

Red-faced, the mom passed her, still hurrying after her child. "Sorry." She slowed for a few seconds as though considering whether to help Heidi clean up the mess or pursue her son.

"Don't worry. I'll take care of this. I like seeing kids excited about reading." Heidi noticed the boy plopped the stories he wanted to check out onto the counter by the lady behind the computer.

Heidi turned to begin picking up the books when a large, blond-haired man handed her several. "I thought you could use some help."

She took the tomes from him. "Thanks."

Within a couple of minutes the cart was stacked and the man bid her a good day. She studied him for a few seconds, trying to figure out where she'd seen him in town. Shrugging when nothing came to mind, she pushed the cart toward the fiction section.

Deep in the bookcases, she stopped to shelve a thick volume on the top one. She stretched up on tiptoes and caught sight of the man who had helped her a few minutes before peering at her from the row over, jingling a set of keys. Recognition dawned in that second, the book slipping from her fingers and crashing to the floor.

"This is Officer Lee Calloway from the Sagebrush Police Department in Texas. I understand you were a neighbor of Lucy Cullen five years ago."

"Yes," the older woman said over the phone. "But I haven't seen her in that time."

"Do you have an address where she moved after leaving Lake Charles?"

"The last I heard was Jackson, Mississippi."

Lee hesitated. "Was she married when she left?"

"No, but she was going to Jackson to get married. She was engaged to a young police officer."

"She didn't get married in her hometown?"

"I wanted her to, but she didn't have any immediate family left here and her fiancé had some living in Jackson. They decided to get married there because that's where they were going to settle. I think a small town near there."

"Do you remember her fiancé's name?"

"Let me see...my memory isn't what it used to be. Just a second. My daughter has returned and she might. She and Lucy were friends while growing up." The woman must have cupped the phone by the sound of muffled voices in the background, then she came back on. "Nancy says it's Scott Nolan."

"Do you remember which police department he worked for?"

"Nancy, who did Scott work for?" the woman yelled.

Lee pulled the phone away from his ear for a few seconds, until he heard the older woman say, "Magnolia Blossom Police. It's a suburb of Jackson."

"Thanks." Lee hung up, then looked up the number for that police department and made another call. After explaining who he was, he asked to speak to the police chief.

"Chief Quincy here," a man with a gruff voice said a moment later.

"I'm searching for a Scott Nolan. I understand he works for you."

"He worked for me for nine years until five weeks ago. He didn't even give his notice. Just up and quit one day and said he was leaving Magnolia Blossom. That he needed a change of scenery."

"Was there ever any reports of him using excessive force on the job?"

There was a long pause. "Only a few times over the years."

"Was he married?"

"Yes, for a while, to Lucy. A nice girl, but last year she left him and served him with divorce papers. After that, he wasn't the same."

"Do you think he abused his wife?"

The man sucked in his breath. "What's this about? Is Scott in trouble?"

Lee told the police chief about what had happened in Sagebrush and Tom Green County.

Chief Quincy whistled. "He had a temper, but usually he could control it. Those few times he used excessive force was in the past two years. To tell you the truth, I was glad he left. I didn't know what to expect from him anymore."

"Do you have a picture of the man?"

"Yes. I can fax it to you."

"Thanks, and if he returns to Magnolia Blossom, please give me a call and keep this between you and me." Lee gave the police chief the necessary information, then waited for another fax to come through.

Five minutes later, he stared at the photo of the man who had asked him for directions yesterday. He snatched up his keys, called Kip, who was lying at Lorna's feet, and hurried toward his SUV, punching in the library phone number.

Before Heidi could move or open her mouth, the man with cold, gray eyes rounded the corner and came to her side, pressing a gun into her back.

"Hello, Lucy. Miss me?"

The sound of his voice, gravelly as if he'd smoked too much, flooded her mind with images and memories—none of them good. She swallowed several times to coat her dry throat and asked, "My name is Heidi. Who are you?"

"You know who I am—I see it in your eyes. Remember, we were married—and as far as I'm concerned still are—for many years. I know how you think. I know your expressions."

The quiet steel in his words chilled her to the bone. "How could I forget you, Scott?"

"Oh, sweetheart, I'm gonna make sure you never forget me again." He poked his gun into her back, inching so close his hot breath flowed over her shoulder as he whispered, "I will kill you and anyone who gets in my way. We're gonna leave here and you're coming willingly or else." He left that last word to hang in the air between them for a moment. "You know what I'm capable of. Don't push me."

"Where are we going?"

"Home. And you'll never leave me again."

Either he would kill her or hold her prisoner on his farm in Mississippi—outside of Magnolia Blossom. Far enough away that people wouldn't hear her scream or come to her rescue. She wouldn't last if she made it back there because she would keep trying to escape until he did kill her.

"I won't allow any interference. Remember what happened to that man last month."

"I wish I didn't."

Every horrific moment played across her mind. Her ex-husband beating the man and strangling him to death, then chasing after her. She'd made it to the man's car and was able to pull away before Scott could stop her. But he came after her in his car. In San Antonio's rush-hour traffic, she managed to get away. Then not far from Sagebrush, she thought she saw his car behind her again. She increased her speed and was putting more distance between them until she had a blowout and lost control of her car. That was when she ended up crashed against a tree on the edge of the Lost Woods.

"No one comes between me and my wife."

She remembered every moment of the fear and stress she'd gone through while married to him, until she finally managed to run away from him in Mississippi and end up in New Mexico where she lived. "I'm not your wife anymore."

"Yes, you are!"

The fierceness in those quiet words embedded the cold deep into her bones. She'd been in this situation many times where he tried to force his will on her. A tightness in her chest reminded her of the times right before she ran away when he had strangled her to the point right before dying.

"Ah, I think you realize the hopelessness of defying me."

No, because she had the Lord on her side. She would get away when the right time came. She would never give up waiting for that time.

"Let's go. Not a word to anyone. We're just walking out of here."

"Shouldn't I get my purse and jacket?" She tried to think of a way to get away from him, but she couldn't place these people in danger.

"Why? I'll supply everything you need. I always did until you became ungrateful."

In the middle of her fear, a calmness descended. All she had to do was bide her time. God was with her. Scott never understood that. Scott thought he knew her, but he didn't, especially the new person. She'd had a year living on her own, putting her life back together. She wouldn't go back to the old life. Ever.

Lucy put one foot in front of the other, looking straight ahead, not making eye contact with anyone. She couldn't give Scott a reason to lose it. He didn't really know her, but she knew him well. He stood on the edge of a cliff, teetering, any small instance robbing him of what little control he had left.

She heard her name being called behind her. She kept walking. Almost to the exit.

"Heidi," the supervisor said, not far from her.

Scott's grip on her upper arm dug in until pain shot through her.

Lucy forced a smile and glanced at the woman. "I'm so sorry. I'm taking my lunch a little early. A friend of mine came to town, and I wanted to help him find a place to stay tonight."

"Sure." Her supervisor scrutinized Scott. "I just wanted to remind you the afternoon reading time is earlier today."

Scott increased the pressure of his fingers on her, the weapon pressing into her side.

"I'll be back for that. I don't want to disappoint the kids."

"Fine, Heidi."

Scott urged her forward, and Lucy hurried her pace, wanting to put as much distance between her and her supervisor before the woman thought of something else to say.

Outside, the cool breeze blew her hair across her face, chilling the sweat on her forehead. Scott directed her toward the Jeep she'd seen on Sunday. If only she had remembered that day who he was. She wouldn't be in this predicament now.

"You're driving. I'll tell you where." He opened the passenger door and forced her inside. "Climb over to the driver's side. Remember I have the gun, and you know I'm not afraid to use it."

A memory—the one that finally made her realize she had to leave him eighteen months ago—invaded her mind. He'd taken her out to the field at the farm where he liked to practice shooting. This time his target was a poster of her nailed to the tree. He took great pleasure in aiming at various places on the poster. Killing her over and over until the paper was riddled with gunshot holes.

"Hurry. We don't have all day. I want to be out of this town." He shoved her hard.

She fell forward, her shoulder hitting the steering wheel, one knee pressed into the driver seat. "Give me a chance to climb over," she snapped, then bit her lip to keep any anger inside. It would only rile him more.

"Don't talk back to me. I have no patience left. You made me come across the country to bring you home. You made me kill a man. It's your fault he's dead."

Lord, help me.

"Is Heidi there?" Lee asked as he neared the library.

"I was going to call you. She just left with a man. I don't think she went willingly. There was something about her smile that seemed false," the librarian said.

Lee's hand tightened about his cell and he accelerated beyond the speed limit. "What did the man look like?"

"Very tall, blond hair. Looked like a body builder."

"Did you see them drive off?"

"Yes, in a black Jeep going east."

"Thanks." He clicked off and called the station. "Lorna, tell the captain that Heidi's ex-husband has kidnapped her from the library. Going east on Sagebrush Boulevard. I'm heading that way." He tossed his cell onto the passenger seat and concentrated on maneuvering safely.

Up ahead, he glimpsed the Jeep weaving in and out of traffic. He made another call to the station. "The black Jeep is heading for the highway along Lost Woods Road. This is a hostage situation. This man killed a person with his bare hands. He's a police officer and most likely has a weapon."

As he increased his speed even more, a car pulled out in

front of him, and he stomped on the brake while turning sharply to miss the vehicle, sending the SUV into a spin.

If they left Sagebrush, it was all over. That impression, along with the memory of how Scott murdered William Peterson, hardened her determination to do anything to get away from him.

"You won't get away with this, Scott. The police know you killed that man at the abandoned gas station. Where do you think you can go? Your picture will be all over the T.V. You know the police will be on the lookout for you and your Jeep."

"You don't know anything. I can get lost and stay lost. Not like you."

"Sure. You keep telling yourself that," she taunted.

Scott blew up, cursing and striking at her. She used the action to swerve toward the wooded area on the side of the road. He tried to jerk the wheel and correct the Jeep's direction, but she pressed on the accelerator. Using his gun, he hit her on the side of the head. Pain burst through her skull. She gripped the steering wheel tighter, darkness hovering closeby. She hung on, resolved that his abuse would end once and for all.

In seconds, the vehicle bounced over the rough ground and plowed straight into a pine tree. The blackness swallowed her as her body jerked forward then slammed back, the explosion of the air bag punching her in the chest.

When Lee's car stopped spinning, it faced the opposite direction, but somehow he hadn't hit anything or anyone trying to avoid the vehicle that pulled out in front of him. Traffic around him pulled over. Heart pounding, he praised the Lord, made a U-turn and headed the right way. At the first few intersections, he slowed to look up and down the cross streets. No black Jeep. Finally, he decided he needed to commit to the road that led to the highway. Heidi's ex-husband's best chance to get away was to leave town.

When Lee saw the Jeep smashed against a tree, a constriction about his chest obstructed his breathing. Sweat beaded his forehead. He swerved off the road and came to a halt right behind the car. Jumping from his SUV, he drew his gun and hurried toward the car, steeling for the worse.

Please let her be in the car alive.

He approached the passenger side, the door ajar, and peered inside. The vehicle was empty. Both air bags had inflated, a fine powder scattered everywhere. The driver's door stood open, too.

Straightening, Lee panned the surrounding wooded area. Nothing. With his jaw clenched tightly, he headed back to his SUV and let Kip out then fixed his leash to him. Although he was a cadaver dog, he could search when needed. As he took Kip toward the Jeep, he called the station to update them on what happened. He needed the Lost Woods swarming with officers and the escape routes blocked. He promised Heidi he would protect her. He wasn't going to let her down.

Instead of going to the passenger's side, as Lee had indicated, Kip circled the back of the Jeep, barking. On the ground near a bush lay Heidi.

Adrenaline surged in Lee and flowed rapidly to every part of him.

Please, Lord. Let her be alive.

He quickened his pace and stooped next to her as she moved her arm, touching her head and groaning. "Take it easy. You're bleeding."

"Scott. He's getting away." She tried to sit up.

He assisted her, supporting her against him. "I've got others coming. Do you know which way he went?"

"In the woods, south. I was trying to get to the road to

flag down help." She glanced around frantically. "I must have passed out."

Lee took out his phone and called for an ambulance. When he hung up, he heard sirens blaring, coming fast. "As soon as help is here, I'll go after him."

"No, I'm fine. You go now. He's got to be caught. He would have taken me, but I was so groggy he knew I would slow him down. Scott is a survivalist, if nothing else. Go. Help is coming."

"No. I'm not leaving."

"He told me when he left that I would never be free of him. When I least expected it, he would find me again." She shuddered. "I couldn't escape him. I can't live like that. Find him."

Torn between staying with her and going after Scott Nolan, he looked toward the road. A patrol car arrived, screeching to a halt. "I'm going. Stay here. Don't move."

She managed a small smile. "Promise."

Reluctantly, he rose and guided Kip to the other side of the car to get the scent he needed to follow. While Kip sniffed around the ground, Lee called the dispatcher to relay Heidi's position on the ground and that he was going south from the car after Nolan. Kip picked up the scent and charged into the denser trees.

Lee raced after his dog, branches slapping against him. Sweat rolled into his eyes, stinging them, and down his face. Lee kept the dispatcher abreast of where he was going. She let him know the captain was organizing a search from all directions.

Kip slowed and began smelling the ground around him.

Breathing heavily, Lee asked the dispatcher, "How's Heidi? Did the officer find her?"

"Yes. Paramedics are on the scene. She'll be all right."

Kip caught the scent again and plunged into a thick underbrush, threading in and out of trees. When his dog came out of the thicker woods, a stream running east and west cut across their path. Kip paused at the edge of the water and sniffed it. Then he plunged into the cold brook and continued east, going from bank to bank, smelling the ground.

The water iced the lower part of his legs and feet, but Lee kept saying, "Find him, Kip. You can, boy."

When Kip led Lee out of the woods, the old cemetery with mausoleums and a chapel no longer in use, stretched before him. His border collie tracked through the rows of graves, taking a whiff of the air every so often. He ended the chase at a dingy, white mausoleum with dead vines on its sides. The lock on the door was broken.

Lee signaled Kip to bark. The vicious sound echoed through the cemetery. "Come out, Nolan. You're surrounded and won't escape."

Nothing.

Lee backed away to scan the surroundings. Kip was rarely wrong. He was here or had been. His gaze lit upon the flat roof that slanted down slightly toward the back of the mausoleum. As he made his way around the building, he caught sight of Nolan lying flat on the roof at the back. The man's head popped up. When he saw Lee, he scrambled to a crouch, aimed his gun at Lee and fired it.

He dove to the side behind a tombstone, the bullet grazing the top of the grave marker. Behind him, he heard several dogs barking. Lee peered around its bottom, his weapon pointed at the area where he'd last seen Nolan. Before the man could squeeze off another round, Lee got off a shot, hitting Nolan in the leg. He tumbled off the roof and fell to the ground, his weapon discharging.

Lucy lay in the hospital bed in an E.R. room, biting her thumbnail. At the rate she was going, she wouldn't have any nail left. By the time she left the scene of the wreck, there was still no news on where Lee was or if Nolan had been captured. The waiting played havoc with her nerves. At least the medication the doctor had given her for her pounding headache was starting to work.

She'd brought trouble to Sagebrush and Lee. Seeing Scott again and knowing all that had transpired in her past with him only made her realize how much she'd fallen in love with Lee. During all of what had gone on this month, he'd been there for her, supporting her, protecting her, caring for her. Being a friend. She'd never had that with Scott.

He'd come into her life when her mother had recently died. Lucy fingered the gold locket and opened it. Staring at a photo of her mother, Heidi, all the heartache with her death washed over Lucy. Tears blurred her vision of the picture of a woman who she'd looked so much like.

Vulnerable, she'd believed Scott's words that she had later realized he didn't even know the real meaning of. He didn't know what it meant to love someone—only to dominate and control. He hadn't cared what she'd thought or believed. The marriage had been all about him. Then when the physical abuse and threats began, she'd started planning to escape—not as easy as she'd originally thought. Once she had left him, all contact concerning a divorce had gone through her lawyer. She'd never wanted to see or talk with him again.

Her mind, crowded with images and thoughts of her past, sent tension spiralling through her, aggravating the pain in her head. She closed her eyes, picturing a peaceful scene—she and Lee by the stream, listening to the sound of the water, talking and getting to know each other. The kiss they'd shared.

Lord, please keep Lee safe.

She started to chew on her thumbnail again but stopped

herself and folded her arms over her chest, tucking her hands under her armpits. The door opened.

She stiffened and looked toward who was coming into the room.

Lee, with a huge smile on his face.

Relief shivered down her limbs.

He's alive—unhurt.

She returned his grin, feeling unspeakable joy. "What happened? Did you find Scott?"

"Yes, ma'am. In fact, he's in this very hospital going into surgery to have a bullet removed from his leg."

"Did anyone else get hurt?"

"No. Everyone is safe, especially you. Nolan won't get out of prison for a very long time, if ever, after he's convicted of murder, kidnapping and attempted murder. He has a lot to answer for." Lee moved toward the bed and pulled up a chair. "I came as fast as I could. I didn't want you to worry. How are you doing?"

"Fine, now."

One eyebrow rose. "Fine? You're not in any pain?"

"Well, a little. Okay, just below a lot, but you've brought me the best news I've heard in a long time. I thought when I left Scott I would be free of him and his abuse. I should have realized he would never let me go. Before I married him, I was a teacher. But once we wed and I moved to his home in Mississippi, he didn't want me to work. That was the start of his controlling ways." Her voice vibrated with emotion. "They only got worse the longer we stayed together. At the end, I didn't have any friends, and stayed at the farm all the time. If it hadn't been for the Lord, I wouldn't have been able to hold it together. He was the one who helped me through the ordeal with Scott, and gave me the courage to escape."

"You always felt you believed, even when you didn't remember your past."

Lucy patted her chest over her heart. "I knew it in here. The Lord had gone through a lot with me. He never abandoned me."

"That's what I like about Him." Lee took her hand. "Are they keeping you overnight for observation?"

"Yes. The nurse left to see about getting me a room. They're concerned because of my previous head injury. Scott hit me with his gun. I guess that was better than shooting me with it, but he couldn't bully me if he killed me. Then where would he get his entertainment?"

He caressed her hair behind her ear. "Where he's going, he won't be able to hurt you ever again. Besides, I hope you'll stay here and let me keep you safe. I wouldn't mind protecting you for the rest of your life."

Her heartbeat kicked up a notch. She knew what it meant to be protected by Lee. "What are you saying?"

"That I love you and want to spend the rest of my life with you."

Tears of joy filled her eyes. "Heidi or Lucy? I'm sure this isn't news to you, but my real name is Lucy Cullen. My mother was Heidi. I took my maiden name back when I divorced Scott. I wanted nothing to do with him, even his name."

"A name means nothing to me, Lucy. I love you. I know we haven't been together for long, but I've never been so sure. We can have a long engagement or a short one. The decision will be yours. A marriage to me is a partnership."

She grinned. "Like you and Kip?"

"Not exactly." He chuckled. "I prefer you not chasing after bad guys. I don't want to go through the close calls you've had this month ever again."

"I agree. I want to live a boring, peaceful life with at least three children."

He quirked a brow. "Boring? With kids? And you say this being a teacher?"

"Okay. You're right. Never dull but a peaceful life. I love you."

He leaned toward her and feathered his lips across her mouth. "That's a much better description of our life to come, Lucy."

Then Lee sealed the proposal with a kiss, deep and long, rocking Lucy to the core, as he always had.

★ ★ ★ ★ ★

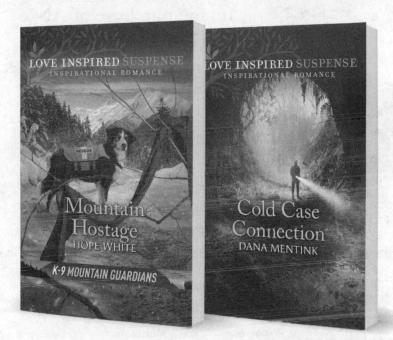

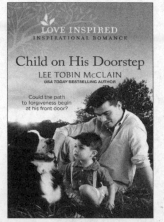

LOVE INSPIRED
INSPIRATIONAL ROMANCE

UPLIFTING STORIES OF FAITH, FORGIVENESS AND HOPE.

Join our social communities to connect
with other readers who share your love!

Sign up for the Love Inspired newsletter
at **LoveInspired.com** to be the first
to find out about upcoming titles,
special promotions and exclusive content.

CONNECT WITH US AT:

f Facebook.com/LoveInspiredBooks

🐦 Twitter.com/LoveInspiredBks

Facebook.com/groups/HarlequinConnection